LAISRATHERA

LAISRATHERA

HER INSTRUMENTS: BOOK THREE

M. C. A. Hogarth

STUDIO
MCAH

Laisrathera
Her Instruments: Book 3

First edition, copyright 2014 by M.C.A. Hogarth

M. Hogarth
PMB 109
4522 West Village Dr.
Tampa, FL 33624

ISBN-13: 978-1499348385
ISBN-10: 149934838X

Cover art by Julie Dillon
http://www.juliedillonart.com/

Designed and typeset by Catspaw DTP Services
http://www.catspawdtp.com/

TABLE OF CONTENTS

PART THE FINAL
CHOICES

CHAPTER 1

For a time during which time had no definition, he knew nothing but a desperate urgency: sleep, mend, mend, God and Lady, stay alive long enough to discharge this duty (what duty) this duty greater than any he had yet shouldered. He clung to life with a tenacity honed by far too many bitter encounters with foes greater than his strength, and renounced death, and cursed it, and held fast, and held fast, and held fast—

—and heard, at last, from a great distance, the musical progressions of a halo-arch in heavy use. Not long now, he thought, ferocious, and fought the chains that bound him, of weakness and pain and injury too close to endings. He pushed so long he no longer remembered any existence other than effort, so when he won free from sodden unconsciousness he woke disoriented. Where was he? He did not recognize the room, nor the halo-arch that prisoned him, hissing and chirping through its diagnostic and monitoring cycles. Some vague voice woke in time to whisper, "Not long now—"

The halo-arch sang a rising arpeggio, signaling his change in status, and Hirianthial struggled to rise as much as he might in order to better espy the person set to the patient watch. She would be there, he thought. She had brought him out of the catacombs. He had felt her fingers on his hair, the tears that had fallen from her eyes to his cheek, still warm as her coursing blood. She would be here; she could be nowhere else.

But the person who charged into the room in the wake of the stranger in a healer's garb was not Captain Theresa Eddings, but her pilot, Sascha . . . and everything in his aura howled the wrongness of it. As the healer checked the readings, Hirianthial pinned the Harat-Shar tigraine with his gaze and said, "*Where is she?*"

Did he imagine the hesitation? No. A syncopation in the conversation that should have beat steady as a metronome. "She's a sector away . . . on your homeworld."

"*WHAT!*"

He had never yelled before, and Sascha's ears flattened instantly to his head. The healer began to speak and Hirianthial ignored him to say, voice hard, "You did not abandon her there. *Among our enemies!*"

"I didn't abandon anyone!" Sascha exclaimed, anger seaming his aura like magma thrusting up against stone. "She chose to stay! Ask your cousin, it's the Angels-blessed truth, I swear it!"

"My cousin is here?" Anger made it hard to think, and the halo-arch began whining.

"Excuse me," the healer interrupted. "Can we have this tête-à-tête later? Like, maybe, when my patient's not still being held together with spit and bailing wire?"

"No," Hirianthial replied. "No, it cannot wait." He glared at Sascha. "Tell her to come. Now."

Sascha folded his arms, teeth bared and fur visibly

bristling at the neck and upper arms. But he forced himself to look away and inhale through his nose, exhale. "Well," he said. "Now I know you love her too, so I won't take it personally. But she's not the only one on your homeworld 'among our enemies,' arii . . . my twin is, too. Keep that in mind before you yell at me again." And then he left, trailing an aura dense with unspoken fears and ferocities.

"Now," the healer drawled. "If you're done, maybe you can give me some of your attention?"

Hirianthial glanced at him, torn between irritation, to be pulled from matters of staggering import . . . and rue, that he was treating someone with such discourtesy. The healer was one of the Pelted, a Hinichi wolfine man with fur the color of iron and eyes like winter skies, so pale they were almost white.

"Good, so your hearing is selective, not damaged," the healer continued. "Before you berate me, Lord Sarel Jisiensire, let me inform you that you arrived here in hypovolemic shock. I'm told you have a license to practice several forms of surgery, so this will have some meaning to you."

"I beg your pardon," Hirianthial said, startled. "How is that possible?"

"It might have had something to do with the spleen that was leaking into your abdominal cavity," the healer said dryly. "Did I mention there were perforations in your intestines? And a lung that was thinking very seriously of collapsing. Someone apparently plumped it up just enough to keep you breathing. For a while." He pursed his lips and looked up at the ceiling contemplatively. "Your insides reminded me a little of a custard someone hadn't baked quite enough to set. You were obviously under a halo-arch for just long enough to keep from dying immediately, but not long enough to actually be fixed." He turned narrowed eyes on the Eldritch. "You may understand why I think your problems can wait."

"But they can't," he said, thinking of his brother's revelations. "And you have done a good job of mending me."

"I haven't—"

"The halo-arch hasn't made a single noise associated with stabilization of a body following surgery," Hirianthial said, raising his voice just enough to convince the Hinichi to be silent. "Nor any that indicate complications from those surgeries."

The healer opened his mouth, then closed it, baring his teeth. "Fine. You're right. But if you know that, you can also tell that it's not reporting normal function either. You need more time here. And especially more time unconscious. Don't make me sedate you to fulfill that condition."

"I promise to rest," Hirianthial said. "But I must speak to my queen first. I must."

The wolfine searched his eyes, then flipped his ears back. "Fine. But the moment she leaves, you had better be unconscious, or trying to be, or I'll be back in here with an AAP faster than you can say 'I didn't sign any consent forms for treatment.'" At Hirianthial's look, the healer finished, dryly, "Your queen signed them for you. She claims to be a family member."

"She is," Hirianthial murmured. And sighed. "I apologize for my conduct."

The wolfine snorted. "Don't. We both know doctors make horrible patients." He tapped the halo-arch. "You know this is the call panel. I'm Healer Rosser. Your other physician is Doctor Mayfield. You have an entire nursing team; if we don't answer, they will."

"I will keep that in mind," Hirianthial said, and then an aura welled into the door that he would have recognized half-dead: the steel in it, the power, and the ardor, red as blood and pulsing with simmering wrath. His expression caused the wolfine to glance over his shoulder and sigh.

"I'll be back," he said, and Liolesa stepped aside to let him pass.

She drew a stool to his bedside and settled on it, pulling her skirts out of the way and then resting her gloved hands on her lap, calm . . . far too calm for the volcanic fury roiling beneath the surface of her aura. Before he could ask, she said in their tongue, "I swear it, Hiran. My soul to the Goddess, I swear it, that I did not compel her, nor even give her the idea. She advanced it to me herself, that she should stay that we might have a people to return to, when we do. But having heard the offer—" And here Liolesa's gaze grew sharp as a blade, "I could no more repudiate her than I could command my heart not to beat. She is human, and not of us, and yet has the heart and the instincts of a true liegewoman. I would not deny her."

"Liolesa—"

"Hirianthial," she interrupted. Her voice was tense, and every word was shaded in the white mode of their language for the sanctity of truth. "*I would not.* It would break the vows between us, liegelady to liegewoman. I pledged my troth, cousin."

He looked away from the blaze in Liolesa's aura, so bright his eyes watered. "You left her behind."

"But not alone," Liolesa said, silvering the words for hope in dark places, and this was surely a very dark place. "I left the vixens with her, and her tigraine, and Urise's acolyte. And she will have allies on the ground. They will educate her on the geography and the resources available to her, and she will bring to them her knowledge of the technologies that will be used against them by the Chatcaava—"

Of course. Of course. Her aura, the raw power of her anger. "You know!"

"I know," she said, some of that anger leaking into her words. "We fled the system after the arrival of a pirate ship, and there were too many coincidences for it to be unaffiliated with the dragons. The pattern is suggestive. You have proof?"

"From my brother's lips," Hirianthial growled. "I should have slain him as you bade me, when he first betrayed the family."

She was silent, studying him; it was a kindness that she did not press him on how much pain they would have avoided had he performed that execution, long ago. But that anger remained; it was impossible not to feel it, like the radiation off the sun. He knew better than to think it was directed at him. "Pirates," he said, quieter. "One ship only?"

"Is not one ship enough?" she asked, each word clipped and shadowed.

For centuries they had kept the secret of their world's location from the universe at large. To have a sole lawless vessel there, and now able to carry that information away. . . . "Where are we?" he asked at last.

"Starbase Omega," she said. "Which is far too far from the seat of the Alliance for me to plead my case with any immediacy. It is also, however, very comfortably far from the conflict that is ripping the borders and spilling, finally, into war."

Then he truly did try to sit up, and was repelled by the halo-arch for his temerity. Wincing, he pressed a hand to his chest and said, "You do not tell me that it has come. Oh, cousin—"

"Our allies are hard-pressed," she said, the words again in the shadowed mode. "The Empire is a good third larger than they are, and I judge it would be a disastrous war for both sides if I had not handed the Alliance an assassin's blade to use on the throat of its enemy." At his look, she smiled, thin. "The heir to Imthereli has vanished into the fray."

"The one you sent before," he murmured, frowning.

"As ambassador to dragons," she agreed. "Who returned their rulers' lover. A duelist, cousin, and half-dragon himself. Unlooked-for aid, and it is in my heart that he will make a difference. But that avails us not at all, for the Alliance no longer has an armada to send to my cause. They have promised they will see what they might spare, and it is that word we await before we ourselves move . . . well, that and the other iron I have in the fire."

"Which would be. . . ." He paused, then nodded. "You mean to call in my kinsman."

She tipped her head. "The Tams have been waiting full long enough for their chance to come home," she said. "Their resources will be of little use if we cannot secure enough time to put them to use, but I have summoned Lesandurel all the same. Once I have gathered what strength I may, we will return at best speed. But we cannot go home without some sword to lift against our enemies, Hiran. Surely you know it."

He did. But he could not resist speaking, his own words clouded with shadows. "You left her amid them, on a world she barely knows. With winter approaching, who has never known a winter."

"Has she never?" Liolesa asked, the searing lava of her aura fading briefly at the distraction of the thought. "How extraordinary. Are you certain?"

Swift as rain coursing he felt the rush of all the memories he'd ever gathered from her mind, by accident or by gift. "Unless you count the ball of ice where the crystals dwelt, then no. But what good can she possibly do, Lia?"

"I don't know," Liolesa said. "But I have done her the

grace of leaving her to make the attempt. You should rest, ere that healer returns to reproach us both. Mend now while you may, cousin, for when we leave I need you on your feet." She rose, skirts hissing as they slid from the stool. "It will not be long now." She hesitated, then added, "I have done with seeing you laid so low, Hiran. Prithee, sleep and fade the memories."

"I will," he promised. And added, quiet, "You said of the Tams . . . 'a chance to come home.' To our world."

"No mistake there," his cousin said—who was also Queen of the Eldritch, and the third to reign since their Settlement centuries ago. "When all this is over . . . our world will be home to more than the Eldritch." And then, in a show of affection that startled him, she touched the backs of her fingers to his temple, and let him feel the sharpness of her worry for him straight through the fineness of the fabric of her gloves. Even her tone of address became familiar. "Now, to bed with thee, I charge it."

It was not in him to argue. If she was right and they were leaving soon, he needed all the rest he could have now . . . because when they left for home again, there would be nothing between him and Theresa but the bodies of their enemies, and he fully vowed to be the one to slay them all.

Reese's breath came in clouds, misting her lips as she stared through the trees. "You're making a joke."

"No," said Taylor from behind her. "No, the map's right. What about it, Belinor-alet?"

The Eldritch youth—a youth who was twice her age, for all Reese knew—joined them at the forest's edge, keeping a proper distance from them. There he studied the vista, shivering in the cold but holding himself with a dignity so determined Reese decided he was maybe closer to half her age instead. In his accented Universal, he said, "She has the right of it, Lady. That is the castle Rose Point."

"Wow," Irine murmured from behind her. "Somehow I expected it to be . . . more . . ."

"More what?" Taylor asked with interest, glancing at the Harat-Shar.

"More less of everything."

That said it all, Reese thought, trembling, and not with cold. When she had put her idea to the Queen of the Eldritch, that she should stay and find some way to do something heroic—what, she had no idea—she and the others had debated where they should set down. Liolesa's Eldritch enemies would expect her to go to one of the two strongholds of her allies: either to Jisiensire in the south or to the western Galares, further inland. The pirates would expect her to stay in the capital and try to take Ontine. Maybe. Right?

What they were all pretty sure of was that she wouldn't head for the land the Queen had deeded her, for the very good reason that it was at the northern edge of nowhere and abandoned. There was no hope of finding allies there; certainly there were no resources ready to hand. It would have made a great ballad, Reese thought: gathering everyone to the flag of a dead land, and from there marching to the capital singing. On horseback, knowing the Eldritch. But it was also a stupid idea, and they'd been betting that their enemies wouldn't think they'd do something stupid.

What Reese hadn't counted on was arriving to find a real castle, still mostly intact. An enormous castle, perched alongside the sea, a beautiful castle. *Her* castle. A castle of her own. Who'd never so much as owned a patch of dirt. Whose only home for years now had been a rattle-trap freighter with just enough crew space to sleep in. And now she had a castle—an intact castle, a large castle—a castle with sheep grazing around it, and in its courtyard.

Wild sheep. Dirty sheep. Were they supposed to be that grayish color?

"Blood in the dirt," she muttered. "I have no idea what I'm doing."

"That's fine," Taylor said. "Just don't tell anyone else." The Tam-illee foxine glanced at her data tablet. "The sheep make for a fine confusion of life signs, and they're probably in and out of here all the time, so a few more warm bodies won't make a difference. Why don't we go take a closer look?"

"Sure," Reese said. "That sounds like a great idea."

Reese watched the woman set off. The Eldritch youth glanced at her. "My Lady," he said. "It will be no warmer inside, but at least we won't be exposed to the wind." Then he followed Taylor, leaving Reese standing beside the trees with Irine, who'd been her irreverent co-pilot, employee and the ship busybody for years now.

"You have a castle," Irine observed.

"I have a castle."

"You don't know how to feel about that." Irine cocked her head, mouth twitching.

"Have I told you yet how ridiculous you look with a shirt wrapped around your head?"

"Yes, well, if my gorgeous ears get frostbitten I won't be able to tell when Sascha's nibbling on them." Irine rested a hand on Reese's shoulder. "Come on. Let's go get settled."

As they walked, Reese said, "I have sheep."

"I think those sheep have themselves," Irine answered. "But I guess if you can find someone to round them up and put them in one place . . . then yes, you'll have sheep."

But the tigraine was frowning. It was such a normal thing, to see Irine frown, such a welcome thing to have some normalcy at that point, that Reese said, "What?"

"I was thinking about us having sheep," Irine said. "To

eat. Tonight."

"You can eat sheep?"

Irine covered her face with one hand and used to the other to keep pushing Reese in the right direction.

They caught up with the others in front of the enormous doors set into the castle wall, where Taylor was consulting her data tablet and Belinor was waiting, huddled in robes that seemed thick enough to keep him warm, but didn't seem to be doing the job. As they approached, he said, "Yon fox is finding whether it be safe to open them. Those doors are centuries old now."

"I'm surprised they haven't rotted," Irine said, and paused. Reese looked past her and hissed.

"My castle's missing a tower!"

"So it is," Belinor said, subdued.

"Why is my castle missing a tower?" Reese asked, trying not to be surprised. When Liolesa had granted her the property she'd expected ruins, so finding the building still upright had been a pleasant surprise. It also made the hole in the castle's side feel like an unexpected wound.

"Because," Belinor said. "This was once the home of Corel." At their blank stares, he said, "The mind-mage. The first mind-mage. The one who went mad, and upon whom Queen Jerisa threw her legions, and they died and watered this field with their blood."

Reese's heart gave a great double-beat as whispers erupted in her head, ancient as childhood stories of the soil of Mars reddening with the blood of fallen patriots. She suppressed the urge to look down at the ground, see for herself her new life and the old mingling. Trying not to shiver, she said, "And then what?"

"And there he would have conquered, had not love brought him low," Belinor continued, looking at the tower. The gray sky and sea reflected off his eyes, winter-dulled.

"But the love of a woman caused him to give himself over to judgment. Or so they say. Some of the tales say he killed himself for remorse for having slain her by accident."

"Wouldn't you . . . well, remember?" Irine asked, trying to be delicate about it. "It hasn't been all that many generations, has it?"

"I wasn't alive, certainly!" Belinor exclaimed. And then peering at her, added, "How well do you remember the events of your childhood? The details? Can you see them clearly in your mind? Could you describe them in the exact same way to more than one person, and know that you are recalling them truly?"

Irine opened her mouth, then closed it and looked away, frowning. "Okay, right. And I'm only a few decades old. Good point."

"You'd think 'committed suicide' or 'was dragged back for a trial' wouldn't be a matter of detail," Reese said, studying the gash in the castle and the long spray of stones that extended out from it, crusted over with sea salt and streaked with rain and rust. "Did the army pull down the tower?"

"No," Belinor said, hushed. "On that matter all the records are clear." They looked at him and he hunched into his robes. "The mind-mage did that, in his fury."

Which is when it really hit her, what Liolesa had done. Indignant, Reese exclaimed, "The Queen gave me the first mind-mage's castle? Me? What, is she expecting me to die to keep Hirianthial sane? If she is, I've got news for her!"

Irine covered her mouth with her hand but her giggles escaped her anyway. Reese glared at her and noticed again just how poorly her glares worked on her crew. "Oh, Reese," Irine said, laughing aloud finally. "You think that woman thinks you'd roll over for anything?" She shook her head, eyes sparkling. "I bet it's a joke."

"The Queen does not jest," Belinor muttered.

Reese glanced at the castle. "Not about something like this, no," she said. Black towers against thick winter sky, the smell of brine, the slap and distant hiss of the sea on the shore. No, this hadn't been meant as a joke. A correction, maybe, of something that had gone wrong. Maybe Liolesa expected them to re-write the story of this Corel, and give it a happy ending this time. And for that to happen. . . .

"Taylor," she said. "Tell me there's a way into this relic. And that you know how to cook a sheep."

The foxine looked up, bemused. "I don't know about cooking sheep, Captain, but I can get us inside."

"That's a start."

In the end, they didn't go through the doors because they were so massive they had to be opened by chains that had locked up centuries past, with rust and age. So Reese entered her new home, the one she'd been given, the one that the Queen had written out a deed for, to make the transfer of ownership official . . . by climbing in through one of the windows.

"This is not how I imagined this happening," she grumbled.

"Think of the story you'll be able to tell your kits," Irine said.

Reese shot her a fulminating glare, and this one actually worked. A little anyway. "Fine," the tigraine said. "Think of the stories you'll be able to tell *my* kits."

They had landed in a narrow corridor, much taller than seemed necessary but close at the elbows. It reminded Reese of the corridors of the *Earthrise*: nice and claustrophobic. She could get used to castles, maybe, if they were built like spaceships. Trailing after Taylor, she drew in a deep breath and wondered why the air wasn't thicker.

Weren't shut-in places supposed to be full of dead air?

And then she found out why the corridor smelled so fresh.

"Angels," Irine whispered as they reached the corner, and stepped out of the rubble into a crumbled courtyard. It had been whole once, Reese thought, halting abruptly at the sight. There were filigreed gates in wilted ruin, evidence of gazebos and arbors, and the remains of low walls and benches. There had been entire buildings in it too, if the wreckage was any indication. But there was nothing there now, but a garden. A garden blooming in winter, a garden that had overgrown every boundary and flowed like the ocean to the interior walls, a garden that in places was as tall as a hedge maze and dense with black thorns as long as Reese's palm.

And everywhere, everywhere she could look, was a profusion of white roses, their perfume mingling with the sea breeze that swept in through the broken wall.

"God and Lady!" Belinor whispered.

"Do . . . do roses do that?" Reese asked. Before her the two Pelted women had flattened ears and low tails, and she was trying not to find the whole thing uncanny. "I thought flowers died in winter."

"Winter roses do not." The acolyte stared, awed, looking toward the crumbled tower where the flowers were twining, sinking roots into the remains of the mortar. "They are rare, though. I don't know of anywhere they grow like this . . . !"

"You won't find anywhere they grow like this," came a voice from above them. "And unless you tell me now what you mean to do here, they will be the last sight you see."

Reese froze. A man's voice—young, she thought—but speaking Universal. Did he have an accent? She couldn't discern one. Had she led them into a trap after all? And then she tried to move, and discovered she couldn't.

Belinor cried in outrage, "Mind-mage! Release us, misbegotten cretin!"

And the chances of their enemies having a mind-mage were . . . what . . . astronomical? Wasn't Hirianthial supposed to be the first in a million years? Reese frowned and said, "I'd rather not talk to someone behind my back."

"I'd rather not let you see me."

She sighed. "Blood and freedom, what is it with you Eldritch and your having to be all dramatic? What, if I see you, you might have to kill me? Or you just enjoy being mysterious? Trust me, I've had enough of mysterious to last me a lifetime."

"Um, Reese—"

"Not now, Irine. I'm not done yet." She pulled against the invisible chains holding her in place. "And can I tell you how rude it is to do this? If you can freeze us anytime you want, then what's the point of threatening us with it? You can't possibly have anything to fear from us—"

"Reese!" Irine hissed.

"And another thing," Reese added. "This is my bleeding castle, and I've already paid blood and sweat and tears for it, so you're the one trespassing! I have a deed to prove it, even. Or I did, before the Queen's enemies made off with it, damn them to all the hells."

Now Belinor blanched. "My Lady, you should not say such things!"

"Even if she means it?" the voice asked again. A man dropped to the ground in front of them, raising a puff of ice from the ground, and turned to them. He looked older than Belinor, but nowhere near Hirianthial's age, and unlike every Eldritch Reese had ever seen, he moved like a cat prowling, like something only half-tamed. The sharp, pointed face, the hair short enough to brush his shoulders, and the knee-length coat in pale gray over gray clothes, all made him look like some sort of snow fox. And he had eyes that Reese immediately liked. Suspicious, yes, but alive. Curious and quick and very alive.

"God and Lady," Belinor whispered. "A renegade priest!"

"A what?" Irine asked.

"Your boy is quick," the man said to Reese. "You should keep him. In a few centuries, he'll be a real wonder."

Before Belinor could speak, Reese said, "You really are abrasive."

"I don't get much company," he answered, studying her with interest. "I'm afraid I don't have much chance to polish my manners."

"You're not howling in terror at the sight of the unclean alien."

"You're not howling in terror at the sight of the evil mind-mage." He glanced at her hand. "And additionally, you are breaking my compulsion."

Reese looked at her own hand, found it half-raised. "I do kind of want to wring your neck for this. I hate being espered at."

"This is something you have experience with?"

Reese narrowed her eyes. "I don't think you've earned that story yet."

He grinned. "Fair enough. And if I release you, you'll promise not to let your tame priest try to kill me?"

Belinor said, "My Lady! Renegades are dangerous!"

"You have that all wrong, boy," the man said. "It's the priests who are dangerous. I should know, yes? And you should too, except you're in the God's garb, so what would you know?" He shook his head. "You have a lot to learn."

Reese snapped her fingers with the hand she was struggling to lift. "Hey. Showy Stranger. Over here. I'm the one in charge. Pay attention to me." Had she judged him right?

Yes, he was grinning. He even essayed a small bow. "Out of the chains, please?"

"Fine. But mind your priest's manners."

"He won't do a thing against you," Reese said. "Will you, Belinor?"

"No, my Lady," the youth muttered, but in poor humor.

"Very well." The stranger waved a hand, releasing them . . . and crumpled, caught in the crossfire of two separate palmers. Irine and Taylor glanced at one another.

"Did we both hit him?" Irine asked.

Taylor shrugged. "Shouldn't matter. Two beams or one, he'll be out a few hours either way."

"Well, let's truss him up," Reese said with a sigh. "No use having him wake up free."

"Ah, but what will being tied up matter if he can freeze us all up like that with his thoughts?" Irine asked as Belinor gaped at them. "I mean, I assume this is sort of what Hirianthial did to those bandits on the colony, but I don't know how to prevent him from trying it again."

"I think drugs make it harder," Reese said. "But I'd rather not drug him. We'll just have to keep one of you out of sight behind him or something and hope we don't need to think our way out of this a second time."

"My Lady!" Belinor said. "You had weapons!"

"We have some weapons," Reese corrected. "Not too many. But yes. We have a few."

"Then slay this creature, while you still can!"

Thinking of Hirianthial, Reese said, "Not until we know who he is and what he's doing here."

"But he's dangerous!"

Reese said, "I noticed. But so are we. At least a little bit." She smiled wryly at Taylor and Irine. To the Eldritch, she finished, "We'll keep an eye on him. In fact, you can keep an eye on him, if you're comfortable guarding him."

"I will do my best, my Lady. But I am no mind-mage."

"None of us are."

Belinor subsided, but Taylor glanced at her. "He may be right, you know."

"Maybe," Reese said. "But he could have killed us all before he even knew we were here. And he didn't." She glanced at the riot of roses and inhaled deeply. "Let's get inside and see what we've got to work with."

CHAPTER 2

"They told me you've been released," Sascha said from the door to the room the Eldritch was only too glad to be vacating.

Hirianthial glanced toward him, then looked away, suffering the unaccustomed swing of his shorn hair against his jaw and the unfulfilled promises it represented. The dangle the crew had woven him barely moved, a long rope down his back: that too, was a promise, but theirs to him, that they'd meant it when they'd said they would stand by him. He composed himself, then said, "Sascha, I am sorry."

"For snapping at me?" Sascha padded closer, pulling a stool with him and straddling it. He flicked his ears forward, aura a settled warm gold, comforting. "I could use an apology for that, yeah."

Hirianthial exhaled and met the Harat-Shar's eyes. "You have it, then. I am sorry. I was . . . not myself."

"I think you were actually very much yourself," the tigraine said. His ears flicked forward. "Worried, are you."

"We've left our own amid dragons and slavers and

traitors," Hirianthial replied. "Perhaps you have some knowledge that prevents you from worrying? If so, I would very much like to hear it."

Sascha shook his head. "If that's a 'tell me something's changed since I was awake last,' that's a no. But you're up, and that's good. That's one of the things we were waiting for. And frankly, you need to be on your feet because your cousin needs you."

"Ah?"

"She's going to explode," Sascha said. "I'm no judge of royalty or anything, but I do know something about tempers, having lived with Reese for years now. And if something doesn't distract that woman, she's going to start punching walls. Or whatever passes for that among you people. Something that sounds more dramatic and genteel."

"We say cutting ourselves to feed the blade," Hirianthial said.

Sascha's ears flattened and he grimaced. "You would, wouldn't you." Hirianthial felt the tigraine's regard as he pushed himself off the bed, trying his feet. Far too weak, he thought. How long did he have before he'd need his full faculties? Not long, and he was no longer a youth to snap back from bodily distress so easily. So it surprised him when Sascha said, "You look good."

"I beg your pardon?"

"You looked like death when we rescued you, so . . . yes. You look much better." The tigraine's tail lashed once against the stool. "Fortunately we got you patched up by the best on the starbase."

"I had wondered. Where are we, then?"

"We're in the Fleet hospital," Sascha said. "When we came barreling in, your cousin took over the comm and, not surprisingly, I guess, royalty gets perks. Especially royalty from an allied nation. Not only that, but the

Earthrise is owned by one of the few holders of Fleet's only civilian citation—for that business with Surapinet and Captain NotAgain—so we got privileged treatment. They're shining the hull as we speak. I don't think Reese will recognize her when we pull back into orbit."

His heart contracted at the thought. Theresa alone, and amid his enemies . . . had they never met, she would never have become their targets.

"You really do love her, don't you," Sascha said, and Hirianthial broke from his reverie to find the tigraine studying his face.

"Sascha . . ."

"You're about to tell me all the reasons why it can't work," Sascha said. "As if I don't already know them."

"You don't," Hirianthial said, firm.

"She loves you, too, you know."

"And now," Hirianthial said, "You are meddling, Sascha—"

"By telling you things you already know?" Sascha snorted. "You called me 'arii'. That means we're friends. And as prickly as she is, the Boss trusts me with her life. That gives me enough right to meddle when the both of you already know something and don't want to look at it." He looked up. "And you know. You *know*, don't you."

The touch of her fingers in his shorn hair . . . the temple she'd pressed lightly against his in her wild despair. The feeling that had been wellspring to that despair, the only one capable of creating such panic and horror in her at his state, at the thought that he might die. He closed his eyes.

"Thought so," Sascha murmured. "Look, we're going to live through this . . . so I'm not going to push you about it."

"No?" he said, surprised.

"If I'm right," Sascha said. "All that we've lived through, and all that we're about to go through, will teach you far better than I could. I'm just pointing all this out so . . . you know. When you do live through it, it'll be on your mind. About how precious some things are, and how rare, and how easily you can lose them." He smiled faintly. "You Eldritch. You think you're magic just because you have the potential to outlive us ten times over. But that doesn't change that it's just potential. You know how often people realize their potential, arii? And that's over things in themselves they can control."

Hirianthial stared at him, stunned. Not just at the words, but at the solidity of his aura. Before leaving the homeworld, Urise had been teaching him to reach the silence of the Universe, where the answers were implied because there had been a Listening in that silence. To see it reflected in the aura of someone his own kind would have called a mortal. . . .

"And how did you get so wise?" he asked.

Sascha grinned. "Thanks for not finishing that 'so young.' By now you should know the answer, right?"

"I fear not."

The Harat-Shar snorted. "By loving. Of course. What else?"

"What else," Hirianthial murmured, feeling it sweep through him like a vivifying wind, like the first breeze of spring.

Kis'eh't peeked in. "Is he awake? Is—oh! You are!"

"I am," he said, and had enough time to realize the Glaseah was running to brace himself. She halted just short of him as if remembering such as he was not to be touched for casual cause, but . . . surely this was no casual cause. So he leaned down and completed the embrace she'd wanted to give him, and she sighed against his ribcage, bringing him the effervescence of her pleasure at the sight of him on his feet, the quiet orderliness of her thoughts, the contentment she felt that things were finally falling into place . . . and the knowledge that she was holding . . . his clothes?

"You have something for me?" he said, puzzled.

"Yes," she said. "If you're up, the Queen asked that you come see her. Apparently you have family coming? And they're arriving now."

"Family," he murmured. "Of course. If you will excuse me? I will dress." He paused and looked at Sascha.

The Harat-Shar laughed. "What, are you waiting for the inevitable joke? 'Do I have to go?'"

"I thought I would grant you the opportunity."

"To tease you!" Sascha grinned. "Maybe things will be all right after all." He paused a heartbeat, then added, "So do I have to go, or can I watch?"

Kis'eh't rolled her eyes and pulled his elbow. "Come on, lecher. The faster we figure things out here, the faster we can deliver you back to your sister's loving arms."

"Sounds good to me."

Hirianthial watched them as the Glaseah led the Harat-Shar away, felt at his fingertips the softness of their auras where they melded with the ease of long friendship. He did not think they would call one another friends, if asked. Family, though.

He looked at the clothes. Pulled from his own room on the *Earthrise,* no doubt . . . but by Liolesa. He knew the moment he touched the long bronze scarf, and not just because he could feel through it the memory of her fingertips. She would have noted the hair Baniel had shorn in the cell, and how naked it would make him feel, to be reduced to the coif of a boy not yet at his majority. And yet, there was something freeing about the lack . . . as if, without it, he might contemplate a life outside his world's expectations. He passed his hand over his nape, hearing the bell at the end of the dangle shiver as he disturbed it.

Hirianthial was escorted directly from the hospital,
over a Pad and into what looked like a hotel lobby, save
that this lobby was maintained solely by uniformed personnel from the Alliance Fleet. One and all their auras
were contracted close to their bodies—discipline learned,
he wondered? Or concern over their military's posture?
But they were courteous to him when they guided him
smoothly from the lobby to the suite where they'd installed
Liolesa . . . who was, after all, a visiting head of state. She
was sitting in what looked like the Alliance version of a
receiving room, complete with a small collection of chairs
around a table and a window. If here the window spanned
from floor to ceiling and showed the uncanny clarity of
space rather than a winter landscape, well. He had been
traveling in the Alliance for over sixty years now, and it
looked natural to him. Even his cousin looked normal in
this setting . . . but then, Liolesa had that talent of making
anywhere she bided her own.

No, it was the stranger facing her, who was rising at his
entrance, who arrested his attention.

Lesandurel Meriaen Jisiensire was not much more
their senior: two centuries or less, Hirianthial thought. But
unlike either of them, Lesandurel had left their world when
he was barely over two hundred . . . and had not returned.
He had stayed among the Pelted and made a home with
them, and kept family—mortal family, nine generations'
worth—and though Hirianthial knew Liolesa had maintained contact with him since Maraesa had passed the
crown to her, he knew very little of a man who was technically a distant kinsman. He hadn't known what to expect
of an Eldritch who'd been so long away, but given his own
experiences with loss and death, he thought to face at least

some evidence of melancholy and the grief of time made manifest in the lives of those who had died before him, over and over again.

But Lesandurel Meriaen was not a melancholic. And while his aura was scored with the memories of sorrow, he was a brilliance to Hirianthial's sight: a calm and an energy and a richness that made Hirianthial suddenly want to touch and see if that energy would feel like velvet and smell like aged wine and taste like flakes of gold on festival bread.

He could not move, facing this evidence of just how wrong he'd been.

. . . and then Lesandurel smiled and touched his palm to his breast, bowing as one would to the seal-bearer of the family. "My Lord Jisiensire."

"God and Lady," Hirianthial exclaimed. "Call me not that."

Lesandurel cocked a brow. He spoke beautifully in their tongue . . . but he had an accent. A Universal accent. "You are no longer the head of the family?"

"He still bears the swords," Liolesa said, silvering the words. She was still sitting, as was her right. She was also, he discerned from her aura with some irritation, amused. "But his cousin now holds the seal."

"Ah," Lesandurel said. "I apologize. I have not been keeping up with affairs at home the way I should."

"Lesandurel just joined me," Liolesa said. "Won't you sit, cousin? This is a conversation you should take part in anyway."

"Are you no longer the Queen's White Sword as well?" Lesandurel asked as he settled again.

"I no longer guard her body," Hirianthial replied. "I appear to be helping her to guard our Body, now." And shaded the final words in white, for purity and abstractions, to evoke a people rather than a person. He caught the edge of Liolesa's approving glance and decided to ignore it; she was already enjoying herself too much, and if Sascha had been right he could bear some mortification to keep her from living too deeply in her anger.

"You have joined a rare brotherhood, then." Lesandurel leaned forward to pick up a cup of coffee from the table. "So, my Queen." He looked at her, growing somber from face to aura, a gray weight settling around him like a cloak. His words slid into shadows. "We arrive at last at that we most feared."

"We have," she said. "What can you give me to the task?"

"A great deal . . . and none of it what you need." Lesandurel shook his head, a gesture less minute than it should have been among their own. His body language was some seamless amalgamation of Eldritch reserve and Pelted openness; Hirianthial found it mesmerizing. "I have money, my Lady. It can buy you weapons, but not people who have been trained in their use. It has bought you ships, but they are couriers, not corvettes. It can buy you intelligence—that has its utility—but the most important intelligence available you will already have access to, if the Alliance is sharing its with you . . . ?" At her dipped chin, he sighed. "Then you have some notion of what transpires. There are some in the family who have gone into Fleet, and while they cannot say much, what they have does not inspire confidence."

"No," she murmured, words shadowed. "It would not."

"I tell you true, liegeman to lady," he said. "What I have made all these years passing was never intended for the purposes of war, but of peace. I have for you builders, my Lady, and engineers, doctors and messengers. We are positioned to solve the problems that developed during the reign of Queen Maraesa, and the ones you identified yourself later. To fight a war . . ." He shook his head again. "That is a matter for your alliance with the Pelted."

"Surely there must be mercenaries," Hirianthial said. "There have been in every culture."

"Mercenaries you would trust with the fate of our world?" Liolesa asked, arch.

"We have few options," he said.

"I am to know soon what our allies are willing to offer us by way of aid," Liolesa said. "Even a single Fleet ship should be enough to deal with a pirate. And after that. . . ."

"And after that," Lesandurel said. "We will build you your infrastructure, my Lady. Money cannot buy warriors. But it can buy a world fixed defenses, and with time the warriors can be trained."

"And you?" Liolesa asked. "Will you come home?"

"If my family is permitted?" Lesandurel smiled. "Maybe. For a while."

She laughed. "For a while."

"A man who has centuries to nurture his investments is rich among people who don't have that luxury." Lesandurel had a sip of his coffee. "It is not unusual for the rich to have more than one residence."

He was—was he?—yes. His aura sparkled with the laughter he was withholding. How could this man have such equanimity after centuries among the short-lived Pelted? Not just living among them, but living with them? Liolesa had teased Hirianthial about beginning to develop a mortal household like this distant House-cousin, but the idea had horrified him. It obviously did nothing of the sort to Lesandurel . . . but he also did not seem heart-lamed, or callous, to be insensible to the pain of people's passage. Nor did he seem as angry about the condition of their world as he thought proper—"You aren't worried," he said suddenly. "About the pirates."

Lesandurel paused, then set his cup down carefully and folded his hands. "No."

"Because?" Hirianthial demanded. "You speak of the death of our people!"

"We speak of the death of the Veil," Lesandurel said. "They are not the same things. And the world is not the people, as you well know, cousin. It is a fine world, and it would be an inconvenience to lose it, but it was not our first and need not be our last. And if I have no access to warships, what I do have access to . . . is lift."

"Lift," Hirianthial repeated, aware that Liolesa was not as surprised by this comment as he was.

"If things become that dire—if in fact, they are so dire already—then it would take very little to move all of us off the world. There are not so many of us anymore. A single colony ship would be sufficient to the task." He tilted his head. "It would use up all the Meriaen fortune, but it could be done."

"With pirates in orbit?" Hirianthial said. "Such a ship would not last long. Indeed, it would merely give our enemies a convenient prize to tow away."

"They must leave orbit sometime," Lesandurel said. "And then there will be an opportunity."

"Too much risk," Hirianthial murmured.

Lesandurel said, "Which has described our philosophy for most of our lives, has it not? And this has served us how?"

Liolesa held up a hand. "A matter to consider after we have put paid to the situation that besets us now."

The chime that sounded then managed an air of diffidence, as did the Tam-illee male who entered at the Queen's permission. Another of Lesandurel's, from the uniform, and the foxine bowed and informed her that she was wanted by some ambassador, if she was available. The

Queen rose and said to them, "I will return anon. I leave you to the discussion of the issue."

"As if there is much left to discuss," Lesandurel said after she'd gone. "Coffee, House-cousin?"

Hirianthial supposed that was somewhat better than 'My Lord Jisiensire,' which while strictly correct put far too many layers of formality between him and this man, whom he did not sense to be his to command at all. Lesandurel, he thought, belonged to the Alliance . . . and because of that, he dared honesty and said, "I do not believe that was the issue she left us here to discuss."

"Ah?"

"She believes I might learn from you something of what it is to have short-lived companionship."

Lesandurel's 'ah' then was softer. He poured a second cup and offered it, and not wanting to be ungracious Hirianthial accepted it. Their auras lapped, though their fingers did not touch, and Lesandurel paused.

"You felt it?"

"That was you?" At Hirianthial's nod, Lesandurel shook himself. "I don't envy you that."

"I don't envy me it either," Hirianthial said. Had Urise come with them? God and Lady knew the priest had needed a Medplex as badly as he had. Surely moreso, given the frailty of the elderly. And if he had come, then Hirianthial had access yet to spiritual counsel . . . and his lessons, which had suddenly become far more important, if they gave him a sword to use against his enemies. Liolesa's enemies. Theresa's enemies. His enemies.

"So why does she want us to discuss it?" Lesandurel was saying. "You have companions of your own already. You don't need to be talked into it, as I see the matter."

Hirianthial looked at him, really looked: at the ease of him, at the depth and layers of his aura, at the calm that lived so well with his vibrant engagement in life. There was nothing languid about Lesandurel, nothing broken and seeping. His eyes, a rare silver, were present in a way Hirianthial had yet to see among almost any of his kind. "How do you bear it?" he said, because he had to know.

"You ask me that, though you have the mien of someone who has known loss?"

"I ask you that because I have known loss, and you must have also. But you are bearing it better than I am."

Lesandurel smiled. "Are you wed, House-cousin?"

"I—was."

"Forgive me—"

Hirianthial lifted his fingers, just enough to still the guest. "You gave no offense."

"I hope I continue not to," Lesandurel said. "Have you children?"

"No."

Lesandurel nodded. "That would be my guess, then. I bear it because I have a large family. A very large family."

"The Tam-illee you have cultivated . . . ?"

"Cultivated!" Lesandurel laughed. "You make it sound so premeditated. I did not intend to "cultivate" a family, House-cousin. I made a friend in a young and uncertain Tam-illee foxine when I visited Earth. And I decided to remain friends with her. She married, and then they had children, and when she died I thought . . ." He trailed off, then looked up at Hirianthial. "That was it, you understand. That was my moment of decision. When I buried her and thought 'it is over.' But then her daughter came to me asked me how it was fair, that I should abandon the children who'd grown up knowing me when they'd so lately lost their mother. And . . . I couldn't."

Hirianthial tried to imagine being confronted by Irine and Sascha's children, did he try to leave after the death of the twins, and felt sympathy like a cramp in his heart. "You could yet have gone," he said after a moment. "No matter their claim. To stay and give up the possibility of a wife and children of your own body—"

Lesandurel stared at him, brows lifted. "When did I say I had given up that possibility?"

"You live among outworlders, and have for centuries."

"And I will live another four or five yet," Lesandurel said. "Whoever said anything about giving up the thought of a wife?" He shook his head. "God, House-cousin. I have time. I fully plan to return and see if anyone will have me." A flash of a smile then, and a ripple of merriment through his aura that shone like the silver of his gaze. "I am waiting for the Queen to remake the world in her image; that will transform me from outré exile to a very rich and very eligible bachelor. And more seriously . . . I will not go back until I can take this, my first family, with me. I love my Tams, Lord Hirianthial. I know them each by name, and have seen them grow and struggle and prevail, love and bear young and die, carry on and carry forth and carry through every possible hardship. If they cannot stand with me at my wedding, I will not have one."

For a very long moment, Hirianthial said nothing. Could say nothing in response to the understanding that he had been thinking enough like an Eldritch to deny himself the company of the Alliance's aliens . . . but not enough like one to realize that, if he survived, if he lived his entire span, he would have time for everything.

What he said at last was, "You did not say 'return home.'"

"I have a home," Lesandurel answered, quiet. "It is in the midst of my Tams. That gift Sydnie gave me, when she welcomed me into her family, and everyone who came after." He set his cup down. "Make no mistake, Lord Hirianthial. I may return to our world to take a wife. I may even buy myself a holding there. But I will never live again on our world. I belong out here, among my own."

Another hesitation, one he felt like a hiccup in his heart. Then he said, "Tell me about them?"

The other man smiled. "I would be glad to."

Some hours later, after Lesandurel had left in the company of three of his foxines, Sascha found him alone there, still sitting, looking out the window. Hesitantly, the Harat-Shar said, "Long day?"

It struck him as ridiculous, a crazy humor: a long day. Days to people of his lifespan were supposed to be short, and they were, and yet he could answer honestly, "Yes." Not because the day had been long, but because the revelations in it had been painfully vast, and he found himself troubled at how deeply he'd erred in so many ways. "Sascha, did the elder priest come with us?"

"He did," Sascha said, still choosing his words carefully. "You want to see him? I can take you."

"No." Hirianthial stood. "Tomorrow, perhaps. It's evening, by starbase time, is it not?"

"Yes. . . ."

"Tomorrow, then. If there is a room prepared for me. . . ."

"Well, you'll laugh," Sascha said, scratching his arm until the fur on it bristled.

Hirianthial glanced at him, brows lifted.

"This is your room, more or less. It's a suite for the Queen, and she said you were family, so if you go through that door—" Pointing. "You get to your bedroom. Hers is on the opposite side." He paused, tail sagging. "Hopefully you're not going to find that inappropriate or something."

"Inappropriate . . ." He shook his head slowly, feeling again the brush of hair against throat. "No. Once upon a time, I was a man who slept in a chamber adjacent to Liolesa's, when I was not standing at her door. If anything, it feels like going back. And going forward."

"How do you mean?"

"You said it once on Kerayle, arii. There's no running from one's problems."

"And if I remember right," Sascha said dryly, "You answered that it depended on whether you were running toward or away from them."

Hirianthial paused, allowed himself a laugh. "I did, didn't I?"

"You are good with the one-liners," Sascha said, and added modestly, "It's why I set myself up for them."

He did laugh then. Then said, quieter, "I have spent almost six decades running from my problem, Sascha. And the Eldritch have spent over a thousand years running from theirs. Now all those birds are returning to the glove, and we can blame no one but ourselves for training them to it." He shook his head again. "Well. I am done with running."

Sascha's ears perked. "Great. Does that mean we're finally going to go kill the bad guys? All of them this time?"

The flare in the tigraine's aura was like the coronal ejection of a sun. Hirianthial hesitated, caught off guard. "Are you so eager then?"

"No," Sascha said. "If we could do it all without blood-letting, I'd be first in line. Battlehells, among Harat-Shar there's a good chance we could have screwed them straight. But somehow I doubt pirates and slavers are going to respond to 'make love, not war.' Right?"

"Yes," he said, quiet.

"Then whatever it takes," Sascha said, meeting his eyes with that fierceness. "To make my sister safe, and my friends."

What could he say to such ardor? Nothing. He offered his hand instead, saw the incredulity that flashed through Sascha's gaze before the Harat-Shar stepped forth and took it. Warm fingers, bare skin on one side, furred on the other, but callused from the work of repairing a ship and strong from moving cargo. Had grief never driven Hirianthial from his world, would he have experienced such a touch? Felt the loyalty burning in it, stronger than stars? Been changed by it, and made more whole?

"For once," Hirianthial said, because it would make the tigraine laugh, "We shall be the rescuers."

It startled Sascha out of the intimacy of the touch; his laugh had a precipitous feel. "Reese will be so confused."

"Hopefully," Hirianthial said, "not as confused as our enemies."

"So?" the Chatcaavan asked, lounging in a chair in his borrowed Eldritch shape, very like a noble in his indolence. Baniel thought it added significantly to the verisimilitude of the body, one that was flawless save for the eyes . . . and the fact that the Chatcaavan spoke only Universal. And his own language, presumably, which Baniel had not bothered to learn.

"So," he said, setting the data tablet he no longer needed to hide on the table. "It is what I expected. The Well repeaters are gone."

"Gone?" the Chatcaavan repeated, quirking a brow.

Strange how similar the expression was, and unlike the more limited espers that comprised the majority of his race, Baniel could read the alien's aura, enough to tell that the emotions matched. Either skeptical Chatcaava arched whatever passed for brows on a dragon's face, or the shape-change was even more complete than anyone thought. "Yes. I had wondered if the Queen had some sort of self-destruct for them, since the arrival of an unwanted ship would have been disastrous if it had been able to use them to send word of the planet's location. Now I know.

They're definitely gone. If we want a message to go out, we will have to send the ship. It shouldn't have to go far to reach a public Well repeater."

"Then send it now," the Chatcaavan said. "No use baiting a trap you can't trip." He flexed his fingers, as if unused to them, though from what Baniel had seen the Chatcaava had fine hands of their own. Tipped with scythe-like talons, perhaps, but not so different as all that. "Will we be able to keep our pets in check until then?"

"The others?" Baniel shrugged easily. "The new queen will serve us admirably there."

The way the other canted his head, though . . . that felt alien. More a predator's motion than a humanoid's. "You think she has the strength to do this? A female?"

"Her sex is immaterial," Baniel answered. "Her ambition and her naiveté are all that need concern us. She wants all the Eldritch to bow to her as their new sovereign and thinks that merely deposing her predecessor should be enough to ensure it."

The Chatcaavan snorted. "Ridiculous. When one usurps a throne, one must kill one's enemies and extirpate their families, possessions and allies. Nothing less will serve."

"It would be the wise course," Baniel agreed. "But I think she is too aware that doing so would deprive her of half the population of the existing Eldritch. She will try everything in her power to keep them from requiring that of her. And then she will fail."

"Because her enemies will fight her?" the Chatcaavan said.

"Oh, I don't know," Baniel said, looking out the window at the cold wind rippling the lake outside the palace. "It would be convenient for me if Liolesa's allies took the battle to her. But you can never be sure with them, with the Alliance influence they've allowed into their heads. They might parley because they believe in talk. Or they might parley to keep Surela from attacking until rescue arrives. Or they might kill her. Or surrender. Who knows?" He shook his head. "No, I dislike leaving such things to chance. There is a man who has been paying court to Surela since she was presented, and whom she has been ignoring for just as long. He now begins to wonder if the Eldritch are ready for a king. I have arranged for him to advance his own plans." He smiled thinly. "It turns out that he has a finer grasp of the potential uses of technology than the woman who's spurned him."

The Chatcaavan chuckled, a low, growling sound. "You are cruel. I approve."

"I'm glad. So, shall we send the ship?"

"Let us," the Chatcaavan said. "Though if it is only going as far as the next repeater, it would be pointless to send gifts . . . and I had anticipated sending the gifts."

"Ah?" Baniel asked, curious.

"My patron would have enjoyed them," the Chatcaavan said. "I would have sent him two, maybe three. Women, though. Your men are too much trouble."

Baniel smiled a little. "Are they? I had no idea. Still, a pity not to make the gift. Unless you'd like it instead?"

The Chatcaavan yawned. "It would be pleasing. The body has needs."

"I'll arrange it," Baniel said. "How many of the men must go with the ship, to fly it?"

"Oh, most of them," the Chatcaavan said. "But then, between the two of us, we can control a great deal. Can't we."

"You are ready for another lesson in mind-magery then?"

The alien reached for him with an alacrity that was more akin to a serpent's, and made a lie of his borrowed body. "Always."

"Very good," Baniel said, and extended his hand. "I love a willing pupil."

CHAPTER 3

Leaving Taylor and Belinor to watch over their . . . prisoner, she guessed she had to call him, Reese took Irine with her to explore the castle. The two of them made a tour through the gardens, as best they could; the paths in it were visible only because they were less choked with thorned vines, and both she and Irine stabbed themselves more than once stepping over or pushing past them. They'd reached a large structure in the middle, with another set of those enormous doors, and inside found something more like the castle Reese expected, with a great hall and stone steps leading up to floors with multiple rooms . . . empty now. Scavenged, she wondered? Had someone removed everything in an orderly way, or had things been stolen? There was detritus in the corners, and a lot of sand blown in through windows that had once held glass, from the jagged teeth and broken black frames. But no furniture, no signs of habitation except for the inevitable nests made by (thankfully) small animals.

They climbed the stairs to the very last landing and

found that it opened on a walkway around the conical roof, and from there they could see . . . forever, Reese thought, her heart pounding. Her agoraphobia? Maybe not. She wasn't afraid. Or she was, just not of the size of the sky and the sea.

"You okay?" Irine asked, gently.

"I . . . um . . . could use a hand," Reese admitted, and was glad of the one the tigraine slipped into hers. She accepted the squeeze, let it center her. "Planets still scare me sometimes. Unconstrained ones, anyway."

"Are you sure it's not the size of your responsibilities?"

"That too."

Irine chuckled. She pointed with her free hand. "Look at that! It almost looks like there used to be something there."

"Like what?" Reese asked, squinting.

"Like a statue, maybe? Outside the castle though!" The tigraine glanced around. "Actually, the castle itself is pretty spectacular from up here. It's big. Like 'fit a town in the courtyard' big."

"I wonder why there isn't a town then?" Reese wondered. "I thought castles had towns in them."

"Maybe this one did before the garden ate it." Irine started pacing the parapet, leading Reese by the hand. Reese narrowed her eyes against the cutting wind, trying not to shiver. She was still blinking against the weather when Irine said, somber. "Oh, okay. That's why there's no town in the castle's courtyard. The town's already outside it."

"What?" Reese exclaimed.

"Look."

She and Irine had been surveying the north, further up the coast. To the south, though, the coast zagged inward toward a forest, and there if she squinted she could see gray roofs. As towns went it was tiny; she doubted it was much larger than a handful of her neighborhoods on Mars. But it was very distinctly a town.

"Maybe it's abandoned?" Irine said.

Reese thought of the Queen's charge. Hadn't she said something about Eldritch here that needed a lady? "No . . . no I think there are people there. Just not many."

"I'm glad we have someone along who speaks the language, then. It will be nice to be able to explain why there's an army marching on them with flaming palmers."

Reese covered her face with her hands, something Irine allowed by letting go of her fingers. The tigraine hugged her. "Come on, let's go back down and see about some food. Maybe we can contact Malia and see how she's getting on with those Swords we sent her to meet up with."

"Right," Reese said, dragging in a deep breath. It cut her throat. "Ugh, why does it have to be so cold?"

"Because you like it cold," Irine said. "Why do you think I had to buy so many socks?"

"A town?" Belinor said when they asked him about it. "I suppose there must be one. There are no castles or estates without towns. But I have to imagine it was abandoned long since. There is no lord here anymore to serve them."

"What do lords do, exactly?" Reese said, sitting on the floor. Someone had managed to light a fire in the great room's hearth. The blaze looked very tiny, given that the fireplace was longer than Reese was tall, but at least it gave some meager warmth to the part of the room they were using.

"They . . . are lords!" Belinor said, confused. "They caretake the people."

"Where's Kis'eh't to say something acid where we need her," Irine said.

"He's not kidding," Taylor said, unexpectedly. She was

sitting behind their prisoner, keeping her palmer trained on him. When they looked at her, she continued, "It's supposed to be a circuit. The people who work the land do that. The people in the castle protect and feed them, get them what they need—"

"Feed them?" Irine asked, skeptical. "Aren't they the ones 'working the land'?"

"Sure," Taylor said. "But it's not enough to feed everyone. And if you have a little bit of one thing and a little bit of another, and a cow and a few chickens, all of a sudden you're doing a billion chores. If you're just raising wheat, and you give part of your harvest away and get back eggs and milk and meat, that's more efficient."

"More efficient is farming with machines," Irine said.

"But they don't have machines here."

Reese shook her head. "Whether it makes sense or not to us, Irine, it's what they do. Still, I can't help but think they wouldn't need protection if their lords weren't fighting over whatever the heck it is they fight over." She glanced at Belinor.

The priest said, "There are no wars like that anymore, my Lady. But there are . . . creatures."

"Creatures?"

"He means monsters," a voice croaked. Taylor leaped to her feet, pointing her weapon at their guest. "Please, tell your fox I don't mean to flex so much as a thought, much less a muscle. What did you hit me with?"

"Two palmers, set to stun," Reese said, watching the other Eldritch blink blearily and try to sit up. He failed and slumped back to the ground.

With a shudder, he said, "Can I at least have a blanket? This floor's damned cold."

Reese nodded to Irine, who brought one from a pack and set it carefully around his shoulders. "You were saying?"

"When we first settled," the man said. "There were more of them. Centuries of harassing them have made them move away. But there are things in the forests here that make short work of people. They're huge, they're territorial, and they can project some sort of aura, and it petrifies people."

"Are you serious?" Reese asked, startled.

"We call them basilisks." He smiled, faint. "That was a job that used up a lot of us, initially. Mostly men. Men died often, defending women and children. It's why we have such a complicated family structure. We came back from a small base of people. If you can call what we've got now successfully coming back." He glanced at Belinor. "Of course, we complicated that process by killing off a lot of the people who showed stronger than average talents."

"This is blasphemy," Belinor said to Reese, shoulders squared. "Blasphemy, my Lady."

"But true?" Reese asked, glancing at the stranger.

"Blasphemy can't be true!"

"I dunno," Taylor said. "His story sounds plausible."

"Who *are* you?" Reese asked finally.

"I'm Val," the stranger said with a crooked grin. "Former priest of the Lord."

Belinor half-stood, his outrage palpable.

"And you left the priesthood because . . . you're a blasphemer?" Reese asked, curious.

"I left because the Lord's priests hunt and kill people with the potential for a mind-mage's talents, and there was nothing I could do to end it. I was tired of killing people innocent of anything but a hypothetical future crime."

A long pause. Reese said, "Um, and they didn't kill you because?"

"Because most of the priests of the Lord have better than average talent, and some of them are mind-mages themselves," Val said dryly. "So in addition to being murderers, we were also hypocrites."

Now Belinor was also staring at their visitor.

"They don't tell you that part, do they," Val said. He shifted against his bonds and grunted. "Do you really have to bind me like this? It's uncomfortable."

"You did just admit to being a murderer," Irine said, tail twitching.

"I won't deny it." He grimaced. "When I was young I believed the stories. Whole-heartedly. I needed to believe them, because I did have those talents." He glanced at Belinor. "You understand, my only choices were to believe myself a monster, or believe that I had been anointed by the Lord to serve His sacred mission. Which would you have chosen?"

"I . . . I don't know." Belinor sounded stricken.

Val nodded. "There you are, then." He closed his eyes. "You have become very thoughtful, Lady of the Castle."

"Reese," she said. "My name's Reese Eddings. And yes. I maybe know a little bit about how hard it is to break away from your social conditioning. Enough to do something everyone else thinks is horrible."

"And this makes you trust me?"

"No," she said, honestly. "I trust you because I like your eyes."

Irine pressed a wrist to her mouth.

"Yon tigress seems to find that amusing."

"Yon tigress has a filthy imagination, and she's always teasing me about not joining her in the gutter," Reese said wryly. "I think you can untie him."

"My Lady! At least ask him what he's doing here!"

"That matters?" she asked the acolyte, confused.

"He is dallying here where he does not belong," Belinor said firmly.

"Because he had so many other places to go?" Irine lifted her brows. "What with the 'people kill mind-mages and apparently hate rogue priests' thing?"

"He's right to be suspicious," Val said. His eyes were sparkling again, and Reese liked it and was instantly wary. And then he finished: "I'm here because I'm the reincarnation of Corel."

CHAPTER 4

In the morning, Hirianthial asked to be shown to Urise's room and followed one of Lesandurel's kin—for he should so call them now, shouldn't he?—to the priest's door. Chiming for entrance, he received not the Alliance's computer-thrown voice, but a mindtouch: *Come, my son.*

Entering, he found the priest . . . in a chair by the window, once again lost in the voluminous folds of his robes, smiling the same smile he'd worn when they first met in Ontine. Startled, Hirianthial said, "It is as if you have merely been transplanted, Elder."

"This chair is more comfortable," Urise said. "Prithee, don't tell the Queen I said so."

"Oh, she already knows." Hirianthial sat across from him. "Given how many of them she has warmed off our world. How do you fare, then?"

"Better than before I left." The priest flexed his fingers beneath the concealing sleeves, making the fabric flutter. "Truly, the medicine of these non-Eldritch astonishes." He lifted his brows. "And you, my son? You look more hale yourself."

"If a touch like a shorn sheep?" Hirianthial smiled a little. "I am as well as could be expected, given the circumstance."

"Which involves the ending of the Veil, yes?"

"You knew?"

"That it would come or that it has?" Urise shook his head minutely, and the words were delicately stippled, part shadows, part silver. "It was inevitable. And nothing less than violence would have served. It has become too comfortable, the Veil. All things must change if they would live."

"So I noted," Hirianthial murmured.

"So you have. And what will you do with that knowledge, mmm?"

Hirianthial looked up. "Beg a few last lessons from you ere I go back, Elder. Where I go now, I must have every weapon to hand."

"Ah?" Urise narrowed his eyes. "Have you given over your horror so quickly, then?"

Had he? He looked at the priest and said, "They sell our own to slavery, to die in the arms of dragons. They use weapons given to them by pirates and drug lords. They have ships, and they have our world at their mercy. Whatever advantage I have, I must use. *Must* use. Everything is at stake."

"And if I told you that you could stand at the head of a battlefield and rip the souls from a thousand men, as Corel once did?" Urise asked, his tone more a question than an attack. And because of that, Hirianthial hesitated, took the idea seriously, tried to imagine it . . . and couldn't.

"I could do such a thing?" he asked, low.

"It was done before. Why not again?"

So it was possible. God and Lady, that a man could be more destructive than a bomb! And yet, if there was nothing between death and all those he warded but his own mind. . . . "Will you teach me?"

Urise sighed. "You already have the trick of it, my son, or you could not have used it in your own defense already. But let us practice other things that might be of use."

"Such as?"

"Such as how to survive the effort," Urise replied, dry. "For if you think striking out against ten men is taxing, wait you until you try a hundred."

"At your convenience, Elder."

"Then we begin now. Recall you the earlier teachings? The Now and the Quiet and the foundations?"

Hirianthial inclined his head.

"Keep those things in the forefront," the priest said. "We shall begin."

"What am I to do?"

Urise eyed him, then said, "Don't fall." And then a gentle pressure settled on his aura and began to push inward. Hirianthial wondered what the priest was about, but obediently kept the force at bay. Slowly, it grew stronger. He continued to hold.

How strange it must have looked from outside: two men, sitting at their ease facing one another, eyes closed, silent, for hours. But as the time passed, Hirianthial began to sweat and then to tremble with the effort. When he collapsed at last, he was startled to find himself on the floor.

Urise leaned over. "What have you learned, then?"

"That I can be crushed by a man a third my weight?" Hirianthial said, bemused.

"Not a bad beginning." The priest pursed his lips. "Go on."

"That there must be a better way to resist than to endure."

"Better," Urise said. "You already endure too much.

Anything else?"

"That you know something I don't," Hirianthial said, eyeing him.

"How is this, then: you collapsed because you were hungry."

"I . . . beg your pardon?" Hirianthial paused, then frowned. "What time is it? We are past the hour? We are!"

Urise chuffed a laugh. "We are expending physical effort, my son. Don't forget it. Now go and find fuel and rest."

"And you?" Hirianthial asked, lifting his brows. "Have you not also expended physical effort?"

The priest looked exactly as he had when they'd begun: pacific, unbowed, with a touch of merriment hidden in his eyes and swirled through his aura. "I have."

Hirianthial folded his arms.

Urise grinned. "Your assignment is to figure why you are tired and hungry, and I am not. And to practice the renitence."

"A riddle!" Hirianthial said, amused. "Very well, Elder. I shall apply myself directly. To that and the renitence."

"After the meal."

"After a meal." He bowed and withdrew . . . and stopped in the corridor, running a hand down the back of his exposed neck and finding it slick. A meal, yes. But *after* a bath.

For a heartbeat, no one moved. Almost, Reese exhaled.

And then Belinor threw himself at their prisoner with a howl of rage, and Irine and Taylor leaped after him. There was a tussle Reese knew better than to interrupt and then the foxine was dragging the youth off Val, still yammering away in his own tongue.

Val was sporting a new bruise—or two—and seeing it,

Reese sighed. "Taylor, why don't you walk our native guide around the castle a bit? Take him to the roof, see what he makes of the town, maybe."

"That sounds like a great idea," Taylor said, eyeing Belinor. "Yes?"

"I will not leave a lady with that outlaw!"

Irine said, "I'll be with her, and I'm armed."

"It may not be enough!"

"If it's not, it's too late already and you should get away so you can run for help," Reese said, trying not to sound as acerbic as she felt. Her hired help was pushy and never listened to her, fine. But the biddable Eldritch acolyte assigned to her started giving her trouble within a day of being assigned to her? Apparently something about her inspired backtalk. No wonder her glares never worked.

The acolyte was waffling, so she said firmly, "Please go, okay? I'd like to get this sorted without the interruptions."

"Very well, my Lady," the youth said, though he looked distinctly rebellious. He did, however, allow Taylor to lead him away. Hopefully she'd keep him for a while.

Reese went to the Eldritch and paused. "To untie you, I'm going to have to touch you."

"And that should matter why?"

Reese exchanged a look with Irine, and their captive chuckled. "I can feel your skepticism like a brick falling on my head. Yes, I know it's hard to believe, but properly trained, you don't have to feel anything through your skin . . . or floating in the air, either. It's true that the Eldritch you've met would have you keep away because they can't control it. But that's what it is: a lack of control. Just like you couldn't walk until you learned?"

"Blood and freedom," Reese muttered. "Can you stop with the shocks for a minute?" She started untying him. "Figures I've finally met an Eldritch with a sense of humor and the personality to go with it. There had to be one."

Val grinned as she released him and rolled, slowly and awkwardly, upright. "Thanks. You tied them tight."

"I'm good with knots," Irine said.

The Eldritch snorted, but said nothing, and Reese sat across from him with the fire at her back. Irine joined her and together they stared at him. She wasn't sure what she was waiting for. Mostly she thought she was tired.

Irine finally whispered, "He looks pretty normal."

Reese laughed and rubbed her face. To Val, she said, "So why are you trying to pull Belinor's chain?"

"Pull his chain?" the Eldritch said, puzzled.

"Upset him," Irine offered. "Tease him just to annoy him."

"Oh!" Their guest looked superbly innocent. "Was I?"

"The reincarnation of Corel?" Reese prompted, dry.

He looked at her, and suddenly she couldn't tell if he'd intended it as a joke. Her heart fluttered.

Val grinned. "Seemed like the thing to say at the time. Besides, it's a good reason for me to be here, where he died."

"His castle," Reese said.

"His castle?" Val snorted. "Who told you that story? It's the official one, I'll grant you that, but it's not the real one."

"Uggggh, just tell me already!" Reese threw up her hands. "You're all so bleeding enigmatic! Get on with it!"

He laughed. "Fine, fine. Have you wondered why Ontine is a palace, but this is a castle?"

"No?"

Irine's ears were flat, though.

"Yon tigress does, though."

She eyed him. "Well . . . it is weird. Architecturally."

"And she's a tigraine, not a tigress," Reese said. "Tigers are animals. Tigraines are people."

"He can call me 'yon tigress,'" Irine said. "It's kind of cute."

Reese covered her eyes. "Ugh, stop flirting with him, Irine. Back to the castle, please?"

Thankfully, Val had let it pass. That was the last thing Reese needed: her Harat-Shar seducing an Eldritch she still wasn't sure of. "This was the original capital. Corel lived north of here, but he occupied it—his solitary self, you understand—and when he killed most of the army that tried him, and finally died here, well . . . no one had the heart to stay. They moved south and started over. Palaces this time, not castles, because they saw for themselves just how useful castles were against the things they were really afraid of, so why bother with the false reassurances? Anyway. A few people remain in town, but nobody's lived in this castle since. And I am here because it's the furthest I could get from the bloodrobes, and distance is a good thing when people have to ride horses to cross it."

"The whats?" Irine said, frowning.

"The bloodrobes," Val replied. He sat crosslegged, but loosely, with the soles of his feet pressed together in front of him. "What one calls our kind, the hunters of men and women and innocent children."

"Oh," Reese whispered, struck by vivid memory. "Baniel."

Val glanced up so sharply Irine half-rose, brandishing the palmer. But all the Eldritch did was hiss, "Did you say 'Baniel'?"

"Please tell me he's your enemy. That sounds a lot like he's your enemy." Reese looked up at the ceiling. "Please, I could use some good luck here."

"Have you come to this world to kill him? Dare I hope?" Val asked. "Because if so, oh, I am with you."

"What did he do to you?" Irine was, Reese noted, no longer aiming the weapon at Val, but trying not to play with her tail, which was her nervous habit.

"He was the one what swept in and made things more

vile," Val said. "And he was the one who turned everyone else on me when I spoke against it." He glanced at Reese. "Called me a traitor to my race, and a renegade, and trust me when I say that the word from him is an epitaph, rather than the epithet it is from your boy."

"You make that sound as if you were important," Irine said.

"Oh, I was, a little." He smiled. "He and I were the only possible candidates for the head of the order."

Another silence. At least this time, Reese was sure there wouldn't be any bodies flying around to end it.

"So do I hear right, that you might want something done about him? And that perhaps you might have com- patriots with modern weapons who might be of aid?"

"Your hearing's not all that bad, but it's embroidering things," Reese said, feeling tired and suddenly cold despite the fire. Or maybe it was because of the fire; she peered at it and found it a lot lower than it was before. "Look, we have a billion enemies—"

"More like fifty thousand, or maybe twenty-five thou- sand, depending on which population estimate was right," Irine interrupted.

"Fine, twenty-five thousand enemies, a lot of who seem to have plenty of modern weapons themselves, plus there are pirates here with a ship in orbit and possibly at least one Chatcaavan," Reese said. "So getting you over to the palace for your revenge isn't going to be as easy as 'hooray, I've got a couple of aliens with palmers, I can go clean up the priesthood now!'"

"No," Val said, studying her with interest. "But it seems I have stumbled on something a lot more interesting than mere revenge."

"You might not think so when you're done hearing the rest of it." Reese sighed and said to Irine, "Call the others down? I think it's time we contacted Malia, if she'll answer, and start making real plans."

CHAPTER 5

"There, my Lady," Thaniet said, tucking a final emerald-topped pin into Surela's hair. "You look radiant."

Surela studied herself in the mirror and said, silvering the words for gratitude, "Thank you. You have a way with the toilette."

The other woman flushed a tender peach at the cheeks. "Oh, my Lady. My efforts were only barely adequate before. Now that you've risen in station, you really do deserve a dedicated lady's maid."

"A dedicated lady's maid wouldn't be you," Surela said. She smiled wearily at Thaniet's reflection. "I prefer your touch to a servant's, and suspect I always will."

Thaniet lowered her eyes, but she was smiling. "You are too kind, my Lady."

All their words had been silvered and gilt; it was always thus with Thaniet. They talked and the world became a brighter, more beautiful place, cradled in the filigree of optimism and faith and gentleness. Would that she could tarry here and talk with someone sympathetic to her aims!

But she could not. "I appreciate the effort you put into it today, particularly, as I now go to unpleasant duty."

"May I ask?" Thaniet said, hesitant.

Surela sighed. She turned from the mirror and surveyed the bedroom she had claimed as her right as the new Queen of the Eldritch and still found it stamped too well with Liolesa's mark for her taste. But there would be time to address that, after she had settled the realm, which was the matter that concerned her now. "I summon the detained, to see if they might be convinced to give me fealty."

Thaniet's hesitation was obvious.

"Yes, I know. The chances of it are low," Surela said. "But what use killing them? They might not become good servants of the Crown, but they might be obedient ones, the way we were to Liolesa until she gave us unforgiveable insult." She shuddered. "A mind-mage. Imagine it. And to think Jisiensire was harboring that seed all along! And that I tried to bring him suit!" She smoothed her sleeves over her arms, trying to still the gooseflesh that had run down them at the thought. Hirianthial was fair of face and manner, and had been well connected and well-moneyed . . . but if she'd known he was a sorcerer. . . .

Shaking herself, she continued in the shadowed mode, "I don't need them to love or respect me. I just need them to agree not to spend their strength testing ours, and die for their pains."

"What does Athanesin say of this plan?" Thaniet asked tentatively.

Surela snorted. "I have not asked him, for it is not his to opine. Besides, what would any man say of such a plan? He will want to kill them, of course, and install some of our own in their place."

Thaniet shivered. "I am glad you are not so blood-thirsty, my Lady. It would be a fell thing, to begin a dynasty with the slaughter of so many people."

"I know," Surela said, the words muted. "And I will not, I pledge you. So I hope they will not prove too intractable. Will you come with me? You may, if you wish."

"I would, my Lady . . . but the priest has asked me to see him. Perhaps I can attend your next meeting? Or do you see them all at once?"

"No," Surela said. "Together they can give one another too much support. I will take them one at a time." She smiled and returned to their silver-gilt world, the words glittering. "You have been a great help. Thank you for it."

"Oh, my Lady," Thaniet said, blushing. "It is nothing beside what you have done for me and my family." She curtseyed, her skirts rustling. "By your leave? I will see what the high priest wishes."

"Go on, then."

Liolesa's office also still felt far too much like *Liolesa's* office, and that was something Surela intended to rectify immediately. The private spaces could afford to wait. The public spaces had to reflect her new rule which, she thought with distaste as she glanced around the room, would be far less tainted by the notions of mortals. Tradition would serve them, as it always had. There was nothing out there for the Eldritch save danger and jealousy and the avarice of people who had not their talents, their beauty, or the wisdom afforded them by their lifespans. No . . . better to remain withdrawn, where they could live their lives in peace. Surela regretted deposing Liolesa in the fashion she had, but the former queen had brought it on herself; by Surela's way of thinking, it was fated that weapons of the very cultures Liolesa had been unwisely courting should end her reign.

All of this was a deeply sordid business, and she very much wanted to be done with it. And hopefully, this next interview would begin that process, so that the world could resume the normal rhythms of life. Surela did not look up when the guards announced Araelis Mina Jisiensire's arrival, but waited until they'd withdrawn to consider her guest.

Unsurprisingly, Araelis was infuriated, obviously so. She had never been deft at disguising her feelings, and in this instance Surela suspected she wasn't even trying. What was to be expected of Hirianthial's successor, though?

"Lady Araelis," Surela said. "Please, join me by the fire."

"You'll have to kill me before I join you in anything," Araelis answered, the words black as ashes.

Surela sighed. "We need not begin this way. I don't expect you to like me, Araelis, but surely we can work together to ensure the prosperity of your family."

"The . . . the prosperity. Of my family!" Araelis stared at her. "Are you in earnest? You expect me to believe that you care anything for the welfare of my family when your puppet priest delivered my cousin all but dead into the middle of the winter court, and for no aim other than to be sure he was denounced? So you could give everyone a reputable reason for having him slain for denying your affections?"

Surela felt her cheeks warm. Maintaining her aplomb was difficult, but she managed. "I did not have him slain for spurning me."

"Oh, tell me a fresh lie," Araelis snapped. "You are a vain and foolish and short-sighted woman. You have invited our worst enemies onto our soil, thinking that once they are paid they will never return. But if you feed the wolf once, Surela, he will be back . . . and he will bring all his kin."

Surela had hoped using Araelis's name would invite the other woman to consider the same intimacy. She was now no longer certain she was glad to have opened that door. "I have been assured that the creatures we've bought have been paid already."

"Oh is that so." Araelis snorted. "Yes, you continue thinking that. Idiot!"

"That is enough!"

"No, that's not enough! Because you *are* an idiot! Do you think the slavers who were picking us off in the Alliance when we dared to leave our world will hesitate even a heartbeat before descending on us now that they know—now that you and that three-times-bedamned priest have *told them!*—where we lie? What do you think Hirianthial was spending his blood to investigate in the outworld before returning here? We have lost too many to dragons, and now you have given us all to them, and the worst of it is that after dragging a false crown onto your head you will still do not the first duty of a liegelady and find us protection against the very enemies you've bought us! Goddess and Lord, but to think that our downfall would be the doing of traitors! I had thought accident would belie us first but you have undone all that Jerisa and Maraesa spent their reigns erecting in our defense!"

Surela leaped to her feet. "That is enough! Whether you accept it or not, I am your sovereign now and you will not speak to me this fashion!"

"You will never be my sovereign," Araelis snarled, the words dripping black and shadows. "And even if Liolesa died tomorrow, you would never be anyone's liegelady, because you will fail in the one paramount duty that only a queen can undertake . . . the protection of the realm." She folded her arms around her swollen belly. "Am I done here, or do you wish to have me executed for my insolence?"

"It is not insolence! You skirt perilously close to treason!"

"Oh . . . oh no. You have not seen treason yet." Araelis

narrowed her eyes. "You have set your sword against the Galare-Jisiensire. Good luck with that, 'Queen' Surela."

"You may go," Surela said, before she said anything more regrettable.

Without thanking her for the dismissal, Araelis departed.

The nerve of the woman! To say such things! As if she knew better than anyone what would serve the world and the people!

. . . still, there was the chance, slight as it might be, that she did know aught that was kept from others. Jisiensire enjoyed a rare closeness with the royal line; perhaps Liolesa had confided something in Araelis, or Hirianthial, that she had not mentioned to the court? This business of Hirianthial observing the acts of outworld slavers sounded plausible.

Fortunately, he was still in the catacombs awaiting the trials of the priests. She could ask. He would not be glad to receive her, but perhaps for the good of their people he could be compelled to give answer. Best to arm herself with that knowledge before attempting her next interview; if Araelis had been less than tractable, and she only of allied family, Surela could only imagine what her reception would be when she attempted the northern branch of the Galares. She sighed and took up her mantle, remembering the cold in the catacombs, and went to ask for escort.

Liolesa found him the following day in the room he'd been assigned. She did not look well, he thought, nor would she until she was home again, but her aura smoothed at the sight of him. He set his stylus down and started to rise, but she lifted a hand. "Don't, cousin. I am the one who intrudes. I do not interrupt anything, I hope?"

He glanced at the tablet and smiled faintly. "Nothing that would not make you laugh, perhaps, to hear."

"Oh? I could use such a tale." She stepped into the room, sat at a chair by the door.

"I am arranging for horses."

A comet-tail of bright amusement skittered over the dome of her aura, silvered her words. "Theresa's horses?"

He tapped the stylus gently against the data tablet, kept his voice even and the color neutral. "Yes. They remember me well on that world."

She hesitated. "I imagine they do," she said finally. "Well, you will not hear me laughing, cousin. I am glad, in fact."

"Oh?"

"Because it shows you have expectations for a future where horses still play a part," Liolesa finished. "Where your lady has time and peace to raise them for me."

"And when you still need them? Will you?"

Liolesa smiled a little. "An Eldritch will always need a horse. Whether she is using that horse for transportation or for pleasure. I'm told you have been to see the priest?"

"Who has resumed my lessons, yes," Hirianthial said, thinking of the one he'd endured that morning. "I have a great deal yet to learn." He added, quiet, "She is not my lady."

"You are still carrying the swords for Araelis, so, no, I expect not," Liolesa said, with far too bland an expression.

"Your attempt to properly educate me using Lesandurel—"

"Worked? Or did not?"

He denied himself the severe look he wanted to award her and said only, "I am not Lesandurel."

"No one would have ever said differently—"

"And I will not do things as he did, nor make his choices. I will make my own."

"So will we all," Liolesa said, her aura flashing dark, like steel turned against moonlight. And then, rueful. "Forgive me, Hiran. There is so little I can do right now, and little joy to be had. I fear I may be indulging myself at your expense, if only to have something pleasing to contemplate in my exile."

Hirianthial sighed and smiled, just a little. "And you find me with the horses, doing the same."

"Well, then . . . perhaps you might show me what you are about, and we can both be diverted by something that does not abrade you quite so much."

On this they whiled a pleasurable hour away, and were in fact still engaged in it when one of the ubiquitous Tams arrived at the door and begged their attention. "My Queen," he said. "The Alliance ambassador has requested your presence for a meeting with a member of the Fleet Admiralty."

Liolesa rose and said to Hirianthial. "Come. You will be wanted for this discussion."

The Ambassador and Admiral awaited them in one of the hotel's conference rooms, a space dominated by its window and the view of the ships that passed beyond its flexglass wall; everything else fell away, an understated sweep of midnight blue carpets and dark brown furniture cut in simple, elegant lines. The twain standing by the window were the sole spots of color: a female Seersa, white fur pied with fire-red, wearing maroon edged in silver surmounted by a black cloak affixed with the Alliance's crest, and a human man, skin dark as chestnuts with a fringe of short black hair, in the stark splendor of the Fleet's dress uniform, cobalt blue and black and gold and silver.

"Your Majesty," the Ambassador said, drawing nigh and bowing. Speaking in Universal—not a given, with the Seersa, for Hirianthial recalled the few people allowed to learn their tongue by treaty stipulation were mostly Seersa. "Thank you for coming. As you can see, Admiral Ogaban has arrived."

"With news, I hope?"

"Good and bad," the human said, stepping forth. He had a mellifluous bass, and none of the unease Hirianthial had often marked among those fresh introduced to the Eldritch; even his aura was a calm burnished silver. "Your Majesty. It's a pleasure to make your acquaintance, though I would have preferred better circumstances."

"As would we all," she said. "This is my Lord of War, my cousin Hirianthial Sarel Jisiensire. Lord Hirianthial, Ambassador Fetchpoint."

"My Lord," the Seersa said, looking up at him. "It's good to see you on your feet. I trust the Fleet hospital met with your approval?"

"They did very well by me, thank you," Hirianthial said, and wondered at his own acceptance of the unexpected title. But then, had he not said that he was committed at Liolesa's side to the protection of their Body?

"Excellent," Fetchpoint said. "Then if we might have a seat? Admiral Ogaban can outline what we can immediately send in response to your request for aid."

"The good news," Ogaban said once they'd settled at the conference table, "is that I can free up a scout to send your way. Our scouts are heavily armed ships with fifty-man complements; they're trained to sneak into hot zones and grapple with enemies that might not want to see them coming. They're just the sort of ships I'd want for a situation like this." He met their eyes. "The not so good news is that I won't have that ship to send for another two weeks."

Hirianthial could feel the flare of Liolesa's aura as she reacted, though no sign of her tumult reached her face.

"I have spoken at length with Ambassador Fetchpoint," Ogaban continued, "about our need to honor the treaty we've signed with you, and what that entails, and how what we're currently offering is not sufficient to the promises we've made you. That we made those promises before we became embroiled in a war on our coreward border shouldn't put constraints on our delivery, even if realistically it does. This is particularly odious because I strongly suspect that what's happening on your world, Your Majesty, is only another arm of the same war. Given that, then, I have a ship en route that should arrive here tomorrow.

"This is one of Fleet Intelligence's quick-insert vessels. It's manned by a single FIA hold, a group of operatives who've trained together and remained together since. I want them to go in and get the intelligence we need so the scout can come in swinging."

"And they could not handle the pirate vessel themselves?" Liolesa asked.

"Not unless it's a lot smaller than we're guessing from your description," Ogaban said. "I won't rule it out, but I won't raise your hopes either. If there's opportunity, they'll take it, but their primary goal will be to prepare the ground for the heavier vessel coming after them."

"And if they find something that requires more than a scout's weaponry?"

"Let's pray they don't, Your Majesty," Ogaban said with a crooked smile. "But if they do, then there really is more going on in your sector than we thought, and we'll deal with it accordingly."

"This vessel," Hirianthial said. "Can it carry passengers?"

The human looked up at him, aura swirled with a sudden queasy yellow consternation. "It's a military vessel, my Lord. It's not equipped for guests."

"It would not be carrying a guest," Hirianthial said.

Ogaban paused. "You mean to assign someone to accompany them?"

"It would be meet," Liolesa said. "To have an observer with you. And wise as well; someone who knows the land, the language, the political situation intimately."

"Ah . . . yes, yes it would," the Admiral said. "And of course, your observer is welcome."

"Two," Liolesa said. "Two observers."

"Two. But I can't in good conscience allow more. It's not a large ship and passengers are an intrusion."

"Two will suffice," Liolesa said. "Thank you."

At the conclusion of the conference, Hirianthial and Liolesa walked together to their suite. He was intimately aware of the strength and solidity of her aura . . . that at some point, her anger had become the impetus for forward motion, now that there was some action she could undertake. So it was, with his cousin: Plan early. Execute presently. Emotion later.

Once they reached the sitting room, he said, "What will you do?"

"Wait for this scout," Liolesa said. "And then go home with her. So I will be two weeks behind you, and I expect you to have prepared the ground, cousin."

"A fine title you granted me, all unknowing."

"You think it so?" She smiled, just a faint curve at the edge of her mouth. "It has not been used since Jerisa's reign, and the last man to answer to it died carrying the war to Corel."

He suppressed the urge to sigh, and his words came out drenched in shadows. "We put too much weight on things that have passed. It is little wonder we are strangling to death in our own history."

"No. But Goddess and Lord willing, we shall be

done with that soon." She looked up at him. "You will prepare now?"

"If the vessel is arriving tomorrow? Absolutely." He folded his arms, regarding her. "And now I wait."

She turned one of the coffee cups on the service. Not innocence, he thought—she was feeling it, feeling the reality of where they were, and the entity they would be courting a closer relation with once this was over, did they live through it. "Mmm?"

"For you to explain."

"Explain . . . ?" She looked up, cup in hand, then laughed, a low sound. "Ah. Which part?"

"Two?" he prompted.

"You and your equerry, of course." At his blank expression, she said, "The Harat-Shar, yes?"

"My equerry!" The notion struck him as ludicrous, and yet there was a tender humor in it: Sascha, who would not mount a horse for fear of it biting him, as an equerry! Him even needing an equerry, when their world did everything possible to minimize wars. His carrying a title as old as Settlement, and dusty from disuse. "Sascha?"

She smiled, all silvered words. "Try you to leave without him, see what happens."

"Someone must carekeep the *Earthrise*."

"Fleet can carekeep the *Earthrise*," Liolesa replied. "And Fleet is a safer place for Theresa's investment than a system threatened by an unknown number of pirates. There is not a weapon on that vessel, is there?"

He thought of the single laser designed to deal with debris and said, "No . . . no, that there is not."

"There you are, then." She studied him, then nodded. "Go you with your man, and see to our world. I will come with the cavalry, and we will put paid to this nonsense and see to the real work."

"You sound so certain of success," he said.

"And so I must be. What choice do we have?" She set the cup down. "It is this or oblivion. Worse than death: slavery and dispersion until we die out. No, Hiran. We must succeed. There is no other option."

"Then I shall do my best to abet you. Only, I pray you, cousin . . . have some useful notion of where we are to go after this to prevent a similar happenstance."

She laughed then, full and rich. "Oh, never fear that. I have a plenitude of plans and always have, and if this is not quite the way I'd envisioned launching them, well . . . I was never so arrogant to think that war might not have been the ultimate catalyst in the end." She offered him her bare hands and he took them, resting his thumbs on her palm. Her fingers were warmer than his; she'd always been thus, like a fire strove at her edges. Liolesa, the woman who was not content to be solely a seal-bearer for a world and its people, but who insisted on being her own sword as well . . . to the point of taking it for a personal emblem. He smiled, fond of her and exasperated both, and turned her hands so he could kiss their backs.

"I am your faithful liegeman."

"And much beloved, at that. Pack, Hiran. At last we are in motion again."

"Yes," he said, vehement. "Yes."

CHAPTER 6

"I am not convinced of the wisdom of allowing this stranger access to our counsel," Belinor said once they'd all been seated around Taylor's data tablet. He glanced at Val. "Even if he has offered us no further harm, he is an unknown. We hardly know his motivations."

"If it makes you feel better," Val said, "I could step outside. Except that I could still learn everything you're saying if I wanted to listen. I could even use your ears and you'd never know."

"You're not helping," Reese told him dryly.

"I thought being honest about my capabilities would make it clear that I am being forthcoming."

Irine coughed into a fist as Belinor turned a scathing look on the other Eldritch.

Val grinned and inclined his head, pressing his hand to his heart. "I apologize, Acolyte—"

"That's better than 'boy,' at least," Taylor muttered as she flicked through the tablet's comm channels.

"—and if there is some way I might convince you I am

here in good faith, only tell me."

"Fine," Belinor said, eyeing him. "Will you swear to it?"

"On anything you like," Val answered magnanimously.

"On Elsabet's sacrifice," Belinor said with zeal, leaning forward. "Swear it."

Val froze in place. Seeing it made Reese realize that he tended to move more than the Eldritch she knew; she'd seen Hirianthial do this stillness, but it was less marked. Was that one of the reasons she trusted the former priest so easily? Because his body language read like Pelted body language . . . or human? Because it made him seem more open?

This stillness, though—the request had meant something. Meant a lot.

Folding his arms, Belinor finished, "You say you are his incarnation. Then swear on her sacrifice, that you will not betray us to our enemies, whosoever they may be."

"Ah," Val said, and sighed. He ran a hand over the back of his neck and said ruefully, "Perhaps it won't be years before he's useful after all, Lady Eddings." Lifting his head, he met the other Eldritch's eyes and answered in their own tongue, a stream of vowels with consonants that only seemed to give them ground to soar from. In Universal, "Repeating for the benefit of our companions: I do so swear, on the Lady Elsabet's sacrifice, that I will not betray any of you to your enemies, whosoever they may be."

Satisfied, Belinor said, "My Lady. It is well with me, then."

"Just like that?" Irine asked, mystified. "You think he's a renegade and a horrible witch and you trust him to keep his word?"

"He claims to be the reincarnation of Corel," Belinor said. "If he can hold such a belief in his heart, then he would never go against the word he swore in the name of the woman who loved Corel, and died for him."

"What if he was joking?" Reese asked, uneasy. "You know. About the reincarnation bit."

Belinor said, simply, "He wasn't."

Reese let that go because dealing with it . . . well, how could she? A woman could only handle so much metaphysical gibberish at a time. "Taylor, you ready?"

"Ready." The Tam-illee tapped the data tablet and it chirped. "Malia."

A few moments later, the other Tam-illee's face formed above the data tablet, shimmering until it solidified. "Taylor? Can you see me? I've got the solidigraph feed off on my side, we're keeping it quiet here."

"We've got you," Taylor said. "Where are you?"

"Out in the woods, west of Ontine. There are some caches out here that the Swords have been maintaining: weapons, another Pad, food and communication gear. We're hiding out while they do some scouting. So far no one's left the palace, but they're sure that Surela won't stay long; they're of the opinion she's going to have to ride out soon to demand the surrender of the Queen's enemies."

"Armed with Alliance weapons," Reese said heavily. She tried not to imagine what palmers would do to people armed with swords and succeeded only because she'd never seen the battlefields of the dead her romances had described when they'd wandered into epic fantasy storylines. What would that look like? The books always said things about the sky darkening with the wings of carrion birds. She rubbed her arm against the gooseflesh. "Have you gotten off any people to warn them?"

"We've sent messengers, yes. Two to each of the Houses, in case something happens to the first."

"Good thinking. What about the pirates?"

Malia shook her head. "We haven't seen hide or hair of

them yet. They must still be in the palace, or on their ship. Grace and Thad are keeping an eye on it and sending us coded message bursts. According to the last one, it's still in orbit."

Taylor roused. "Are they using active sensors? That could lead the pirates straight to them if they're not careful."

"They've had the computer set up a random schedule," Malia said. "It only activates briefly, at irregular times, just to double-check that they're still in position. Then it shuts off. Trust me, they're laying as low as they can. The last thing they want is to fight off the entire complement of a pirate ship by their lonesome, in a base so small there's nowhere to hide." She smiled, tired. "So, Reese . . . what's our plan?"

What was her plan? "Blood, I'm not sure. There's so much to do."

"How many enemies do you have, Lady?" Val asked, bemused. "If I can ask."

"Who's that?" Malia said.

"Another native we picked up," Reese said. To Val, she said, "We have four separate problems here." She lifted a finger. "One is the woman who deposed Liolesa, who is apparently her mortal enemy, and is probably going to go out and try to kill—or subdue, I guess—all the pro-Alliance Eldritch on this planet. Number two is the pirates who brought all the weapons here, and who are apparently still here. Number three is your Baniel, who did the betraying—he brought the pirates here, and gave their weapons to Surela so she could do her coup."

"And number four?" Val asked, sounding fascinated.

"May or may not be on world . . . but somewhere out there, there's at least one Chatcaavan involved in this," Reese said.

"Chatcaava," Val said. "That is a shapeshifter, yes?"

"You're remarkably well-informed for an Eldritch," Irine said.

Val shook his head. "Not all priests held with the isolationism, Lady Tigress. I certainly had no use for it."

"What about the heir?" Taylor asked. "Isn't she problem number five?" She glanced at Malia. "If Surela goes for the heir, wouldn't that cement her rule?"

"Does that matter with Liolesa gone?" Reese said. "She's at the nearest starbase by now. No one in the Alliance is going to believe Surela's the new queen when the old one's organizing an armada to come back and kick her out of the palace."

"It's not about convincing the Alliance," Taylor said. "It's about what the Eldritch think."

Reese forgot sometimes that these Tam-illee were as Eldritch as they could be while still being Pelted. These things mattered to them. Maybe it mattered to the Eldritch too. She glanced at Val and Belinor. "What about it?"

Belinor had grown wide-eyed and a little gray, but he said, "I believe the Navigatrix is correct, my Lady. The Queen's allies are in favor of a deeper connection with the Alliance, and as such they are not likely to accept the Queen's absence as anything but a temporary issue. She is still the Queen to them, off-world or on. Surela taking the Heir would grieve them, but change nothing legally."

"But would Surela think so?" Taylor pressed. "Maybe she wants a quicker answer to her problems."

Malia frowned and shook her head. "That, I don't know."

Reese rubbed her face and sighed. "Look, let's talk about problems we can solve. We have . . . what, about forty Swords? Is that right, Malia?" At the Tam-illee's nod, she continued. "All right. Forty soldiers with modern weapons. Do we have a Pad?"

"Two," Malia said. "The Swords took the one from the

palace library after you fled over it, and they have one here. There's at least one more on-world, but it will be with the pirates. We haven't seen any shuttle traffic between the ship and the ground, so they must be using one to get back and forth."

"Two Pads we can use, then," Reese continued. "And we have us, and three more Tams, two manning the outpost and one there with you, and the communication gear to link them. What can we do with that?"

"Do we have useful sensors? Maybe we can track people's movements?" Irine said.

"There's no satellite in orbit anymore," Malia said. "And no Well repeaters; the Queen destroyed them all on the way out."

What could they possibly do against so many? "Let's assume Surela leaves, and takes her minions with her—"

"Minions," Irine interrupted. "I like that. Sounds properly sinister."

Reese ignored her. "Can we deal with the pirates? We're the foreigners. It seems right we should deal with the other foreigners. Do we know how many of them there are?"

"No, but if we could find out, that would be very helpful," Malia said, pursing her lips. "Only problem is they're in the palace, and the palace has the priests."

"I can handle the priests."

They all looked at Val.

"You," Reese said, uncertain. "By yourself."

"Oh, your lad will help me. Ah, Belinor? What say you? Us against the bloodrobes?"

Belinor eyed him, then said with prickly dignity, "Very well."

Reese was already saying, "So that won't work—wait, what?" She looked at Belinor. "Are you kidding?"

"He froze us in place, my Lady. All four of us, without

harming us. It is easier to kill than it is to hold fast," Belinor said.

"And you know this because everyone learns about the whole forbidden evil mind talents?" Reese said, brows rising.

"No," the youth said, patient. "I know this because anything that requires fine control is harder. Tell me, my Lady: is it harder to strike someone with all your might, or is it harder to judge the blow and pull it and then hold it thus?"

"Well, when you say it that way," Reese said. She considered Val. "You're serious, then. You're good enough to take on an entire palace full of priests."

"Not only am I good enough, you will need me," Val said. "I can lead you into the palace through the catacombs my order uses for prisoners."

"Oh!" Belinor exclaimed. "Yes, my Lady! That is a fair notion. There are several secret ways. It gives us a better hope of infiltrating the palace, if we do not come in through the gates. And it avoids involving the servants, which is a perilous cruelty."

Reese's heart seized. "Wait, I thought the servants would have . . . I don't know. Crept away by now? Are they still there? Liolesa's servants?"

"Of course," Belinor said, puzzled. "No one would dare hurt one of them, my Lady. No, nor the commoners either. Nobles do not involve their commonfolk in these fights. To do so would be to invite disaster."

"There not being so many of us that we can afford to throw every last person at a quarrel over someone's insulted pride," Val said.

Reese glanced at Malia, who nodded. "They're still there."

"Felith," Irine said, her ears sagging.

Seeing the look on Reese's face, Belinor said, "Be at

ease, my Lady. Even the usurper queen is not so mad as
to involve anyone but the nobles and the guards each
House is permitted to levy. There is rebellion, and then
there's anarchy."

"I don't know," Reese muttered. "Surela was stupid
enough to go after Liolesa."

"That's a fair point, though," Taylor said, thoughtful. "If
we do get into the palace, we'll have allies. Unless Surela's
killed the families of her enemies, the ones who came for
the court, they're all going to be confined in their suites.
And they're actually nobles of their respective Houses, so
they're free to act on the Queen's behalf. If we could free
and arm them. . . ."

"But it would take us weeks to get there . . . wouldn't
it?" Reese asked. "I don't know distances on land—"

"We have two Pads," Malia said. "If this is the plan we
want, then we'll set one up here, cross it with the spare,
and set up the spare there. Then you can walk over it to get
back here, or we can figure out some coordinates near the
palace that suit better. But we've got to be sure that's what
we want to do; once we've got them placed, that's where
they're going to stay. We don't have any other spares to
create a new launch point."

Irine said, "So once we do this, we're committed."

"But we don't know how many pirates there are," Reese
muttered. "If there's more than ten or eleven of them, we're
done for."

"Maybe, maybe not," Taylor said. "But what are our
other options? We've done what we can to warn the
Queen's allies, and we can't make a big difference in a clash
between several hundred people. But if we can roust the
pirates from the palace and free the hostages there. . . ."

"And if we set up a Pad tunnel between here and the
Swords' hiding place west of the palace," Irine said, "We'd

have a place to run. You know, if things blow up."

"I hate to tell you this, Irine," Reese said, "but if this blows up, I don't think any of us are getting out. Except possibly as slavebait."

Irine hunched her shoulders.

"What do you think?" Taylor asked.

"I think . . . I need a little bit to think," Reese said. "This is a big gamble."

"It's a big gamble, but we promised the Queen we'd do something," Irine replied.

"'We' did, did we?" Reese eyed her.

Innocently, Irine said, "Well, we did empower you to make decisions for us. You know. You speak for us and all that."

Reese started laughing as the Eldritch watched, mystified. To them, Taylor murmured, "It's not usual for us to accept liegelords."

"What a bizarre world you must live in, my Lady," Belinor said.

"That's one way of putting it." Reese sighed. "Can I get back to you in half a day, Malia-alet?"

"That's fine. We're not going anywhere. But I wouldn't wait much longer than that, Reese."

"Fine. Stay safe."

"Will do. Malia out."

Silence, filled only by the crackle of the fire. Reese could feel the heat beating at her back, but it only made the front of her body feel colder. Why did it seem more biting with the data tablet quiescent on the stone floor? Was it the sudden deprivation of the reassuring technologies that had surrounded her all her life? As poor as Mars was compared to the average Alliance world, it still existed because of technology far beyond the reach of most Eldritch. She shivered.

"I had not had the experience of Alliance machinery." Val reached for the data tablet, paused to glance at Taylor, and at her nod picked it up. He examined the slim slate. "Like a page of a book, but a window into worlds. Amazing."

"You really need to sleep on this, Reese?" Irine asked.

She wanted to say 'I'm talking about throwing all our lives away on a chance.' She wanted to say, 'I'm not trained to be a soldier. You're not. Taylor's not. The two Eldritch—who knows? But against modern weapons? What chance do they have? What chance do any of us have?' But instead she looked up at the distant rafters, at the wan light filtering in through the windows. She inhaled the air, cold and sharp and pungent with the smell of burning wood and the more distant perfume of the salt sea.

"No," she said. "But I may need to walk on it." She got up. "I'll be back."

"Take someone with you," Taylor said. "It's not safe—"

"If it's not safe here, it's too late for any of us," Reese said, shaking her head. She resettled the folds of her long jacket and went for the faraway door into the great hall . . . heard her boot heels clicking on the stone and echoing. Blood, everything here seemed designed to magnify its own significance, didn't it?

Didn't mean it wasn't significant. She shivered.

"Elder." Hirianthial went to one knee alongside the priest. "I am gone with the morning. Perhaps you had heard?"

"I had not." The priest studied him with kind eyes. "You go to do the Queen's work, yes?"

"I do."

"Ah." Urise nodded, softly silvering the words. "That is good. It is not well to leave the sword in the scabbard at times like this."

Hirianthial managed a wan smile. "You say this knowing how this sword may meet the test?"

"I do!" The priest's eyes grew merry, and his aura streaked gold with pleasure. "I am sure of you, young lord, even if you are not."

"I would be surer of myself if I'd had more time for lessons," Hirianthial said. "As it is, I fear I go half-clouded in my own ignorance. I have not yet unriddled your lack of fatigue, Elder, nor do I know how to resist your pressure successfully." He managed a whimsical smile. "I don't suppose there is some way by which I might magically learn all that you might teach me in a moment?"

He'd been expecting another of the priest's gentle witticisms; to see instead darkness cross the elder's aura like the shadows of clouds gliding over the back of a field startled him. "Elder? Did I speak poorly?"

Urise held up a hand. "No. No, but what you ask can be done."

Hirianthial leaned back, the hands he'd folded on his knee tightening despite his best efforts.

"Knowledge can be imparted mind-to-mind, at speed," Urise said. "But it is knowledge, my son. It is not experience. Do you know the difference? Between the description of a thing and feeling it—seeing it—for yourself?"

"I do," he said, quiet. "But I would think that knowledge transmitted mind-to-mind would come with the experiences of the teacher entwined."

"It does. With the *teacher's* experiences." Urise slipped his hand back into his sleeve. "In some ways then, it is harder for the student, for he must draw the teacher's experience apart from it, the teacher's emotions, before he can assign his own. And even then it is only knowledge until it is experienced."

The priest's aura remained dimmed. Hirianthial

considered it, then looked at Urise and said, "There is aught else that bothers you. A risk."

"A minor one, perhaps, in that I go not with you," Urise said. "But such a sharing creates a yoke between teacher and student, and some teachers have exploited it to use their apprentices for their own ends. Some have even killed their apprentices, drinking too deeply at the fountain of their energies. That requires proximity, however, and I—" He smiled, and there was the merriment again, so welcome after the shadows. "—I think I shall stay here until the conflict has finished. War is for the young. Besides, I like these animal people. It is diverting, looking at them . . . so many bright colors."

"They are beautiful," Hirianthial said. "Elder—would you consent to this sharing?" In response to the other's gaze, he continued, "I know not what I go to, but every weapon I can use I must have to hand."

"You are certain," Urise said. And sighed. "Yes, of course you are. The young always are. Well, then, now will do as well as any."

"Now?" Hirianthial asked through his amusement at being called young.

"Just so." Urise shook his sleeve off his hand and offered it. "We shall have it done now."

Hirianthial drew in a breath and rested his palm against the priest's. He felt the knobs of arthritic joints, the dry, lined skin, but no emotional data, and was not surprised; he had no doubt Urise could have withdrawn his presence even from the air around him, if he'd wanted not to be seen. A handy skill, that . . . perhaps he might absorb it with this last lesson.

"Relax," Urise murmured, and Hirianthial let his head rest forward. His hair curled close around his chin and he felt the drag of the dangle as it rose up against the back of

his tunic. Kis'eh't's prayer bell whispered, bringing memories dire and gentle, and he sank into the acceptance of
life's vicissitudes. To love was to be vulnerable to pain. To
laugh was to be sensitive enough for tears. To be open to
joy was to be despair's fair prey.

/Yes,/ Urise said. /Yes, when you can bow your head to
these things, you are on your way, my son./

/But not there,/ he surmised.

/No,/ the priest replied: humor and sorrow both,
swirled together in a spiral like the helix of life. /No, for
you there is a much more important lesson. But first things
first./ And then the knowing spilled into him, water poured
not from a pitcher, no . . . this was knowledge accumulated
over a lifetime well over a thousand years long. Knowledge like a great river falling over cliffs to the sea, so much
that he felt it sweep him away . . . and instinct told him
not to fight it, not to reach for any one thing. A hundred
million droplets, but they could only be grasped the way
the sea was: as a great gestalt. It was not his gestalt, but he
welcomed it all the same. And if it sat in him uneasily, he
accepted that as the condition of the gift. What he could
absorb, he would, and he would pray it would be enough.

Slowly he became aware of the priest's palm against
his. It was how he realized he'd lost the world entirely . . .
and that he was sweating.

"So much," he managed at last, and his voice had gone
to rasping.

"Too much?" Urise asked.

"I pray not, no. And the gift is without price," Hirianthial said. "Whatever I keep of it."

"And none of it," Urise said, "None of it will be of any
use to you until you learn the final lesson. And I would
rather not have imparted it to you this way, but we are
short on time and long on need. So hark you, young lord."

He leaned forward. "You cannot wield the power of the world if you accept its weight on your shoulders."

Hirianthial frowned. "I beg your pardon, Elder. That sounds a great deal as if you counsel me against responsibility, against duty."

"No." Urise shook his head. "I do not. And until you understand the difference, not all the learning will help you, because you will hobble yourself. You take too much on your own shoulders, Hirianthial Sarel. It is not humility to assume every responsibility is yours to bear. It is not wise. And it is not just, nor kind. You must let go of your need to feel that everything that befalls you is yours to mend, for at the root of that assumption is a great flaw: the belief that you can control everything. Continue to nourish that flaw and it will grow into the fault that will shatter you as surely as the sword poorly made."

"I would never . . . !"

"Have you not?" Urise lifted a brow. Then he smiled and sighed, shaking his head. He touched the backs of his fingers to Hirianthial's cheek. "Arrogate to God and Goddess all that belongs to them, my son. Give away that which belongs to others to them. To you, the rest may come."

"I promise to try," he answered, still struggling to accept the words. So tempting to reject them out of hand, but knowing the depth of the priest's experience, viscerally now, he could no more do so in good conscience than he could turn from any other teaching.

"Good. Now go and make ready. I shall stay and look at the furred peoples." Urise grinned. "They truly are diverting."

Hirianthial found a laugh and gained his shaky feet. "I expect they are. Until I see you again, Elder. Thank you."

"Go in Their care, my son."

꜒

He packed next, and there was little to pack. He felt the absence of his swords painfully, but there was nothing to be done for it; no doubt they were somewhere in Ontine, perhaps in his brother's untender care, or even lying in the snow by the lake. But he had been brought to the starbase with the clothes on his back, and not even that had survived the fight that had necessitated his arrival. There had been spares in his quarters in the *Earthrise,* at least, but not much more since most of his effects had accompanied him to the Jisiensire house on Noble's Row. But it was well that it took so little time, for that left him enough for a different errand. That his lessoning with Urise had left him feeling strange and unsure of his edges somehow made that errand more urgent, for he knew Reese's people had helped him through similar episodes. That is where he went next.

"So is there news?" Sascha asked after he entered. The *Earthrise*'s crew was sharing a single suite in the hotel, and Kis'eh't was sitting in the shared common room with Allacazam cradled in her forepaws. Bryer was a mounded silhouette near the window, like a vast bird of prey with furled wings.

"There is," he said. "One of Fleet Intelligence's smaller ships will be here tomorrow to pick me up, and then we are returning home to gather information for the scout ship Fleet will dispatch when it is free, in two weeks."

Kis'eh't tsked softly beneath her breath. "A lot can happen in two weeks."

"It is why they wish to send the smaller vessel," Hirianthial said. "To see what might occur, and give warning."

"Makes sense," Sascha said. He stretched, tail curling behind him. "I'm already packed."

From the window, Bryer said, "Me too."

"I . . . am not sure there is room for three," Hirianthial said, startled.

"Four," Kis'eh't said.

"Aw, no, arii," Sascha said. "Who'll keep an eye on the ship?"

"The ship isn't going to be vandalized in a Fleet slip," Kis'eh't said dryly.

"And Allacazam?" Sascha pressed as Hirianthial listened, bemused.

"So we'll stay on this new ship while the rest of you go off doing your 3deo hero bit." In Kis'eh't's lap, Allacazam turned a sunnily amused yellow.

"But the Queen?" Sascha asked. "Who's going to keep the Queen company?"

That stopped Kis'eh't. She frowned, opened her mouth, then closed it again.

To Hirianthial, Sascha said, "She's been chatting with your cousin. I think they like one another."

"She's a smart woman," Kis'e'h't said, feathered ears flicking back. "I like smart people. They're relaxing to talk to."

The thought of Liolesa discoursing at length with the short, phlegmatic Glaseah tickled Hirianthial through his fatigue. "Did she also meet the Flitzbe?"

"Of course. I promised Reese I'd look after him, so he goes where I go."

"And what did my cousin think of him, pray tell?" Hirianthial wondered, his mouth quirking.

"I think they found each other interesting," Kis'eh't said. She scowled at Sascha. "That was a low blow."

"Maybe so," Sascha said. "But I get the feeling there aren't going to be many berths on this ride, and you're not going to like the fight, arii. And it really is true that if we all leave, there won't be anyone with the Queen. Not from our ranks, anyway."

The phrasing piqued Hirianthial's interest. "Our ranks?"

"Sure," Sascha said. "'Our' ranks. Reese's people. Reese is the Queen's vassal, and we're her whatever you call it: employees, retainers, whatever. Her people. We're her symbol of her commitment to the Queen, right? So we need to show our support for the Queen while she's out here in the Alliance, so she won't be alone. No offense to that priest we brought, but he's Eldritch, and she's not among Eldritch, right?"

He stared at the Harat-Shar, surprised, and his expression must have been leading, for it made Kis'eh't chuckle. "You've been listening to me about the feudal systems after all. And here I thought you were busy kissing on Irine."

"I was busy kissing on Irine," Sascha replied modestly. "But I'm so good at it I can multitask. Harat-Shariin talent, you know. So what about it, arii?"

"It's well-reasoned," Kis'eh't said. She smiled. "Goddess, I am turning part-feudal myself if I can be pleased that I now feel useful."

"You need not be feudal to want that, arii," Hirianthial said. "But if it helps, I will say that Sascha is correct. I would never have thought it, but the symbols will stand, and she will feel it."

"All right." Kis'eh't nodded. "I'll stay here with Liolesa and Allacazam. We'll wait for this bigger ship and come back with her. You two are in charge of keeping Hirianthial in one piece until we can get him to Reese."

"Can do."

When had they decided that two people would be accompanying him? Much less that they were doing so to be his defense? "I beg your pardon?"

Bryer shook his feathers with a hissing rustle and stepped away from the window. "Will be done."

Sascha said. "All right, good. That's settled. When do we leave, Boss?"

"I am not—" He stopped at the sight of their gazes: Bryer inscrutable and unblinking, Kis'eh't amused, and Sascha almost challenging him to disagree. Theresa had always been their 'boss,' and no such title had ever devolved to him, and could not, unless they had decided he and their mistress were sharing power. Did they understand the feudal system enough to know what they implied?

No question of that.

He sighed, exasperated and amused. "The ship arrives tomorrow. I will arrange for Bryer's passage."

Sascha grinned, ears perked. "There, see? Wasn't so hard, was it."

"It's almost as if we can read your mind," Kis'eh't added blandly.

Hirianthial shook his head. "What is she to do with the lot of you."

"Unfortunately nothing I'd suggest," Sascha said, grinning. "But Angels willing, I'll be around to keep suggesting it until she gives in or finds me a few wives to keep me busy."

CHAPTER 7

The prisoner was gone.

Surela stared at the empty cell and turned to the guards who'd led her into the catacombs, her guards, in her livery, men she'd been sure were at very least competent at their duties. "Has he been moved?"

"No, my Lady," her guide said, his nervousness palpable. "He was here when last we were informed."

She glanced down the corridor, hating the chill and the damp and the moisture that gleamed on the floor and made her small, tidy heels feel unsteady beneath her. "You there," she said, spotting a priest in the Lord's dark robes. "What has happened to the prisoner?"

"I cannot say, Your Majesty."

"Cannot say?" she asked, astonished. "You deny knowledge to your own Queen?"

"Your Majesty," he repeated, impassive. "It is not for me to say. The High Priest has sealed the matter."

"Oh has he," Surela said, lips drawing back from her teeth. "You may go." To her guide. "We return."

Her mind roiled with frustrations as they mounted the stairs leading back into the palace. Hirianthial gone! Where? Had Baniel killed him already? She had given him to the priesthood, of course—a mind-mage could not be suffered to live, much less one that consorted with mortals—but that was before she'd understood him to have knowledge that she needed. She wondered suddenly if Baniel had known about these things, and if that was one of the reasons he wanted his brother dead so quickly? She paused on the stairs, and her guards halted immediately, waiting on her pleasure.

A foreboding came to her then. "Take me to Liolesa," she said to the guards. No, surely she was wrong . . . Hirianthial had been Baniel's to dispose of, but the Queen—the former Queen, she reminded herself angrily—had been her prisoner. Baniel would not have touched her—

There were no guards waiting at the suite. She flung the door open and stared at the empty room. To search it would be futile, she knew; Liolesa was gone. But she ordered it done anyway and returned to her study while they worked, and there she brooded and grew more and more wroth until they delivered the inevitable report that the Queen was gone.

"Get me Baniel," she hissed.

He arrived—in his own good time, she noticed—and by then she was so infuriated she didn't even wait for the guards to close the doors before saying, "What did you do with her?"

"I beg your pardon, Your Majesty?" he said. How she hated his urbane manners and the cold green glitter of his eyes! Would it be worth it to throw him in his own cell for a while? Could she keep him there? Except then who would conclude the transaction with the mortals and send them away? She would have to sully herself with the arrangements.

"Where is Liolesa?" Surela said. "And Hirianthial? Or did you kill him already?"

"He was mine to kill."

"This sidesteps my question. Where are they? *Answer me!*"

"Gone, Your Majesty," Baniel said. At her expression, he finished, unperturbed, "Escaped."

"*Escaped!*"

"Off-world, in fact."

She stared at him, shocked that he could admit to this catastrophic failure with such equanimity. Did he truly think himself beyond punishment?

"That is all you have to say for yourself," she said, the words black with anger. "You have allowed our enemies to escape—and to the mortal worlds, where they can gather aid and return to crush us—and you have nothing more to say? 'They're gone'? Really?"

"You are overwrought, Your Majesty," Baniel said. "We are in no danger, I assure you."

Despite herself, she felt a faint fascination at this continued evidence of his delusion. "Go on. I would like to hear how you have derived this conclusion."

"They have gone to seek aid. But they will not find enough to win back the world."

"And how is that possible? Do not these mortals have thousands of their own vessels?" she asked, trying not to grit her teeth.

"Ten vessels, a thousand, a million . . . the numbers are meaningless, Your Majesty, if they cannot be deployed." He smiled. "It is a matter of mortal politics. I assure you I am well versed in them, and I can say with certitude that the Alliance will not have the resources to devote to our little . . . fracas."

"And if you are wrong?"

"But I am not. Fear not, Your Majesty. I have the matter well in hand. Though if you like, I could educate you on the matter? I can send for our mortal allies and have them explain at length. I am sure they'd be pleased to meet a Queen, see a royal study. Drink sweet almond liqueur. Such opportunities come infrequently to people of their quality."

The thought of letting such creatures into the palace proper made her shudder. Bad enough that they were presumably wandering the catacombs. And yet, to trust him with the entire future of her endeavor . . . what would it matter if she succeeded in winning Liolesa's former allies to a sulky acceptance of her reign if the woman could return on some spacegoing warhorse and depose her? And too, the matter that Araelis had spoken of . . . she knew so little. They had consorted with mortals to make her coup possible, and to her all mortals seemed alike. Did that mean that these mortals were allied with the ones Araelis suggested were interested in pillaging their world?

Who had Baniel made his deal with?

Could he be trusted?

"Your Majesty," he said, softening. "I know you are concerned. But I would not let harm come to you, when you carry all our hopes for a world free of the interference of mortals. Most of them will be departing this evening to protect our interests abroad. They will bar Liolesa's way, I pledge you. Let me continue to be your obedient servant in this so that you need not soil yourself with the details."

"Departing," she said, wary. "Do they mean to return?"

"Only once, to collect their pay. I cannot pay them of course until they fulfill their contractual duties. These mortals can be led by their love of money, Your Majesty: dangle it before them, and they are completely predictable.

No, they are well in check. They will take care of Liolesa and my brother, and then they will come for their money, and then they will be gone and we may continue in peace." He tilted his head. "What will you do about the rebellious Houses?"

"I will have a talk shortly with the Delen Galare," Surela said. "And after that . . ." She looked out the window. "We will see. I may ride forth to demand allegiance from them."

"And the hostages?"

"They are not hostages," she said, irritated. "They are guests . . . guests, until they see reason."

"Your guests, then," he said, inclining his head. "Will they be staying?"

"What else? It's the winter court." She eyed him. "Almost I think you would have me kill them. Do all men have this bloodthirstiness? Is it inherent to the sex?"

"Oh, I would never suggest such a thing," Baniel said. "Surely your way is the best."

"Yes," she said, still considering him. "Very well, then. You may go."

"Your Majesty," he said, bowing. "Thank you for the opportunity to assuage your fears."

"Keep me better informed, Baniel. This is a command, not a suggestion."

"Of course."

She watched him go, uneasy. Her enemies hated her, of course, and would lie to her at any opportunity; she did not put it past Araelis to do such. But she began to wonder if Baniel was as much her ally as she'd thought. It had not escaped her that he had preferred to address her as 'Your Majesty,' which was a less intimate title than 'my Lady,' when traditionally the Queen was everyone's liege-lady. Was this subtlety a rejection of his relationship with her . . . and the duties that came attendant?

Surela sent for Thaniet and a meal and went to sit before the fire and weigh her options. None of them seemed very appealing.

The coat the Tams had supplied Reese with did a good job of insulating her from the chill, but very little to shield her from the strangeness of feeling it outdoors. The *Earthrise*'s dry, recirculated air, vacuumed clean of any smell, had been artificial, something she could control. It was an entirely different experience to stand outside and know that she couldn't wish away the weather. That it was moving according to some magical collection of variables that planets had and she didn't understand well enough to predict. That it had a smell—floral and briny and wild— and a texture—moist and clinging—and that it would continue to have, and be those things no matter what one small human woman decreed.

Ordinarily, she would have found the idea appalling. But somehow she still liked the Eldritch world. She liked listening to the surf in the distance. She liked the crazy ramble of unlikely-looking roses. She liked the intransigence that seemed bred into the bones of anything that had to do with the species. Her crew would laugh, but it made her feel a little bit related to them; stubbornness, even in the face of approaching disaster, was something she could appreciate. Reese petted one of the flowers, finding the petals silky until the cold numbed her fingers, and then she hid her hands away in her pockets again.

And then there was the sky.

What had Hirianthial called it? Io . . . gev . . . something. The sacred caul. She stared up at it and wondered where he was, and Liolesa, and the rest of her crew.

"My Lady is melancholic."

"Am I your lady?" she asked, waiting for Val to draw up

alongside her.

"Point," he said. "I have not offered and you have not accepted. But I like you, Lady Eddings. I haven't met a human before. You have a presence."

"Oh, do I." She eyed him.

He laughed. "And you are unconvinced. That's fine. I don't expect otherwise."

"Are you out here alone?" she said. "Did they really let you wander off like this?"

"Oh no. Yon tigress is following at what she believes to be a discreet distance." He smiled crookedly. "Her thoughts are very busy with a fierceness of devotion."

Reese smiled at that. "Yeah, I'm not surprised. So why did you follow me out?"

"To ask you to please make the attempt," he said, surprising her with his sobriety. "I would very much like to help you."

"You have a debt to repay," she guessed.

"I do."

She looked out over her castle—her castle! And said, "How do you say it? The roses. What are they called?"

"*Me'enia,*" he said. "Say each vowel separately, Captain . . . most of our words are that way. Meh eh nee ah. Roses. But these are special. They are *lioyasea,* white roses, the roses of sacrifice. They bloom only in winter, the cruelest season, and grow only by the coast where there are storms. And it's said they were born of Elsabet's blood when she died here."

Reese looked at him. "Is it true?"

He cocked a brow at her.

"You know. If you're the reincarnation of Corel. You'd know. Right?"

He smiled a little and leaned toward the nearest vine. With a twist of his hand he broke the branch off and presented her with the flower. She noticed a drop of blood on the side of one finger where a thorn had dragged through the skin. "We have to make our own legends sometimes."

She took the flower, mindful of the thorns. "It's dangerous."

"Picking the roses?" he said—misinterpreting her willfully, she was sure. Wasn't he? "Of course. But if you don't try, then you have no rose."

"You can leave them out here to grow on their own, and enjoy them from the nice, warm keep," she said dryly.

"Ah, you could. But then you couldn't smell them, wouldn't feel the rush of having picked something yourself, and conquered your fears. What's a scratch, after all, compared to that?"

"On a world with no real medicine?" Reese snorted. "A scratch could be worth your life."

"Even on a world with medicine, death comes to us, and rarely expectedly." He smiled. "And sometimes it doesn't, no matter how intently you wish it."

She glanced at him sharply, but before she could speak she heard Taylor calling. "Reese! Reese!"

"What is it?"

The foxine joined her, her breath coming in white pants in the deepening gloom. "It was Malia. They've gotten a coded burst: the pirate ship's left!"

"Left!" Reese's skin went cold. "They went for reinforcements."

Irine joined them as Taylor said, "They must have. And we're not sure when they'll be back but we've got our window. If we want to get in there now, while there are fewer of them to fight. . . ."

Reese clenched her free hand, far too aware of the thorns on the rose she held with the other. Crazy world, to have things like this in it. Gardens and renegades and too many challenges and a climate she couldn't control and a future she couldn't predict. And yet . . . hadn't she already made the commitment?

"Tell Malia to come on through," Reese said. "We don't know how long we've got, so let's not waste any time."

CHAPTER 8

"There are three of us," Hirianthial said. "I hope that's not a problem."

The Seersa woman in the black and dark blue uniform looked up at him, then at Sascha and Bryer. "No," she said. "That'll be fine. You're the national I was told to expect, the Eldritch Lord of War, yes?"

"That's correct. Hirianthial Sarel Jisiensire, and the first name is sufficient. These are members of the Laisrathera House and go to meet their seal-bearer. Sascha and Bryer."

"That's fine," she said. She smiled, and it lit her eyes; a handsome woman, he thought, short like all Seersa and very fluffy, with white fur and a delicate face. "My name's Solysyrril Anderby, Commander of Hold 17. If you'll come with me? We're departing in half an hour and I'd like to get you battened down before that."

"Of course."

As he followed her toward the docking platform, Sascha whispered, "That was painless."

"Surprisingly so," he agreed, having expected more of

an argument himself.

The Harat-Shar drew abreast of him, glancing over a shoulder to make sure Bryer was still following. "Also . . . members of Laisrathera?"

"The name of Theresa's new House."

"Reese has a real name to go with the castle?"

Hirianthial chuckled. "She cannot have a castle without one."

That occupied the Harat-Shar for several moments as he paced Hirianthial. Then, "Wait, can I be part of it, if we're not related?"

"I'll explain later," Hirianthial promised.

"I'll hold you to that."

The ship awaiting them was a thing of sleek menace that could be read through its bulkheads. Hirianthial did not need to see its exterior to sense the purpose that animated it, that had necessitated all its lines. It was not an uncomfortable vessel, nor as small as he'd been expecting, but there was little wasted in its design. And he was grateful—and surprised—to discover he did not have to dip his head down to fit through the hatches; he had been on vessels that had necessitated doing so and not enjoyed the process.

"This way," Solysyrril said, pointing them down a corridor. "You've got the last two compartments. Split them up however you're comfortable. Once we're underway we'd be pleased to share a meal with you, and maybe you can tell us what additional background you have on the target."

The thought of designating his homeworld a 'target' discomfited him, but Hirianthial said only, "That is generous, Commander. Thank you."

"So, berthing," Sascha said. He glanced at Bryer. "You care?"

"No."

He snorted. "Of course not. So you and I will take one and you can have the other, arii."

Hirianthial glanced in the first compartment, found it larger in size than he'd expected, but not so large that he was glad to be spared the necessity of bumping elbows with someone else. "Very well. And thank you."

Exactly on schedule, their vessel left the starbase, and this Hirianthial recked only because of a flash of the lights lining the ceilings and a chime that rippled through the ship's internal speakers. He had become accustomed to the *Earthrise*'s many flinches, shudders, and vibrations, and not being able to sense them left him feeling strangely off-balance. Not long after, they were invited to the mess and introduced there to the remainder of Solysyrril's team. She was their commander, and a linguist and diplomat, but in addition the hold had two analysts and fieldwork specialists, a human named Tomas and a snow pard Harat-Shar named Narain (whom, he noted, immediately looked at Sascha with interest so poorly concealed it was probably not intended to be concealed at all). A Ciracaana served as healer, and Hirianthial saw the value of the tall hatches, for at nearly nine feet tall the centauroid's head was easily higher than the Eldritch's. And their navigator was a creature he'd not yet seen, though he'd had a seminar on them in medical school: one of the allied alien species, the Faulfenza. This one, Lune, was a fog-gray female nearly his height with a gentle demeanor, a muzzled face that swept back into long ears with two orange tips and a heavyworlder's easy strength and solidity.

"So," Solysyrril said after introductions had been made and the meal begun. "What can you tell us? Anything would help. Our mission brief was. . . ." She trailed off, looking for a word.

"Brief," Narain supplied, wry.

"Yes. Brief." Her smile was lopsided. "We've had a crash translation here; we were on duty elsewhere and pulled off it precipitously."

The Veil, he thought, would be well and truly torn by the end of all this. And his brother would have had a hand in it. Would that count for or against him? Ah, but would it matter, when through all his other acts Baniel had forfeited the stay on his life Hirianthial had awarded him? He steepled his fingers and drew in a breath. "'Anything' is rather a long telling. I will begin with the situation as it exists, and then you may ask me questions that seem relevant to you."

"Good plan," the Seersa said, nodding. "We're all ears."

He smiled at that and began, noticed Sascha listening just as attentively as the intelligence operatives. Bryer, of course, remained unreadable, but remembering his admonition on the *Earthrise* about their duty to protect, Hirianthial knew the Phoenix would retain everything that mattered.

"That is how it stands," he finished after a recitation that had seemed long in the telling for something that felt as if it had happened so swiftly.

"That is stunningly awful," Narain said, leaning back and sighing.

"Such a professional assessment," the human replied.

Narain snorted. "That *was* a professional assessment. My non-professional assessment wouldn't have been fit for Soly's ears. Or Lune's." He shook his head. "So we've got a scout incoming in two weeks? How much harm are we talking about to the infrastructure in that time?"

Hirianthial frowned. "The physical infrastructure?"

"Any infrastructure," Tomas said. "Social, political, geographical. He's asking what the delay is going to cost us."

"I don't know," Hirianthial admitted. "It would depend

on the capabilities and intentions of the pirate vessel."

"And your usurper's not going to destroy anything?" Tomas said. "No demonstrations, no battles, none of that?"

"I would be deeply surprised did she do so," Hirianthial said. "She cannot rule when the world is in disorder. And while she could send forth her guard to enforce her will, she cannot use them in broad conflict while they're armed with modern weapons. They would destroy everyone who opposed them, and she cannot afford a bloodbath."

Jasper, the Ciracaana healer spoke for the first time. "Can't she?" He looked at the others at the table. "Would take care of her opposition handily. No one left to say no to her. So she kills off a chunk of them, unfairly—who's going to rebel against her, knowing that they're going to die the same way?"

"I think the 'no one left' is the operative phrase there, though," Sascha said. "There aren't so many Eldritch that she can go and kill them off in job lots."

"How many are we talking about here?" Tomas interrupted. At their glances, he clarified, "People fighting. A few hundred thousand? Ten thousand?"

Sascha looked at Hirianthial, who cleared his throat and said, "Between herself and her allies, Surela can put eight hundred men in the field. Perhaps a thousand, if she strips Imthereli bare."

In the silence that followed, he sampled the auras of the Fleet personnel and found them regrettable—as much for what they implied about the viability of his people as for how clearly they demonstrated the miniscule scale the Eldritch had become accustomed to operating at.

"A thousand soldiers," Tomas repeated. "That's it."

"Each House is permitted to raise a personal guard equivalent to five percent of its population," Hirianthial replied, quiet. "My cousin's enemies consist of three

Houses—four, perhaps. There are two other neutral parties who may or may not be swayed toward Surela's cause, but they would add only another five hundred to the total. The Queen's allies can field seven hundred and fifty men; combined with the Swords, who are her personal protection detail, and the palace's guards, that would make some nine hundred in total. Those are the numbers we have to work with."

"Five percent total." Narain's ears were sagging. "You're telling me you have a total population of . . . what, fifty thousand people? In your entire species?"

Hirianthial inclined his head.

"Like I said." Sascha was playing with his fork. "She can't afford to kill them off in job lots."

"Are you sure?" Jasper said after a heart-beat's pause. "She might not have all that great a handle on genetics. Maybe as far as she's concerned, starting fresh from a smaller population base, one that supports her, is a good thing."

Sascha glanced at Hirianthial, who shook his head. "No. It is not in her temperament, I think. She wants her enemies to agree that her reign is just. Especially her enemies, because she was once Liolesa's enemy and remembers what it was to be ruled by a Queen she detested. She wants. . . ."

"To be accepted," Solysyrril said, and made a face. "Is that it?"

"I believe so, yes. She has taken the crown in violence; to be bowed to by her enemies as well as her allies will give her the legitimacy she craves, the legitimacy she fears she will always lack because of how she took the throne."

"Well," Narain said after a moment. "That makes our lives a little bit easier, anyway."

"A little," Solysyrril agreed, but she sighed. Shaking

herself, she continued, "So, the three of you, if I can ask: what skills do you have that we can borrow?"

"I'm a pilot," Sascha said.

"Excellent pilot," Bryer murmured, surprising Sascha into splayed ears and wide eyes.

Clearing his throat, Sascha said, "Um, right. I'm a pretty good pilot, and can do some engineering. Not much with fighting. Those two fight."

The Seersa glanced at Bryer. "You're Eye-trained?"

The Phoenix dipped his head, and her brows lifted. She looked at Hirianthial, still wearing her startled look.

"I am no Eye-trained Phoenix, I fear," Hirianthial said. "But I have some talent in that regard. I would need a sword to use most of it."

"A sword we can get you," Solysyrril said. "What weapon do you need to get the rest of 'most'?"

"The other I have already," he said. "I can read minds from a distance."

Another pause then, but not the appalled silence he'd been expecting. The professional interest with which these aliens regarded him was somehow more comforting; he could almost see them running likely scenarios through their heads.

"How long a distance?" Tomas asked. "Could you read the minds on another ship?"

"I have not made a good test of it, but I doubt it. I would have to try."

"But do the targets of your mind-reading know you're doing it?" Jasper asked, curious.

"Not unless I wish them to—or they are similarly trained."

"Huh." Narain tapped his fingers on the table. "That could be awfully handy."

"You with the professional assessments lately,"

Tomas said.

Narain grinned. "You got a more accurate one?"

Tomas considered, then offered, "Holy Hell, tell me more?"

Narain nodded sagely. "Very professional."

Solysyrril snorted. "All right, that's enough. Sascha-alet, could I trouble you to join Lune in the fore when we're done here? We're going to be dropping Fleet-issue repeaters on our way in since your Queen destroyed hers. If you have some expertise in that, the work will go faster."

"Sure!"

She nodded. To Bryer, she said, "Do you need weapons?"

"Not that you may supply."

"Fine. Then Lord Hirianthial, if you'll join me I'll take you to the armory. The rest of you, duty stations, please. And try not to spill the coffee this time."

The crew dispersed, and though their movements and conversation remained casual there was steel beneath the affable exteriors, down in the aura where its weight and sharpness hinted at long training.

"They mesh well together, your people," he commented as he followed the Seersa down the corridor.

She smiled. "They should. It's how the organization's designed. Each group's carefully selected for personalities and skill sets, and then we stay together until we retire, or move to administrative jobs. Our hold's been together almost ten years, and honestly it feels like ten days. Time just melts away when everyone's in the proper place, doing something they're good at with people they like and trust."

"I am surprised you have attempted to integrate us into that matrix, given how carefully it was fostered."

The Seersa paused in front of a hatch, aura darkening to a sober gray. "We serve a very specific function for the Alliance, Lord Hirianthial. When you do fieldwork, you're trained to take advantage of everything to hand. Honestly, it's a wonderful luxury to have the time to evaluate you all prior to putting you to use; most of the time we're grabbing for the nearest tool when we're already in the thick of it. Part of success, then, is being able to improvise." She grinned and color streaked her aura, confetti-bright. "We get good at improvising in this business."

"I imagine so."

"I'm hoping," she continued, "we won't need your skills, or the Phoenix's. But I'm not feeling very optimistic on that count."

"It doesn't bother you," he observed. "What I can do."

She glanced up at him. "Should it?"

"It has others."

"Ah." She shook her head. "Alet, if you really can read minds at a useful distance, you could make the difference between us making a mistake that kills us, and us living. Your talent doesn't bother me. Very much the contrary." She smiled. "I suspect the people it does bother assume that you're interested in what's going on in their heads . . . but that strikes me as egocentric. As if you'd be interested in what's in any one person's head? And that's setting aside the impracticality. A person only has so much time. You think he's going to waste it all going through the infinite number of thoughts passing through the brains of all the people he meets?" She snorted. "It's fear that talks when people say such things to you, alet. And the one thing we can't afford in our line of work is to let fear cloud our thoughts."

As he stared after her, wondering whether it would be his week for the Pelted to bring him up short, Soly stepped into the room. He followed her, and halted there at the threshold, startled at the racks of weaponry: not just the small hand-sized palmers in military-grade editions, but

larger rifles, stun and snare weapons, grenades, body
armor and shields.

"God and Lady," he exclaimed. "Do you truly need such
things often?"

"Often?" Solysyrril shook her head. "No. But when
we do, we really need them." She went to one of the walls
and took down what looked to be a mere hilt. "Here. It's
not a sword like you're used to, I'm guessing, but it's what
we have."

"And it operates by some Alliance magic, I presume."

She chuckled. "I guess it might seem that way." She
turned the hilt to face him and said, "Here, where your
thumb and first fingers go . . . these are the controls. You
can get a broad beam or a thin one, a long beam or a short
one, and a cutting edge or a blunt one. And you can vary
that with the sliders, from most to least of one thing or
the other."

Hirianthial stared at the innocuous hilt. It was
unadorned, a slim haft of gray metal with plain grip and
guard. It was long enough for his hand, but that was all;
it did not have even a pommel for counterweight or decoration, only a socket as if something was meant to be
screwed into it. It looked like a toy . . . but then, so did the
palmers, and he knew very well how deadly they were.

"How does one tell?" he asked finally. "What one is
wielding? With so many choices?"

"The color," she said, and flicked it on with a chime.
And then there was a blade there, a flattish beam of purple
light. "It's a solidigraph—that's how it works. Both the
visual aspect and the physical. Here, try it."

Try it! He was torn between an aesthetic horror at the
contemplation of this unwanted upgrade to a weapon he'd
been trained to use all his life . . . and a fascination, impossible to quell, at the sheer unlikeliness of the thing. When

he took it from the Seersa's hand, it weighed nothing; felt like an extension of his palm and yet it was a blade. Experimentation with the settings shifted it through the entirety of the color spectrum, widened or narrowed the breadth of it, and changed its shape from very nearly a club to something so thin he lost the sight of it briefly while turning it.

"How before God does one remember all the options while busy with one's enemies?" he said, astonished.

She chuckled. "That's what practice is for. We have a room set aside for exercise and training; you're welcome to use it."

"I think I must." He turned the weapon off, noting the chime. "Does it always sing?"

"You can silence it," she said. "And you can add weights to the grip, if you want to change the heft." Her ears flagged. "It's not ostentatious, I know. Consumer models are far prettier to look at. But the Fleet model can recharge by kinetic energy, when you're swinging it, through induction in a gem grid, via solar power, or by batteries, and the solidigraphic generator is so efficient I've never heard of one running out of power. That's not a weapon that will fail you."

"I admit to surprise that you even have swords," he said. "It was not a weapon I thought common to the Alliance."

She folded her hands behind her back as he tested the controls. "Oh, there are thousands of competitive sword tournaments, and that's just sports. We have a lot of cultures that prefer edged weapons, and Fleet itself has always issued its command officers swords. It's a hold-over from the first days of the Pads, which reacted badly to palmers. We've since solved that problem, mostly, but we've kept the sword habit." She took down one of the other hilts and turned it, pointing at the empty socket. "You're issued a pommel based on which service you're in, and your specialty. So I would have a Fleet Intelligence design, with the dark stars and our motto, but someone from Fleet Naval would have the hawk and stars, and theirs."

He thought of the ornamentation on the Jisiensire swords and studied the modesty of the Alliance version. No, not modest. Austere, perhaps. Strange how both his culture and theirs obfuscated their steel. One would not look at the haft he was holding and think something so simple could be capable of slicing off a man's head, and his House set had looked like museum pieces: relics not appropriate to real use, to real blood, to sweat and a man's hand.

"Thank you," he said, bowing. "I will take good care of your weapon."

"Good," she said. "I'll show you the practice room. You can get to know it better there."

CHAPTER 9

The new day had not been promising. The confrontation with the Northern Galare contingent yet loomed, and much as she wanted to postpone it, Surela knew it would have to be done today. Thaniet, though sent for the previous evening, had not attended her, and the page she'd sent to fetch forth an explanation for this absence had returned unable to locate her. And now Athanesin had begged a meeting from her, and she could only imagine what new triviality he wanted to inflict on her; he'd been animated by the success of their coup and the receipt of the foreign weapons, and had attempted to sing their praises to her far too many times—men! What did the weapons matter so long as they fulfilled their function? Why trouble her with the details of their operation?

No doubt this would be more of the same, but much as he annoyed her he was still one of her strongest supporters. So after breaking her fast, she summoned him to the receiving room. They exchanged courtesies, as two long-acquainted would, and then she sat in one of Liolesa's fine chairs in front of a warm fire and waited, with poor grace, for the newest lecture on the possibilities the mortal technologies opened to them.

"My Lady," Athanesin began. "I know this might not be the proper time for this. But I find it hard to wait any longer, and so I will not."

The first words, aggressively gilt with the man's enthusiasm, drew down a cloud of foreboding, and by the end of this recitation, Surela's teeth were clenched so hard they hurt. Would he really do this to her now? Goddess and Lord, let him be working up to some less ridiculous topic, something less outré—

He went to a knee before her and offered a medallion emblazoned with the Sovenil family seal. "I have admired you all these many years, Lady Surela. I knew then that you were a woman of intelligence and wisdom, as well as beauty and wit. And I know you did not honor my attentions because you were consumed by your plan to fulfill your ambitions. You have done so, as brilliantly as I have come to expect from someone of your quality. I know it is hardly usual to do this, but I put my pledge before you, now. Take me to husband, Lady! How better to consolidate your rule than to take a royal consort and beget yourself a daughter to hold the throne behind you!"

Shocked, Surela gave voice to the first objection she could reasonably speak without revealing the depth of her revulsion. "It is custom to choose a niece for heir, and my sister has a husband—"

"But no daughter, no, nor son yet, and she may never. Why hold to customs that no longer suit your vision for our world? You have taken power for yourself, Lady. You could invest it in your bloodline, direct, and have the training of your heir yourself."

Of course. Because what she most wanted to do was

waste her time raising a child when she should be running a kingdom. Surela said, "Lord Athanesin, this proposal is . . . is incredible. I hardly know what to say."

"Say you'll consider it," he said, resting the medallion on the table. "I know I am precipitous in advancing it to you, particularly when it is for you to make your interest known. But I feel I can serve you, that I would make a good partner to you, a faithful lieutenant to carry out your aims. In fact, before you decide one way or the other, I beg you, give me leave to prove my worth to you."

"Prove your worth," she repeated, numb.

"Let me lead your men to Jisiensire," he said, his fervor lighting his eyes. "And bring them the news of the change in dynasty. Let me prompt their obedience, and bring back a liege gift from them. Think of how useless rebellion will seem when faced with an entire army in parade dress, banners flying! Just the sight of it will resign them to the inevitability of their surrender. To you, Queen Surela. My Lady. Please, let me do this for you."

Now she stared at him, finding his vehemence unsettling. "I was planning to lead that army myself. Liolesa would have."

"You are not the pretender queen," Athanesin said. "And it would not be seemly for you to ride out yourself. You are above such petty squabbles. I pray you: give this assignment to your truest liegeman. I will make it happen for you, and prove to you my worth. Whatever you answer then, I will accept."

She considered his bent head. The thought of marrying him was absurd. That was one habit of Liolesa's Surela thought well worth keeping. Men were troublesome and vain and needed constant attention, and given swords they inevitably turned to rattling them at one another to have something useful to do. And babies! Not that she didn't find them pleasing, but to spend nearly a full year of her life burdened when she had so much to do already? The whole idea was ridiculous. She would never marry him. Telling him so outright would probably be the easiest course, but . . . it would also create more instability at a time when she needed all the stability she could foster. Acquiescing to his test would also get him out of Ontine, and away from her, so she might not suffer his constant attentions.

"Very well," she said. "Go forth to Jisiensire, and carry my standard there. I await the results of your expedition with interest."

"Thank you, my Lady! You will not be disappointed!"

Left alone in the sitting room, Surela sighed. The petty irritations of ruling a kingdom were somehow more exhausting than the petty irritations of ruling a family. She drifted to the window and looked out on the court-yard, waiting until she saw Athanesin cross it, cloaked against the threat of snow. Preposterous. Marriage! As if she would ever. It was the sort of insult she would share with Thaniet . . . if she knew where Thaniet was. That she didn't was ridiculous. Could her pages not find a single lady-in-waiting?

She would look herself. And if she found her quarry where the pages failed, well. She would have words with the palace staff.

The last time Reese had seen someone arrive from Pad-enabled nothingness, she'd been a little preoccupied by the pirates who'd been manhandling her in her own cargo bay, so her recollection of it was distinctly fuzzy. Watching it this time made her stomach twitch, and she rested her hand on it out of a habit that being healed of her digestive issues hadn't quite broken yet. It was one thing to see someone appear over a Pad, knowing that the

Pad was doing the magic. It was another to watch a Tam-
illee woman appear out of nowhere, without any warning,
without any device to reassure you there were sound sci-
entific principles associated with the sheer unlikeliness of
her having melted out of the air.

Malia shook herself, then glanced around. She found
the nearest part of the great room with a patch of sunlight and crouched down, unrolling the Pad she'd brought
into the light. Tapping it awake, she waited for the colors
to stabilize to the blue of an open tunnel, then looked for
Reese. "All go, Captain. And we should be quick. We don't
want to run these on active for any longer than we have to
without a quick way to power them back up. The sun will
keep it on standby indefinitely, but frequent transits are
going to rip through the power cells, and recharging them
off solar alone is going to take forever."

"Right," Reese said. She waved Irine through. Belinor
paused for only a moment before passing over. To her surprise, Val glanced down at the Pad once, then followed the
younger priest without comment or hesitation. She went
next, Malia last.

Her first impression of their destination was not of
trees, but of the dim gray-green twilight created by their
clustered boughs, and of the *smell*: bright, evergreen and
pungent, carried on moist air so chilly it hurt to breathe.
Reese shivered and rubbed her arms. "Why does 'cold'
have to feel different in so many ways from what I'm
used to?" she complained to Irine, who was watching
sympathetically.

"I don't know," Irine said. "But I admit it's novel feeling
like my fur has a purpose beyond decoration for once."

It was surprisingly difficult to make out the camp amid
the trees, despite the lack of underbrush; most of the activity was underground ("Finally, someone who knows how

to build," Irine said), and the men who came up from those hidden boltholes no longer wore the white uniforms Reese had last seen them in, but were dressed in a grayish green color, with hoods to cover their shining hair and smears of paint to mar their perfect white faces.

"Eldritch in camouflage," she said to Irine. "I would never have imagined it."

"They seem pretty serious about all this," she agreed.

"Thankfully," Reese said, and followed Malia into one of the holes.

Down below she found the bustle she'd been expecting above . . . and a maze of high corridors hollowed out of the dirt and shored up with wooden beams. She narrowed her eyes as she kept up with the foxine, stepping out of the way of Eldritch on their way to patrol duties. Catching up with Malia, she said, "They seriously had all this built out in the event of a rebellion?"

"Actually, Lady," said a voice in front of them in accented Universal, "These tunnels lead into the catacombs under the palace and are much older than any plans Queen Liolesa had for them."

Reese found herself in a small cave-like room, a nexus for activity if the number of doors leading into it was any indication. At the round table in its center were Olthemiel and Beronaeth, the Swords who'd helped her rescue Hirian-thial from beneath Ontine. Olthemiel was the captain of the Queen's Swords, she remembered; Beronaeth's rank hadn't ever been revealed to her but she guessed him to be Olthemiel's Sascha, someone who acted as a second. A less mouthy one, probably. "The same catacombs they were keeping Hirianthial in."

"That's correct," the Swords' Captain said. "Welcome to our camp, Lady. We have fresh intelligence."

"Oh?" Malia said, joining them at the table where

Reese was surprised to see a small holo-map. Maybe not the highest fidelity, but still much newer technology than she'd expected.

"Yes," Olthemiel said. "Lord Athanesin has departed with nearly all the soldiers beholden to the usurper queen."

"Nearly all of them?" Reese said, startled.

"Where were they going?" Val asked from behind her.

Olthemiel glanced over her shoulder, but if he thought anything of her having arrived with an extra Eldritch he gave no sign. "They are heading south." Looking at Reese, he finished, "To Jisiensire's seat."

Irine's ears flattened. Reese squeezed her arm and said, "Still armed with our weapons?"

Olthemiel inclined his head once.

Irine shuddered. "It's going to be a massacre."

"They could surrender," Reese muttered.

"Jisiensire?" Malia said. "Never. They loved Sellelvi."

"The usurper queen may have given orders not to have anyone killed," Olthemiel said. "We haven't been able to ascertain Athanesin's orders."

"She didn't go?" Irine asked, startled.

"She remains in the palace, last we heard," Beronaeth said.

"And the prisoners?" Malia asked. "Lady Araelis's contingent, and Lady Fassiana's, and House Mathanith's?"

"Still inside." Olthemiel smiled. It was the first smile Reese could remember seeing on him, and it was grim. "An opportunity, thus."

"Let me guess." Reese rested her hands on the top of a rough chair, flexing cold fingers on the wood. "We sneak in and half of us help them break out and the other half go chasing pirates, and if it all goes to hell than everyone's so busy trying to figure out which threat to deal with that at least one part of the mission succeeds."

Olthemiel inclined his head. "You are not new to this, I see, Lady."

"Won't that be dangerous?" Irine's ears were still flat. "We're talking about . . . what, a bunch of non-combatants? Women and children, maybe? And it's cold. And how will they get far away enough to have a chance to outrun the pirates if we don't catch them all?"

"The risks are manageable, particularly if you are willing to house them. If you are?"

Surprised, Reese said, "Me? You're asking me? Where would I put them?" She thought wildly of the *Earthrise,* anchored somewhere half a sector away.

Taylor, behind Reese, said, "We did just leave a Pad at the castle."

Malia nodded. "If they can get away from the castle, they can flee over ours to Laisrathera. There's shelter there, and it's far from the Queen's enemies."

"As long as they don't use a Pad or a pirate shuttle to chase them there," Irine said, ears flattening again.

"The risks are manageable," Olthemiel said again.

Reese wrapped her arms around herself. "I don't know. If Surela hasn't killed them yet, why would she start now? Liolesa's still showing up with the cavalry. All we have to do is wait—"

"While slavers converge on our unprotected planet?" Olthemiel said. "If they arrive before the Queen does with reinforcements, we are lost. If she arrives before then, that still won't stop what's happening now . . . and if the usurper queen has not killed off the hostages yet, that does not mean she may change her mind . . . or that one of them will give her unforgiveable insult."

Reese said, slowly, "I can't help but think, though, that if we show up to kill the pirates and free the hostages, Surela's not going to care enough about the aliens to protect them. Which means most of her energy's going to be put toward stopping the escape. And if it fails. . . ."

Olthemiel met her eyes. There was sympathy there, but it was a thin veil over the steel in his gaze. "It is their duty, Lady, to protect their families, and their world. It is what it means, to be a seal-bearer. If they are called upon to make the sacrifice that rids us of the pirates and our betrayers, then they will have served as duty requires."

And this is what she had to look forward to as a lady of her own Eldritch property? Reese tried to hide her shudder. Could she die to protect people she was responsible for?

"It is the plan we have," Olthemiel said. "It is made immeasurably more feasible by the Pad at Laisrathera and your having someone willing to guide us into the cat-acombs through the secret ways." He glanced at Val. "I presume this is the man?"

"At your service," Val said, touching his palm to his chest and dipping his head.

"And you have vouched for him?"

"I do," Reese said.

Olthemiel nodded. "Then the sooner we leave, the better. Let us discuss the particulars of the plan, and if we are all agreed, make the attempt tonight."

Reese wanted to cry, *I'm not ready!* But when would she ever be? And somewhere east of her, near the sea, the people who'd almost killed Hirianthial and betrayed his entire people—people she was just starting to like—were free and, as one of her books would have said, up to no good. The sooner they got in there and messed with their plans, the better.

Baniel spared the crumpled body in the corner of the room no mind, though his nostrils did flare at the smell of blood. The evidence of violence was pleasurable, at least; the more of his kind who died due to the incompetence of his brother and cousin's protections, the more clear the demonstration of their failure. And if those ends were sordid, so much the better. He did not plan to be here when Hirianthial arrived to vent his fury on him, so he would have to make do with imagining his brother's horror when he discovered what the Chatcaavan had made of the women Baniel had been sending him. Hirianthial had always been good for taking on unnecessary guilt. Perhaps this time it would drive him to suicide? That would neatly solve a great many problems.

Folding his hands behind his back, he said to the Chatcaavan, "You have news?"

"I do," the alien said. He was still in his borrowed shape, but he was licking his bloody fingers with a tongue Baniel found an appallingly bright color, and somewhat too long for good taste. "Relief should be here shortly."

"Relief?" Baniel said with interest.

The alien nodded. "I have had a message tube."

Interesting that he hadn't noticed it coming . . . but then he was unfamiliar with the method. All the communication he'd undertaken had been via Well repeater; the less common practice of sending the remotes physically was not something he would have chanced, given the likelihood of Liolesa's foxes noticing it. Which prompted the thought: "Did the foxes notice?"

The Chatcaavan snorted. "If they're still in-system, you mean? I doubt it. A tube is a small thing, and painted for stealth. They would have had extraordinary luck."

"Luck does happen."

"Then let them see that we received a tube," the alien said with a fluid shrug. "They can't decrypt it. Unless they somehow know pirate codes." He grinned. "Do they? That might make the game more interesting."

"I doubt it," Baniel said. "So . . . the relief comes?"

"It does. And I doubt your petty Pelted will be ready for it." Another grin, this one with teeth. "We have had good luck in the unclaimed zones, laying our traps for the freaks' Fleet. Good prizes, yes. And one is coming here."

Baniel's brows lifted. "That sounds promising."

"It will be glorious," the alien said. "And deeply amusing. There will be bloodshed." He licked another finger, thoughtful. "The other vessel will not return."

"Ah? So they go to carry the news of the location out."

"Yes. But to those in our organization." Another of those shark-like grins. "This is a secret I intend to keep for myself, until I can properly fortify my new demesne."

How deeply gratifying to know that the ruin of Liolesa's dream, and Maraesa's and Jerisa's before her, was now irrevocable. No more convenient secrets: now all the villains and thieves and ruffians and slavers of the universe would converge here in search of prey. Baniel appreciated the Chatcaavan's desire to keep the world a secret . . . but all it would take was a single one of those pirates whispering the knowledge in someone's ear for a little extra money, and not even the dragon could keep it from exploding across the universe. In that, the Eldritch would have accelerated their own demise, for centuries of prim refusal to divulge the location of their homeworld would have incited in almost everyone a raging curiosity to finally learn its whereabouts.

"I noticed our pets have been shifting position," the Chatcaavan continued. "Have you set in motion your plan to destroy your enemies?"

"Let us say I whispered a few interesting notions into Lord Athanesin's ear," Baniel said with a casual flick of his hand. "He hardly needed it, though. Do you know it was his idea to send the entire army partway down the continent via Pad?"

The Chatcaavan arched his eyebrows. "An army. Via our single-person Pad."

"Even filing through one by one, it was faster than riding there," Baniel said. "I was impressed by his grasp of the technology. I hardly imagine the Queen knows what he's done; she thinks he'll be gone for weeks. In reality he's already there, and probably destroying his enemies with commendable zeal."

"And will return triumphant, having won a victory she does not want?"

"Just so," Baniel said, amused by the idea. "And hot to marry her, if you will believe. She will deny him, of course, and then we will be rid of Surela."

"And in her stead we will have a far less controllable king."

Baniel laughed at the Chatcaavan's scowl. "Athanesin? Oh, please. He's violent and cunning, yes. But he's not smart. You perceive the difference?"

"I have some notion of it, yes." The alien considered him. "You are certain you can leash him?"

"I don't need to," Baniel said. "But if he ever proves troublesome, I will invite him to a conference about the state of the priesthood, and he will emerge from that meeting with a mind firmly devoted to my purposes." He smiled. "You should know by now how useful our powers can be."

"I prefer their more obvious applications." The Chatcaavan considered the wreck in the corner. "All this subtlety . . . I have been warned about you Eldritch and subtlety. You all think too much."

"Mm. Thinking has its rewards, as I have been teaching you."

"Yes, speaking of this teaching. . . ."

"You are done with your entertainments?" Baniel

glanced at the woman. "I may have that sent away, then?"

The Chatcaavan dismissed her with another of those liquescent shrugs. "I am done with it, yes."

Baniel called for a guard—one of the five pirates that had remained on-world—and had the woman taken away. "Yours," he said. "If you like such things." Then he turned back to the alien and cupped his face with long hands. "Now. Fall into me, and I will show you more." He smiled thinly. "You will see why we have such subtle minds."

"Go on, then," the Chatcaavan said with a hiss. "Turn me into an Eldritch. If you can. It would be safer for you."

"Nothing about this is safe," Baniel promised. Especially for his 'student.' But then, what did aliens know of the bonds between teachers and their pupils? All that mattered was that, did he need it, he would have a weapon against his alien. His pet alien. The notion was almost as pleasing as knowing what Hirianthial would suffer on his return. "But that's well, eh? We are not safe people."

"No," the alien agreed, baring his teeth. "We are not."

CHAPTER 10

Hirianthial arrived to the room set aside for practice and found it already in use, knew it initially by the searing streams of the combatants' auras, so bright they left afterimages. It took him a moment to discern the bodies through those banners: Narain and Tomas, sparring at a speed he found breathtaking. Narain landed on the floor on his back, was already reaching for the human when Tomas went for him, sent the human sailing over him with a foot to the solar plexus. Tomas landed and laughed through his panting. "Dammit, arii. No one else in the universe is going to try distracting me by tickling my groin with his tail."

"You never know," Narain said from the ground, his voice a purr. "Lot of us Harat-Shar out there."

From a corner, Sascha snickered; he was sitting alongside Jasper, the Ciracaana, observing.

"Stop letting it distract you and I'll stop doing it." Narain rolled to his feet with a bonelessness that recalled his feline antecedents. "Another round?"

"Nah." Tomas handed him a towel. "I'm done for now." He looked up and added, "Ah, Lord Hirianthial. You need the gym?"

"Salle," Narain muttered.

"Gym," Tomas said firmly, ignoring his fellow analyst.

"I came to practice," he replied. "With this sword your commander was kind enough to lend me."

"Ah, holoblades. Can't help you there, never got the hang of them," Tomas said.

"We don't have a specialist in them, do we?" Narain frowned, thinking.

"No," Jasper offered from the sidelines. He flexed a forepaw, claws inching from their beds, and then folded it again. "So Elements forbid any of us get into a situation where a duel has to save the day."

Tomas snorted. "If we did, we'd just set the thing to bludgeon and win the hard way, that's all."

"Or sic you on them, Jasper," Narain added. "Let 'em try to chop through nine feet of Ciracaana. You'd kill them while they were still working on it."

Jasper rolled his eyes. "Your command of biology is underwhelming."

"I know. You suffer so much." Narain grinned and bowed to Hirianthial. "The floor's yours. Should we clear out?"

Given how much of his training had involved either a tutor or group sessions, it was hard to imagine finding their presence as distracting as, apparently, Narain's tail was to Tomas. "It may not be very interesting to watch, I fear. I am out of practice, and not long off a biobed."

Jasper's ears pricked. "Oh? I didn't know this."

"The Fleet base hospital had to sew all his internal organs back together," Sascha said. "He won't admit to it, but he probably should be resting, not jumping around."

Hirianthial cleared his throat . . . and surprised himself

by finding his mouth twitching.

Sascha added, "And he's a surgeon himself, so he should know better."

"That so?" Jasper said, glancing at Hirianthial. "You didn't mention being a doctor to Soly."

He hadn't, had he? Had he renounced his vows so easily then?

No, that was too easy. All that he had learned at the Alliance's knee, about medicine, about life, about the ethics that defined the existence of a healer, remained, saturated through him like water in soil. But there was a time for everything, and he had accepted that for now he needed to set the healer aside in favor of the fighter. Once he and Liolesa had swept their world clean of their enemies and Lesandurel arrived with his army of relatives to set up the fixed defenses, then he could turn his hand to kinder endeavors. He looked forward to helping Araelis with her child—all the Eldritch with the children they'd found so hard to conceive and carry to term. He could be happy with that life . . . once he'd earned it.

"I fear I will have little call for those skills for the nonce," Hirianthial said. "Sascha is correct, though. I should know better."

"But he'll still do what he wants anyway. He's like Reese that way." Sascha eyed him. "They make a good pair, what with all the stubbornness."

Hirianthial didn't suppress his sigh then.

"You see?" Narain told Tomas. "Everyone needs a Harat-Shar. Who else is going to tell them what they need to hear?"

Sascha offered, "They're so stubborn we needed two, even. My twin would tell you so."

To Sascha, Hirianthial said, "And if I promise to stop when I am winded?"

"Then I'd say, 'sure, as long as you let the doctor stay and make sure you're honest about when you need to stop.'"

Hirianthial pressed a palm to his heart and dipped his head to Jasper. "If the healer will oblige."

"Sure," Jasper said. "I've never seen an Eldritch fight."

"You've never seen an Eldritch at all until this one walked in the airlock," Tomas observed.

"Like I said. I've never seen an Eldritch fight."

Guffaws then. The camaraderie in the room had a warmth, like the residual radiated from a hearth still nursing its embers. It reminded him of the Swords, when he was one of them. He smiled to himself, then considered the sword and its settings. He chose as close an approximation to the length and breadth of the Jisiensire sword as possible and set himself to the exercises. They were . . . very different, when the sword had no weight. Partway through them, Tomas interrupted with a question, which he answered absently. And not long after, Narain had a different comment. Soon they were interrupting him at intervals which, he noted with resigned amusement, always seemed to coincide with when he was breathing too hard.

He stopped finally and eyed them. Their auras were blemished with secrets, and even Sascha's had the taint. "Tell me how you are doing this."

"Doing what?" Narain swished his tail, assuming an expression of innocence.

"Deciding when to throttle my exertions."

Both of the analysts glanced at Jasper. Jasper lifted a hand, exposing a small medical monitor. "Heart-rate, metabolic rate, oxygenation."

"From a distance?" Hirianthial said, startled. "We had no such equipment where I trained."

"Fleet hath its privileges," the Ciracaana said, unperturbed.

"Then how do you know?" he asked the analysts.

"He extends a finger against his foreleg," Tomas said. He grinned. "We have our ways. Actually, we've had our ways for so long most of the time we don't have to talk them out beforehand."

"It's a little like telepathy that way," Narain agreed. "No offense to you, if that seems presumptuous."

"A Harat-Shar apologizing for presumption," Tomas muttered. He folded his arms and said to Jasper, "Maybe the Eldritch broke him."

"If he's broken, I can fix him," Sascha said with a grin.

"Is that a promise?" Narain eyed him hopefully.

"It can be? Right now maybe?"

"Deal," Narain said. "Bunk's this way."

Sascha waved to Hirianthial. "See you, arii. I've got an appointment with an Eldritch-broken Harat-Shar and I'm the only one with the expertise. You know how it is."

Hirianthial laughed. "I have some notion, yes."

"Well, unlike some fuzzies I'm on duty in ten." Tomas nodded to Hirianthial. "Thanks for the demonstration."

"Of course."

Which left him alone with the Ciracaana, who studied him so pensively Hirianthial finally said, "There is something on your mind."

"And you divined that entirely without reading it?" Jasper smiled, resettled his bulk. The long catlike tail stretched out along the wall, mottled like his namesake, twitched once at the tip. "The monitor says you're too soon from a sickbed to be using a sword on someone anytime soon. You know that, I imagine."

And was tired of people reiterating it, but he was too polite to say so. "I had the notion, yes."

"So you know if you overexert yourself, you're going to collapse." The Ciracaana met his eyes, and Hirianthial recognized the look for the one healers all over the Alliance had cultivated: that combination of professionalism and obstinacy that brooked no patient protest.

"That may be overstating the matter."

"But not by much," Jasper replied. He pushed himself to all four feet, stretching, and that was a sight to see: the only other centauroids in the Alliance, the Glaseah, were compact, stocky creatures that barely came up to Hirianthial's ribs. Jasper's legs were longer than Hirianthial's arms, and his entire body seemed poured, like something liquid. If someone had elongated a great cat and then given it a fox's face, it may have approached the unlikeliness of Jasper's appearance, but it would somehow have failed to capture that surreal grace. "You know why I push the matter, alet."

"I have some idea, yes."

"Because we're going into dangerous waters, and you're the only local we have to guide us," Jasper continued. "If you aren't honest with yourself about your limitations, you can't be honest about them with us, and that might land us in a situation where your weaknesses betray us all."

It was not an accusation, and yet he struggled not to take it as such. He had already failed too many people in his weaknesses; the intimation that he was repeating his mistakes was too keen a barb. He forced himself to breathe through his reaction and replied, at last, "It is my world, alet. To fail at its defense is unthinkable."

Jasper considered him for several more moments, then sighed. "I can't tell if that's a 'yes' or a 'no,' and that's how you people are advertised, isn't it. Very well, Healer. I will take you at your word and hope I don't regret it."

"As do I."

Surela wasn't sure whether to be stunned at the

invitation awaiting her in her office or infuriated at the presumption: Fassiana, head of the Delen Galares, had asked her to take tea in the rooms where Surela had ordered the Galare entourage detained. She sat abruptly on a chair, the invitation clutched in one hand. The nerve of the woman! To offer with such nonchalance, as if she still had the right to entertain! And yet, Surela had always admired that about Fassiana, her absolute self-assurance. In fact, Surela found her frankly intimidating in a way Araelis could never manage. Fassiana was beautiful, with a demeanor that would not have been out of place in a princess . . . graceful, self-disciplined, tranquil. Surela had heard she'd not always been so, but for as long as she'd known Fassiana, the other woman had been a model of regal behavior.

She looked at the invitation. She had not found Thaniet yet, a situation that was beginning to distress her. Athanesin was gone, for which she was grateful—she had some peace now—but Araelis remained obdurate. She knew she'd been putting off the confrontation with the northern Galares, and apparently Fassiana had decided to take that matter into her own hands.

The invitation was perfectly correct. Had she been Liolesa, one of Fassiana's allies and relatives, it would have been unremarkable. But Surela was neither, and Fassiana had no reason to speak with her, much less pretend to civility. Tea! Really!

And yet . . . this was the first time one of her enemies had reached out to her. If Fassiana was willing to make the effort, maybe she should as well.

Accordingly, two hours later, Surela visited the suite devoted to the northern Galares' entourage and was graciously received by its servants and shown to a fine table, glittering with cut crystal and polished silverware.

Fassiana was standing alongside her chair—calculation, that, for it neatly sidestepped the question of whether the other woman would have stood for her as she should have when visited by her Queen. It was too much to hope that this might represent a true effort toward amicability, and Surela found she did not want to be disappointed . . . so she spoke first, before Fassiana had the chance to do so and reveal that she thought herself Surela's equal.

"Thank you for the invitation."

"Thank you for accepting it," Fassiana said, the words politely neutral. "Won't you join me?"

"I'd be delighted." Not quite a lie. At least, not as much of one as Surela had hoped. She did not want to crave this woman's approval quite as much as she felt she might.

They sat, and the servant poured for them, brought them cakes and cream. For a brief time there was only the chime of spoons meeting the lips of plates and the click of cups returned to their saucers. Then Fassiana dismissed the servant and clasped her hands beneath her chin, studying Surela in a way that became, very quickly, uncomfortable.

"So you have dispatched your army."

And what a tedium it had been, standing at the balcony in the wet chill of a dull winter afternoon, watching as the column processed before her in the courtyard and then made its slow progress out of the palace grounds and off through the city to the nearest road south. "They go to collect allegiance from Jisiensire."

"And you know they will never give it, as their seal-bearer has already rejected you?" Fassiana poured for herself again, her tone conversational.

"It is their duty—"

"To bow to you?" Fassiana shook her head minutely. "You know better, Asaniefa."

Watching her, Surela said, "I bowed to Liolesa."

"Queen Liolesa did not steal the throne from you."
When Surela began to speak, she held up a hand. "Be
honest, Surela. Did someone yank the throne from you
now, would you meekly bow your head to them?"

"That would depend on their policies toward the
aliens," Surela said, trying not to seethe. Why did all of
Liolesa's allies believe they would be protected from the
consequences of their cheek?

"Ah, yes. The aliens." Fassiana spread clotted cream
onto her cake and pushed aside one of the tart red berries,
leaving it smeared with a white swirl. "Tell me, how do you
find the food?"

"I—the . . ." Surela gathered herself and said, "You set a
fine table, thank you for asking."

"Berries are such a fine talisman against the winter
doldrums, aren't they?" Fassiana scooped hers up on her
spoon and offered it. "Another?"

"Ah . . . thank you?" Surela took it, perplexed at the
change in subject. "I am fond of raspberries."

"As am I," Fassiana agreed. "Have you a sense of where
they're grown?"

"No? Though I suppose now that the entire kingdom is
my responsibility and not Asaniefa alone I shall soon learn."

"Mmm." Fassiana reached over to refill Surela's tea,
which was gratifying, as was the continued graciousness
of the conversation. Even the studied neutrality of the
word shadings couldn't detract from it. "And the cream is
particularly fine today. Don't you agree?"

"Very much."

"I'm told the cakes are made here in the palace. A very
delicate touch they have with the sugar. Not overwhelming."

"The kitchen staff has great talent," Surela said.

"You grow wheat in Asaniefa, do you not?"

"Some," Surela said. "Not much for export, I fear. We

tithe of other crops."

"It does not strike you as strange," Fassiana added. "That Ontine has berries in winter."

"No?" Surela glanced at the other woman. "There have always been berries in winter."

"At Ontine," Fassiana said.

"At the winter court." Surela paused, then laughed, hiding her nervousness. "You are going to tell me that Ontine has some magic garden that will not work without a Galare on the throne?"

Fassiana calmly ate a piece of her cake. Then set her spoon down, tapped her lips with her napkin, and said, "Yes."

Surela stared at her. "I was not aware that you had such poor taste in humor, Lady Fassiana."

"That is because I do not." Fassiana met her eyes. "I was not making a joke, Surela. This food—the flour, the sugar, the berries, the cream—all of it was imported."

"From some other fief?"

"From the Alliance."

Surela sat back, fighting anger. "So Liolesa had alien taste in food. What else is new? I will end our foreign dependence on these aliens and we will resume eating what we grow!"

"Then you will doom us to starvation, because we cannot grow enough to live on."

The cup Surela set down clattered when it met the saucer, but by then she didn't care that Fassiana might know she trembled. Let her think it wrath! Surela herself was fairly sure that was the cause. "You say amazing things, Lady Fassiana. Notorious things."

"Only because they can be proven," was the unperturbed reply. "Go ask the Royal Procurer. Check the almanacs, and the ledgers. See you where our food comes from, Surela. And then tell me how you mean to solve the problem without the aid of the aliens."

"And if I find a solution?" Surela asked. "Assuming that the problem even exists. Will you bow to me then?"

Fassiana said, "Go check the books. You will learn something about the kingdom you purport to be yours."

Infuriating. Ridiculous! Surela rose and managed a frosty, "Thank you for the tea." But she left before waiting for a response, and hated that Fassiana had driven her to such a petty discourtesy, like a spoiled child.

From that suite she went directly to the library, where she demanded the ledgers that showed the amount of the royal tithe. Sitting beneath the cupola's windows, she began paging through them and reading . . .

. . . and reading. . . .

She sent for a lead and a sheaf of papers and began making notes, and ordered the census records brought to her. The almanacs she drew down from the shelves herself. As the afternoon waned, more books joined the ones already scattered on the desk in the library, and by evening she sent for the Royal Procurer, wishing that the Chancellor hadn't hidden himself off with the Heir—she should do something about that, but later—for the Chancellor would have been able to give her a broader view of the issue. But the Procurer would do, and he arrived shortly after her summons.

Surela tapped her lead against the paper and said, "If we ceased to buy food from the aliens, how much of our population could we feed?"

The Procurer hesitated. He was a thin, small man with delicate hands and great hollows in his cheeks, and a perpetually surprised expression caused by the natural arch of his brows. But he recovered from his hesitation immediately and answered, "Fifty-five percent."

Surela clutched the lead. "Fifty-five percent."

"Yes, Lady Surela," he said, and she let the improper form of address go while she grappled with the horror of the figure . . . which he compounded by continuing, "That is by crop-weight only. Unfortunately, given factors involving the livestock, it is closer to forty."

"Forty . . . percent?" she asked carefully.

"That's right."

"Because of livestock," she repeated, to have anything to say in response to this unbelievable situation.

"That's correct, Lady Surela. We can eat the crops we manage to grow here, though they are not as nutritious as the ones we can import." The Procurer tucked his hands into his sleeves as he spoke, for all the world as if lecturing on a topic of less earth-shattering significance. "But our livestock situation presents several challenges. Our domesticated fowl cannot survive on the insects of this world, so we buy insects to feed them. We have a few experimental greenhouses where we attempt to cultivate the insects, but those projects haven't succeeded on a large enough scale to make the importation of insects unnecessary. Also, the ruminants cannot thrive on the grass here. We can feed some of our livestock on the produce we grow—swine do better on some of our crops than we do, in fact—but if the majority of their diet is grass-based, they must be fed imported hay. Without those imports, we would have no horses, Lady, nor what few cows we've managed to maintain. Goats manage well enough, but they are easy prey for the wildlife here. . . ."

"Stop!" Surela pressed her fingers to her brow and tried to breathe. "How can this be possible?"

"I fear it is a matter of numbers, Lady," the Procurer said. "We are too few to farm the amount of land we would require to live without aid . . . and this world is not ours.

The crops that have adapted to the foreign environment kept us from dying out, but as you no doubt know yourself from the management of Asaniefa, we are not as fertile as we should be, nor do we thrive. It is what the Queen has been attempting to understand with her fertility projects."

"Her what?"

"The research she has been funding?" the Procurer said. "In the Alliance, in an attempt to understand our low birth rate. I do not know much about that aspect of her endeavors, Lady Surela. The Chancellor would. Perhaps you can ask him when he returns."

"Of course," she managed. She set the lead carefully down on the desk. "So . . . you mean to tell me that for centuries, we have been eating from the mortal table, and that otherwise we would have long since died."

"Since the reign of Queen Maraesa, yes."

She looked down at her books, her notes . . . wondered suddenly whether the paper she'd been writing on had been made here. She touched its surface, felt the dust from her lead on her fingertips. Clearing her throat, she said, "You may go."

After he left she carefully shelved all the books and sent the census back with a servant. Once she'd cleared the table of everything but her notes, she sat down again and stared out at the sullen winter twilight. It felt far closer than it had last night . . . and as the snow began to drift from the clouds, she put her head in her hands.

CHAPTER 11

The part of the plan Reese had not been anticipating involved walking. A lot of walking. It hadn't occurred to her to notice the lack of horses in the underground camp, but she guessed it made sense; who kept horses underground? They didn't like that, right? What did she know about horses, anyway . . . and she would have to learn. If they survived all this. Of course, if they survived all this she could just ask Hirianthial. . . .

Reese tried not to think about Hirianthial because it made her chest hurt. She needed her chest not to hurt when she was about to throw herself into crazy danger.

No horses meant they hiked from the site of the camp east, toward the sea, and they left in the mid-morning, when the light was diffuse and gray and the wind cut straight through her coat and made her limbs clumsy. She wondered if it was normal not to be able to feel her nose and trudged after the column of Swords in silence, grateful Irine had elected to come along. Malia and Taylor had stayed behind to coordinate via telegem with both parties and the backup they were sending toward Ontine to help the escapees. As much as possible, they didn't want to use the telegems, though. Reese was hoping the pirates were as careless as they were in stories, but knowing her luck Baniel had hired some kind of hyper-vigilant super-pirates who'd notice the first whisper of unauthorized telegem traffic. Belinor had elected to come too . . . to keep an eye on Val, maybe? Reese didn't know, but she was oddly comforted by the steadfast acolyte's presence.

After two hours of hiking through the forest, they crossed a pitted path Olthemiel called a road despite its lack of pavement and headed gradually down a narrow, crumbly path shrouded in more trees. The shadows, the moist wind, the cold . . . Reese couldn't remember when she'd been more uncomfortable in her life. But in the distance she could hear the boom of the surf and she found she was eager to look at the ocean again. Had Hirianthial ever told her the word for sea? She couldn't remember. How many vowels would it have? She smiled a little, wondering.

The light waned and the path became a trail, and the trail a suggestion, a place where the sea grass hadn't grown in over rocky soil. They continued to descend until at last they broke away from the trees and found themselves on a beach, where Val, who'd been leading the expedition, pointed out their ingress.

"You have got to be kidding," Reese said.

"Not at all." He flashed her a grin. "How do you think it went unnoticed?" Tucking a line of rope through his belt, he began to climb.

Their way in was a hole in a sea cliff at least six stories over Reese's head. She scooted close to Irine, tucking her hands under her armpits to keep them warm. "Are we seriously going to have to climb that? Because I'm not a good climber. I don't think I can climb. What is it with us and cliffs, anyway? The last cliff we climbed . . . that wasn't a good memory."

"Fear not, Lady," Beronaeth said. Kindly, she thought. She wondered what her expression looked like, to have prompted that much concern. "The priest will send down the rope once he's made the ascent and the rest of us will go up aided. Pulled if necessary."

She wanted to be too proud to be pulled, but when her turn came around she found the rocks too slippery and cold for the mittens built into the sleeves of her coat. Her boots couldn't find purchase either, and the distance was too daunting. So she suffered herself to be tied into a harness and lifted, and spent the entire journey staring east. It had gotten dark while they'd been making the trip, and all she could see of the ocean was a hint of star-gleam on the waves that sounded on the shore. It was like being in a dream, one composed of the racing of her heart and the discomfort of uncertainty and the voice of the sea, the smell of it, brine and salt and so, so cold.

She wondered if she could pinch herself and wake up back on the *Earthrise,* with all this over and everyone safe.

"It's a little underwhelming," Reese muttered to Irine once they'd both made it up.

"I don't know." The tigraine swept her gaze over the narrow, craggy cave. "I think it looks just right for a secret entrance. Not too ostentatious or anything."

Reese snorted and padded after Val and Olthemiel.

"From here," the former priest was saying, "we should maintain silence unless absolutely necessary. I will guide us to the intersection I mentioned, and from there you go to the captives and we will head on through the catacombs."

"After waiting the necessary time."

Val nodded. "We'll give you your lead, Captain."

Satisfied, Olthemiel said to Reese, "Lady?"

"It's a little late to be messing with the plan now," Reese said. "Let's get moving."

Reese remembered very little of what followed, except that she'd been expecting hallways, like the ones that led out of Ontine into the catacombs, or that had been hollowed out of the ground at the Swords' campsite. But Val brought them through a maze of passages, some so tiny that she had to squirm to make her way through them. She left scraped skin on a few of them, even.

"Here," came Val's voice in the dark.

Some shuffling. Reese could barely see Olthemiel's face by the sticklights Malia had passed to them all before they'd left. The Captain was looking up at something; abruptly, he nodded. "I see it." Faint humor. "You didn't mention having to climb."

"It's not much of a climb," Val said. "Just pull yourself up half a body-length and you'll be under the servant's quarters."

"Understood. Lady?"

"Here," Reese said.

He regarded her carefully. "Still well?"

"Fine," Reese said. "I like small spaces."

Shadows edged the little smile. "And you are petite enough to use them well. We go, then. You remain well with the plan?"

"Twenty minutes, and then we head for the pirates' den," Reese said. "Assuming they're somewhere near the priests."

"Or we can get the information out of the priests," Val said, low.

"Right. What he said."

"Very good," Olthemiel said. He touched his palm to his breast. "Go with God and the Lady."

"Freedom bless your errand, Captain."

He paused, surprised. "Yes. I very much hope so." Turning to the men he said something sharp in their tongue and they were away, leaving fifteen of their number to back-up Reese's part of the mission. She sighed and slid to the ground, putting her back to the wall and hugging her knees.

"What are you thinking?" Irine asked, sitting next to her.

"You'll laugh."

"Try me?"

Reese glanced at her and smiled wryly. "That I don't remember what it's like to feel warm?"

Irine huffed. "Yes. Me too."

"What, no 'now you know how I feel?'"

The tigraine smiled. "I guess that doesn't feel too important right now. You know, what with the 'we might end up dead by the end of the day' business."

Reese sighed a little. "This is not how I planned to go."

"Did you? Plan to go? Actually, did you ever plan anything beyond our next stop?"

The innocent question made her thoughts scatter, left a blank in her head in their wake. Had she ever had an idea of what she wanted her life to be like? The end game, the thing she'd be able to do once she could stop running the *Earthrise* to make up for past debts? What came to her lips then was, "No. I never had any idea what to do with my life." She rubbed her knees, trying to get the ache out of them. "Though 'living in a rose-choked castle surrounded by Harat-Shar kittens' was certainly never in sensor range."

"Sounds like a pretty good life to me!"

"To me too, actually."

Irine glanced at her, ears pricked in surprise. Then she shifted closer and rested her head on Reese's shoulder. For a moment, Reese tensed . . . then she let it go. Let herself rest her cheek on Irine's hair, and was surprised to find it cold. She'd had no idea hair could be cold.

"What about you?" Irine said.

Val, who'd been sitting across from them with his wrists resting on his lifted knees, glanced at them, surprised. "You're asking me?"

"Sure."

"What I expected of my life."

"Yeah?"

Sitting a short ways down the wall from Val, Belinor looked up.

"That I would grow old in the priesthood. I would guess. To eventually take the high priest's mantle? Maybe. That was treated as an inevitability, so I never questioned it."

"But did you want to be a high priest?" Irine asked, curious.

He flashed her a smile. "I don't know. I've never been one, so how could I decide?"

"If you run your life based on that philosophy, you'll never do anything," Irine said. "Except, I guess, the things that your parents made you do before you had any choice, so you've already experienced them. Don't you have experiences you want to have had before you die?"

Val considered this, eyes still focused on the corridor where it dwindled into the dark. "Yes, actually. I believe I do."

"And?"

Val grinned at her suddenly. "I've never kissed a woman."

Irine canted her head. "Have you kissed a man?"

Belinor exclaimed, "God and Lady!"

"Guess that's not okay here," Irine said.

Val was laughing. "No, not very."

Irine nodded, ears pricked. "Do girls with fur count

as women?"

"Goddess and Lord!"

"Good job," Reese murmured to Irine. "I haven't heard that one yet."

Belinor was flushing, the Eldritch skin so fair it was easily read even in the low light. "One does not kiss priests."

"Why not?" Reese asked, curious.

"Priests and priestesses don't marry," Val offered. "It's considered a distraction from their work. This is, in fact, the same reasoning that allowed Queen Jerisa to beg off from marrying, and the Queens after her, since technically all queens are the titular heads of the Church."

"A kiss isn't marrying," Irine pointed out.

"A kiss is a carnal distraction," Belinor said firmly.

"I could use a carnal distraction." Val grinned at Irine. "If a furless mind-mage counts as a man to you, Lady Tigress, then I am willing to have the new experience. Particularly since there's no guarantee I will have the chance again."

"To kiss a woman?" Belinor muttered.

"To kiss anyone."

"Good a reason as any," Irine said, and crawled across the corridor. She stopped on her hands and knees in front of Val and paused, waiting; when he didn't flinch, she leaned into the glow of his sticklight and touched her fingers to his jaw. It was a sweet, chaste brush of lips, but it was beautiful. Reese hugged her knees and thought that romance novels hadn't prepared her for anything, and that surprised her because now she had the sense that she wanted to be prepared. That she wanted to try.

Val opened his eyes and met Irine's and smiled. "How about that," he said, low. "I like fur."

Irine giggled and backed away, curling back up against Reese's side. Reese could sense her happiness.

"And now, ten minutes," Val said, sounding vastly

pleased with himself.

Belinor eyed him.

Reese didn't want the time to pass. She didn't like sitting in the corridor, in the cold, with her backside getting colder and damper and her nose getting more numb and all the possibility of failure (and worse) in front of her. But she didn't want to move through the next few hours either. She kept her cheek on Irine's hair, when the tigraine put her head back on Reese's shoulder, and thought about how heavy a head could be, when a body could also be so fragile. She shivered and pressed her nose behind Irine's ear.

"What are you thinking?" Irine whispered.

"That you smell like wet cat."

"That's because I am a wet cat."

Reese paused and the Harat-Shar began to giggle. Amused and a little exasperated, Reese said, "What?"

"I actually made you wonder if that was some sort of dirty joke." Irine grinned. "And here I thought I'd never get you to think that way."

Reese huffed. "Hush or I'll bite you."

"And I'll—"

"Like it, yes, I know."

Belinor was staring at them now, and Val smiling but still staring down the corridor with an innocuous expression. Well, let them hear. Reese hugged Irine and waited out the last few minutes, and then it was time.

"Come on," Val said, and they started, and this was the beginning of what Reese hoped to be the ending. The right ending.

Their passage through the hidden catacombs beneath Ontine felt like nightmare for Reese, the mundane kind filled with halls she could never escape from and a pervasive dread that spurred her heart and made her body shake. She hated that kind of nightmares, wished suddenly and powerfully for Allacazam's chiming reassurances. Where was he, she wondered? Would she ever see him again? Was Kis'eh't feeding him enough? Too much?

"Stop," Val hissed.

The entire column froze. Reese waited for soldiers or priests or enemies . . . something. When none were forthcoming, she whispered, "What is it?"

Val backed away, rejoined them in the dark behind one of the turns. "The pirates are in a different part of the palace."

"From what we expected?"

"From Baniel. The pirates are in the catacombs here. Baniel's upstairs, in the palace."

Reese frowned. "We need the pirates gone."

"And Baniel, right?" Irine whispered over her shoulder. "He's the traitor. The one who made the deal with the dragons."

"We need them both," Val said. "So we will have to separate."

A breathpause. Then Reese said, "Oh no. No, the moment we do that we're going to die. How does it make sense to split up? Half the people sent to fight the same number of enemies? We need to stick together!"

"And for the most part, we will," Val said. "You and the others will go after the pirates. I will go after Baniel."

"You. Alone. Against the guy who got you thrown out?" Reese said, skeptical.

"Me, alone," Val agreed, meeting her eyes in the dark. "Because if I bring more and he can turn their minds, then I will be fighting not only him but my own allies."

Her heart gave a sickening double-thump to make up for the beat it missed. Reese pressed her fist to her chest to steady herself and swallowed bile. "Okay. I can see that being . . . um . . . not the greatest scenario. But you can't go without any backup at all." She thought of snow and roses and the anger that had allowed her to move an arm despite Val's pressing attention. "I'll go with you. I have some luck resisting compulsions."

"Some." He studied her, frowning. "But I don't like the idea of being responsible for your safety, Lady."

"I don't like the idea of you going alone, either!" Irine said.

"You won't take any guards?" Reese asked.

He glanced at them, saw their silent regard. To her, he said, "Have you martial training?"

"Um, no."

He nodded, short hair twitching around his neck. Maybe hair that short could look normal on an Eldritch, if Val had it. Maybe she wouldn't be so shocked by it next time she saw Hirianthial. Which she would. Damn it. But Val was talking. "Then you I will take. I'll have no chance against trained soldiers if Baniel can command their minds against me. But a small woman. . . ."

Irine sniffed. "She probably weighs more than most of them!"

Reese eyed her. "Not that much more."

"And she's armed! You can't ask her to leave her weapon . . . !"

"Now that I'd rather not," Reese muttered.

Val glanced at her. "I think this is ill-advised."

"I think you going off alone is ill-advised," Reese said. "But you're in charge of this expedition, and if you say Baniel might be capable of . . . of mind-controlling us so that we turn on you, I can respect that—"

Belinor folded his arms and said, "Is this your death-wish, then, Corel Reborn?"

Complete silence. Val looked slowly over his shoulder

and narrowed his eyes, and in profile Reese could see the gleam in them, dark and angry. Astonished, she said, "Blood, he's right?"

"No." That from between gritted teeth. "But I would prefer to go into danger this severe in a way that does not endanger innocents."

"Especially innocent women?"

"I'm not an innocent woman!" Reese said, irritated.

"Yes, you are," Irine whispered.

"Irine!"

The tigraine put a finger to her own mouth, quieting her, because the men were still . . . arguing? If something as fiercely controlled as their exchanges could be called arguing.

"I am not suicidal."

"I think this sounds like a very noble form of suicide," Belinor said. "The hero, slipping through the corridors alone to meet his fatal nemesis, and probably dying while killing him. The least you can do is take Lady Eddings so she can drag your body back."

"Ugh, this is ridiculous! We're wasting time!" Reese said. She pointed at Belinor. "You, Irine and everyone else go take care of the pirates. Val, you lead me to Baniel. You keep him busy—I shoot him. Everyone got that?"

A tense stillness followed in which Reese was far too aware of how round Irine's golden eyes were, and the fear that made her ears tremble flat against her skull. She gripped the tigraine's shoulder and said firmly, "I'll see you on the other side of this."

"Right." As Val began giving the second group directions, Irine bit her lip, then said, "Hey, one thing, okay?"

"Sure?"

Irine opened her jacket and pushed back the flap at an angle, drawing out a long, thin needle from a compartment so tiny Reese could barely see it. "I have spares. So take this one."

"You want me to have a. . . ." Reese trailed off, then remembered their conversation while trapped in the closet on the *Earthrise*. "A door hook?"

Irine laughed. "It doesn't have a hook at the end and you'll never bend it. It's too strong." She took Reese's hand and set the pick on it, folding the human's dark fingers over it. "Last time I put a pick in Hirianthial's gift, he needed it. You might need one too. You never know."

"Where do I put it?" Reese asked, bewildered.

"Did you replace the knife you lost?"

Reese grimaced. "No."

Irine slid the pick out of Reese's fingers and bent, tucking it into her boot. "There. No one will ever know it's there."

"I hope not," Reese said and hugged her tightly. "Soon, all right?"

"Promise," Irine answered, and then joined the group as they formed up. The last Reese saw of them was Irine's too tight shoulders . . . and Belinor giving the renegade a significant look before departing.

"What was that about?"

"I should never have said that bit about Corel," Val muttered. Sighing, he continued, "Come, Lady."

"Reese. Just Reese." But she followed him as he resumed their interrupted journey.

Had Olthemiel and the other Swords gotten all the hostages out by now? How far were the pirates, and when would she see any enemies—

Reese started as they turned the corner and found a full hallway, tall and hung with lanterns, and right before them, a man in red robes, walking. Val reached back and took her wrist and strode past him, and he didn't even flinch. Didn't even move out of their way . . . ! As if he hadn't even. . . .

"No," Val murmured once they had turned down a different hall. "I told him we weren't there, and he believed me." A flicker of a smile. "Much easier to do with only two of us. Explaining away a troop would have been somewhat less successful."

"Somewhat!" she whispered.

"It's fine," was the distracted reply. "And it will only get easier as we go from the priests, who are after all trained to some level of competence. Once we are upstairs, it will go quickly."

"Your pet has done what?" the Chatcaavan asked. His tone was more mild curiosity than affront, which was perhaps for the best, given the news. Not that Baniel cared either way what became of the Eldritch, but he suspected his alien ally would have preferred to cage them and send them to whatever God-forgotten planets the dragons used for their harems.

"Slain the House." Baniel set the telegem aside and stretched before going to the sideboard for a glass of cordial. "Rather with prejudice."

"Like a male should, then. I didn't think any of these freaks were capable of showing any horn at all."

Baniel snorted. "I thought you'd be more disappointed. This reduces the number of potential slaves available."

"More slaves can be bred," the Chatcaavan said, uninterested. He held out a hand, expecting a glass of his own. "Yes? That is how you beget your young?"

"I assume the begetting is not dissimilar, since I have seen what remains of the women I've sent you." Baniel poured him some of the cordial, because courtesy seemed associated with weakness in the aliens. He did not mind

the creature underestimating him; it was what had allowed
him so many hooks into the Chatcaavan already.

"Oh, the act." The alien shrugged his liquescent shrug.
"Of course. Similar enough, anyway. I meant you need to
lie with one another to get your heirs."

"You don't?" Baniel asked, amused.

"No."

He paused between sips.

"We Change," the alien said, and something about the
word made him feel its weight, even in Universal. "We can
get young on other species. Our seed fools their bodies into
nurturing it until it develops, but it is born Chatcaavan."

"And do your women also transform the leavings of
alien males?"

The alien snorted. "What do I care for what females
do or do not? But we are not like you, freak. We do not
sell our own to our lessers. Even if they are no better than
possessions to us, still they are better than that."

To that, Baniel could only reply, "How pleased I am not
to be a woman, then."

The Chatcaavan smirked. "Were you a woman, alien
ally, we would not be having this conversation at all."

Yes, he had seen that. Once, and that was enough; he
left the work of clearing the refuse afterwards to acolytes.
He cared very little for what became of his enemies, but
blood made a dreadful stain and he found the stench of
violent death distracting.

"So this male you've found with horns," the Chatcaavan continued. "Now that he has destroyed his enemies,
what does he plan?"

"Now?" Baniel snorted, amused. "He plans to make the
long trip back to Ontine with his victorious army, a journey
that will take weeks—longer, if the weather worsens. It was
brilliant work to use the Pad to transport his army there,

but he perhaps did not think through the consequences of having to return the long way." He grinned. "He may even have failed to adequately plan for that journey. We may be rid of some number of his people, completely by accident."

The alien sipped his drink, amused. "You are enjoying yourself."

"It gives me a certain pleasure to watch the demise of people I hate. I imagine you understand."

"I do. What I don't is how you can hate all of your own people. Is there no creature you value?"

Baniel considered, then smiled. "Myself."

The Chatcaavan guffawed, a very inelegant sound for the shape he had wrapped around himself. Lifting his glass, he said, "To the best and first investment."

"Indee—"

He stopped. That aura . . . oh yes, the woman. Had she really returned? And at her side, a clot of studied nothingness that could only be. . . .

Baniel started laughing. "Ah, my ally. Come, we have guests. Let us prepare to receive them."

"Stop," Val said.

Reese froze, heart racing. She could taste her pulse in her mouth, under her tongue—how did that work? She was ready to be done with this kind of 3deo action hero stuff. She'd had enough of it the first time she'd had to sneak through Ontine. Doing it a second time, even if the halls were practically deserted with all the winter court activities canceled, had only made her more nervy.

When Val didn't move, she whispered, "Is there something wrong?"

"There's someone in the room with him. I want to see if he leaves or not." He glanced at her. "Might as well sit down. We can afford to wait. Give the Swords time to get the people out."

"Sit? What if someone finds us?"

"No one's going to find us." He put his back to the wall and slid down. "No one's going to bother Baniel in his own den without permission."

"Then who's in there with him?"

"I don't know. I can't read him."

Reese glanced at him sharply.

"It happens," Val said, unconcerned. "Some people are harder to read than others, especially if you don't know them well. Just relax, Lady. Catch your breath. If he hasn't left in a handful of minutes, we'll go in."

"And you'll freeze them and I'll shoot them."

"Yes."

Reese rubbed her arms, looking nervously at the tapestry across from them: some kind of horrendous battle scene, of course, involving unicorns and banners and corpses. She hadn't seen anything like it on the lower floors; maybe that's why it was up here? Maybe Liolesa thought it was ugly. It was. "Baniel . . . do you know if he's as strong as Hirianthial?"

"His brother?" Val looked over at her, curious. "I didn't think Baniel's brother had talent."

Of course . . . he wouldn't know, with the talent having developed while Hirianthial was off-world. "He's a real mind-mage. Like 'kill people from a distance' real."

"Ah? This is new. If we'd known the high priest's own brother had had such talents. . . ."

"You all would have killed him." She glanced at Val. "Killed Hirianthial."

Val said, "Yes." Considering her, he finished, "That upsets you."

"Of course it does," she replied, testy. "Murdering people for having an ability that's only potentially lethal is wrong."

"But especially this person?" He smiled at her expression. "Is that how it is, then?"

"I wouldn't read anything into it," Reese muttered, folding her arms tightly. Even on the third floor the rooms were cold. Wasn't heat supposed to rise? It was very obviously not rising here. The first thing going into her new castle during renovations was definitely central heating. "I'm only human."

"So were we, once."

She eyed him past the braids crumpled against her hunched shoulder. "You admit that pretty easily, given how long it took for us to drag it out of Hirianthial."

Val smiled. "I am a renegade, yes?" He closed his eyes, and Reese could see his eyes flicking beneath the lids. "I think we'd better be going. Are you prepared?"

Her hands were shaking, but blood, she had a gun and these people weren't expecting them and wouldn't be able to move. "Let's get this over with."

"Come on, then."

It all went wrong from the moment Val pushed in the door. Reese didn't even remember ending up on the floor unable to move, but it gave her a horrific and very clear view of Val on one elbow and both knees, curled down beneath the foot Baniel had planted between his shoulder-blades. She could see the fabric of Val's gray coat creasing around the heel.

"The wanderer returns," Baniel said. "How predictable. Don't! Even think of it. You won't succeed."

"You were never this strong!" Val gasped.

"Things do change." Baniel smiled and ground his heel against Val's spine. "How charming it would be to torture you. My newest ally would approve. But you are a touch too troublesome to leave alive for even the short amount of time it would take for you to die."

Nothing changed in the tableau; not the figure seated in the chair behind Baniel, not the priest himself, not Val. Even so, Reese could feel a pressure in the room, pushing on her skull until her eyes and cheekbones started throbbing. Val had turned his face away from Baniel and his eyes were shut, not in pain, but as if in puzzlement.

Abruptly his eyes flew open, and there was shock there.

Oh! A voice hissed up through her bones where they met the floor. *Lord and Goddess! I give you this, I pray you give it to him if he is what you say he is—*

She wanted to say 'what?' but there were no words, only the sudden shock of a blow so powerful she half expected to have been thrown on her back. But there was no blow, and when she gathered herself to look at Val and ask what the hell he'd been on about, she met his eyes just in time to watch the spirit in them gutter and die. His body sagged beneath Baniel's boot and the priest kicked it aside.

"And that is how we deal with our enemies, mm?" He walked to her and crouched, close enough to touch her, his robes puddling near her cheek. "Captain Eddings. You would have been better off staying far, far away." His hands slid over her back, down her arm, found the palmer and freed it from her hand. He searched her coat pockets until he liberated the telegem; despairing, she watched him turn it in his fingers. "Not alone, then, I am guessing. Don't worry. We'll take care of your incursion."

He had his own telegem, she saw, and a data tablet, and he used them to summon two guards—Eldritch, at least, so maybe the pirates had died? Blood, let something good have come out of this! The guards bound her hands behind her back and paused at her face, looking to the priest for guidance.

"No, leave her mouth free. She can yell all she wants."

Baniel smiled at her. "In fact, I'd like her to howl as hard
as she can, at the top of her voice . . . and her mind." He
lowered his head until he could look directly into her eyes.
"Do that for me, Captain Eddings. Dwell on your dear
Eldritch healer. Call for him. Beg him to come to your
rescue, the way you did so wonderfully before. That would
do very, very nicely."

How fast could she go from dismay to active nausea?
She thought her heart had time to beat once.

"Take her to one of the cells. And don't harm her."
Baniel stepped over Val's body and settled in his chair.
"For now."

As they dragged her away, Reese thought about
screaming and clenched her teeth.

A most satisfactory day, Baniel thought after taking
the guard's report. The "escape" of most of the Eldritch
hostages would probably win him a tiresome interview
with Surela, but having them out of the palace suited him;
trouble that needed management should be less proximate
to his own location, lest it become too immediate for his
tastes. He preferred to pick his kills and personalize them
to the last detail, and sudden outbreaks of violence did not
afford him the luxury of indulging himself. No, let Surela
work herself into a froth over the abrupt scattering of her
rivals. And Athanesin! It was to laugh. Truly they did the
work of dividing their own forces admirably with very little
help from himself.

Speaking of dividing his forces . . . he sat across from
the Chatcaavan and waited patiently for color to flare back
into the aura. When the dragon spoke, he sounded groggy.
"What happened?"

"I fear you fainted," Baniel said.

"Fainted!" The alien pushed himself upright in the

chair and froze, eyes closing. "Ughn, my head."

"I wouldn't make too many sudden movements. You have been unconscious for nearly an hour."

"An hour! What did I miss?"

"There was a fight." Baniel threaded his fingers together. "I fear your five pirates are dead."

"Ah?" The Chatcaavan slowly rubbed his head. "Doesn't matter. Ship should be in orbit by now. Have you called?"

"Not yet. I wanted to see to your health."

"Yes. My health." The alien frowned.

"Perhaps it is some malady relating to the shapechange?"

"Perhaps." Uncertainty, though.

"You should retire, maybe. Rest a little. Or would you like us to put you under the medical equipment you brought . . . ?"

"No." The Chatcaavan bared his teeth in a grimace that looked out of place on his Eldritch face. "That won't be necessary. But I think I will have that rest." He stood and eyed Baniel. "You were helpful."

"We are allies."

The alien considered him a moment longer, then shrugged. "So we are. Call the new ship. Have them send down reinforcements. Tell the new ones not to be pathetic enough to die to these puling freaks."

"I'll be sure to relay the message."

The alien nodded once, curt, and left the room . . . without ever suspecting that most of his responses had been scripted for him, if not in words, than in emotions. Allies! Baniel snorted and went to pour himself a cup of warmed wine. Oh yes. The Chatcaavan was quite the ally, supplying Baniel with the power and reach to slap down his enemy. To think that Valthial had survived! And crept all the way back here to make an ending to an old rival? Amazing! But not, perhaps, as amazing as his having died so easily. When Baniel had told the Chatcaavan to imprint the Eldritch shapeshift pattern off his brother, he hadn't realized just how strong Hirianthial was. It was to feel himself a god! Was this what had given his brother that unassailable self-assurance when they were younger? Surely not, when Hirianthial was a master of taking on unearned guilt.

No, he had to believe that Hirianthial was too timid and had been bred too well on stories of duty and sacrifice to ever fully take up the powers that he now had to hand . . . and that Baniel now had as well, through the bond he'd created with the Chatcaavan during their sessions.

Yes, that had worked exactly as he'd hoped.

He took a sip of the wine and smiled over the lip, savoring the memory of Valthial's shock as he'd fallen. So good. Good enough to almost make him want to oversee his brother's demise personally.

Speaking of which. He had a new crew of pirates to bring to heel. He took up the telegem and called for them. They were indeed in orbit, and very eager to send down replacements for the pirates who'd died, particularly if they might be able to partake of the local . . . culture.

Really, sapients were all so much alike. It almost took the pleasure out of manipulating them. Almost.

CHAPTER 12

"I trust you've found the journey satisfactory," Hirianthial said, amused.

Sprawled in one of the mess hall's chairs, Sascha grinned. "Oh, I think I've spent it a little more enjoyably than, say, some people I know who've been holed up in the gym."

Bryer snorted from the corner, where he was tucked into his own wings.

Hirianthial ordered himself a cup of tea from the genie and sat across from the Harat-Shar with the mug it delivered him. Warming his fingers on the ceramic, he said, "Truly, arii. Tell me how you find them."

"The Fleet people? Like all Fleet people. At least the ones I've met. Competent. Professional. A little keep-apartish from the rest of us mere civilians, but not intentionally." Sascha straightened up, rolled his shoulders. "It's more of a different-families-brushing-elbows thing. Cultural. Something. But I'd trust them in a fight. That's what you're asking, isn't it?"

"I suppose it is."

"I wouldn't worry on that count, then. They don't have a stake in this the way we do, but they care about getting the job done right. Speaking of which. . . ." Sascha put his cheek in his palm. "You can tell me more now about how I end up as family in an Eldritch House, or whatever. How's that work?"

"All Houses are first formed thus. One begins with the named seal-bearer—that being the person charged with making the decisions for all the families who look to her— and then she chooses what satellite families she allows to bear the name. Those who are expected to do the duties of nobles are lifted into the House itself. Everyone else living on her land becomes a tenant who looks to her to fulfill those duties. So if she decides that you are to help her, as no doubt she will, then you will end up a junior member of a noble House, and all your children will be also."

"Seal-bearer," Sascha said. "Because, I guess, there's a seal? Like something you stamp on documents?"

"Exactly," Hirianthial replied. "The seal-bearer is almost inevitably a woman, because women are the continuity of families: in a society without reproductive technology, the only proof of bloodline comes through the matrilineal line."

"And men get to be glorified studs?" Sascha grinned. "I might make a good Eldritch after all."

He chuckled. "Hardly. Men carry the swords." At the Harat-Shar's snort, he said, "And yes. They do their part to continue the species. With far less frequency and variety of partner than you would probably enjoy."

"Oh, I don't know. I could settle in with a single person, if it was the right person," Sascha said. And amended, "Well, and Irine. I wouldn't give up Irine." He glanced at Hirianthial. "So those swords you had . . . that was your job for your old family."

His . . . old . . . family. Hirianthial paused in the act of bringing the mug to his lips and tried to decide what he felt about having his life before the *Earthrise* relegated to a musty past, one he could no longer reclaim. His old family. His former life. He flexed his fingers on the mug's handle and said, "I performed that service, yes."

Sascha's ears flipped back. "I said something wrong, didn't I."

"Talk too much," Bryer said from the corner. "Disturbs the center."

"No, it's well." Hirianthial shook his head, heard the bell tinkle against his back. "I am just concerned about what is to come."

"Yeah. That makes three of us."

"Not concerned."

"If you weren't concerned, you wouldn't be lecturing me," Sascha said to the Phoenix. "You've known me long enough to realize that I've always talked too much, and chastising me disturbs your peace more than it does mine."

Bryer huffed, but there was a brief gloss of alien amusement skating over his flat aura, so quick it looked like a sheen on his feathers.

"You have made a Phoenix laugh," he observed.

"What can I say," Sascha said. "I am magic."

A chime sounded, drawing their attention. Then Soly's voice: "Bridge to mess. Lord Hirianthial, we'll be dropping out of Well shortly. If you'd join us?"

"On my way."

"This is it, if we read the directions right—" Soly paused for the Faulfenzair navigator's dismissive sniff. The Seersa smiled. "And we always read the directions right. Look familiar, alet?"

"You have the right of it," Hirianthial said, standing at her side. "We're home."

"Is home always this quiet?" Tomas said from the comm station.

"We would usually have been hailed by the Far- thest Wing, the station on the moon," Hirianthial said. "Have they?"

"No, but we're running Dusted," Soly said. "No one's going to be able to see us except by very, very rare accident."

"You're hiding from the pirates," Sascha said from behind Hirianthial.

"We figured it would be better if we saw them before they saw us, yes."

"Only problem with that," Tomas muttered. "I don't see them."

A long pause, during which the ship continued to coast in-system. Finally, Hirianthial said, "You don't see the ship?"

"No. It could be on the other side of the world—"

But the human sounded skeptical. Hirianthial won- dered what sensor technology made him so confident of that evidence so distant from their target.

"Keep an eye on it." Soly sat in the chair in the center of the small bridge and crossed her legs. "We're still a few hours out. See if you can find this moon station while we're going in."

"Aye, sir."

"Alet? Would you and your man like to sit?"

There were extra seats at the back of the bridge, two on one side and none on the other where the chairs had been removed; there were restraints, however, and Hirianthial imagined they'd been arranged for Jasper's use. Hirianthial glanced at Sascha, but the Harat-Shar met his eyes with an aura as obdurate as a stone. "We'll wait here with you, thank you."

Wait they did, in a silence that felt tense with the focused attention of the Fleet personnel at the fore of the bridge; their auras melded into a smooth whole, making him wonder at what it meant, that such things happened. He'd noted it in Sascha and Irine, the closeness that became a psychic melding, unnoticed by those without the talent. He had no doubt it had happened between himself and Urise when they'd done the teaching. Could more than memory make the transit between people? He wondered if all camaraderie was actually dimly sensed psychic connection.

Tomas broke the silence to say, voice clipped, "That station's gone."

Hirianthial started from his reverie. "Gone?"

"There's a hole in it. Looks like someone put an entropy packet through the wall."

"God and Lady," he whispered. Had the Tams still been in it? He prayed they were all on the planet with Reese.

"So the pirates were here . . . and left?" Soly glanced at Tomas. "Still no sign of them?"

"Not even any emissions traces. If they left, it was a while ago."

If they'd left, how long would it be before they told everyone where to find his homeworld? The time between now and the arrival of the Fleet reinforcement suddenly seemed far too long.

"So they're gone," Soly murmured. "They have to have left people on the surface to hold it against the natives, and we don't know what kind of equipment they might have. Stay Dusted and put us in orbit, Lune. Above the capital. Let's have a look at what's going on."

"Aye, sir."

Hirianthial tried to relax. There was nothing he could

do about the vessel that had escaped. And if they were gone, there was some chance that he could help Reese clean up the situation on world with a minimum of fuss. Perhaps even within a day? He could hope. That would give them time to sit with the Fleet personnel and make plans for whatever pirates would be returning. He watched idly as the world grew in the ship's forward viewscreen. It would be difficult if they had to hold the world against more than one ship, but—

A siren screeched, startling them all.

"Sir! Collision alert!"

"*What*? What the hell is out there? An invisible asteroid?"

"It's right on top of us!"

Abruptly the world vanished from the screen, replaced from edge to edge with the flank of an enormous ship.

"What the hell!" Soly said.

Their ship shuddered, seemed to hold its breath . . . and then wrenched so hard Hirianthial had no time to see the bulkhead that met his head and drew down the dark.

"I beg your pardon," Surela said to the guard, astonished. "You will say that again."

"Your Majesty," he said, words black with remorse. "Most of the hostages have escaped."

She wanted to correct him, to tell him to call them guests, or at best, detainees . . . but *guests* did not escape their suites. *Prisoners* escaped their suites. And her prisoners had done this. "Escaped. Escaped how? Escaped where?"

"Into the countryside, Your Majesty. The Swords . . . the Swords managed to find their way into Ontine and helped them out through the servants' halls. Or the windows, in one case." He was staring past her at the wall, his posture so rigid her own back ached, staring at him. "We have caught twelve Swords, Your Majesty, among them their captain. The others escaped with the hostages."

"How many hostages?" Surela asked sharply.

"Escaped?" He cleared his throat. "Some sixty-seven, Your Majesty."

"Sixty. . . ." She stopped, appalled. She didn't know the exact numbers of the Galare and Jisiensire contingents, but there had been less than ninety of them. Gathering herself, she said to him, "I have no words to describe the magnitude of your failure."

"No, Your Majesty."

"You will guard the remaining detainees," she said. "And the Swords. Until they escape you as well, the way apparently the Queen, her mind-mage, and the hostages have managed in the past. Goddess and Lady! Are all of you inept? I should replace you with the aliens! At least they haven't failed us yet!"

He glanced at her, then back at the wall and said, diffident, "The aliens are dead, Your Majesty."

Her pause then was long enough that she could measure his tension. She watched him swallow, throat moving above the high collar of his uniform. "Dead."

"Yes, Your Majesty. There were six of them, and five of them died to Liolesa's Swords. The only one that remains is the high priest's guest."

"I presume you have sent someone after these escapees?" Surela said after a long moment. What did she care for the fate of aliens, anyway? "It's winter. I can't imagine they've gone far."

"Your Majesty, we have and . . . we are so far unable to locate them."

"In the new snow," she said. "You tell me that over sixty people have vanished, leaving no trail in the new snow. Without provisions or coats or horses to ride. And you can't find them."

"No, Your Majesty."

"I am speechless," she said at last. "And surrounded, apparently, by amazing incompetence. Remove yourself from my presence while I contemplate the discipline, any discipline, sufficient to your correction for this debacle."

"Yes, Your Majesty."

He bowed and backed out of her study . . . Liolesa's study, damn it all, for she had not had time to redecorate, and she wondered now if she'd ever have the time with all her enemies slipping away from her into the wilderness where they could make mischief. At least Athanesin was taking care of Jisiensire's allegiances. She sighed and sat heavily in her chair, rubbing her brow. Ridiculous. And through the servants' corridors! She couldn't punish the servants, not without winning herself a reputation; servants would band together against a noble who turned on them no matter their master or mistress. But she would have to turn them all out somehow before they found some new way to betray her.

Goddess and Lady. It beggared her imagination that Liolesa had ever had such problems. Then again, she had fomented a rebellion beneath Liolesa's very eyes and succeeded in a coup. . . .

What woman was even now sitting in a warm and distant parlor, contemplating Surela's removal?

What a useless, horrible, ghastly day. She was ready to be quit of it, and supposed as Queen she had the luxury of doing so. Exiting the study she headed for her rooms, yet another suite that reminded her far too much of her predecessor. On her way, she contemplated how she would fix that. Perhaps it was time to move the royal suite to the opposite side of Ontine. She could convert the rooms that had once been Asaniefa's and move her family into the suite opposite it. At least then she'd be surrounded by her allies. Goddess knew how she could afford to sleep soundly at night if the guard she'd instated was not capable of keeping an entire phalanx of Liolesa's soldiers out of Ontine.

She was very glad to shut the door on them. On everyone. On everything. She did it with prejudice and flounced into the bedroom, throwing her shawl onto a chair and stopping short in shock.

There was a body on the floor beside her bed.

"What is the meaning of this!" she cried. "Do my enemies now resort to grotesque messages to instill fear in me?" Backing away, she turned for the door to call for someone to remove the corpse.

Then it spoke.

"Mistress. . . ."

Surela's hand froze on the door. "Thaniet," she whispered. And then, horror cresting on an enormous wave: "*Thaniet!*" She flung herself toward the body, falling to the ground alongside her liegewoman's head. There was not a place on her body that was not smeared in blood or bruised some hideous color. Surela could barely think of touching her, fearing to make it worse. "Oh, Thaniet! What has become of you! Where did you. . . ." But there was a smear of blood leading from Thaniet's body toward the wall, where one of the servants' doors was ajar. "Oh, my dearest. Oh, what has become of you!"

"Please," Thaniet said, and her voice was so hushed Surela bent to hear it. "Lady. So important."

"I'm listening. I promise!"

"Alien . . . is your enemy. Wants . . . this world . . . to sell us all. . . ."

Surela's mouth set in a hard line. This she could well believe, though her heart dropped to hear it. But her liegewoman was not done.

"Priest . . . too. Priest has . . . given it to him. Plot . . . your downfall . . . Athanesin . . ."

Now she felt faint. She swallowed.

". . . wants your crown."

"No," Surela whispered.

Exhausted, Thaniet let out a long breath and did not speak again. Was she breathing? Oh Goddess, let her breathe! Surela hovered, frantic. Her one ally in all this mess, who had nearly died to bring her the news that she was beset on all sides, and a good woman besides, a true woman, her only friend, who had stood by her in every circumstance. . . . "Oh no, no," she said, hands fluttering as they touched the sodden hair. "No, you mustn't die, Thaniet. There is no justice in your death. You deserve better . . . !"

Nothing on this world could heal wounds this grievous. So much blood! But if Thaniet was right, and she had to believe it, then she could not go to Baniel to ask for help from his pet aliens. To reveal that Thaniet had survived . . . he would kill her. But it was past bearing that Thaniet should die. Who. . . .

Her shoulders squared, even as her nausea redoubled. She thought she would faint, but somehow she didn't. She leaned down and kissed Thaniet's temple. "Hold fast, dear one. I will get you help. I pledge it. Only hold a little longer." She rose and pulled down a blanket, tucking it around her liegewoman's body. A quick survey of herself found no blood spots, nor dishevelment—she could not afford to be stopped—and pulling her shawl around herself she left her apartments. Outside, she said to the guard, "You are aware of the escape?"

"Yes, Your Grace."

"Was the Lady Araelis one of those escapees?"

"No, Your Grace."

"Excellent. Take me to her."

The trip to the Jisiensire suite took too long—Surela could feel the blood growing cold and sticky on the fingertips she kept balled against her palm—and too little a time for her to compose herself. She used the precious few moments between the guard announcing her and her first step to square her shoulders, and entered the room of one of her worst enemies to beg for aid.

But she did not have time to draw breath for the request before Araelis stole it from her, by looking at her, and Goddess and Lord, that *look*. She thought she'd seen Araelis's anger. But this . . . this was something more horrific, a towering, bleak hatred that sent her stumbling back toward the door, reaching behind herself for the handle because she was unwilling to turn her back on that much wrath.

"You," Araelis hissed. "You monster-keeping *bitch*!"

Surela stopped, shocked by the epithet. "I-I b-beg your. . . ."

"Pardon? *Pardon?* NEVER." Araelis said, advancing on her. Surela backpedaled until she was pressed against the door and couldn't move. There were tears streaking the other woman's face, and that made the utter implacability of her hatred the more terrifying. "That you would dare to ask such a thing after what you have done . . . !"

A new thing. It had to be a new thing, because her usurpation of the throne had not incited this much emotion from Araelis. But what had she done? Nothing! It was Araelis and Fassiana and the Swords who had done something! "If you mean to tell me I should have held still for your escape, I cannot apologize. I had to try to stop you—"

"Escape?" Araelis paused, her eyes losing focus. "What do you . . . you think that has any bearing on what you've done? What you've done! You destroyed my House and you dare think it unworthy even of notice?"

Surela lost a breath, her mouth gone suddenly dry. "I have not destroyed your House."

"You sent your pet monster to the task and he did well enough," Araelis snarled. "Do you think I would not put the blame on your shoulders? Particularly since he used the Pads your pirate friends brought with them? You ordered them slaughtered like kine! Every one of them! They've fired even the tenants' cottages!"

"They've what?" she breathed, feeling faint.

"Athanesin, damn his soul to an immortal hell. Has done your bidding. And left me with nothing more to lose." Araelis withdrew.

"I sent Athanesin to compel Jisiensire's obedience!" Surela cried. "Not to destroy it!"

"Then you should have kept a tighter leash on him."

She was shaking now. Jisiensire destroyed? She had not wanted that. Had not wanted anyone *killed.* She could not rule dead people. She could not win the hearts of corpses. She'd wanted Athanesin to intimidate them! It was what he had promised! And to abuse the common folk . . . that was past bearing. One caretook the commoners! It was their duty! To do otherwise . . . that was sacrilege, a stain against one's immortal soul!

"This can't be true," she whispered.

Something hit the wall beside her and bounced to the floor beside her shoe: one of the mortal contrivances, the one that permitted talk over long distances. "Call him yourself and find out." When she didn't reach for it, Araelis sneered. "Take it. I don't need it anymore. The last person who could have answered me died using it to tell me what you've done. There's no one I have left to talk to."

With numb fingers, Surela gathered it from the carpet

and straightened. Such a small thing, to have brought such devastating news. And if it was true—

It had to be true. Thaniet had said, hadn't she? Athanesin wanted her crown.

Thaniet.

"Lady Araelis," she said, hoarse. "There is a matter."

"A matter, is it?" Araelis laughed bitterly. She sat carefully at the table meant for receiving guests, and made a throne of it with her anger as mantle. "Oh yes. Tell me this 'matter.' Let me guess. Your allies are turning against you?"

She flushed. "My liegewoman, Thaniet. She is . . . she is horribly injured. I had thought if perhaps you had any mortal instruments capable of aid . . . I ask this not for me, but for her, she is a good woman, she does not deserve to die because . . . because of her allegiance to me."

"Doesn't she?" Araelis asked.

Surela said, "Please. For her sake. I beg you to have mercy for her."

Araelis smiled without humor, without even pleasure. It was a hideous expression when inspired by irony and pitilessness. "Your 'mortal' allies probably had their way with her and left her for dead, is that it?"

"Yes."

"You are not insensible to the lesson there?"

Surela found she was trembling, hated that it was fear and misery and horror. "No."

Araelis studied her. "How I would like to have those instruments, solely so I could deny them to you. So I could hurt you, in some small part, on the level that you have hurt me. My own baby's father dead in the fire-gutted estate that has housed Jisiensire since the end of Jerisa's reign . . . and you the author of it all? Oh yes. I would love, very much, to force you to suffer and know it was my hand that struck the blow. But alas for you—and your hapless

liegewoman—I have no access to 'mortal' medical technology. Nor does Fassiana, before you ask her."

"Thaniet is an innocent," Surela said, pleaded.

"And she will die because of your acts. She will not
have been the first." Araelis rested a hand on her belly. "I
tire of looking at the face of a butcher. Go away, Surela.
Don't come back."

Surela let herself out and adjusted her shawl around
her shoulders to give herself an excuse not to look up
at the guards standing their posts at Araelis's door. The
mortal device caught on some of the floss embroidery and
she tugged it free before setting off down the hall, feeling
the hard edges against her skin. To whom could she speak
to corroborate the news of this atrocity? Jisiensire put to
the torch . . . what was Athanesin thinking! What would
keep their enemies from doing the same to them, now that
they had begun this? If nobles could destroy one another's
populations, what would be left of their world? It was not
done, and he had done it!

And who now would help Thaniet?

Back in her bedroom—Liolesa's bedroom—Surela
settled alongside her liegewoman's still form with the
washing bowl from the dresser. Dipping a towel in it she
began to gently clean Thaniet's face. She worked her way
down the woman's body, slowly, stopping to pour out the
water and fetch fresh, and to heat the towel by the fire.
The depredations she found wreaked on Thaniet's body . . .
that such animals had been allowed to touch such a good
woman! And that she might be the proximate cause of this
. . . this and everything else!

She had been very sure of herself, that the aliens were
the enemy, and to keep them away the only course. Their
violence and cruelty did nothing to sway her to a different
opinion; she did not want to see Thaniet's injuries repeated

on a hundred bodies, a thousand. But she began to wonder how one could stop them. She was Queen, and Baniel, though her ally, was not controlling these creatures. Athanesin was using their weapons to kill off the population in swaths, and then who would be left to defend them when the aliens came in force? Because she now understood that they would.

What did she do now? Give the crown to Athanesin? He would take it when he arrived, if that was his aim. She could offer to marry him . . . but what guarantee was there that he would not do to her what others had done to Thaniet? A man who could fire the cottages of farmers could do anything.

"Oh, Thaniet," she said, hushed. Was she crying? No. No, she was not. But the feeling in her breast was like anguish, and rage, and terror. There was no crying because she could not push tears past the ball of emotion in her breast, the one that made her tremble as she went gently over broken ribs and shattered bones.

What could she do?

It took Thaniet three hours to die. It was poor comfort that she at least passed on wrapped in warm furs, clean, with her head on the lap of a friend, but it was all Surela could give her. When she was sure of her own legs, she gently set Thaniet's head on a pillow and followed the blood trail through the door.

It took her some time to find a servant, but she stopped him when she did. "I need help."

Did she imagine the hesitation? Probably not. These people were Liolesa's, and no doubt would never be anything else. But the man did answer with neutral politeness, "Of course, Lady."

"Thaniet . . . Lady Thaniet . . ." Surela paused until she

could talk without trembling. "She has died, and I fear if I send for the priests to take her they may not bury her."

This hesitation was longer. Unhappily, the servant didn't seem surprised by her fears. They'd known, she guessed. Of course they had. Baniel had supported her, and they didn't trust her. His uncertainty, then, had to do with her breaking ranks with her own allies. She swallowed her pride and said, "Please."

"Of course," he said again, gentler this time.

"My bedroom."

"Yes, Lady."

At least he hadn't flinched when she'd called Liolesa's bedroom her own. As far as Surela was concerned, though, Liolesa could have it back, and all the memories of Thaniet's death with it.

The servant returned with three others and a maid. Surela insisted that Thaniet remain wrapped in the furs and waited until they'd lifted the body to tuck them more carefully around her lady-in-waiting's body. Then she kissed the cold brow and said, in the white mode for sanctity and holy vows, "Go you to the Goddess, and forget all the suffering you knew here. And forgive me."

To the servants, she said, quiet, "Go. And thank you."

For how long she stood alone in that room, she didn't know. But she had a debt now, and a duty to attempt to make right some of the errors she'd committed in—yes, Araelis and Fassiana had been right—her witless arrogance. She wanted no part of aliens yet, still thought them best set apart, found the thought of them disgusting, in fact. And she had no idea how to get rid of the ones who'd entrenched themselves in her world. But she could make a start.

The guards outside her room were in Asaniefa's green and electrum. She had to hope they were more competent in numbers than they had been apart. "Fetch me twenty of your fellows," she said. "And meet me at the study. Arm yourselves. We go to arrest the high priest for treason."

CHAPTER 13

By now Hirianthial had woken in so many cells that he was utterly unsurprised to find himself in another, and this, somehow, made him want to laugh. Pushing himself upright, he assessed his condition: undamaged, other than a few desultory bruises and scrapes . . . novel, given his usual state in captivity. Unarmed, naturally. Not hungry or thirsty, so he hadn't been here long. And surrounded in smooth metal with a halo field for a fourth wall, without so much as a bunk or a drain. An Alliance facility, then, and not meant for long term captivity. Through the floor he could feel . . . not a vibration or a hum, but something like to them, which suggested engines, and so a ship. Somehow, Soly and hers had run into an enemy ship.

Reese's words came back to him, about their having to stop meeting in prisons, that cells didn't suit him. He murmured agreement as if she could hear him, setting a palm on the wall and then passing it over the cool metal, uncertain what he was seeking but prodded to the act all the same—there. Bryer was on the other side of the wall.

How many customs did he contemplate breaking? And yet he did, and without regret or guilt. Why was that? Some memory—not his—of the mindtouch between welcoming souls not being hardship—Urise's? He could almost hear the priest now: *Must all touch be coercion?*

He knew better. Hirianthial closed his eyes and reached. */Bryer./*

A sense of assent, wordless.

/You're hale?/

An affirmative.

/Do you know aught of where we are?/

Exasperation? Nothing so extreme. More like a feeling of friction in the Phoenix's emotions, tagged with the thought that he was the only one capable of finding out, so why was he asking Bryer?

/I will return./ He withdrew from that contact and rose, pacing the cell. Sascha was on the other side, with someone unfamiliar . . . Narain? They had been put in the same cell? */Sascha./*

A start of surprise so sudden it felt like a jab with a practice sword. Hirianthial touched his side where he'd taken one such hit too many and smiled a little. */Sascha, it's Hirianthial./*

/It is you! How . . . you . . . oh, don't look over there—/

Over there were memories that involved Narain. */You don't appear to be doing anything worthy of embarrassment,/* he commented, amused.

/We're not now. We might have been before . . . you . . . wait, you're talking to me./

/This does seem to be the only way to do so. Narain is with you? Does he know anything?/

/I'll ask./

Hirianthial leaned a shoulder against the wall, eyes closed. Sascha's mental presence felt furry to him, comfortable and blood-warm and a little tingly; he registered the latter on his tongue, like peppers, or mint, or champagne. Very different from Bryer, who had been cool and diffuse, like fog. He was still sorting the impressions when the tigraine returned.

/Um, can you hear me?/

/Here, arii./

/Right. Narain says we ran into . . . I don't know if I believe this, but battlehells, here we are . . . a Fleet battlecruiser. A stolen Fleet battlecruiser, Dusted, in orbit above Ontine. And they scooped us up because, you know, battlecruiser./

/I don't, actually?/

A hint of a different voice, very distant. Sascha said, /They're about four times—ten times? Make up your mind, sweets—fine. The Fleet Intelligence ship holds fifteen people. This one has a crew of four hundred, usually. They're way, way bigger than us./

/A Fleet battlecruiser,/ Hirianthial repeated. He frowned. /Does Narain know what pirates are doing with one?/

/He says there have been rumors that pirates were trying to get hold of Fleet ships, but not that any of them had succeeded./

/Well, now they know./ Hirianthial looked out into the hall. /Four hundred people, he says./

Another pause. /He says there might not be four hundred pirates. That you can drive this ship with twenty-five people and fight it with fifty. You just get into big trouble if someone actually hits back./

A different voice now, thin and distant and also, somehow furry . . . but lusher and cooler than Sascha's, and overlaying a mind of astonishing clarity and depth. /Most of a cruiser's complement is redundancy, and science-based./

/Narain,/ Hirianthial said.

/At your service, alet./

Sascha now. /Can you tell how many people are on this ship? I mean . . . can you . . . feel it?/ A hint of embarrassment, as if he felt guilt for asking.

Could he? He drew in a breath and reached—

—and found himself on the floor and did not remember sitting so abruptly. His tailbone hurt. /Only vaguely,/ he answered when he was sure of himself. He recalled the ballroom at the opening of the court and the way that group of over three hundred had felt to him, their weight, their presence. /There are not four hundred, though. Or if there are, they are dispersed./

Narain again, with that cool swiftness of thought. /If we can get to a computer, we can find out. But someone's got to let us out first./

/I had noted the lack of guards at the door . . . ?/ Hirianthial glanced again at the halo field barring his exit.

/Fleet doesn't post them. There will be a station at the end of the hall, and that'll be the only exit. The person there will have surveillance on all the occupied cells and can control their disposition./

A person in a station. That he could do. Hirianthial sought the flicker of an unfamiliar mind, passing Solysyrril and her people until he sensed the enemy. And . . . then what? If he put the man to sleep, or killed him, they would not be freed. *Does everyone need killing?* A good question. Not relevant, however. He hovered over the ugly tent of the pirate's mind. Not greasy, the way the Rekesh of Keryale's had been, nor cold and stark like Surapinet's, the drug lord. A man with an unexamined mind, thoughts edged with occasional cruelty and a great deal of boredom. Just a man.

Ask him for help, came the voice from memory.

Help! A pirate!

Killing is a far greater intimacy, but you court that quickly enough, my son.

Hirianthial half-opened his eyes, lost the sense of the distant mind and made an irritated noise. Urise had said nothing about his teaching surfacing in the form of phantom conversations, but then again . . . would he have? He could well imagine the priest's amusement. *You would not have believed me.*

No, he admitted, he wouldn't have. He closed his eyes and concentrated, and this time . . . he asked for help. Slipped into the unfamiliar mind and was polite. *Turn off the force-fields,* he suggested. *There is no one there to guard. Nothing on those monitors you see. No reason to keep them up.*

The pirate resisted him, not because he felt attacked, but because he was puzzled by this contradiction between his thoughts and reality. Hirianthial leaned on him, made the reality he was crafting more real than the one the pirate was living . . . succeeded.

The halo fields died as he opened his eyes, just enough to watch. Then he sank back into the trance and suggested the helpful pirate sleep. A great deal. And soared free of the claustrophobic smallness of the man's mind as it passed out of consciousness.

He was once again sitting. And now very hungry, in a way that also made him aware that he wasn't quite healed yet from Baniel's attentions. His ribs ached, and he passed a hand over them once, sighing. And then he smiled, imagining Reese's reaction. 'Fine, you opened your own cell this time, but you haven't rescued yourself yet.' "At work on it, my Lady," he murmured, and then Sascha peeked in.

"You did it!"

"I did. Where is your roommate?"

"He went to get the others. They're all heading straight for that station so they can mess with the computers." Sascha padded in and crouched in front of him, tail curled behind him for balance. "You look a little peaked."

"I have been better," Hirianthial admitted, and then smiled. "You have seen me worse, though."

"I have!" Sascha's brows lifted. His expression matched his aura, not awed, but something like. And glad, too, strangely. "And . . . you think this is funny?"

"Funny . . ." He trailed off, then shook his head, hair brushing his neck. "No, that would be pressing the matter. But I am . . ." What was he? Not amused. Not buoyant. Not pleased. A little of all of those things, but they were expressions of a single feeling. "I am done with cells, arii. And I am done with letting other people put me in them. And for some reason, this strikes me as something to celebrate."

"That you're through being a victim?" Sascha grinned like sunrise. "Okay, sure. I see that. Hells, I'm glad to see it. Do you need help getting up?"

"Let me try first." He pushed himself up and paused, assessing himself. Tired, hungry and sore, but serviceable. He needed Urise's trick of not needing to eat or rest to power these abilities, but the memories associated with that knowledge overwhelmed him, thousands over thousands of them, confusing and vast. It would have to wait. "I appear to be steady. Let us go to our allies."

"Right." Sascha paused, then added, "Ah, if we die before the day's over—"

"We shan't."

Sascha cleared his throat, one ear sagging. "Right. But just in case we do, can I just say. . . ."

Hirianthial waited.

". . . you can pet my mind anytime."

"Sascha!"

The tigraine snickered. "Now I feel better. Come on, it's down this way."

Shaking his head to hide the smile, Hirianthial followed, and Kis'eh't's temple bell sang at the end of the hair-dangle.

Bryer was standing outside the guard station's door, watching the corridor, and all the Fleet people were indeed inside, crushed together over a single console as Narain manipulated it. When he and Sascha entered, Tomas said, "That mind-reading thing is a lot more handy than you suggested it might be, Lord Hirianthial."

"I am never sure how much it is capable of," Hirianthial demurred. "So I thought it best not to overstate the ability."

"As long as the surprises keep being good, you just keep on keeping on."

"We can certainly use some good surprises," Soly muttered, her tail flicking behind her in agitation.

"Is this a bad surprise, then?"

Soly looked up at him; she was leaning over Narain's shoulder with one small hand on the console, and he had never seen her look so grim—or was that her aura he read? "Alet, these pirates have a Fleet battlecruiser."

"So Narain told me. I presume this is not a vessel easily captured."

"Easily—" She choked on the rest of the words, her ears slicked back. "No. No, it's not, and Fleet keeps very careful tabs on all its ships. Particularly its capital ships. We've had evidence that the pirates were trying to capture something, but the only battlecruisers lost have been on the border with the Empire. Fighting them, not fighting pirates."

"Ostensibly," Hirianthial guessed.

"Ostensibly. It's not a secret that the Empire's been

encouraging pirate activity on the border, but if they're looking the other way while lawless men are stealing Fleet ships of this size . . . or even encouraging them. . . ."

"They want to split your attentions, no doubt."

Soly sighed. "No doubt. Yes. But we have got to live through this, alet, because someone has to know."

"Looks like we've got just over a hundred people aboard," Narain interrupted. "Eighty of them are in engineering. Fifteen up on the bridge . . . the rest of them are moving around."

"One hundred and eight?" Tomas said, squinting over the tigraine's other shoulder.

"One hundred and eight to nine," Sascha said. "That's . . . uh . . ."

"Long odds," Tomas said.

"Yeah."

A pause as Narain worked the console, scowling at it, and everyone else frowned at one another.

"So what do we do?" Sascha asked finally. "Find the nearest Pad and escape?"

"If we do that, we're leaving a manned floating fortress in orbit above the planet," Soly said, tense. "A Dusted one. The scout that's due here will show up and die: or worse, get captured itself. Plus, anything we do on the planet will be useless if they have this much backup available."

"Can this thing go atmospheric?" Sascha asked.

"No. It doesn't have to. Its weapons will."

Another ugly pause.

"The only thing for it, then, is to take the ship," Hirianthial said.

"Us. Against a hundred and eight pirates?" Sascha eyed him skeptically.

"Could be done," Narain muttered. "Maybe."

"It's that group in Engineering I'm worried about," Soly

said. "We could take the bridge and lock them out of the computer, but if they're physically there they can kill the power themselves."

"Likely result in their deaths," Bryer said from the door.

"They're not going to kill themselves just to get to us." Tomas nodded to the Phoenix. "He's right on that. They can work past the computer lockout from Engineering, but it would take time."

Softly, Lune said, "They have tools there. And suits." When everyone glanced at her, she said, "They can walk on the hull, to reach the bridge. The tools are meant for such work. They could breach."

"Hells," Soly said. "What a mess."

"What about our ship? It looks like it's in one of the landing bays." Narain brought up a diagnostic. "Not damaged either, beyond a few surface dings. Maybe we could haul it out of the ship and keep an eye out for walkers?"

"And what if they have a Pad in Engineering? They often do." Soly frowned, tapping her fingers on the console.

"That clot in Engineering's going to be trouble," Tomas said. "This ship's got guided entropy packets. I say we secure the bridge and then take out Engineering."

Hirianthial had expected an electric silence in response to that comment, but instead Narain frowned. "Unless we're careful, or lucky, or both, that's going to kill the power to the ship. We won't be able to use it."

"No, but neither will they."

Hirianthial said, "There is no way to render them unconscious?"

Soly shook her head. "Like gas them? The ship's not set up for that. There's no way to block the ventilation. Any sort of dangerous chemical leak like that is taken care of with a vacuum system: it sucks air out, it doesn't trap it in place."

Tomas said, "If it's one hundred and eight to nine, we don't have a lot of choices. We absolutely can't leave this thing operational up here, and we can't get a message out without alerting them—that's game over for us, and not much better for Fleet, given how few ships they've got to send out this way. We either have to destroy a part of this ship, or destroy the whole thing, and I'd rather live."

"Hard to argue that," Narain muttered.

"Show me Engineering," Hirianthial said, suddenly. "Is it a single room?"

Narain looked up, surprised, but Soly waved an encouraging hand at him. The pardine brought up a schematic, floating it over the console. "It's got a lot of compartments, but the actual power plant needs a lot of room, so it's got a big space in the center."

That it did, though the power plant occupied the prominent central space. And yet . . . surely that would be close enough. His power seemed to flow outward in a circular radius—was it spherical? He shifted the schematic with his hand and saw that the compartment was several levels tall. The whispers in his mind gave no report on whether he could extend his influence upward as well as outward. He had to imagine he could—*costs more*—but yes, that it would be more effort. He closed his eyes, paying closer attention to the hissing memories he could sense but not experience. Was there a flaw in this plan? *You will not be able to pay for it easily.* Everything had a price. If he managed even twenty of the eighty, that was something, wasn't it? *But not enough.*

"Lord Hirianthial?" Soly asked, cautious.

"If we could take Engineering, that would be a goodness," he guessed.

"A lot better than gutting it, yes. If we could keep the

ship intact then we'll have one more to use against the ones your escaped pirate might be bringing back as rein-forcements. We might not have enough people to fight this ship well, but the armament on it is overkill against the typical pirate."

"Unless, of course, they're bringing more battlecruis-ers," Tomas said, quiet.

"Not something we can control," Soly said. "But we can foresee it, yes. And having this one if they do will help. Especially if we can trick them into thinking we're one of theirs for long enough to get them to turn their back on us."

Sascha, who was watching Hirianthial, said, "You're thinking of doing it on purpose, aren't you."

"Shouldn't I?"

"Doing what on purpose?" Soly asked, ears switch-ing forward.

Ignoring them, Sascha said, "I dunno, Boss. To hear Reese tell it, it lays you out flat."

Jasper spoke for the first time. "There is a Medplex in this vessel. A significant one."

Hirianthial glanced at him.

"I'm qualified to use it."

"And you're going to need it why?" Soly asked.

He told them.

To their credit, the Fleet personnel recovered more quickly than he anticipated. Tomas spoke first. "Sounds like it would be easier to take them on in smaller groups. That might work out better, actually, if you sneak in and take down a handful at a time."

"Until you get to the main compartment," Narain said, frowning.

"Not necessary," Lune offered. "If all the groups are taken care of first. This sounds like less strain for the God's gift."

Hirianthial glanced at her sharply, but Soly was already nodding. "I can see that. I don't like it, but I can see it." She folded her arms, tapping her fingers on her upper arm. "All right. Here's the plan. We're going to head to the bridge with the intention of taking it. We'll stop on the way at one of the upper level Pad stations to send Lord Hirianthial to Engineering. Narain, you go with him. I want you to do sensor duty. Find clots of people in Engineering and guide him to them. As much as possible, take care of the small groups first. If Lune's right and that saves him from over-taxing himself, so much the better. If it turns out it doesn't work that way, then at least you'll have winnowed them down before you need to get out." She studied their group. "I'm assuming your people want to stay with you, alet? So you three are together, and Narain. Lune, Tomas, Jasper and I will take and hold the bridge. You give us updates as you can. If things go bad, get out and we'll lock the compartment down."

"Splitting up is a good idea?" Sascha asked, hesitant.

"We can't do this otherwise. If Engineering finds out we've locked them down before you're done down there, you really are done. And if you fumble Engineering, they're going to fortify the bridge against us." Soly shook her head. "No, we're going to have to do it at the same time, as much as possible. We all clear?"

When no one objected, she said. "Good. Let's go raid an armory."

There was surprisingly little chaos in the woods near Ontine where the former hostages were filing over the Pad on their way to Reese's castle. Beronaeth was overseeing the operation alongside Malia and Taylor, who'd brought the Pad in accordance with the plan; they hadn't wanted to risk losing it to the enemy by bringing it into Ontine, and definitely didn't want Surela's guards to know they'd used it to whisk the hostages away once they'd been smuggled out by the servants. Olthemiel and Belinor had stayed behind to point the hostages in the proper direction and clean up the evidence of their passage.

It was all going very well . . . except Reese wasn't back yet.

"Where is she?" Irine paced, shoulders hunched and arms tucked close against the cold.

"She'll be by, alet," Malia said. "Give her time."

"She and Val have been in there a long time already. We're almost all back by now! How long can it possibly take to kill one person?"

"They might have needed to wait until the halls were clear to make their way to him." The Tam-illee sounded unperturbed. "The priest was further into the palace than the hostages, Irine . . . no convenient windows or anything. Give them time. Trust them."

Irine eyed her. "You wouldn't say anything like that if you knew the things we've been through in the past year or so. Pirates, slavers, drug lords, firefights in space, firefights on the ground, firefights in palaces, broken arms, broken insteps, dead aliens . . ."

Malia's ears sagged.

"I'm not exaggerating any of it." Irine chafed her arms. "If we're working up to this as a finale, then I think I have the right to be nervous."

"It will be well," Beronaeth said from his position alongside the Pad. "Everything has gone as planned thus far. You and the Captain killed the enemy aliens—"

"And he's still back there too, and Belinor," Irine said. "How long can it possibly take to get all the hostages out?"

"It takes the time it takes," Beronaeth said. "Surela has few guards. They can't be everywhere."

But the night wore on, and the flood of hostages slowed to a trickle, until one of them said, "They caught us at the last. The seal-bearer remained behind and sent us on; we are your last group."

Beronaeth was stiff. "And the Queen's White Sword? And the acolyte accompanying him?"

"Still in Ontine, as far as I know."

"Go on through, please."

"Is that it?" Irine hissed once the last of the hostages had passed over the Pad. "Your captain's missing, so's mine, along with both our priests—" She remembered Val's mouth forming a smile against her lips as they kissed. "They're just . . . missing in action, and that's fine?"

"Of course it's not fine," Malia said. "But we can't charge in there after them."

"Then what can we do?"

Beronaeth looked troubled. "We cannot go back in now. They would be expecting us."

"But we can go back in at some point, right? And rescue them?" Irine looked from him to Malia, agitated. "Well? We rescued some of the hostages. But we can't let them keep Reese! Do you know what Hirianthial will do if he comes back and finds her dead? You think Corel was bad the first time around? You just wait until you see Hirianthial mad. He set fire to a slaver's house, and that was *before* he was a mind-mage. There's not going to be anything left of that palace!"

Malia rubbed her knees, causing the data tablet on her lap to shift. "Irine, we haven't heard anything from the Far-thest Wing in a while. That means we've lost our window. The pirates are probably back."

"Probably?"

"I can't see anything in orbit without help from the outpost, and it's not responding." The Tam-illee grimaced.

"Look, we don't know who's out there, what kind of sensors they've got, whether they can find us or not. We have to play this carefully—"

"We don't have time!" Irine glanced at Berona-eth. "Well?"

"It would be a significant risk to return to the palace now," he said. "Without intelligence, we have no idea how things fare inside, and this is a different situation now than the one we built our plan upon. We knew then how many men the usurper queen had, and how many pirates. Now we know neither of those things, nor the disposition of our people."

"And how are we going to get that intelligence if we don't go look?"

"We will have that intelligence," the Sword said firmly, his accent growing heavier. She hoped that meant he was finally as agitated as she was. "But we must choose our methods with care. And right now, what we needs must do is retreat. They'll be looking for us, and we must give them no clues as to where we have gone."

Irine helped the Tams with the comm equipment, though the rolled-up Pad went to one of Beronaeth's aides. There weren't many of them left to head back through the woods toward their original campsite, but each of them had been given a different route to take, and instructions for the clueless, like her, on how to minimize her tracks in the snow, or erase them with fallen branches from evergreens. She had her own trail, and her own frond, and as the faint sounds of her compatriots faded into the trees, she glanced over her shoulder at Ontine.

Soldiers were expensive in a culture with little food. Malia had explained it; how there wasn't an army on this world, because people who did nothing but learn how to fight well had to be fed and maintained by people who farmed and hunted and gathered, and there just wasn't enough food to go around. Surela had been able to draw her own levy to Ontine, and perhaps that of her allies, but it didn't amount to a lot of soldiers. And most of them had to be somewhere south of here, playing at war with Jisiensire.

Irine glanced at the trail she was supposed to follow . . . and turned her back on it. Hell if she'd let Reese die there alone. Or Val. A man shouldn't die after only having had one kiss.

The cell they'd thrown Reese into had absolutely no furniture, no windows, and only one door, which meant (to her startlement) that when that door shut it was too dark to see. And it was made of stone and damned cold, and she couldn't help the feeling that she'd been imprisoned in a closet. Weren't cells supposed to have drains? Or places to chain people up? There should be bars, too, so that her keepers could torment her with verbal abuse. And there should be Blood-damned light so she could see it all and figure out how to use all the bits and pieces to come up with a plan to get out. That's how it was supposed to go. It would have been easier than being shoved in a room alone with no idea who was out there or what they were going to do with her. It gave her no distraction from the catastrophe that got her put here in the first place, and from her fears for Irine and the others.

And Val—Reese paced, tried to control her breathing. He'd died so quickly . . . ! She'd been staring into his eyes when the light had gone out of them.

What had gone wrong? Baniel shouldn't have been able to control them the way he had. Val had been expecting some power, though Reese had never seen Hirianthial's brother using it, but that much?

She couldn't imagine Val making that big a mistake. He didn't seem the mistake-making kind.

And now . . . now she was stuck here until someone opened that door and gave her the chance to escape. She absolutely had to escape because the alternative—letting Hirianthial walk into a trap to rescue her—was unthinkable.

Reese had thought she'd had some sense of what it felt to need rescue the way she'd always accused Hirianthial of needing. When Baniel had dragged her off the Ontine balcony, she'd found the powerlessness infuriating and the realization that she'd done exactly what he wanted her to even worse. But she'd never been in a cell before, at least, not by herself. She looked up at the ceiling, wishing she could see it, and shivered.

It wasn't until she sat down and scooted backward, hoping to set her back against a wall, that she felt the stickiness on the floor. Visceral memories assailed her—the heat of her own tears, the puddle under his head, the light spilling from the door at exactly that angle—

Baniel had thrown her into the cell he'd put Hirianthial.

Reese dropped her head on her knees and didn't cry. But she did start shaking, and once she started it took a long time for her to stop.

How long she spent in the dark, fighting with her own terror, she didn't know, but it was long enough that when the door finally did open, her cold-stiffened joints dumped her to the floor on her first attempt to lunge for the exit. Her second attempt brought her to the door where the guard smashed her down.

No one said a word. They just dropped a body in the room with her, and left a candle: no candle-holder, just the wax pillar, as thin around as her littlest finger. She couldn't imagine it lasting long. The door shut on her and the newest inhabitant of her domain, and she stepped closer to see what unfortunate had joined her.

"You!"

Surela looked up and scrambled back until she reached a corner.

Reese stared at her, shocked . . . for all of a heartbeat, before anger in all its welcome familiarity crested and swept all the other emotions away. "*You!* You're responsible for all this!"

Before Reese could work toward the fullness of her tirade, Surela surprised her by saying in accented but competent Universal, "I am. And here I reap the harvest of my error."

"What?"

"And an error I have made. Does it please you to hear it, human?" Surela looked up at her with remorse that also seemed resentful. Reese congratulated her for pulling that combination off.

"My name isn't 'human,'" Reese said finally.

"I thought it would be kinder than 'mortal.'"

"It's not," Reese said. "But at least it's not a lie you're telling yourself."

Surela began to speak, then looked away. Bleakly, she said, "No. We are as mortal as you. And I will discover that soon enough."

"What are you doing here, anyway?" Reese asked, folding her arms over her chest. "Did Baniel get bored of you? Decide he wanted the throne himself?"

"No," Surela said. "I tried to arrest him, and he decided to take issue with it."

Reese paused. "Wait. You? Decided to arrest him? Didn't he put you in power?"

"He did, yes." Surela shifted, then settled and began spreading her skirts around herself and neatening the folds. Her hands were trembling; Reese wasn't glad to have noticed it, and the fear it betrayed. "But I discovered he was plotting to replace me with Athanesin who, I suppose, is more amenable to mortal technology and mortal ideas. Baniel also apparently intended to sell us all into mortal slavery. Though how he thinks Athanesin will agree to that, I have no notion."

"Unless your Athanesin is more depraved than you thought, I doubt he will and I doubt Baniel cares," Reese said, watching Surela warily. "This is a man who conspired to have his own brother given to Chatcaavan slavers."

Surela shuddered. "His brother was a mind-mage."

"He's a man." Reese welcomed the anger back. "A man worth a thousand of you."

"He can kill people from a distance, without touch!"

"You killed actual people, and none of them were attacking you!"

That made Surela sway, touch her hands to her face. Surprised by the strength of the other woman's reaction, Reese finished, a little less aggressively, "So tell me which of you is the real murderer."

Surela turned into the wall and said nothing.

Reese sighed and retreated, sitting in her own corner. If the situation hadn't been so harrowing, it would almost have been funny, ending up trapped in a room with the author of all this mess. Though she guessed she had to be fair. It was Baniel who was pulling all the strings. Surela was just one more tool, and she hadn't known it until he'd tossed her in here with one of the 'mortals' Surela found so revolting. The mighty did fall, after all, and how they fell when they did.

After what felt like hours, Surela said, "I did not mean for any of this to happen."

Reese discarded several possible responses to that,

most of them bitter or cruel. What she chose instead was, "Don't you people say that how you begin a thing dictates how it ends? So how are you surprised that something you started with betrayal ends with it?"

Surela looked up from her folded arms, eyes wide.

"Don't tell me you didn't think of that."

"I. . . ."

Reese sighed and hugged her knees. "Let me guess. The rules apply to everyone but the righteous."

Surela was silent. Then said, low, "You have a tongue like a whip."

"Yeah. I've been told." She thought of Hirianthial and the twins and tried not to notice the prickle in her eyes. She'd see them again. She had to.

Surela wasn't done. "I regret putting us in this situation."

"Do you really?"

"As much as I regret admitting it to a human."

That . . . she laughed. She didn't expect to. "Yes. I bet you do."

"Do you know . . . what they plan . . . ?"

"For us?" Reese shrugged. "Your guess is better than mine; you were the one out there most recently."

"So they have not come for you."

"No." Reese thought of Baniel's words and shivered. "No, I think they're going to keep me here until all this is resolved, either way."

Surela glanced at her sharply. "You know something . . . ?"

Reese said, "Even if I did, I wouldn't tell you. Being cellmates with you doesn't make you my ally, Eldritch." At Surela's flinch, she said, "Doesn't feel any better from the other end, does it."

"I. . . ."

When the other woman trailed off, Reese said, "But we

can agree to try to fight our way out if they open the door again, can't we?"

Shoulders tightening, Surela said, "Yes."

"Good. That's one thing, then. But I'll make this clear now: when Liolesa gets back and beheads you, or whatever barbaric thing you people do here to execute criminals, I'm going to be in the front row. For what you did to Hirianthial, and to her, and most of all this world."

"What do you care what happens to this world?" Surela muttered.

"If you think I want to see anyone given over to slavers. . . ." Reese shook her head. "Maybe you can afford to live in your little bubble where terrible things happen to other people and that's not your business. The rest of us don't work that way. We're a *community*. We protect one another from people who prey on us. We've got one another's backs. Because anything else leaves us all easy pickings for pirates and murderers and criminals."

"So you do this out of selfishness," Surela said.

"We do it because we've seen what's left of the people taken by slavers," Reese replied, voice hard. "And we wouldn't wish it on anyone. And that includes terminally stupid, stuck up bigots like you and all your people, and by that I mean *your* people, Surela. Because people like Liolesa and Araelis aren't stupid enough to think the slavers are going to come for only their enemies. They've spent their lives defending you along with all the more worthy and grateful people, because they knew that they couldn't keep half the world safe. It's everyone or no one."

"It was never my plan to involve aliens," Surela whispered.

"Except as tools to your own end," Reese said. "Even now, you're trying to talk yourself into believing in a universe where you had some noble reason for what you did. Just admit it, Surela. You were selfish and willfully ignorant, and you brought the doom the Eldritch have been trying to hold off for centuries before you were even born right on their heads. You invited it in the bleeding door! And here you are in a cell for it. Did you really expect any differently?" Reese hugged herself against the cold and rubbed her running nose against her shoulder.

"All I wanted for us," Surela said, voice trembling, "was for us to be left alone."

"And I'm sure you expected to be, because you are born to wealth and privilege and it never occurred to you that being left alone is something only the powerful can have, because it takes power to defend yourself against all the people who want a piece of you, no matter how trivial that piece. The rest of us know that freedom has to be paid for in fresh blood, eternally, over and over." Her anger ran out, left her feeling hollow and tired. "I just wish you'd known that before you started all this . . . but I guess everyone has to learn that the hard way."

Surela said nothing for so long Reese assumed their conversation was over. She was glad; her sides ached as if she'd run a race, and she felt heartsore, and she missed her crew terribly. Allacazam would have been a great comfort right about now. Hirianthial, she was sorry to admit, even more so.

But Surela did speak. "Tongue like a whip."

"You'd better hope that's the sharpest thing you get hit with. I wouldn't get your hopes up though." Reese thought of Hirianthial. "I've seen what pirates like to do with Eldritch."

Surela shuddered. "I know," she whispered. At Reese's sharp glance, the woman finished, "I saw what they did to my liege-woman."

There seemed no good answer to that, so Reese said nothing.

CHAPTER 14

On the way to the armory, Hirianthial fell back to pace the Faulfenzair navigator. Her aura had a texture, like smoke against the fingers, warm and pricked through with unexpected embers. He would have thought such an impression would distress, but he found it strangely appropriate to her.

"The God's Gift," he murmured to her as they followed Soly down another of the enormous vessel's many corridors.

She had an accent . . . a lovely one, breathy and musical, somehow evocative of her aura. "Your ability, yes? A gift from the God. I assume you have your own name for Him."

"Does your god give gifts, then?"

"Of course," Lune said, unruffled. "To defend ourselves when we were new, Faulza granted us the mindfire." She held out her hand and the air rippled around it, waves of heat visible to both his natural sight and his finer senses where it lit her aura with licking flames.

Startled, he said, "Is that as hot as it looks?"

"It will burn flesh, but not metal."

"Not your flesh."

"It would be a curse and not a gift if so." Lune glanced at him as they jogged. "You have some confusion?"

"We do not call my abilities a gift from any god, where I'm from," Hirianthial said.

She flicked her ears. "If not from the God, from where does such a gift arise?"

A good question. "I suspect," he said slowly, "we believe it arises from ourselves."

Lune huffed, a sound that dimmed her smoke-drawn aura. "Forgive me. That sounds delusional. Hubris . . . that is the right word. Yes? To believe all good things come from oneself?"

"Some would say this gift is no good thing," Hirianthial replied. "At best, neutral."

The Faulfenzair glanced at him. "This seems unbeliev-able to me. Also, asking for sorrow. Why invite sorrow? Life is long enough to contain enough without asking for more. You should know, yes? You are a little longer lived than us."

"A little?"

"Soly—how long do I live, in your years?"

"Eight hundred, I think? Seven?" Soly paused, con-sulted her map. "This way, we're almost there."

"Seven hundred years!" Hirianthial said, stunned.

"Not so alone in the universe after all, eh?" Sascha said from behind him.

Shaking himself, Hirianthial hurried after the others.

The battlecruiser's armory was not as large as Hirian-thial had expected; apparently the vessel did not have a single centralized facility, but scattered them throughout. There was light armor here, little more than a padded tunic, and of heavy armor nothing; but there were weapons, and even the swords. He accepted one and a tunic; the rest of the party armed themselves, and they found the nearest Pad station.

"You're going to walk over this into Engineering," Soly was saying. "Give us ten minutes to secure the bridge, then move out. Do what you can. Report at intervals. And try not to leave too much evidence."

Narain snorted. "I've been through the training, arii."

"You have, but the rest of them haven't." She smiled and swiped his shoulder, which he ducked. "Take care of them, Spotty."

"And try not to tickle too many groins with your tail," Tomas added. "I'd hate to see you lose it."

"Awww, and all this time I thought you found my tail-tickling annoying. . . ."

"I do, but it doesn't change that they're my tail-tickles to be annoyed by. I'm not letting any pirates steal my prerogatives."

Narain grinned. "Good luck."

"See you on the other side of it all," Soly said, and led the rest of the team out.

"And now we wait?" Sascha guessed.

"Ten minutes," Narain agreed. He considered Sascha. "Long enough for a little fun to get us through the next few hours of blood and gore?"

Sascha pursed his lips. "Someone might walk in on us."

"That's what your Phoenix's claws are for. . . ."

Sascha started laughing. "I like you. You should meet my sister."

"She pretty?"

"Just like me, but a girl."

"Promising!"

Hirianthial leaned against the wall, arms folded, and listened to the banter, the way it smoothed out the auras of both Harat-Shar, bled the tension out. Bryer was unflappable, as always, crouched alongside the Pad and staring at the door from the side of his head. It left him alone, to his thoughts of an alien race that treated its ability to burn others as a gift from a God who wanted them to have some defense. Against what, he wondered? He had not asked. Creatures, like the monsters that had beleaguered the Eldritch settlers? Each other? Aliens? Did the target matter?

What he'd said to Lune had been only truth: no matter what gods the Eldritch purported to worship, they began with themselves. All good things rose from within, like the engineering that had set them apart from humanity on the voyage out from Terra. All evil, also. Hirianthial considered his fingertips, imagining flame licking them. At his shoulder, Urise seemed to wait, an ineffable presence. A man who believed; no question there, not with the ocean of the priest's experiences filling him. What would it be like to believe oneself the recipient of a divine gift? Did that lead one, inevitability, to pride and cruelty? Or to a responsibility to use the gift with respect, because it had been bestowed with love?

Of course, his people had already descended to pride and cruelty, bigotry and xenophobia, entirely without the excuse of belief in a god. Their whole religion was a sham, a way to swaddle the killing of the talented in the raiment of legitimacy. The way, no doubt, Surela was attempting to swaddle her own reign. What was it about his people that they were prone so to this error?

"We lost him," Narain said.

"It happens." Sascha bent down until he could look up into Hirianthial's lowered face. "Hey, arii? Still with us?"

"I am, yes. Is it time?"

"It is."

"Let us go, then."

"Right. And remember . . . as much as possible, let us do the work, Lord Hirianthial. If we need you, we want you to be topped up."

"Understood."

It took exactly five hours for Malia to get worried enough to beep her. Irine touched the telegem at her ear and tapped back a 'fine' response and immediately started looking for cover. She was hugging the palace's basement beneath the balcony that led to the lake; there were sunken windows along its edge that suggested a way in, if she could find one that hadn't been shut tightly enough. Guessing that Malia was going to want words with her, though, she found the deepest corner and cuddled up into it, puffing out white breath. While she'd been sneaking back she'd hardly been aware of the cold; now that she wasn't moving, it felt a lot more acute.

Hopefully the conversation wouldn't take long and she could move on. She hugged her knees and bent her head into them, scanning the lake's edge. There were scrapes in the snow where the bodies Hirianthial had left had been pulled away—into a pile, in fact. Why hadn't their graves been dug yet? Maybe the ground was too cold to get a shovel through?

The telegem hissed to life in her ear. "Irine! Where in Iley's name are you?"

"Under the ballroom balcony."

"What!"

"I'll be fine," Irine said. "We need to get off this channel before someone hears us."

"Irine, you've got to get back here!"

"And I will. When I'm done here—"

"Irine! If they take you and someone reads your mind to find out where everyone's gone. . . ."

That she hadn't thought of, and it put her fur on end. She clenched her teeth against their sudden need to chatter. "I guess I shouldn't get caught then."

"Come back. Right now. Before you blow operational security to the moon and back."

"I can't."

"Irine, they killed everyone at Jisiensire! They're not going to bat a lash adding you to that count!"

Her heart lurched. "Everyone?" Irine asked, fingers tightening on her shins. "All Hirianthial's kin?"

"Everyone. We just heard. And that army's coming back this way. We're going to get word to the rest of the allies. Tell them to start heading north. . . ."

"Sounds like you've got work to do," Irine said. "I do too." In the distance, the pile of bodies seemed to waver. Was it snowing? She blinked to try clearing her eyes. "Angels with you, Malia."

"Wait, Irine--!"

She shut the telegem off manually and tucked it in her pocket. She couldn't afford to let Malia dissuade her. Her vow had been to Reese, not to the Tams, and not to the Swords. And Reese needed her. She crept out of her hiding hole and skirted the edge of the palace, grateful for the lack of technology that had deprived the building of the sort of external lighting that might have exposed her. All she had to worry about was the moon and starlight, which, granted, was reflecting off the thin snow . . . but then, she was used to that. The sand near her house was nearly white too, and on a moonlit night it could be blinding.

She checked the next window, found it solid and sneaked to the next. On her way, she glanced toward the bodies.

One of them was moving.

Irine froze. For a moment, she thought about zombies

and the uneasy dead and her adrenaline spiked . . . and then, through the uncertain light, she saw someone lift his head, short hair swinging around shoulders streaked dark in the chiaroscuro of the evening.

"Val?" she hissed, shocked. Checking the windows for lights and finding none, she darted across the distance as light-footed as she could run, her tail low to scuff the marks behind her. As she approached, the smell became more obvious . . . not as ripe as she'd expected, but still unmistakably blood and gore. And there, on top of the pile, was Val, struggling weakly against the bodies on top of him. "Angels on the battlefield! Val!" She lunged for him and dragged him out of the pile, falling backwards with the Eldritch in her arms. He didn't move . . . just dropped his head on her chest and breathed, hard.

"Fur," was the first word he said. Then, "Smells good."

"Not what Reese told me a few hours ago," Irine said, sitting up. She glanced at Ontine, found the dead between them and easy view . . . good enough. She propped him up and cupped his cold cheeks in her hands, looking at his face, frantic. "Are you hurt? Badly?"

"Nowhere you can . . . can see," he managed, hanging against her. He groped for her arm, caught it and leaned. "Goddess . . . God . . . Lord and . . . Lady . . . damn it all. Damn it!"

She shook him gently. "Talk to me. What happened?"

"Baniel!" Val snarled, panting. "Baniel has a protégé and is sucking power from him. I expected to find him as he was, not augmented!"

Irine's mouth dried. "You mean you're out here because. . . ."

"Because he nearly killed me. Thought he had, or he would have finished the job." Val shuddered. "The cold nearly has."

"And Reese," Irine whispered.

"Safe, for now." Val slumped. "In his care, but untouched. He will use her to bait the trap for his brother. Because they love one another, don't they."

"Yes," Irine said, all her fur standing on end. She swallowed. "Okay, well. We've lived through situations this bad before. We can do it again."

He peered at her. "And I find you here why, Lady Tigress?"

"I'm Reese's girl," Irine said. "And Reese is in there. I don't care about anyone else. I'm going after her."

"And it's true, that Lord Hirianthial is on his way? Your captain and our enemy both seemed convinced."

"Battlehells, yes."

He nodded slowly. "Then maybe the two of us can put ourselves to use on his behalf. Do some reconnaissance. Ah?"

"You don't want to send me back?" Irine asked, wary.

He snorted. "What would that accomplish? You will only wait until you think I'm not looking, then creep back. I can shield you from notice. And you—"

"Yes?" she asked. "What can I do?"

He winced as he staggered to his feet and almost fell. Startled, she leaped to her feet and put her shoulder under his before he could topple.

"You can help me walk," he said. "God, but he nearly tore the soul from my body and it's not convinced it wants to come back."

Irine tried petting his arm gently, and when he didn't object said, "You feel unsteady to me, Val."

"I am," he said. "Let us hide under the balcony then, while I catch my wind."

"Right," she said, and looked past the mound of bodies at the achingly white expanse between her and the palace. She grimaced. "It's going to be a long trip."

"Make it now," Val said, head against her shoulder. "No one's watching."

She glanced at him. "Sure of that?"

"Achingly."

"Huh." She resettled his weight against her shoulder. "Maybe we'll make it out of this alive after all."

"I can't recommend the alternative, having nearly experienced it."

"I bet." She started off. "Hold on, Boss. We're all coming."

The candle had long since burned down and left them in darkness when the door opened again. Even blinded by the sudden light, Reese scrabbled to her feet and launched herself at it, only to be thrown to one side. Shaking herself against the disorientation, she prepared for a second attempt, only to find the door already shutting.

She was alone. They had taken Surela.

No loss there, she told herself, sinking to the ground again and rubbing her aching head. Probably changed their minds about needing her for something. She fisted her fingers in her braids to keep her hand from shaking. How long were they going to leave her here? She'd never been afraid of the dark—she was a merchant trader, for blood's sake, she spent her life plying a dark far more abyssal than this—but something about the closeness of the room and the pressure of Hirianthial's impending entrapment and the memory of his body lying on this very floor. . . .

How had he borne being hemmed up like this so many times? Was imprisonment something one got better at with practice? Or was it just a matter of his extended lifespan? Maybe it brought patience. Reese scrubbed her eyes. She could be patient. Damn it all. She could live through this. They hadn't hurt her. She had all her faculties. She just had to wait for the right moment.

The next time they opened the door, she vaulted for it and got a quarter-power palmer shot to the leg for her trouble. She fell abruptly and was pushing herself up when they shut the door again. They'd left another candle this time . . . and Surela.

And Surela.

"Blood and all hell!" Reese scrabbled over to the other woman on her hands and one knee, looking over the body. Some blood but not a lot. The dress was a mess though, and there were bruises . . . Reese had ample experience with how badly Eldritch skin bruised. She hovered over Surela, grimaced, chanced a touch on one of the tattered sleeves. "Surela?"

The woman's lashes parted, just enough to gather the candle's gleam. Then she jerked upright so abruptly she smashed her head into Reese's.

"Blood in the—damn it, that hurt—wait, wait, it's just me!"

Surela had pushed herself to the corner, her back to the wall and her arms wrapped tightly around herself. "*Don't*—!"

"I won't, I won't touch you," Reese said. "I just wanted to make sure you were still conscious."

"You were . . . trying to help me?" the other woman asked, the last word ending on a squeak of disbelief and, Reese thought with a flinch, hysterical tears.

"I want you to stand trial," she said finally. "And if Liolesa decides you need to die for what you've done, then I want her to kill you cleanly. I don't hold with torture."

"Is that what that was," Surela whispered.

Reese glanced at her, at the way she was holding herself, at the bruises, the torn dress. "Yes. I know. I've seen it before."

That made the other woman look up at her, and her face held something other than hysteria finally. Confusion?

"With Hirianthial," Reese said.

Surela shuddered. "To a man!"

"Bad things happen to men too."

"Not the same," Surela whispered.

"Looked pretty bad to me—"

"A man," Surela hissed, "can't be gotten with child against his will."

Reese leaned back, shocked. "Your own guards . . . ? They attacked you?"

"No!" Surela pressed her face into her hands. She was trembling violently enough for Reese to see from across the room. "No, they would not dare. Even now."

"I can't imagine Baniel. . . ."

"No. No, it was the pirates." Surela glared at her. "As you should have guessed, given what you are to your paramour."

"My. . . ." Reese stopped, then frowned. "Hirianthial's not my *paramour*. Who the hell has a paramour these days, anyway?"

"Your lover then—"

"He's not that, either! And what on the red earth does that have to do with children, anyway?"

"Because, you idiot, humans can get us with child," Surela snarled.

Reese stopped short, her skin gone cold beneath her long sleeves. In the silence, the other woman began to weep into her knees.

"Oh, hell," Reese muttered and rubbed her face.

So the next time they opened the door, Reese threw herself not at it, but at Surela, and put herself between the Eldritch and the guards that had come for her. Her act startled them enough that she managed to get one good swipe in . . . but then one of them pinned her. She fought, stamping on his foot with hers and managing a glancing blow. She used the slight lessening of the pressure on her arms to pull free and knock the other guard to one side, and that's how she earned herself a half-power palmer stun. To the side, this time. She fell heavily and even then she tried to grab for an ankle. "No!"

They kicked her to one side and dragged an astonished Surela off anyway. Crumpled on the ground, Reese wept, and wasn't sure if it was frustration or horror or pain. She hated Surela, but she was so tired of the bad guys *winning*. How had Hirianthial managed the patience? Was she failing him by not being up to it?

Next time, she would try harder. At what she wasn't sure. Something. Everything.

CHAPTER 15

They walked over the Pad and into two pirates, both of whom fell to Narain and Sascha's palmers before Hirianthial could so much as lift a hand—and that was for the best. Because all around him, the walls felt *alive*. He wanted to touch them, because he knew there would be a heart-beat in the metal and he wanted the tactile proof of it on his fingertips. To rest them against a wall and then to his lips, to smell the blood-quick brightness of it.

Things that are loved live, a voice whispered, raising the hair on the back of his neck, now so exposed.

"Hey, Hirianthial? You with us?"

"Yes," he said. "Yes. I was just. . . ." He paused because both Harat-Shar were watching him, their worry palpable, like shrouds of cold fog. "This part of the ship feels very different to me."

"Lots of enemies, maybe?" Sascha asked, careful.

"No. No, it feels . . . there is power here."

"Lots of that," Narain agreed as he checked the door, palmer at ready. "Clear here. We can move. You done with the prisoners?"

Sascha said, "Just let me get something to tie them up wi—"

"Done." Bryer rose, the talons on his feet bloody. The auras deflated with the spill of blood, and Hirianthial wondered at his calm at the sight: no, not calm. His own pleasure.

Sascha hissed, "Now if someone finds them, they're going to know we're here!"

Narain glanced over his shoulder and said, "They'd know if they found them tied up too, arii. And I hate to say it, but at least dead they can't be used against us. It's a billion to nine, remember?"

"I know, just . . ." Sascha growled and rose. "Never mind. Let's go."

Go they went, and as they did, Hirianthial's sense of the ship grew with it. Or perhaps not the ship entire, but only this section. He felt the caress of air from the vents like breath on his bare neck and glanced up at it, distracted. "Narain," he murmured. "Is there aught special about an Engineering section?"

"Special?" The Harat-Shar paused, consulted a data tablet, tucked it away. "Wait. We've got five moseying on this way. We can catch them at the cross-corridor if we move."

They moved, and there was a silence, in which the ship seemed to listen. Then they attacked, and Hirianthial did not spare attention for his comrades because the sword he had only used in practice woke in his hand and beheaded his opponent without any effort on his part at all—only to swing, and then a death. The backswing took his second foe from shoulder down, slicing the collarbone and leaving the man with a mouth to scream, so he suggested as the sword sheared through: *Don't.*

And the man didn't.

Bryer had slain his as well, with hands gone ruddy halfway to the elbow. The two down with palmer burns were also dying, if less messily.

Hirianthial stared at the sword, which was a revelation. Lighter than steel and more deadly, and more obedient as well, it suggested its own demeanor immediately. His House swords had been proud weapons, demanding discipline and hardship before yielding their power to a bearer. This sword was retiring, the perfect servant, waiting to see if he would be a cruel or gentle master, but resigned to either. It made him feel an overwhelming urge to protect it.

Things that are loved, live, Urise's memory insisted. Turning the blade off, Hirianthial said to Narain, "The section? Do people care about it? More than perhaps the rest of the ship?"

"What? Oh. Yes." Narain chuckled: true humor, for while his aura was subdued there was no horror in it. This was work to Narain, even the killing. "A good part of a ship's complement does science and research. They're just there for the ride. The command team . . . their thing is the people, all the people. But Engineering keeps the ship running. They get a little fanatic about their ships."

And these pirates had ripped the ship from its devoted crew.

"What was her name?"

The Harat-Shar was once again scouting the corridors, checking his data tablet as Bryer pulled the bodies into a nearby room. "Pardon?"

"The ship's."

Startled, Narain met his eyes: bright blue, wide. Paler than Reese's, and that she might come to mind now . . . he flexed his hand on the hilt of his demure blade, reminding himself to be present.

"Oh. Of course." The Harat-Shar nodded. "The UAV *Moonsinger.*"

"Romantic name for a warship," Sascha said.

"The battlecruisers all have names like that," Narain said. "They're not just warships, after all. They do other things. This way. There's another group, we can ambush them."

Narain found the trespassers alone or in groups of two if he could help it. When he couldn't, Hirianthial helped, and the sword answered him easily, almost too easily. He found himself distracted by it as they made their way toward the core of the section. When had he ever had a weapon that had cost so little physical effort to employ? Even his mind asked more of him when he used it to attack. And yet how lacking in pretension! The bare hilt, the unremarkable color, the naked socket awaiting a pommel, as if born longing for a master.

And if the sword was not distraction enough, the sense of the walls around him breathing grew more intense the further in they went. There was distress to go with that life. The ship missed its crew. Had it hunted pirates in its day? For it loathed them, the way one loathed disease. The ship had bones, and he felt its grief in the hollows of them, and they all led back to the Engineering core.

"You're good with that thing," Narain said after they'd dispatched another two stragglers. "Maybe you won't need to use your head at all, ah?"

"Wouldn't that be simpler," Sascha muttered, helping Bryer drag their latest bodies into yet another room. "Had no idea Fleet ships had so many conference rooms. What do they do, have meetings all day?"

"You have no idea," Narain said, long-suffering. "It's a cultural weakness. We love consensus."

"How many more of these people do we have to deal with?" Sascha asked, expressing the fatigue

Hirianthial thought he should be feeling, rather than the curious serenity.

"Looks like . . . sixty?"

"At least we're making a dent in them."

"Next group?" Bryer asked, interrupting.

"Right. This way."

They resumed their cautious progress, and Sascha fell back to pace him. "Doing all right?"

"Fair," Hirianthial said. "I think I may be less healed than I'd hoped."

Sascha snorted. "Like we all told you."

"Just so." He smiled. "Perhaps I merit the stubborn label after all."

"You're the only one who didn't know it, if you doubt it at all." Sascha glanced at the hilt in Hirianthial's hand. "And . . . um . . . no regrets? You know, from the healer half of you."

"Do I look it?"

"No. No . . . that thing with the sword . . . you've been doing that forever, haven't you."

"It feels like it, some days." Hirianthial glanced at him. "Does it distress you?"

Sascha managed a wan grin. "Actually, it's kind of sexy. Who doesn't like a man who can handle himself?"

"Or a woman," Narain added.

"Or a woman."

Hirianthial thought of Liolesa, of Araelis, of Reese, and smiled a little. "Indeed."

"We'll see them again," Sascha added, quiet. "We will."

"I know it."

"Next group should be up—" The hall flooded with red light, strobing, and a great shudder rocked the floor beneath his boots. A distant grinding noise interrupted the heart-throb beat of his awareness of the ship, and then a voice began to speak, echoing, repeated endlessly down the corridors.

"Alert. Alert. Repel Boarders."

"Rhack!" Narain hissed, ears flattening. "They're locking down Engineering. Something went wrong." He touched his telegem, tail lashing. "No answer there, either. Battlehells!"

"Can we get out?" Sascha asked, balling his fists.

"Not with the bulkheads down. If it was an environmental alert the Pad access would work, but not for intruders. Come on. We've got to find a bolthole and regroup—"

Two of their enemies sprinted into view and halted, lifted their hands. And there was no time, and far too much distance. The flashing lights slowed as Hirianthial reached toward them, hand open. He felt the pulse of their nervous systems like a web he could grasp and he did, stilling it. They breathed. Their hearts flexed. Blood rushed through their arteries, spilled into capillaries. But the higher functions were his, and his mind ran through the silver net, dendrite to axon, clouding the synapses.

Stop, he whispered, and they froze, and he held their lives in his hand.

Two palmer bursts killed them where they stood, and the shock of it staggered him. He would have fallen had Sascha not thrust a shoulder up under his, taking his weight. "Easy there, lean on me."

"You might . . . might wait to kill them until I have done with them," he gasped.

"Is it bad for you?" Sascha peered up at him, his worry a cold cowl draping him.

Was it? He felt his heart skip several beats. He was disoriented; the shift in the color of the light and the constant message repeating didn't help. "Yes."

"Then you'll have to kill them faster—or let go of them

faster. Pick one."

Bryer said, "Lecture later. Keep moving."

Sascha tried a step forward and they staggered. Hirian-thial grimaced.

"Not the first time we've done this," Sascha said. "We're gonna be fine."

"Right."

"Because otherwise Reese will kill you."

That made him smile. "Right."

They found an empty briefing room and paused there; Hirianthial was grateful for the chance to lean on the table and try to draw his shattered concentration back within the limits of his skin. As he breathed through the strange-ness and the cold, Narain and Sascha bent over their stolen tablet.

"They're not answering at all?"

"No, which means we have to assume they can't." Narain was flicking through displays on the tablet so quickly Hirianthial couldn't read them. "So it's up to us to stop them."

"By . . ."

"If we can get to one of the core control panels, we can use the mass ejection routine. That'll kill the power to the ship, once the batteries drain. Failing that, we blow the section."

Hirianthial felt Sascha pale; the energy drained out of his aura, leaving it flush to his pelt. "I'm guessing we don't get out in some kind of miraculous life pod escape in that case."

Narain looked at him.

"How many?" Bryer said. "People left."

"About fiftyish here in Engineering," Narain said. "But the rest of the crew's going to be converging here now that they know where to look."

"We are trapped," Hirianthial said, quiet. "Between those approaching and those already here."

"About the size of it."

"Then we make for the core," Hirianthial said. "And do what we must."

Sascha shuddered. "Right. Let's get on with it, then."

Narain glanced at his tablet. "And . . . there goes the lock-down on non-essential access." He tossed it aside. "We're going to have to play it by sight."

"Mine," Hirianthial said, lifting his head. "And we can go now, and best we do so." He flexed his fingers on the sword hilt and pushed himself upright. "I will take point."

"You sure?" Narain asked, as Sascha said, "I'm not sure you—"

"I can, and I must." He smiled, faint. "The ship is in distress. We go."

Bryer rustled his wings and stepped past the two Harat-Shar. "Wasting time."

"Right," Sascha said with a sigh.

The klaxon, the red lights, the sense of urgency that seemed to throb in the very walls . . . it made him raw even before he stretched himself out to sense their enemies. It blunted the length of his reach. But a corridor he could do, enough to keep them from happening onto their enemies, and he guided them inward, stopping only to kill, with sword more often than mind. Every death scored him though, too close, too violent, and him too open to all of it. Bryer was his anchor, for the Phoenix remained calm, a cool void at his back. The two Harat-Shar cycled through fear and adrenaline and rage so quickly it gave him vertigo.

Over all of it, the ship called him toward the core. Yearned for him, as a patient did a surgeon bearing the scalpel. It needed so badly that he found himself walking

toward a bulkhead more than once, as if he could pass
through it straight to the heart of the vessel.

"Stay on target, alet," Narain murmured, catching
him once.

"Forward," he said, and found the corner.

There were injuries, inevitable ones, palmer burns and
bruises; Narain took a blow to the nose that bled carmine
streaks onto white and gray fur, and the pain that lanced
Sascha's wrist was so bright it bled through his aura into
Hirianthial's. "Sprain," he said. Shook himself. "Immobilize
it, if you can."

"Us and what Medplex."

"We're almost there," Narain said, tired.

"Think we can make it?" Sascha asked, cradling
his hand.

"Honestly I'm shocked we got as far as we have." The
pardine flexed his fingers on the wall. "If we can get in . . .
and if we don't get shot at . . . and if I can get into the
system before they lock me out. . . ."

"That's a lot of ifs."

Bryer said, "One at a time." When they glanced at him,
he gaped his beak in a grin and said, "We handle them.
One 'if' at a time."

Narain guffawed. "Humor from a Phoenix. Now I know
we're in trouble."

"We need to move," Hirianthial interrupted.
"They're coming."

They moved, then. They kept moving, until the pattern
pushed through his confused hyper-awareness, shoving
aside the ship's distress and his companions' dense auras.
He paused, weaving until he caught his balance.

"What is it?" Sascha hissed, ears flattening.

"They're herding us." Hirianthial glanced at Narain.
"Can they communicate with one another?"

"Of course. We're the ones they shut out."

"Then they know where we are, and they are herding us toward an ambush."

A pause that stressed the lack of silence. The computer's automated alert sawed against the ship's ethereal distress in his head.

"And that ambush is . . . ?"

"Ahead of us. In a large open space."

Narain nodded. "Which is where we have to go. The core. Of course." He shook his head. "I'm not sure we're going to make it out of this after all."

Won't see my kin again. Shimmering memories, like fish seen beneath the surface of clear water: Soly, Tomas, Jasper, Lune. A pastiche of camaraderie as fierce as a family's love. It sank beneath the spear-point wound of Sascha's anguished, *My sister . . . !* So much pain there, not only for himself, but for her, for abandoning her.

Bryer's serenity stole through the grief. *It will be good to see the Eye with open eyes. It will be good to be free to fly.*

And all around him, the *Moonsinger's* urgent grief: *COME COME TO ME*

With a shudder, Hirianthial said, "There is a chance. We must be swift."

Corel had killed an army. Surely he could manage the enemies crowding them in. If he could only get to an open space . . . he couldn't concentrate with the racing pulse of the ship urging him inward.

"It's your game now, alet," Narain said. "Lead. We'll guard your flanks."

Where now? he asked, and the ship urged him on. He led, and they followed, and as much as possible he avoided the people converging on them. It needed running, and he was already short of breath: tired of gripping the sword that submitted, tired of seeking with outstretched mind, tired of danger and odds too great for any one person to best. He was tired, he realized, sudden as the piercing of a blade to flesh, of *losing*.

Not this time.

Narain grabbed him and threw him back, away from the palmer shot that would have hit him, and fired past him. He felt the Harat-Shar take a searing shot, glancing off the arm. Sascha caught the other male, steadied him. "Keep moving!"

They kept on, but now they truly were running, and there was no safety in flight if they were not running towards something—

—what had he said to Sascha once?

Running doesn't solve anything.

That depends on which direction you run.

They burst from the final hall and into a vast chamber, milling with people, and none of it mattered because in the center of the room was the beating heart of a battlecruiser, and the moment he was in range it reached for him, met his spectral fingers, knitted him into a matrix larger than any single person. Power from this room ran to every inch of the ship, from head to stern, and his awareness exploded outward on those arteries. All around him he sensed not just the people in the chamber, but everywhere else: on the way here, on the bridge, in the weapon bays.

Time paused between breaths as the knowledge smashed into him, and with it the flames of all those distant souls.

I cannot! he thought, astonished. Couldn't possibly be feeling it. Couldn't possibly control it. Couldn't possibly live through manipulating it, when the control needed to incapacitate a handful of people had laid him out so completely.

And yet, the power was there, and so was salvation.

You can, a whisper answered.

You must! the ship seemed to plead.

Around him, Sascha and Narain and Bryer were inhaling. For how much longer, if he did nothing?

It's not about you. Chiding. The voice of a loving if exasperated father. *It was never about you. It was never about your ability to shoulder things alone. IT IS NOT FOR YOU TO DO ALONE.*

Stunned, he held a breath.

The silence that Urise had taught him to descend to . . . the silence of the Divine, Who was listening because He had fashioned others to speak for Him. The ship, waiting for a voice, offering to show him the way.

Not you, the priest whispered. *You did not give yourself this gift. You take too much on your own shoulders alone, my son, but it was the Divine who gave you the gift. Make yourself the instrument of that Voice, and* be not alone!

Time shivered, lurched forward. Hirianthial opened himself to the gift, and to the One working through them, and the silence filled with a great and endless *YES.* He lifted his face to it as he closed his fists on the flames, and snuffed them.

Silence. The heart skipping? No, time had contracted again to a single point. He felt the wonder of it, and slid to a knee, and then to both . . . and to the ground. Beneath his palm, the ship sang a thankful lullaby, and he let it.

CHAPTER 16

The next time they opened the cell door they were pointing their palmers straight at her. Reese eyed them balefully, every limb trembling with the need to dart past them, and maybe also—a little—with weakness from the last time they'd hit her. She was waiting, she told herself, for the first flinch, the first hint that they might lower their guards. It was a good story. She kept telling it to herself as they set a bucket on the floor, along with a crust of bread and a cup of water.

"Drink first," the guard said. Eldritch, she noticed, but he spoke Universal well enough. "Use the bucket. Then we leave you with the bread."

"Use the . . . in front of you?"

He smiled. "We could leave it in the room with you."

Put that way . . . but who used a bucket for things like that? Of all the things the Eldritch could have chosen to throw away, why indoor plumbing? Reese couldn't imagine consigning herself to a lifetime of chamber pots, particularly one the length of an Eldritch's.

She was, however, thirsty. And she couldn't fight her way out of this situation without energy.

After they left she gnawed on the bread crust until her jaws started hurting. Bread the consistency of leather was another thing she'd thought her books had exaggerated. She chalked it up along with corsets, ill-fitting shoes, and horses being more fractious than advertised. One of these days she'd have a talk with the authors of her penny dreadfuls about all the lies they were perpetuating.

That left her, again, with the wan candle barely pushing back the dark, wondering how much time had passed. Somehow she managed to drowse off, and woke up only when the guards shoved Surela back into the cell and slammed the door behind her.

Any thought Reese might have had about escaping shattered at the sound of Surela's sobbing. All her knowledge of the Eldritch fanaticism about touch fled her, too. There was no letting that much hysteria go uncomforted. She dropped to her knees beside the other woman and took her hands. "Here. You're here. They're behind that door. It's over for now. It's over."

Surela pressed her face into Reese's shoulder and wept, and with a sigh Reese wrapped her arms around the Queen's enemy and awkwardly petted her shoulder, her hand, her back—and came away wet with something hot. Her fingers twitched.

"You're bleeding? You're bleeding! Turn around, let me see. . . ." She peered over Surela's shoulder and saw long, thin gouges in pale flesh. "What on the good red earth . . . ?"

"C-claws," Surela gasped into her vest. "He had . . . he had *claws*. Oh, Goddess, he wasn't even human!"

Given Surela's opinion of humans . . . and then Reese actually heard the words. "Claws?" she said, trying to duck down to look into the other woman's arms. "Was it the shapechanger?"

"He was a beast!"

"Chatcaava," Reese whispered. "Blood and *freedom.*"

Surela wept until Reese's vest was wet all the way to the skin, saying something nearly incoherent until Reese finally caught some of it amid the sobs. "I-I have b-b-been ruined!"

"You've been raped," Reese said with asperity, still holding her. "That doesn't make you ruined."

The woman didn't answer for long enough that Reese thought the matter closed—and a good thing, because she didn't want to be feeling any sort of righteous anger on behalf of Liolesa's enemy. But with a last shivery sniffle, Surela finished, "It does here." Without lifting her head from Reese's chest, she wiped her nose with the side of one trembling wrist. "Though I suppose it matters not at all. Either the aliens will kill me, or Liolesa will." She shuddered. "Goddess, the claws. And the eyes. To be touched by something with a maw. . . ."

"Sssh," Reese said, touching her hand again. "Don't go back there. You're here for now, and here nothing will happen to you."

"Until they come for me again."

"Yes," Reese admitted. "Until they come for you. . . ." She trailed off and touched her boot. Had they searched her before throwing her in here? Baniel had taken her telegem and her palmer, and if that had satisfied them . . . her groping fingers brushed against stiff metal and she inhaled. Irine's pick was still in her boot.

It was her only weapon. If an opportunity arose . . . but she wasn't the one being dragged out of the cell. And in this one thing, she and Surela shared the same goal. Didn't they? Of course, if she told Surela and the Eldritch decided she wasn't able to kill her attackers, then the next time

Baniel rifled through her mind he might find out Reese was armed. Assuming Baniel bothered to oversee the depredations being visited on the woman he'd sponsored to the throne. Somehow Reese doubted it; he'd probably offered her as a prize to the pirates and his guest, and that had been the limit of his interest. But was she willing to bet on it?

Could she in good conscience not, knowing what they were doing to the other woman? Treason might deserve death, but did it merit torture?

That she knew the answer to.

"And if I told you that the next time they dragged you to the Chatcaavan, you would have a weapon," Reese said, quietly. "Would you use it?"

Surela looked up sharply.

"Would you?"

"You have a weapon?" Surela asked sharply. "Why haven't you used it?"

Reese pulled the pick out of her boot and showed it to the Eldritch: a metal needle nearly the length of her forearm. "They would have to come too close. It needs to go through someone's throat. Something gruesome and decisive. And you could only use it once before they took it away from you."

Surela's eyes focused on the dim glitter of the metal. "I . . . I would have to stab him."

"You would have to stab him while he was on top of you," Reese said softly, to make it clear what she'd be signing up for. "And it's not likely you'd survive the experience, unless they wanted to keep you alive for something else. But it's something. And if it's the Chatcaavan you get, and not just one of his hires . . . that would be a big step toward fixing things."

"It would not rectify everything."

"No. But it would be something. And right now, it's something only you can do because they don't seem to want me."

Surela lifted eyes dulled with fatigue. "Leaving you thus is his way of tormenting you. If he gave you some torture to endure, it would distract you from sitting here, fearing, feeling guilt for being whole. Pain would at least give you the opportunity to feel some pride, that you might be fighting through something, that you are fighting at all." She shivered, forced herself to sit up. "He gives you nothing to fight. I think he knows that would hurt you worse than suffering."

The insight startled her. "Did he tell you that?"

"No," Surela said, eyes lowered. "You did, when you touched my skin. And Baniel is nothing if not a master of manipulating the emotions of others. He did it to me quite handily."

"Oh hell," Reese muttered. "I don't want to like you. Stop seeing the error of your ways, all right?"

Surela snorted, a sound perilously close to a sniffle. "Fear not. I still hate aliens. If anything I hate them more now. If I somehow kept the throne after this debacle, I would raise an army in such numbers I could conquer the known worlds and send it against you all to keep you at bay."

Reese considered that in silence, running her fingers along the length of the pick. Finally, she said, "Who would you get to build it?"

The Eldritch looked up at her and scowled. And then, suddenly, barked a laugh. "Ridiculous. It's all so ridiculous. How easily I walked into this trap! There is no doing with you, and no doing away with you without involving you. And all we wanted when we fled Terra was to be left alone!"

"We're not all so bad, you know."

"Enough of you are."

"Should I remind you who threw us in here? You people aren't all paragons of virtue yourself."

Surela stilled. "No. No, that we are not." She lifted her chin. "May I take it?"

Reese met her eyes, wondering if she could read anything in them, and not seeing much but anger and hurt and fear and the pride that was stitching the other woman's tattered spirit together. Sadly, she could empathize with all those things.

She passed the pick over. "Hide it somewhere they won't find it."

"Don't fear," Surela said. She picked at her tattered bodice, finding a place where the seam had ripped, and from a broken channel drew a long, thin white bone. The needle replaced it, and once in was completely hidden. "They create their own destruction," she said with grim satisfaction. "Just as I did." Surela offered her the bone. "To replace your weapon, until I can give it back."

It was more 'if' than 'until,' but Reese didn't say so. She took it, and thanked the other woman, and together they settled in to wait. It was strangely comfortable. Seeing Surela like this had exhausted Reese's need for revenge, had in fact shamed her for feeling it so strongly. Now all she felt was tired.

"I'm going to rush them again," Reese said, conversationally. "Otherwise they might wonder why I'm not fighting them."

"Perhaps they'll think you'd learned the futility of attempting it."

Reese snorted. "If Baniel knows as much about me as you think he does, he'll realize that's completely out of character for me."

Surela glanced at her. "You are so obstinate, then."

"Oh, you have no idea." Reese smiled a little.

The other woman rested the back of her head against the wall, eyes closed. The dim light glowed on her skin, save where the bruises were darkening. "It would take a stubborn woman to bring Hirianthial out of his shell."

Her first instinct, to snap that Surela had no right to say anything about Hirianthial 'the evil mind-mage,' faded at the thought that Surela had known him for much, much longer than she had. "He loved his wife, I hear."

"He loved at all." Surela sighed and smiled. "It was his best quality. And I say it about a mind-mage . . . and yet he seems far less evil to me now than my own confederates." She was silent a while, then said, "Will you take him for your lover?"

Ordinarily she would have had a flustered and angry retort for such a personal question, but in the dark, with the future uncertain, it didn't seem worth it, to fight over it. So she said, "I don't do casual things. I want a husband, not a fling. And what could I be to him, but a fling? I'll be dead before he gets used to me."

Surela glanced at her without moving her head. "You'll live longer than his Butterfly."

"Maybe," Reese murmured. "But she died young and beautiful. I'll die old and decrepit."

"Do you think that's how he remembers her, in death?" Surela sighed and rubbed one eye with the heel of a hand, a gesture so vulnerable, so *normal* it almost made her seem . . . human. "I pledge you, his lasting memory of Laiselin was of her used up by the mortal agonies of childbirth. If I am not mistaken, that is not a hardship that will ever afflict you."

"That's another thing," Reese said. "He'll want children. . . ."

"Which he can give you," Surela said, irritated. "Haven't

you been listening to me? We can mate with humans. Both sexes. You lie with him, you will get yourself with an Eldritch child."

The idea was bizarre. "You mean I'll end up with a snow-white baby?"

"Who will outlive you, yes."

"Who the hell came up with that idea?" Reese asked, indignant. "What if I want a human baby?"

"Then find yourself a human man," Surela said. "But we are . . . designed . . . to propagate, given the right circumstances. We were human once. It helps us, to ensure the continuation of the race."

Reese shivered. "So you hijack wombs."

"And seed, if you want to be coarse. Men no less than women are fodder for the process." Surela smoothed the broken lace over her knees. She was trembling now. "So no righteous rage over the inequality of it."

Softer, Reese said, "I'm sorry. I don't mean to remind you—"

Surela held up a hand. She drew in a careful breath, then continued, "So you can give the man his heirs, if you are willing. If you are great enough of heart to give birth to children who will live many years beyond your span."

Reese set her chin on her knees, hugging them, and said, "Children should outlive their parents, shouldn't they? And if you're a good parent, you want them to flourish." She thought of her mother's cold gaze, the sound of her voice when she'd declared Reese's disinheritance. Thought of the eucalyptus that had been cut down, and her memories of napping in the boughs of that tree. Then she frowned. "If I could have his children, why did you say the hardship would never afflict me?"

"Because you have mortal technology, yes?" Surela looked away. "Would that we did, and I might have used it on behalf of my liegewoman." She was pleating the lace now, forming neat patterns broken by the rips. "There are some things of your making that are worth having."

"And some things of yours that are worth leaving behind," Reese said.

"Perhaps."

Reese didn't push it. It was strange enough that Surela had been trying to allay her anxieties about Hirianthial, a man she'd supposedly wanted for herself before deciding he was some kind of religious anathema. Reforming the woman entirely of her anti-alien sentiments would have been too much. Particularly since Reese didn't feel like grappling with her feelings about whether she liked Surela or not. She didn't *want* to like Surela. But then, how many people had not wanted to like her? And how many times had she blundered into mistakes because of her own willful denial of reality?

She'd never committed treason. But then again, she'd never been backed into a corner with her fears before. Not the way she was now. She had come here to murder someone, after all, and barely a year ago the idea of so much as hitting someone had nauseated her.

Why the hell did things have to be so complicated?

After a time, Surela said, quietly, "Thank you."

What could she say to that? "You're welcome."

The candle burned to a puddle. The guards returned for Surela, and Reese fought them for her, or at least, that's how she couched it in her own mind. Truthfully it was more like she threw herself at the nearest guard and got a face full of palmer for her efforts. They dragged Surela off and the candle guttered in its own wax and finally died.

Would Surela kill the Chatcaavan? Would she even have the chance? Was Hirianthial coming? Reese curled up on her side and hid her head in her arms. Damn Baniel, but he was right. There was barely a bruise on her body and with every pulse of her heart all she felt was guilt and anger and a rising desperation at her own powerlessness.

"This is my war too," she whispered. "When will I get to fight?"

CHAPTER 17

"And this plan makes sense how?" Irine hissed.

"One . . . it gets us out of the cold." Val swayed, grabbed for her hand. "Two, it connects us with the people most likely to be able to help us. Three, it gets us into Ontine—"

"Where Baniel is, and all his minions," Irine reminded him.

"Baniel won't be expecting me to be alive." Val put his back to the palace's foundation, his breath coming in white pants. She joined him; the moist cold of the stone went straight through her jacket and into her blood, and she shivered. She could imagine this weather being delightful . . . once she lived somewhere with artificial heat. Maybe she could talk Reese into installing heated floor tiles, since the castle was half-ripped up anyway. A clan of Tam-illee engineers could probably do it in a few days.

If they survived. Which brought her back to the Eldritch who was holding her hand so tightly her skin ached beneath the fur. She could feel the tremor in his wrist through their joined palms.

"I can keep him from seeing us because of that," he continued at last. "That is the limit of what I can accomplish, however. I need my strength back, and for that I need warmth, food, water."

"Kisses?" Irine said, idly, missing Sascha.

"Only if you're insensible to the fact that I smell like a corpse."

"Right. You also need a change of clothes. And a bath."

He chuckled, then glanced at her without moving his head. "This is what we have, Lady Tigress. Unless you have a better plan?"

"I was thinking of climbing to the roof and letting myself into the attic. Assuming there is one. But I don't think you're up to climbing."

"Now? No." He looked up. "A pity, since it's not a bad plan. We will have to go with mine instead, and trust to the largesse of the servants of Ontine."

Irine sighed. "I hope you're right about their loyalties."

"I'm not at all worried about their loyalties. Their safety . . . that, I question, and the sooner we know one way or the other, the better."

"Well, if it's all we've got, let's get it over with."

He nodded and started off, and she followed.

Getting into Ontine, then, was as easy as keeping close to the foundations until they found the door to the kitchens. There were guards, but they'd all been stationed outside the perimeter, and with the moon playing tricks with the light and their hugging the walls, no one looking from inside the palace was going to see them without a lot of luck. Irine figured the Angels owed them some luck by now, and maybe they were listening because someone opened the door at Val's furtive knock. He didn't say anything, just moved a little so that Irine's face was visible.

"Come in," the woman said in Universal. "Quickly."

They were ushered into a room and the first thing Irine thought was that it was warm, warmer than the rest of the palace had been. Three fires were burning in the same wall, and over them were doors, and along the tables lining the wall were loaves of pale bread rising. It was a dim room, tinted in sepia, and there was no wind, no ice, and no humidity. It felt a little like Heaven. Irine sighed. "I'd almost be fine with you giving us to that imposter woman as long as she kills us here."

"We will not," the woman said, startled. "We would not. We are Queen Liolesa's, to the bone."

"She is making a jest," Val said. "It was not meant as insult."

"No." The servant deflated. "And you have all been hard used, and the news only gets worse and worse."

Irine glanced at Val, found him looking at her. She cleared her throat and said, "Maybe you should tell us then. And . . . if it's no trouble, we could use something warm to drink. And Val needs to eat."

The woman's name was Maraleith, and the news was worse than either of them anticipated. Irine was glad she hadn't asked for food for herself because she was sure she couldn't have eaten after hearing it. Malia had mentioned some of it, but it had seemed so incredible . . . and Malia had not had details. "So . . . you're saying that Hirianthial's family—his entire family except for what's here—is gone."

"His family and his people," Maraleith said. "Slaughtered by that murderer Athanesin and his lackeys. I can only imagine he will be marching for Galare next."

"We can't do anything about Athanesin and his army," Val said, already halfway through a bowl of stew. "But we might have a chance here. What do you know of things here? After the escape?"

"Oh, it's terrible how things have gone." The woman shook her head. "The Queen's White Sword, good Captain Olthemiel, captured with a priest and several of his men! And they have not been killed, but imprisoned in the audience chamber—it is whispered that the pirates mean to take them off-world and sell them, if you can imagine such a horror! Nor is he there alone . . . they have put the remainder of the Queen's supporters in there with them, including the Lady Araelis, and she pregnant!"

Irine laced her fingers together to keep from chafing her tail. "And the woman who replaced Liolesa's going to let them?"

Maraleith's eyes went round. "How can she stop them? She was imprisoned herself, for attempting to arrest the high priest."

Val frowned, rested his spoon back on the lip of his bowl. "Did she?"

"She did," Maraleith said. "Such a sad thing, that. The aliens killed her liegewoman, without so much as telling her they'd taken her for their own. But loyal Thaniet crawled through the very walls to give warning to her mistress and died in the woman's arms."

"So who's in charge?" Irine asked, confused.

"The high priest and his pet alien, and all the pirates they have brought down since." Maraleith refilled Irine's cup from a teapot. "Some thirty-odd, I'd say. We don't have exact numbers, since we've boarded up all the doors in the passages."

"You have?" Val asked, startled.

"We had to," Maraleith said, solemn. "We won't serve pirates and criminals. I won't have my girls and boys in their sight, where they might be coveted. These people are animals. Have you seen the dead outside? They won't even bury them properly . . . just toss them in a pile like refuse.

It was why Asaniefa asked us to tend to Lady Thaniet our-selves. She knew we would give her a proper burial."

"Why haven't they come looking for you?" Irine warmed her hands on her cup, uneasy. "It's not like you're hidden."

"Up until now Surela and her people, and the hostages, have been staying in the palace," Val murmured, frowning. "So Baniel would have needed someone to feed and clean up after them. Now that most of the hostages are gone and Surela's been dethroned. . . ."

Maraleith went grey, but she topped up Val's cup with commendable calm. "We know we're in danger. But someone must stay to help the Queen when she returns."

"And now someone shall." Val looked at Irine. "Because there's a task within our measure."

"What could that possibly be, with us against thirty people?" Irine asked, ears flattening.

"Ah," Val said, grinning. "But what if it was fifteen of us against thirty? Or more?"

Irine squinted at him. "You want to free Olthemiel."

"Oh!" Maraleith exclaimed. "If it could be done!"

"I think it may," Val said. "Would you be so kind as to bring me another piece of your fine bread, Mistress? There are some spaces I haven't filled up yet."

The woman chuckled. "It is good to feed someone with a healthy appetite. And you want to talk alone, I imagine. Don't worry, I shall find the furthest loaf in the kitchen and spend considerable time deciding how to tear it."

Irine blushed. "It's not that we don't trust you. . . ."

"But rather that the less you know, the less our enemies can learn from you," Val finished.

Maraleith nodded, the curtailed gesture that Irine had once found so hard to read. "I know. Trust me. I have some sense of the enemies that have come calling for our Queen. I will be in the pantry if there is need. You should not see anyone else for some hours at this time of night."

"Thank you," Val said.

"So you want to waltz through the heart of the palace, avoiding all the guards and pirates, and somehow sneak thirty or forty people out, more than half of whom aren't fighters?" Irine folded her arms, trying not to dig her nails past the fur on her upper arms. "You sure you're up for that?"

"It's worth a try, ah?" He grinned at her. "They won't be expecting it, so it will come as a surprise to them."

Irine huffed. "It'll be a surprise to them because it's dumb and not likely to work." She raked a hand through her hair, sure that she'd left some of it in unruly tufts and not caring. "What about Reese? Can you tell where she is?"

The Eldritch sobered. He set his bowl aside. "Would that I could. But I can't stretch myself that far right now, not without giving myself a bad case of the faints." A crooked smile. "Not really something I'd care to court."

"Because . . . you got hurt?"

"Because I strained myself in the first fight against Baniel," Val said. "Think of it like a ripped muscle, Lady Tigress, and you'll have some of the sense of it. I can flex it a touch, but too much and the pain stops me."

"How long does it take to heal from that?"

"More time than we have." He sighed. "I am sorry I can't tell you about your captain, Irine. Chances are she's still alive, though. She's too great a liability to your Lord Hirianthial, if I read the situation right. There's no question that Hirianthial will return, but if Baniel has your captain he can use her to split his brother's focus."

Irine grimaced. "Right. Just what we need." She sighed. "So you can use your abilities a little, is that right? Is that's what going to keep them from seeing us?"

"Oh no. No, I imagine what's going to keep them from

seeing us is that we'll use the servants' halls to get there. We'll send the staff away so they won't be targeted for retribution if we're found, though. There's no point in them staying and becoming hostages to pirates, especially since I don't think Baniel's protecting them anymore. If he ever was. That might have been Surela's doing, not his."

"I don't get it." Irine shook her head. "What's his angle? The servants are a danger to him, aren't they? Why didn't he have them all killed?"

"I honestly think. . . ." Val looked toward the fire, then jerked his chin toward it. "That's what he wants. To see the world burn."

"But why?" Irine asked, aghast. At his lifted brow, she said, "I've run into drug barons now, and thugs, and slavers, and pirates, and as horrible as they all were they were in it for themselves. They wanted something. Burning up the world just to see it burn . . . what's the profit in that?"

"That's exactly the profit in it," Val said, quiet. "To destroy something is power. To know you *can* destroy it . . . that is an aphrodisiac. That is what he derives from all this, Lady Tigress. The knowledge that he can cause the demise of an entire people. Surely you are aware that such people exist."

"I guess I knew," Irine said, soft. "I just thought they were so rare I would never meet one."

"Now you have." Val sighed and managed a smile. "My only regret is that you didn't meet one that was also stupid. A dumb thug does localized harm. A smart one. . . ."

"Can rip down a world." Irine squared her shoulders. "All right. If it's all that we can do, then we should. I'm guessing after we free these people we can take them back through the same corridors? Maybe lead them out to where Malia and Beronaeth are waiting."

"It will do. We will tell Maraleith to clear the building.

Most of the staff is up before dawn, and the ones who aren't they can rouse. That will give us . . . oh, I'd say three hours to rest before we make the attempt. We don't want to try it before we're sure they're free of the palace."

"Sounds about right." Irine pushed herself to her feet. "I'll go find her and tell her. You finish eating. Then we can sleep." She managed a smile. "I won't even tease you about sleeping with you, though I should. It's in the racial profile."

"I would think the stink of me would drive any thoughts of it from your head."

"That's what bathwater is for. And trust me, you're getting that even if I'm not tumbling you, because I'm not sleeping next to the smell of rot. I'm surprised you could eat through it . . ."

Val said, "You can get used to anything."

"Yep. Doesn't mean I should." She grinned, and even tired she found she meant it. Maybe things would work out? But if they didn't, she was trying. Better that than to die in a hole alone. Especially not alone. "I'll be right back."

"I look forward to it."

Strangely, she thought he meant it. That made her smile too.

"What is it exactly that you see in her?" Baniel asked, curious. "She is a woman like any other. Much like the last one you used and discarded, even."

"Ah, but that one was not a queen," the Chatcaavan said. In his false shape he was reclining on one of the chaise longues, hands folded behind his head, one knee up, slouched in an indolence that was too overt to pass for a real Eldritch . . . even had he been fully clothed, which he wasn't. Baniel found the revelation of the scars crossing the alien's sides and chest intriguing. Were those the Chatcaavan's, expressed into the new shape? Or were they his brother's, stolen with his pattern?

After a moment of pleased contemplation, the alien finished, "This one thinks herself strong enough to rule. It amuses me."

Baniel found that a curious comment, but let it pass. "Many people believe themselves to be greater than they are."

"Ah, but how many are so delusional as to think themselves fit for a throne when they are so obviously not?" The Chatcaavan grinned lazily. "You yourself do not believe she was ever worthy. Do you deny it?"

"Of course not. But she wouldn't have served so well had she been half as competent as she believed herself. Tools should not think for themselves." Baniel drifted to the window and stared out into the dark. Was his brother here yet? Liolesa? When would they come? The waiting bored him. If he wasn't careful, he'd begin destroying something just to occupy his time . . . and there was nothing left worth destroying that was not already in the process of coming apart on its own. It was never wise to overdo the management. "Shall I have entertainment brought in for your men?"

"Let them wait. It will keep them irritable." The alien half-lidded his eyes. "They are very pleased with themselves, having brought such a ship to me, and have become lackadaisical in responding when I require response. I need them to remember what we are seeking here is cargo, not diversion. The merchandise is not to be touched."

"There are commoners aplenty in town."

"Later, perhaps. Let them earn the privilege." The alien sat up and stretched, languid. "In a few days perhaps I will tour the ship. You could come with me, see your ride out of this system. It is fit for a king, truly."

"If I wanted to be king. . . ." Baniel turned from the

window. "Later, perhaps."

"Then I go to amuse myself with the woman who thinks she could straddle a throne. After that, I shall enjoy myself killing the pregnant one." He grinned. "You could join me. It would be good for you."

Baniel smiled. "I fear I have no taste for failures."

"Hah! Then you must have a very empty harem. I leave you to the contemplation of your virtues and the beds they empty."

"Why, thank you. That is a fine compliment."

"From one predator to another," the alien said, and slid from the chaise longue.

As he reached the door, Baniel said, "Lackadaisical, you said?"

"The ship sleeps in orbit. I would punish them for it, but they are too few for the prize they have captured. There will be time to discipline them properly . . . perhaps when I have a few of my own kind among them to show them." The alien cocked his head. "You disagree?"

"I only wondered. I would hate to have such firepower in the hands of those who have decided they need not answer to you."

The alien chuckled. "Let them rebel if they dare. They already fear others of my kind walk among them, hidden in their shapes, waiting to punish their defiance. They frighten themselves into compliance . . . prey, all of them."

Baniel chuckled. "Let me guess. A rumor you sowed yourself."

"Nothing of the kind." The alien grinned. "But when they birthed it themselves, perhaps I did nothing to discourage it. Best to know who could be cowed by such rumors, eh?"

"Just so. Enjoy your night, then, what remains of it. Lessons tomorrow, perhaps?"

"Eagerly."

"Mm." The door closed behind him, taking the alien with it and, Baniel knew, any hope of that lesson on the morrow; Surela had the creature well and truly distracted. The situation suited him, however; he had everything he needed, having established the link and tested it. Further instruction would only arm the alien, and as much as possible he wanted the Chatcaavan helpless to resist any of Baniel's efforts. His brother, he knew, would be returning soon. Might even already be here, for he was not so dismissive of a ship's silence as the alien. Perhaps it was in combat with whatever forces Hirianthial had mustered in his absence.

And then he would be coming here. Of that, a certitude, for his brother was nothing if not predictable. He pondered the possibility of contriving a trap that would kill Hirianthial without any further oversight from him— it would certainly be safer to take his leave of the world (and not by using any convenient vessel offered him by an alien and his crew of thugs). But he would never be sure of Hirianthial's demise if he didn't witness it. The other predictable thing about the man, lately anyway, had been his ability to live through all the lethal obstacles Baniel had arranged. Granted, his survival through the last one had been engineered, but that was only because Baniel wanted to see him hurt before he died. A weakness, Baniel thought: his own. But it was his last, and soon he would tend it, and have no more. And then . . . the universe awaited.

He glanced through the window at the firmament. *Where are you, O my brother? How long will you make me wait?*

A shiver coursed his spine that owed nothing at all to the cold.

Waking to the sound of a halo-arch's pings and musical murmurs wasn't new. What was new was that the song they were generating wasn't some dirge describing a physical state unequal to consciousness. He was, he thought with amusement, becoming more deft at this fainting from mortal injury business. He'd also had the grace to lose his grip near a modern medical facility, and the *Moonsinger*'s was no doubt impressive.

From a distance, muffled footfalls on carpet sounded, and then a shadow hove over him and was followed by a face. Jasper's mouth gaped in a foxish grin. "And the unlikely hero awakes. Hello, Lord Hirianthial."

"Hello, alet," he answered. "Is it terminal?"

"Now that I've stitched your spleen back together? You're fresh as a new cub. And apparently as accident prone." The Ciracaana tapped the halo-arch, retracting it. "Need a hand?"

"No, I think I need the practice sitting up by myself." He smiled a little and tried it, and other than a faint tremor in his wrists and a slight queasiness, found himself remarkably hale given the situation he last recalled. "I take it the Medplex is not currently under siege by pirates."

"Wouldn't that be dramatic. No, the surviving pirates are all trussed up in the brig, and still unconscious—any idea how long that's going to last?"

"No?"

Jasper huffed. "I thought I'd ask, since you're the one responsible for their state."

"Am I." A memory of power and beauty and oneness that sent a flutter of feeling through him, warming his skin and prickling at the back of his neck.

"Lost the last few minutes of the fight, eh? Not unusual. Well, other than some nicks and scrapes, and the whole 'spleen repair failing, probably from stress' part, you're good to go, and you were the last one I was sitting watch on. Everyone else is up on the bridge."

"Was anyone. . . ?"

"Hurt? Sure." Jasper's ears sagged, and his smile was whimsical. "Happens in this line of work. Hurt enough not to mend up? No. Everyone's fine, Lord Hirianthial. And they're all waiting on you, though you won't catch them saying so."

"Then if you give a moment to orient myself, I will join them."

"Of course."

Alone, Hirianthial pushed himself to the edge of the bed and steadied himself, hanging his head and drawing in a breath. On the exhale, he spread his awareness out from core, tentative, waiting for the headache and pain.

Nothing.

Somewhere in his mind, the memory of a priest was chuckling. *God does not break His tools.*

Which explained the spleen how? he wondered.

Ah, but mortal flesh can only bear so much.

He snorted, smiled and touched his side. No doubt. Like the several wounds he'd probably taken in the fight without noticing in the adrenaline surge that had accompanied their peril. He could do with a touch more awareness of his physical state--he would keep that in mind, the next time he needed to reach for these abilities. The God gift, as Lune would have him call it, and agreeing with her he set his hands on his knees and composed himself, and said prayers he had not had the heart for since his wife's death: gratitude, and pledging. The gift must be used wisely.

And, Urise whispered, *you did not kill with it.*

"I am no Corel," he agreed, quiet, and went to find Jasper, and the others.

When he arrived on the bridge, all conversation stopped. Six faces turned toward him, their auras flaring: curiosity, pleasure, relief, a strange and powerful possessiveness. He was still sorting the impressions when Sascha hit him with an enthusiastic embrace he should have expected, shattering all those nascent thoughts with the strength of his joy: that he lived, that they all lived and had been reprieved. "Oh, Angels, arii!"

Hirianthial smiled and bent low enough to rest his nose briefly against disheveled golden hair. "There, now. No harm done, as you can see. For once."

"We were going to die. I knew it. I *knew* it." Sascha leaned back and stared up at him, earnest. "And then they all just . . . fell down. What did you *do*?"

"We're curious too," Soly said from behind the Harat-Shar. She and the others were sitting at a small table near the back wall, by the lift, framed by the read-outs above unmanned stations that whispered and flickered through their automated procedures. The Seersa's aura revealed a creamy orange curiosity, not quite intense enough to be more vivid, and no disquiet, which he found astonishing. Concern, perhaps, but for him and not because of him. "It was you, wasn't it?"

To say that he was fairly certain it was the God and Goddess working through him would probably not move the Pelted; the Alliance had its devout, but they were rarer than those who navigated their lives with little interest for the Powers. Lune would understand; Tomas . . . who knew with humans? The only one he knew well swore by the blood of patriots, by war and revolution. He chose a less fraught explanation, then. "I was not certain it was within my measure, or I would have said something. But I believe the urgency of the situation was . . . inspiring."

"Inspiring." Soly's mouth twitched.

"Almost dying does have a way of inspiring people," Narain agreed with a look of attempted sagacity.

"Seriously, though." Tomas leaned forward, interested. "What did you do? Can you do it again?"

"Probably," Hirianthial said. How easy would it be without the ship lending him the knowledge of its bones and marrow? "But it is not something I would do lightly."

"Knocking out eighty-seven people at once? I imagine not." Soly considered him. "How did you figure out how not to hit us, though?"

He looked down at Sascha, who had not yet let him go, only stepped to one side with a possessive arm still curled around his waist. Then he surveyed them all and felt only confusion. "How could I have? You are allies."

Tomas guffawed. "Just like that. Might as well be magic."

"A disciplined mind manipulating reality is not magic," Jasper retorted.

Bryer huffed. "Is right. No magic." He cocked his head. "One with the Eye, knows all things."

Hirianthial paused, arrested by the words. Then said, quiet, "Not all things. But the things that matter at the time, perhaps."

A ripple of pleasure traveled the Phoenix's close, dense aura. "You understand."

"A little more than I did before." Hirianthial glanced past the others toward the fore of the bridge, past the ramp leading to the overhanging balcony and the spreading stations that oversaw the ship's many functions. The view was beyond description; it would take the Alliance to substitute a three-dimensional display the height of his townhouse for a mere window looking out on space. The tank held several displays in addition to the swollen curve of his homeworld, its clouds in thick woolen tatters over its surface. "As I am the last awake, perhaps you might tell me how things stand?"

Soly nodded. "You know the pirates are in the brig."

"So Jasper said."

She leaned back, threading her fingers on her solar plexus and looking toward the display. "The first thing we did after cleaning that little problem up was see if we could get the computers to cough up a history for how this ship got into criminal hands. . . ."

"Tomas's doing," Narain said. "And mine. A little. Once I woke up."

At the sparkle of anxiety in Sascha's aura, Hirianthial glanced down at him with a lifted brow. The tigraine grimaced and said, "We were in sorry shape coming out of that fight."

"It was fine," Narain said to Sascha—not to Hirianthial, interestingly, "I've had worse."

Soly cleared her throat, drawing their attention back. "As we suspected, she was taken on the border in a skirmish that led into a very neat trap, and she's been missing for three months now. The crew was. . . ." She stopped, ears slicking back. "The crew is gone. We might recover them, but the trail we have to follow is probably snowed under by now. It'll be for someone else to do." She paused, gathering her thoughts from the distress that had shattered them. "There was a crew of one hundred and fifty pirates on this ship, and only a hundred and fifteen aboard. The remainder are down there, with the Chatcaavan. There's been no communication in or out of the system that we can tell, but this ship received word of its new assignment from a different vessel. We're assuming that's the pirate that made the original trip here. That ship was scheduled to continue on, so we're guessing reinforcements are on the way."

"Guessing," Tomas added, "Because it wouldn't be safe to plan otherwise. The probabilities that they're sending another warship here are low, though. This vessel is big enough to handle a world without any modern defenses, and its holds are large enough to transport some number of captives. If anything, they'll be sending a cargo ship through, not another fighter like this."

"Assuming they have more fighters like this," Soly said, tail lashing. "Which their communication records suggest they might."

"But we're not taking any chances," Tomas finished.

"I appreciate it," Hirianthial said.

"We've sent news of this upstream using the locked repeaters we dropped on the way in. Fleet needed to know about this three months ago, but better late than never. And there's a good chance they'll send a skeleton crew in to help us man this thing against anyone who might be coming on her heels. That sews up the situation in orbit . . . which leaves things on the ground." She looked up at him. "There have been fires."

Such small words, to rip through him like a blade. Fires in winter—never. "Fires."

She nodded. "There are some burned out places, and what looks like a small contingent moving up a road. Maybe about four hundred people. The other big locus of activity is further north, but I use the word 'big' with reservations . . . it's only about sixty people. Everywhere else is quiet, and there's no one outside. The palace is still intact, but if you have any allies there, they're not broadcasting their presence."

"I imagine not." Burnt-out places and an army, for four hundred soldiers together comprised an army among a people as lacking in strength as his. And where was Theresa? Surely in hiding, for if the Tams had seen the arrival of this ship in orbit they would have waited for the contact the Queen had promised, using the secure code she had given Malia to ensure their identity. "But we should have allies on the ground, if you can direct me to a comm station."

"Right. This way."

The moment of truth, then. He felt Bryer's shadow at his back, and Sascha was positively hovering. He tapped in the code and waited, and the panel chirped through its seeking protocol and then chimed acquisition.

Behind him on the tank, Malia said, "Oh, thank Iley, thank Him, you're *here.*"

They turned, all of them, and took in her expression. Sascha said, "Where's my sister? Where's Reese? What's gone wrong?"

Malia's ears sagged. "I hope you're sitting down."

CHAPTER 18

"Now what?" Narain asked after the Tam-illee had signed off to minimize the chances of the pirates noticing the communication traffic.

"More like what first?" Soly turned to him. "Lord Hirianthial? Your guidance would be appreciated on the matter. Apparently your allies in the north are taking shelter somewhere without much by way of resources. Are there soldiers among them we might recruit to deal with the situation in the palace? Or should we investigate the contingent traveling up the road, since Malia wasn't sure about them?"

Oh, he knew. Athanesin gone meant Athanesin had taken the majority of Surela's supporters . . . and they were returning from Jisiensire.

They had set fires.

And Theresa lost . . . no, worse. Theresa in the hands of his worst enemy!

He stood, leaving the chair swinging with the force of his departure, and folded his arms, back to the others.

The world continued to hang in serene indifference in the corner of the towering display, its clouds thicker than when he'd last looked. He thought of smoke. He thought of prison cells. His blood pounded so hard in his temples he thought he would lose his sight to the headache, and did not mind that he might, if he could only reach out a hand and twist those fires to other ends—

A hand touched his arm, brought with it a shocking coolth that ran his skin as swift as a sedative through a vein.

"Control," Bryer murmured. The Phoenix was standing next to him, and he had not sensed the other come. "The Eye is stillness, not the storm."

But what he wanted was to destroy—

Listen to him, something breathed in his ear.

"Like a scalpel," Bryer said. "Not the crushing gale. In this, the healer must meet the warrior."

Hirianthial slowly looked at him. The Phoenix's calm continued to streak through his body, slowing his pulse, draining the headache.

"Be whole," Bryer said. "Or fail. Your choice."

He closed his eyes and addressed the Seersa. "If you have resources to Pad north from this vessel, alet, those would be appreciated. They have gathered at a ruin, and while there is a town at its foot it is not large enough to have food or board for so many refugees. And it is cold there, and there is no heat. Have you something you might do to ameliorate the situation?"

"Supplies we can do," Soly said. She sounded more subdued. "What then?"

"Then the palace," Hirianthial replied. "Where the Chatcaavan is, and no doubt the remainder of the ship's pirates. They will not have gone with the army, and I doubt anyone would have wanted them at large in the country-side. If Malia is correct and Olthemiel and some of his men may be alive, then if we free them we have near even odds. Once we have put paid to that problem, we can attend to the army. It won't be able to come nigh in time to stop what happens at Ontine, and is too far from any of my cousin's allies to menace them either. We have some latitude there."

"All right. We can do all that. I'll coordinate with Malia about the supplies, get things moving. When do you want to attend to the palace?"

"Now," Hirianthial said.

Malia did not hug him when he stepped through the Pad tunnel and into the cold, close shadows of the trees over the Swords' camp, but she did throw her arms around Sascha when the Harat-Shar arrived on Bryer's heels.

"I'm sorry, I'm so sorry, she didn't *listen* to me!"

"Not your fault," Sascha said, ears low. "She doesn't listen to anyone when she's made up her mind. I should know."

"She's alive," Hirianthial said, without thinking, and both Pelted lifted their faces to him, frozen in their embrace. The need in Sascha's eyes made him evaluate the sensation, test it for truth, and everything in him whispered back, soft, *Yes.* "She is."

"Where. . . ."

Hirianthial looked toward Ontine, skin prickling. Not just Irine, but other things. Grief and blood soaking into soil. The cold of thin wet snow, clinging. A howling abnegation that he could touch only from this distance without flinching. And somewhere, in that mélange, the smallest of embers, dampened. Theresa? Why could he barely feel her when her yell for help had pierced him like a lance the day Baniel had thrown her over the balcony? Even at this distance, he should be able to sense her more clearly, and he couldn't. Had she given up?

. . . or was she trying not to call him?

He inhaled suddenly.

"Reese?" Sascha guessed, moving toward him.

"And afraid of bringing us to her. A trap, naturally."

"At least she's alive." The tigraine's ears flipped back. "You could maybe tell her you are too?"

"No." He shook his head minutely. "If it is a trap, and it must be, then technological communication won't be the only thing they're monitoring. Right now it's likely Baniel does not know we have arrived. I would prefer to keep it that way if he's expecting me."

"So what do we do?" Malia asked.

"Whatever it is," Narain said from behind them, "we'd better do it quickly before they figure out the ship's not responding." He dropped the rolled-up Pad he'd been balancing on his shoulder with a grunt. "Damned things are heavier than they look . . . anyway, Soly sent me. She says the re-supply is going well and they're keeping an eye on the group coming up the road. At the speed foot-soldiers walk they're at least two weeks away, though. I'm supposed to give you advice on infiltration of enemy terrain, at speed."

"And   your   recommendation?"   Hirianthial asked, curious.

"Honestly? Can you climb in your enemy's window and slit his throat while he's sleeping?"

"If I knew the room he'd claimed for his own, I would find that a meritorious suggestion."

"Why are black ops never as easy as the 3deos make them look." Narain managed a grin. "In that case, I guess we go over the strength we've got—"

A chime sounded from Malia's ear, and all of them stared at her. She touched the telegem, startled. "Is that . . . Iley!" Flicking it on, she hurried, "Who is this? This channel's supposed to be dead!"

"And it might have been if the servants hadn't been double-checking their work and found it in the Queen's empty suite."

"Val!"

Sascha took a step toward her. "Ask him about Irine!"

"Val—"

"I don't have much time. We're about to break the Swords out of the audience chamber. If you're planning any heroics—"

"We're on our way," Malia said. "Give us as much time as you've got."

"Fifteen minutes."

"We're moving. Tam out." To the rest of them, "I'll muster Beronaeth and the Swords. You—I don't know you but you're in uniform. Configure the Pad!" And then she was running for the camouflaged entrance to the tunnels. Narain was already at work unrolling the Pad and waking it.

"Oh Angels." Sascha wrapped an arm around his own middle, tail lashing. "I'm nauseated."

"You're worried," Hirianthial said. "Don't be."

"Just like that!"

Bryer said, "Will get through this. Or all die. Worry will cloud you to right action."

"Well that's encouraging."

"You'll be united with Irine on the other side of the Pad," Hirianthial said and made the gift. Had Urise not said? He took too much on himself, and there was no need. The weakness in the self was meant to be compensated by the strength in others. "Breathe, Sascha. I need you steady."

Startled, Sascha turned round golden eyes to him, ears sagging.

"I mean it," he added, quiet.

The color seeped back into Sascha's aura, hardening, and his spine straightened. "Well, then. I'm good."

"I knew you would be," Hirianthial said, and then Malia was there with the Swords, what remained of them, still disciplined despite the holes in their ranks. As they filed past, Beronaeth stopped before him and bowed, hand to chest. "My Lord."

"Second," Hirianthial said, switching to their tongue and burnishing the words gold. "You have served your Queen well in her absence. I have had report of it."

"Perhaps, Sire," Beronaeth replied, though his cheeks flushed. "But we have not done, yet."

"Not yet, no."

"My Lord . . . have you a weapon? I may make a loan to you if not. We have spares."

"I have a sword," Hirianthial said, and was surprised to discover he did not want to part with it in favor of the sort he'd grown up wielding. "It has served me well thus far. But a dagger would be useful."

"Then take mine, please." Beronaeth drew it and offered it on both palms. Like all the blades issued to the Swords, it was simple, its only ornamentation the white leather grip—and that was ornamentation enough. He remembered how quickly it frayed and discolored, and how often he'd had to strip it and replace it with fresh. "I would be honored to aid in your defense."

Careful of the other man's hands, Hirianthial lifted it free and inclined his head. For once he was glad of his language and its nuances and shaded the answer with the white mode: for symbolism, for the purity of the transaction, for the shared understanding. "Thank you."

The flush deepened on the man's cheeks, but he merely bowed again and excused himself to see to the others.

"Lord Hirianthial?" Narain called. "We've got the Pad set for some Angels-forsaken dirt hole under a balcony, if you and yours are ready."

Time was wasting. He strode to the Pad, over it, and into the shadow of Ontine.

"This is crazy," Irine hissed. "How can no one know we're here?"

"Because," Val said, "We are in the servants' corridors and no one uses these by choice. Even the servants."

Irine would have argued that point when they'd first set out, since the corridors along the exterior wall of the palace seemed no different to her than the ones on the *Earthrise;* a little narrow and very plain, but otherwise unremarkable. Now that they were in the interior halls, though, she understood; to get through them she had to turn sideways and keep her back flush to the wall, and there was no room for her to stretch her arm all the way in front of herself. She didn't think of herself as a claustrophobe, but this was taking cozy a little too far. "Still, it seems a dangerous oversight. If your enemies can be sneaking around in the walls without you knowing . . ."

"You are thinking like an alien, Lady Tigress," Val said. "An alien would treat these halls as escape routes. An Eldritch would never think of it. Some things are just not done among us."

"Like betraying your entire world to slavers?" she asked, ears flipping out.

Val paused, then shook his head. "No, that's the sort of act that proves the truth of it. If you're going to break the rules, you break them in the biggest way possible, in a sweeping, dramatic way. You make a statement. You can't make statements by crawling around in the innards of a building like a menial."

"Okay, I can see that." She shivered. "Tell me we're there."

"Almost."

Her elbows scraped against the unfinished stone

of the wall. "How are we going to get Araelis through these things?"

"I think the easiest answer to that is, 'we don't.'" Val stopped, lifted his lantern. "We hope the Queen's Tams and her Swords arrive in time to allow us to lead them out the normal way. Quiet, now. This is the door, I think."

"You think," Irine muttered.

"I'm not at my best in the dark."

She grinned suddenly, her anxiety dampened by the retort she thought but didn't share. Of course it didn't matter; she saw Val's head swing toward her, his arched brows.

"Just wondering," she said, innocent. "A girl can wonder, right?"

He shook his head, grinning, and touched his fingers to his lips to encourage her silence before exerting a gentle pressure on the door . . . just enough to crack it open. He squinted through it, then slid away and gestured for her to look.

The audience chamber was smaller than she had been imagining, and it was full of Eldritch seated and bound . . . full of them, and no one else. Irine frowned and eased the door closed again. "I don't understand," she whispered. "Where are the guards?"

Val's expression was some amalgam of amusement and wariness. "If I had to guess . . . they're outside the room, guarding the only entrance. If they stood inside the room—"

"—a room full of twenty or thirty people, then it doesn't really matter if you think they're securely bound. If any of them got free and got someone down, she'd have a weapon." She nodded. "I guess it makes sense if you don't have enough people to post in the room to make sure it's not worth the risk. And there's always a way around bondage, unless you're really, really good at immobilizing people." She rolled her lower lip between her teeth. "But there are more people in there than I was expecting. And that green and goldish color. Isn't that . . ."

"Asaniefa's mark? Yes. But I imagine if Baniel imprisoned her, her personal guards would take issue."

She frowned. "If we let them loose, they may hurt us."

"Or they may ignore us and go rescue their mistress," Val said. "Confusion to our enemies." He squinted through the crack. "We remain unworthy of notice, and I will hold that cloak over us until we assess the situation. I am going to open this door, Lady Tigress. If you are ready."

"As ready as I'll ever be."

He nodded and pushed it open.

It was a ridiculous plan, Irine thought, and it shouldn't be working . . . but she was sure there was time for it to go horribly wrong. She snuck in after Val, staying close, and true to his promise no one so much as looked their way. Olthemiel and his Swords, much the worse for their imprisonment, were bound wrist and ankle in one corner, and Liolesa's remaining supporters in another. Asaniefa's unfortunate loyalists were near the throne . . . and what a throne. Irine stopped to stare at it. So much gold filigree and carving should have looked overblown and tasteless, but the lines were so delicate and the velvet so lush against it that she couldn't help but appreciate the set-up. The Eldritch were like that, she thought. At turns glorious and ridiculous. She could appreciate the whimsy of it.

Val was bent alongside Olthemiel, whispering something as he worked on the captain's bonds. But he stopped abruptly at something the captain said, face growing hard. Startled at the change in expression, Irine stole to his side. "What?"

"Help the Captain," Val said, and was over the nearest

body before she could ask. Frowning, she started working at the (badly planned) knots securing Olthemiel.

"It is the acolyte," Olthemiel offered. When Irine looked up, he said, tired, "He is a priest, and defied them. They did not treat with him well."

"Oh no," Irine whispered, and looked for Val. She found him bent over a body. The white and pale blue of Belinor's robes made the blood streaking them devastatingly easy to see. "Is he. . . ."

"It is fortunate you're here," Olthemiel said, grave. "Your medicine can save him. Ours. . . ." He shook his hands, flexed his fingers. "I will see to my feet and my men. Do you go to the women, now."

"Right," Irine said, biting her lip. Poor Val. And Belinor. She liked them for one another, and wondered if that would ever happen. Probably not . . . but they had to get out of this in one piece so Belinor could live to make the decision, one way or the other. Leaving Olthemiel to free his Swords, Irine stole to the hostages and looked for Araelis, and couldn't find her. Frowning, she scanned the group for the most expensive-looking clothes and went to that woman instead. Was Val's 'don't notice us' field still in force? It hadn't worked on Olthemiel, but Val had been addressing him. Bending in front of the stranger, she said, soft, "Can you see me?"

The woman had been looking past her, and now her eyes snapped into focus and she inhaled. "Goddess!"

"Just a Harat-Shar, I'm afraid," Irine said, and started on the rope around the woman's wrists with the knife Maraleith had given her. "Who are you? And where's Lady Araelis?"

"I am Fassiana Delen Galare, head of the northern branch of the family," said the woman, her Universal as clear as Irine's own. "And . . . I do not know what happened to Lady Araelis. She was not brought here with us. You are our rescue?"

"One very small bit of it," Irine said. "The rest of it should be hitting the palace a few minutes ago."

"A few minutes . . . *ago*?"

It was incongruous, the stream of men in white with bared swords filing past the proofing counters. Hirianthial stood aside with the servant who'd let them in, waiting with Narain, Bryer and Sascha until the Sword's Second halted before him. "Go meet with Olthemiel," Hirianthial told Beronaeth. "Kill the enemies you encounter. We cannot risk their rising again in our wake."

"We go, my Lord!"

"Well they're taking off like kits in trouble," Sascha observed. "That leaves us to figure out the rest of this operation. Where are we going?"

"To find your captain, and anyone else my brother might use against us," Hirianthial said.

"And the four of us are going to be enough to handle any trouble?"

Hirianthial arched his brows.

Sascha said, "Right. Man who shut down a battlecruiser by thinking at it." He looked at the kitchens. "What direction, then?"

"Where do you suppose?" Hirianthial asked. "If you were cruel and wanted to rub salt in someone's wounds."

Sascha wrinkled his nose. "I'm not really into cruelty. Different wiring, I didn't get it."

"You were there when she found me."

All the Harat-Shar's fur stood on end. "Okay. Yeah. That makes sense. Let's go."

They reached the narrow stairwell leading to the catacombs when the sounds of the fight started echoing down the cold halls, but those noises were distant and diffuse compared to the sudden scarlet that spilled through his awareness, like blood from a severed artery. Beronaeth had the fight in hand, from his sense of the confusion; he left the Sword to it and gave himself to his own.

The first priest in the robes of the killing sect went down beneath the Alliance's obedient sword, and the blood hissed off it in a mist on the backswing. Behind him Narain and Bryer took on two more approaching from the rear, and Sascha remained flush to his side, untrained but guarding his flank in answer to an instinct older than sapience. The Eldritch in the catacombs did not carry any foreign weapons; they had given themselves to Baniel and the Lord's works, not to Surela and the pirates, and it made the fighting fair—more or less. What the priests lacked in weaponry they made up for in numbers, and as their screams rang through the halls, they brought fresh groups to replace the dead.

"How many of these people are there?" Narain barked, smacking back against a wall to avoid a knife swing before putting a boot to his attacker's middle and shoving him away.

Hirianthial swept the head from him for the Harat-Shar and said, "The sect of the Lord? I don't know. Most of them will have been centered in the Cathedral at the capital."

"Let's get this over with before we kill them all. Groups of three or four are fine. If they decide to rush us, that'll be trouble."

"Not enough trouble to stop us," Hirianthial said, and led them around the turn into the final hall. Quiet: until he sensed the packed masses in the rooms lining it. "'Ware the doors!"

And then there was time for nothing but the fight, and for the first flickering exchanges it was all physical effort.

Then one of the priests pushed with his mind, and it became a weaving of light and will: identifying those who wanted to cripple with their thoughts before they could succeed while keeping the ones closest to him from stabbing him. He broke through the back of the pack before Narain and Bryer had finished with the middle and paused. They had it in hand, so he took the key down from beside the only door that mattered and flung it open. The light from the corridor flooded the bare floor, raced over the woman sitting in the corner, arms tight around her knees. She lifted her head and he felt her heart stumble, and then the phoenix blaze of her joy, rising twined with streamers of disbelief and hesitation.

He answered the latter by crossing the room in two steps and gathering her face in one hand. A pause long enough to meet her eyes and be sure of his welcome, and then he kissed her, like coming home, because he was, at last.

CHAPTER 19

Surela hadn't come back.

Reese thought she would have been glad about that; Surela wasn't great company, and as one of the authors of this mess Reese was still nurturing one of the famous Eddings grudges against her. But the silence in the cell was far more oppressive than Surela's company had been, and the darkness once the candle burned out felt closer and colder, and she hated having too much time to think . . . about whether Surela had succeeded in stabbing her rapist, or whether he'd found her out and killed her first, about whether anyone was coming to rescue her and if Baniel would kill them for it, and most of all about herself and whether she'd ever been fair to anyone she loved, enough to make them *want* to rescue her.

Which of the twins had it been that had accused her of being more prickly than a cactus?

Reese rested her cheek on her knees and tried not to hate herself for all the things she'd left unsaid. She hadn't told the twins she loved them for their irreverence, and their love of life, and their acceptance of her. She hadn't hugged Kis'eh't and thanked her for being the steady core around which everyone else revolved. She hadn't made it clear to Bryer that his advice had always helped her— maybe he already knew, maybe Phoenixae were a little psychic themselves that way. Allacazam . . . what would he do without her? Would he miss her?

She hadn't apologized to her mother. Hadn't even realized she owed her mother an apology, because as much as Martian custom had imprisoned her, it had given her mother and grandmother and aunts and nieces a structure that made sense, that they valued. Defying it hadn't made her better than them. It had all been a sad misunderstanding, one of those ugly times when people's needs conflicted and no one won. If she got through this, she would send the money back that she'd borrowed. It wouldn't replace her in their hearts, but she'd promised she'd make the money back for her family, and it would be the least she could do to make up for what she couldn't give them.

And Hirianthial.

All the things she hadn't told him. All the things she hadn't apologized for, the verbal abuse and the anger and the fear, the distrust he had never earned, her condescension at his frequent failures because she'd never understood—never been willing to admit—that the things he was striving against were so huge that failure was possible. Reese had never let herself try at anything bigger than the *Earthrise*. Maybe because fleeing Mars had been the very least she could do to maintain her sanity, and she'd been too frightened to aim for anything bigger, to really chase her dreams, dreams that involved someplace to call home, someone to love her, children sung to sleep by their father as well as their mother.

She'd flubbed it all, and Baniel had thrown her in this

cell to force her to face it, thinking it would hurt her . . . but she'd needed it. Needed this moment with her back to the wall and no way to make excuses for anything.

Reese lifted her head and breathed in once, slowly, the way Bryer would have recommended. Out again, letting it all go.

All she had to do was survive this. If she did, she promised herself and all the other faces hanging in her mind's eye, if she did . . . she would be braver. And she would trust other people to forgive her for the mistakes she'd inevitably make, trying to do something more honest than get by.

Now if only she would survive this.

Her epiphany energized her, and she took to pacing. Reese counted the width of the chamber (sixteen steps, toe to heel), and the length (thirteen and a half). She felt along the walls again for any discrepancies or hidden doors, and earned herself only friction burns on her fingers. She examined the door again and found it annoyingly impervious to her plans for escape. Running out of things to do, she returned to pacing until she got tired of hearing the sound of her own boots on stone. Then she sat, and the hours crept on, and she lost track of them. She napped and woke and slept. Paced and sat and hugged her knees and cursed and waited and hated the waiting.

The door twitching in its frame made her look up. Surela, maybe? Another chance to rush the guards, at least. She was just thinking it when the door swung open completely, something her captors had never allowed. Reese blinked in the sudden light, frozen, until the shape in the door resolved into familiarity. An Eldritch—her Eldritch—streaked in red and holding a holo-sword still active, its length coruscating with lilac sparks and weeping webs of blood.

He was the finest thing she'd ever, ever seen, and she

was about to tell him so when he crossed the room faster than she could find the words. That hand that cupped her face was long enough to stretch from jaw to temple, and the thumb on her chin shocked her senseless. But she was aware enough to understand the look he gave her as a request, and with all her heart she answered it.

He kissed her.

There was fighting outside in the halls, distant sounds of effort and violence. The stench of blood and sweat and the uglier smells that came with death clung to him. The palace had to be convulsed with battle for him to be here, looking like this.

And yet, ridiculously, the only thing she thought was that she'd never been kissed, that Hirianthial was kissing her, and that it was better than anything she'd ever, ever, ever felt and blood in the soil but the twins were going to crow, and did she mention he was good at kissing?

She became aware that the kissing had stopped and that he was shaking, his brow against hers and his mouth . . . he was smiling. He was trying not to laugh. Her own lips were trying to turn up too. "What?" she asked. "What is it?"

"Thank you," he said, and the husk in his baritone almost distracted her from the words. "For the evaluation of my performance—"

Reese flushed. "Ah, I didn't mean for you to . . . well . . . um—"

"Given how long it's been since I last practiced, the endorsement is appreciated—"

"Hirianthial!" she exclaimed before he could keep going and make her light-headed from blushing, and now she was laughing. "Blood, would you stop that?"

He grinned against her cheek and gathered her into his shoulder. "Ah, God and Lady, Theresa! You aren't harmed?

They didn't—"

"Nothing. They haven't done a thing to me except throw me down here to entice you to come, and you have and, oh freedom—"

He touched his fingers to her lips. "Enough. I know he's waiting. Our allies are clearing the palace, but all their efforts will be meaningless if we leave Baniel free."

"He's a killer!" Reese blurted.

"Yes."

"No, you don't understand." She gripped his arms. "He can do some of the things you can do, I saw it—"

He was staring at her, frowning. "Wait. What is it that I see in your eyes, that is not you?"

Reese froze. "W-what?"

"Sssh. Be still." He touched his fingertips to her brow and she felt something . . . pulling, stretching, an ache like a splinter being tugged from her body. It dragged and then suddenly was gone, and Hirianthial rocked back on his foot, eyes wide. When he focused again, he said, "Val. The man who contacted us. You trust him?"

"He died for us."

"For a dead man he's remarkably mobile," Hirianthial said. "And clever, to put a warning in you."

"He did what!"

"Later, Theresa. Reese." He ran his fingers down her cheekbone. "Later for everything. If . . . you are willing?"

"Oh, God, yes," she said, catching his hand. "Please?"

"Then let us deal with our Queen's enemies, and make the time."

"Yes," she said. And then, because there was every possibility they might die, she finished before she could lose her nerve, "I'm so sorry, I didn't mean to, but oh, I'm in love with you—"

That made him very still, but not one of those bad

stillnesses. This one was like . . . like . . . someone who'd seen a unicorn in a forest, caught fast by something unexpected but longed for, something beautiful. Hirianthial brought her fingers to his mouth, kissed the back of her hand, and the warmth of his breath on her skin raised all the hair up the back of her neck. "Oh, Theresa. I love you also. And I find I am not sorry for that, so do you not apologize. Never apologize."

Did she squeak? She might have squeaked.

"Now come," he said. "We have work to do. Do you have a weapon?"

"A what?" She shook herself. "No . . . I . . . no."

He pulled a knife from his boot then and offered it to her, mouth twitching into a partial smile. "Another then, to replace the last."

"I keep losing your knives," she said, rueful. "And you're a single-dagger man—"

That pause was startlement, and then he kissed her hair quickly. "This time, I think, you may be ready to keep my offering." Folding the haft into her hand, he said, "Now, we go, ere it is too late."

Blushing, she said, "Yes."

He pulled her along by her hand—held on to her hand!—and it was sweating. Strange to think that Eldritch could sweat. She'd never observed him to sweat.

"You have never observed me in a fight this hard before either," he said, and for some reason his reading the thought seemed more like a way to save time, and a pleasing intimacy, than anything else, and that was all she had time for before she was outside the cell finally, the damned cell she was very ready to never see again, and maybe she would ask Liolesa to burn the thing down as a liege-gift or something. You could burn stone if you made the fire hot enough, couldn't you?

"BOSS!" Sascha wrapped his arms around her. "Angels damn it all! Reese!"

"Here," she said, fighting tears. "Here, one piece, promise." She looked past his shoulder and found Bryer, and if the Phoenix wasn't smiling exactly, his crest eased down and spread a little in the way she associated with his pleasure. "Where's Irine and Kis'eh't?"

"We left Kis'eh't with the Queen. Allacazam too. Irine's up there somewhere with some Eldritch boy. . . ." Sascha pushed back to look at her with frantic golden eyes.

"I promise," Reese said. "One piece." And added, "I love you too."

"Aw, battlehells. Save it for your prince."

"Different kind of love!"

"Damn . . . !"

She fought her laugh, afraid it would come out hysterical. "You haven't changed at all."

"It hasn't been that long. Narain? How's it looking?"

"We're good for now," a stranger said, another Harat-Shar with a gray pelt and a uniform that looked like something out of Fleet and had probably been prettier before being streaked with gore. "Unless you sense something, Lord Hirianthial?"

"No. But we mustn't tarry."

"Right. Lead the way."

"You behind me," he said to her, his eyes very grave and very intense. "And not to part."

"No," she promised.

He nodded once, a sharp jerk of his chin that set his hair swinging around his neck. "Then we go to cut down my brother and have done. This way, now, with a quickness."

Baniel felt the violence pouring through the corridors like sweat from a straining body. He closed his eyes, face lifted, then went down the hall. The door he wanted was unlocked and he did not knock to announce himself, but strode in to sweep the suite with his gaze.

"What is it you want?" the Chatcaavan said without interest from the divan. Under his arm, Surela turned her face away.

"Our enemies have arrived," Baniel said. Where had the alien put the woman? He'd parted her from the pack he'd had trussed in the audience chamber; Baniel had seen him do it. Hopefully the creature hadn't killed her yet. "If you wish to partake of the battle, you should finish what you're doing. I'll be in the ballroom."

"Is it likely that we will lose?" the alien asked, amused.

"Not very, though anything is possible." A muffled noise from the bedroom. Ah, finally. "Your presence is not required if you wish to remain here with your divertissement."

"Oh, I will come. I am almost done."

"Good. I have need of some of your property."

"Ah?"

Baniel strode into the bedroom and found Araelis bound and gagged in a corner. He drew his knife, slashed the ties hobbling her, and pulled her roughly upright. "You may die," he said to her. "Or you may come quietly. Or you may struggle, and I will put this knife through your abdomen. Many choices. Pick now."

Her eyes widened and then she snarled at him, lips drawing back around the fabric in her mouth.

"I thought you would make the wise choice." He took her by the elbow and dragged her in his wake.

"Leave her intact," the Chatcaavan called.

"If she does not remain intact, it will be her own doing."

The Chatcaavan snorted. Baniel left him to his pleasures, judging that Surela would keep him for long enough that it wouldn't matter. If the oldest texts were right, the alien would have just long enough to resume his pleasures before the link Baniel had been fostering so carefully emptied him of everything useful. But first, the trap wanted baiting.

He'd thought he had power enough, in his intellect, in the stupidity of others that made them so ripe for manipulation. The brushes he'd had with the power he'd borrowed from the Chatcaavan had acquainted him with a force far more potent. He was amenable to the notion of stealing that ability permanently, though if the exchange failed he would not be sorry. Corel's legacy came with significant pitfalls, if Val's little story was any indication. Himself he knew he could rely upon.

Pleased that everything was working as arranged, Baniel repaired to the ballroom to await his brother, bringing a furious Araelis with him.

Irine and Sascha's reunion wasn't pornographic only because there wasn't enough time for them to strip, Reese thought. As it was, their kiss was enough to scandalize everyone who caught sight of them, except the other Harat-Shar who (true to form) watched with a big grin and commented when they'd finished, "Finally, something worth seeing on this trip."

"Who's this?" Irine asked, wide-eyed.

"A man I like," Sascha said. "Maybe you should marry him."

"Hmm."

"Hey, Narain, got any wives yet?"

"I've been a little busy."

"He looks likely," Irine said, and leered at Narain.

Reese shook her head and went to see the ghost. Val was standing to one side, looking gaunt and exhausted . . . a lot like a corpse, in fact. She wondered why he was holding position so avidly . . . and then saw the body behind him. She stopped.

"Belinor," Val said, hoarse.

"Not. . . ."

"Not yet, no. But soon, if we do not win this thing." He drew in a breath, shaking. "So we should win this thing."

She nodded and said, soft. "We will." Then added, because it was beyond belief that she'd seen him *die* and yet he was standing here, looking at her with tragic eyes, "Did Corel resurrect himself or is that trick specific to you?"

Behind her, Hirianthial said, "Corel?"

Val managed a weak smile. "I'm no deity, Lady, I assure you. I just wasn't quite as dead as Baniel believed." He looked past her. "Lord Hirianthial."

"And you are. . . ."

"Valthial Trena Firilith," the other man said. "Former priest of the Lord."

"And dire enemy of my brother, it would seem."

"And all his works."

"Where is everyone?" Sascha said, pulling Irine after him by the hand. "I thought you were going to free Olthemial and the Swords?"

"And we have," Val said. "Along with everyone else . . . that would be the noncombatants, whom we've sent through the servants' halls, and Asaniefa's guard, whom we sent to kill pirates for taking their lady."

"You freed Surela's minions?" Reese asked, appalled.

Val met her eyes. "They've taken oaths to protect their liegelady and the last time they saw her she was being manhandled by pirates at the behest of the high priest. They don't want us. They want them. And I have to say they were doing a pretty fine job of getting them last I looked around the corner."

"It's a bloodbath out there," Narain said, trying futilely to wipe his uniform. "Knives are rhacking messy."

"So we have two sets of Eldritch fighting the pirates," Reese said. "Just because things weren't hard enough to figure—"

Hirianthial's face jerked toward the wall.

"—out?" Reese finished. "Hirianthial?"

"Araelis," he hissed. "He has Araelis." His eyes narrowed. "Nearby. The ballroom."

"And you are not going to dash off in there alone!" Reese exclaimed, fretful.

That brought him back, though his eyes remained disturbingly flat. It made their color look more like blood than wine. "No." He smiled lopsidedly. "I think I've had my lessoning about attempting these things alone."

"That's the trap," Reese added, to make sure he understood.

"Indubitably. But he is there to be taken, and he must be." He shook himself, and said, chagrined, "And here I have said we shall not be parted. But I need you to go find as many of our allies as can be spared and bring them to the ballroom. And if you can find the Chatcaavan and dispatch him . . . it's unlikely he is apart from Baniel, but if he is, then he must be dealt with. Captured, preferably, or killed if he resists."

"And while we do that, you go after your brother," Sascha said, ears flat.

"Don't worry," Val said. "I'm going with him."

CHAPTER 20

What had he learned of this stranger in the short time he'd been in-system? How much did he have to know? The power that radiated from Valthial was so hot he expected the tautness of skin that came from too close proximity to a fire, and there was a lodestone weight in it that pulled toward justice that almost, almost disguised the blood-flecked shadow Hirianthial could find no name for. It echoed like memories buried so long they'd rotted clean, leaving only bone and whispers. A perfume glided through it: roses.

"Yes," Hirianthial said at last. "Yes, I think you will."

"At your service." Val touched a hand to his chest and inclined his head in what should have been a caricature of a bow and instead felt real. To them both, he thought.

Returning his attention to Theresa, he said, "I won't engage unless needful, but the quicker you bring reinforcements. . . ."

"I understand." Her aura jangled, discord and nause-ated colors. "Don't do anything too heroic without me."

"I'll keep an eye on him for you," Val said. "But see to Belinor. I beg you."

Reese said, "I will. And you do that. Come on, fluffies, we've got a round-up to do."

"On it, Boss."

He forced himself not to watch her go, the one brightness in all the swamping dark. Instead he crouched alongside the acolyte and brushed a hand over the clammy flesh. His touch whispered back cruel stories of blows and wounds and torture. "How did you survive the culling of the talented?"

Val folded his arms behind his back. "By being one of the people executing it."

"You were a killer."

A hesitation, but there was none of the ambiguity and skidding colors of someone working up to a lie. Hirianthial thought the other man was looking in himself and hating the view. "Until I woke up one day to what I was doing." Val met his eyes. "There was no excuse for my actions. I thought it was necessary; I was wrong."

"And this bought you my brother's ire."

"He tried to have me killed, yes." Val paused. "That was the first time. The second time he almost succeeded, which is why I smell like a corpse. I'm lucky they were throwing the dead in a heap outside instead of burying them or he would have had me."

Hirianthial glanced at him. "A rather more exciting life than the average Eldritch."

Val snorted. "Given how little things change around here . . . yes. Though things are changing now."

Thinking of Liolesa's words to him when he first returned after the misfortunes on Kerayle, he said, "It appears the priesthood has had its purge after all."

"Thank His name, and Hers too. So, how are we going

to do this? You got my message, I'm guessing."

"That Baniel is tapping the Chatcaavan? Yes." A hissing whisper from his borrowed memories: Urise's disapprobation. Dire warnings of power wielded without finesse, death sentences, unpredictable results. "I'm guessing they're together."

"No idea. If he already stripped him, then the alien's dead. If he hasn't, then it's easier to have him to hand, but not necessary." Val glanced down at him. "It really is a trap."

"Let us go spring it, then."

"Without your lady's reinforcements?"

"Baniel will want to have words first. He has been waiting a long time for this."

Val rubbed his nose, streaking it with dust. "He never seemed the talkative type."

"He's not," Hirianthial said. He touched Belinor's brow, whispered a command: *Hold fast.* Then he rose, waking his sword. "But confronted with the two of us? I think he will be inspired."

The fighting in the halls had moved toward the wing of the palace where Asaniefa had been housed and the ballroom was a short distance from the audience chamber. They met no trouble, and didn't need to. Hirianthial knew what awaited them there, and that was trouble enough.

At the end of the echoing emptiness of the ballroom, standing in front of Liolesa's padded bench on the dais, was his brother, looking no worse for their separation, for the battle, for all his machinations. It would almost be unfair, save that he no longer feared this fight. The execution he had owed his brother had been delayed, that was all . . . the blow was finally falling, and the ending pre-ordained.

/You're awfully confident./

Startled by the sending and hiding it, Hirianthial said,

/You would talk to me this way?/

/Seems better than out loud, where we're sure he'll hear us./

/And you're certain he won't hear this./

Val snorted. */If he can we're rhacked either way./*

Hirianthial paused because he wanted to laugh and thought that would be a bad way to begin this encounter. */Learned Universal completely, did you?/*

/Very nice language. Like it better than our own./

"Extraordinary," Baniel said. "And here I thought you were dead. Nicely played, Valthial."

"You're an arrogant bastard," Val said, switching into their own tongue and splashing the words with conde-scending swaths of black and shadow. "You didn't even bother to check to make sure I was dead. You just assumed. That sort of thing gets you killed, you know."

Araelis was lying in a heap of skirts behind the bench, but her dress was intact, without even tears on the hems. Not hurt, then, but not conscious either, Hirianthial noted. Probably to make it easier for his brother to kill her.

"Did you really come here to talk?" Baniel lifted his brows. "You of all people? The oh so obedient minion, who consented to murder because his betters commanded it and he needed to believe? You really want to exhume our history? In front of your newest ally?"

"My newest ally has my mettle," Val said. "But I'm not here to dig up old corpses."

"No?"

"I'm here to figure out why you're the one stalling. Did your fickle alien throw off your yoke? Or did you kill him before you could suck all the power out of him?"

Hirianthial extended a feather-soft hand toward his cousin, felt her stir. */Araelis,/* he whispered. */Can you run?/*

No words in her bleary response, but she was rousing.

"Ah, ah," Baniel said. "No, I think not, my brother." Araelis vanished from his awareness as if cut away. "Very well, if you wish. Let us begin this, and have it done."

Hirianthial gathered himself and launched the attack, met unexpected resistance. Tested that resistance, found it strong and smooth to the touch. He explored it and then exhaled, emptying himself. Let his brother hold fast against the divine silence. No mortal shield could deflect the power that lived in the dark spaces between stars, and in their molten hearts.

Val's shout ripped across the hall. "NO!"

He opened his eyes, saw the knife in Baniel's hand darting toward Araelis, slowing as Val exerted himself on it.

No one expects a knife, the whispers in his head suggested, and he woke his sword and ran the length of the ballroom, to end the struggle, to commit to the execution too many years in the arrest. He reached the dais, swung, and missed when Baniel leaped inside the range, close enough to almost smash into him, the knife reversed. The forearm Hirianthial used to deflect the attack took a long slice—and from his own dagger, the missing Jisiensire knife, to boot—but missed, and none of it made sense of the leaping triumph that blazed from his brother's mind.

"Oh yes," Baniel hissed. "Give it to me, brother!"

His life? Baniel's?

Fingers skidded, slick, over the cut in his arm.

. . . and reached into him, forcing a bond and swallowing the power that was pouring into him from the welling calm, the Divine, the energy that had no ending, swallowing and swallowing until appalled, Hirianthial cut it off, choking his brother's grip and by then it was much, much too late.

This he learned when Baniel threw him halfway across

the room with his mind alone.

"You too, pathetic thing." Val froze in place and Baniel grinned. "Stalling, was I."

A furtive test demonstrated that he could move, so Hirianthial cautiously tucked his feet beneath himself and watched his brother. The aura around him was so dense it crimped the air around him—he had no doubt even the mindblind could see it now.

"Tempting to take the rest," Baniel said. "But this is more than enough. Now truly we finish this."

He could almost feel the wave poised to crash over him when a warm wash of energy flowed through him. Startled, he looked toward Val, who met his eyes.

/Take it, or we're both for toast./

As Hirianthial drew it in, Val added, /And don't open that first channel again or he'll take it all./

Was that true, he wondered? Could all he have learned about no longer relying on his own poor energy have come so quickly to naught? Could divine power be stolen?

Anything can be stolen, was the soft answer. *And anything abused. The gift is made unconditionally. Otherwise, how would They know Their own?*

Hirianthial made a shield out of Val's offering and met the crashing wave, and the battle was well and truly joined.

The halls were *gory.* She hadn't even known that was possible, but Reese was appalled at what the battle had done to them. The pirates had palmers, which tended to cauterize the wounds they made when set high enough to kill . . . but where they missed, they'd dug divots out of the wall and sent shards of stone flying like shrapnel. And the places where people had been reduced to fighting with swords or knives . . . the rich carpets had been ruined with blood and fouler things, and the walls were smeared with it. When she had to step over a shattered statue, something in her broke. She reached for someone's hand, anyone's, and got Irine's. One squeeze steadied her and she dropped the tigraine's fingers to resume being strong and lady-of-her-own-castle-ish. "There don't seem to be many people left."

"The fighting's probably closer to where the pirates were staying," Sascha said.

"Up the stairs, then."

They took the nearest stairwell and then they could hear it: the yelling and squeak of palmers and the harder, wetter sounds of bodies falling.

"Shoot first, ask questions later?" Reese guessed.

"Kind of hard to bring back reinforcements if we do that," Sascha said, peering down the hall. "Come on."

Olthemiel had solved their problem by having his men tie the remains of the ropes that had bound them to their arms like sashes. They met up near a different stairwell, beside a window.

"Asaniefa's guard have taken on the pirates," he said in response to Reese's question. "And mostly killed them, or been slain. There are some few left, from what I've seen. And yes, we can go to the Lord's aid, and will do so directly. Only—"

"Only?" Reese asked, not liking the hesitation.

"We have not seen the shapechanger."

"You might not," Sascha said. "He might be masquerading as one of you."

Reese thought of Surela and shook her chin once to rid herself of unwanted imaginings. "Where's Baniel been staying? Have you been able to find out?"

"Up the stairs again. He has liked an aerie, that one, on the top floor overlooking the lake."

"Right. Go bail out Hirianthial, please."

"At your command, Lady."

"And that leaves us to do what?" Sascha asked.

"We're going to rescue Liolesa's enemy."

"Really?" Irine said, making a face.

". . . and kill the Chatcaavan."

"Okay, that I can get behind," Irine said. "Lead the way."

There was no question in Surela's mind that she was dying. She was no apothecary to understand how, but the creature had bled her too many times, and she'd grown weak with it, so light-headed she sometimes thought she imagined her durance at his hands. But always, the alien reminded her.

He liked defiance. She'd had that from him through his skin the first few times he'd attacked her: how he'd relished her loathing and the revulsion she'd felt at his touch. How her indignation that an alien would dare use her in such a fashion excited his lust. And she'd managed to sustain those reactions for a while, letting her anger and incredulity carry her past the screaming despair that would otherwise prey on her . . . the despair she'd briefly let the human woman see in the cell.

But he had worn down her resistance, replaced her defiance with a dull exhaustion, and she could sense the arc of their interactions as he saw them playing: now that he had ruined her, he would kill her. As she'd lost more of her will, he'd become more violent, until she knew she could not have attacked him and won even with the alien's borrowed tool.

. . . but then he'd had Araelis brought in, and his mind had clouded with plans, not of rapine, but of torture and infanticide.

Surela had ceased to care about the distinctions between Eldritch Houses. The politics that had once dominated her life had fallen away in significance beside the far greater menace that she had invited into their world in all her hubris. The only thing that mattered, seeing Araelis's bloodless lips and wide eyes, was that the Chatcaavan intended to inflict himself on another Eldritch woman, and the only thing stopping him was the completion of his entertainment with her.

So she fought him. With nails on his borrowed Eldritch skin, with her teeth, with flailing limbs. She pushed past her lassitude and dizziness and forced him to re-evaluate just how far gone into meek death she was. And as she guessed, it enflamed him.

There would come a time, she prayed, that he was so certain that all she had to use against him were those nails and teeth . . . and then she'd have the opportunity to wield the needle. She could feel it against her back where he'd rolled her onto the dress he'd finally shredded to expose her.

"Second wind, eh?" the alien hissed into her ear. "I had no idea you would be such a fighter, false Queen." He stroked her flank with fingers that felt too sharp, and when she looked down she saw talons, not fingers. Would he shift on her, then? she thought, terrified. In her? She tried desperately to push him off, only to see him toss his head and begin to pant. His talons became fingers again. For an instant, this puzzled him, but his emotions surged again through his skin: no, of course. This was the shape he wanted to use. Nothing else would do.

Surela stared up at him, paralyzed, like an animal in the sight of a predator. What was happening to him? And did it constitute an opportunity?

Goddess, she prayed. She shifted away from the ruins of her corset, giving herself some room to reach it. *Let me have my chance!*

⊁

"You're saying you like her?" Irine asked, voice rising.

"No," Reese growled as she vaulted the stairs. It felt good to be moving, to be able to move without hitting a wall and having to double back. "Yes. I don't know. Hell, how did you know you liked me? I wasn't a great find or anything."

"I'd prefer to call younger Reese a work in progress."

"Well, then, Surela's a work in progress, she's just got further to go." Reese leaped onto the landing and would have darted into the corridor, but Bryer grabbed her.

"Me first."

"Fine."

Reese hung back to let the Phoenix precede them, but it was unnecessary . . . the silence on the top floor made it clear no one had come up this way, that in fact the battle soaking the carpets downstairs belonged to some other universe. "Great," she said. "Now all we have to do is open every door until we find them? We might be here forever!"

"Might as well get started, then," the new Harat-Shar said, and reached for the first.

Every door they tried spurred Reese's heart faster. They had to find the alien; for him to not be with Baniel couldn't mean anything good. She felt the time passing and her absence from Hirianthial's side like a wound, one the borrowed knife in her hand made her frantic to fix. That desperation was driving her when she tried the door that dumped her into the right suite. The noises from the adjacent room turned her stomach, but she recognized them and didn't wait for the others to come, didn't call them, didn't want to warn the Chatcaavan she was coming.

She appeared in the door, took in the scene, and forgot all of that in her rage. "*STOP THAT! STOP THAT RIGHT NOW!*"

The alien's head jerked toward her, eyes round . . .

and in that moment, Surela groped along the bed, hissed, and lunged.

Flicker of silver.

Gout of pale fluid.

The Chatcaavan howled and reared back, sliding off the needle that had impaled the eye. He covered it, head turned away, and Surela fisted her hand on the metal and drove it into his neck. When no blood met her jab, she hauled it up through the flesh until she reached something—vein, artery? What did Reese know about it?—and then she tore the creature's neck open with a scream that brought the others crowding in behind Reese.

"Quick!" Reese said, lunging for the dying alien. The Fleet Harat-Shar caught the Chatcaavan's shoulders and pulled him away, leaving Reese to catch Surela before she slid off the bed.

"Oh, Goddess, oh, Goddess, is he dead, tell me he's dead, tell me I killed him—"

"He's dead all right," Narain reported. "Battlehells, what did you stab him with?"

"Was that my pick?" Irine asked, incredulous. "You gave my pick to her!"

"She was the one getting raped every few hours," Reese growled, and hunted through the layers of sheets on the bed until she found one that wasn't stained. Dragging it around the naked woman, she said, "He's dead, Surela. Really dead, he's not going to touch you anymore."

"Araelis! Baniel has her—"

"We know. Hirianthial's gone after them. It's all right, you've done everything you had to."

Surela collapsed into her arms, sobbing, and Reese no longer thought it was strange to have the Queen's enemy hiding her face against her vest. A work in progress. Maybe they were all works in progress.

"We've got to get back," Sascha reminded her.

"I know. Narain, she needs a healer. Is there someone who can . . . do you know . . . she needs help, she's bleeding. . . ."

The Harat-Shar crouched alongside the Eldritch and squinted at her, then nodded. "There's a Medplex in orbit we can use, though I've got to arrange the logistics if someone hasn't already for the other wounded. I don't know where our Pad is."

"Can you find out? Quickly?"

"W-what?" Surela said, sniffling. "What do you discuss? Did you say healer? I want no healer!"

"You're weak," Reese said. "You need medical treatment."

"I want to die here."

Reese refrained from shaking her, but it was a near thing. "We had this discussion already. You're not ruined!"

"The Queen will execute me anyway," Surela said, wiping her eyes.

"Then at least you'll die cleanly, on your own two feet, in a nice dress. Not torn apart by a Chatcaavan not five minutes after he's raped you," Reese hissed.

Surela flinched back, eyes wide. And then she laughed, reluctant, and if it was a little shrill at least it was a sign of life. "You know how to galvanize an Eldritch, human woman."

"I've had some practice," Reese said. Sourly, she finished, "A lot of practice by now." To Narain, "You handle that, all right?"

"Time is wasting," Bryer said.

"Yeah." Reese glanced at the body of the Chatcaavan, still wearing the Eldritch façade. "But this had to be done."

"I'll take care of her, and the body," Narain said.

"Let's go, then." Reese pushed herself to her feet. "God knows what that bastard is doing to Hirianthial."

Surela's voice stopped her. "Captain Eddings." When Reese turned, the woman drew in a breath. "There, in the remains of my gown. There should be a centicore amulet. Take it and use it in my name; tell the people who still owe their allegiance to me to surrender. Show them the shield on the back and they will know it for mine." She lifted her chin. "Save their lives. Please."

Startled, Reese said. "I will."

The other woman nodded and turned away, huddling into the blanket. It was Irine who retrieved the medallion, handing it over, because Reese couldn't move; she stared at Surela, then shook herself when the tigraine tapped her shoulder. "Time to go."

"Right." And she did.

CHAPTER 21

In a people not given to intimacy or personal commu-
nion, Val knew how to throw wide the doors to his heart.
He gave of his power unstintingly, seemingly without fear
for the memories and attitudes that wound through it and
all they revealed of him . . . and everything he gave, Hirianthial took and made a shield of it, because his brother had
grown monstrous. The energy he'd stolen in blood and
brotherhood a few moments past twined with the leeching
of the Chatcaavan who, Hirianthial realized as he strove
against that pressure, *was* him: his potential, his ability, the
nerve-fire uniqueness of his own mind ripped from him by
the alien shapechanger, and it was this pattern Baniel was
using against him, his own strengths countered, his weaknesses magnified. That he could step toward his brother
at all was victory, because the short distance Baniel had
thrown him was nigh unto unsurmountable while beating
that attack away, the one that wanted to writhe into him
and make him give up, give in, die.

But he had to cross the distance. The sword in his hand

was yearning to answer his need, hot against his palm. He had only to wield it, and they would be quit of this peril.

One step. Another. A third the distance.

One step. A next. Halfway there.

All of Baniel's energy narrowed to him, and his limbs slowed. Grew weak. He forced them forward anyhow. His brother had not borne witness to the tribulations that had afflicted Hirianthial on his sojourns off-world. Did not know how they had tempered him, had made him insensible to pain and weakness. In what fight in his recent memory had he had the luxury of a healthy body, unfettered by wounds or sickness? His suffering had made him strong. He knew how to ignore it.

One step. Another.

Another.

Val collapsed, and the strength that had been bolstering Hirianthial vanished.

"Finally!" Baniel hissed, and the pressure crushed him. He fell to one knee. The sword's tip hit the floor and gouged it. Liolesa would find that remarkable, he thought. Or irritating, depending on her mood.

"No more thoughts of her," his brother said. "You won't see her again. Now, let me see what you have left to give before I kill you."

To deny him ingress would have taken power he did not have. His thoughts became a confusion as the invasion commenced: his personality, his brother's, interwoven, melting. He retreated, hid himself behind a wall he'd learned to build from a Flitzbe who'd used it to safeguard his soul while he healed, but he knew the wall would not last.

O Lord and God, he whispered, head bent. *O Lady and Goddess. Just one chance. One, I beseech you. Just one.*

His memories began to dissipate. His spirit buckled.

The onslaught was stripping him away, and still he held the sword, and braced his hand against the cold floor. His knees ached. His heart labored. But he held himself still, very still, praying for the moment.

Baniel was so deep in him that when the Chatcaavan died he felt the wound rip open, bright fountain of gore and golden hope. His brother staggered, and the attack wavered.

Hirianthial sprang from his crouch, lunged, redoubled. The sword sang as he swept it in an arc, and on that first cut it was barely visible as it passed through air and skin, but on the second it exploded from flesh in a mist of blood droplets that it flowed behind it in mist-draggled coils.

Baniel's body toppled, the head rolling off the dais, leaving Hirianthial listing over it, breathing hard. Then he flicked the weapon off. Araelis was alive and breathing, but Val was fading. He ran to the priest and dove for that flickering spirit, and now he could open himself to the Divine and he did. He gathered the lax body into his arms, brought with it the failing soul . . . saw again that darkness wreathed in it and knew it for a clot of memories that had somehow adhered from history and myth. He thought to brush it away but a hand closed on his wrist.

"Leave it," Val said, voice rough.

"And if I said to you that you were no Corel?" Hirianthial asked, gentle.

"I would still ask you to leave it." Val managed a smile. "Call it my hair shirt."

"Because you need one."

The man grinned, a foxish look for all the exhaustion sucking the vibrancy from his skin. "It'll come in handy if your Queen ends up appointing me high priest. And I'm not about to bet against that happening."

Since Hirianthial wouldn't have either, he left off, but

to say, quieter, "Thank you."

"Thank me by telling me this is over. Or almost over. Please God."

"It is. Briefly."

"'Briefly.' Figures," Val muttered, before his head rolled into Hirianthial's palm and he fainted.

"Hirianthial!"

And there, just on time, he thought with pleasure, was Reese, sprinting for him with every intent of knocking him over if she didn't pull up, and she barely managed. Hovering, she said, "What happened to Val? Where's Araelis? And where's—"

"Um, Boss, I think you shouldn't look—"

"Oh," Reese finished, staring at the dais. She looked for longer than he would have thought necessary; her pulse had accelerated, something he could taste off her aura, feel almost as if his lips were on it, on her neck. Then she swallowed and squared her shoulders, shaking him from the reverie. "So that's that, finally."

"On that count, yes," Hirianthial said. "But there is another matter left to address before my cousin arrives."

"Two, actually—"

He frowned, looking up at her.

"Yours first," she answered, sheepish. "I'm not sure how you're going to feel about mine."

"Athanesin has sacked my land." To say it out loud . . . he could barely believe it. Such things were not done. "If at all possible we should find what survivors remain."

"And then kill him, right?" Sascha said from behind Reese. "Because we kill people who torch towns."

"And then it is my right and duty to call him to account for it," Hirianthial said, quiet. "And I shall."

Reese didn't like the look in his eyes, but . . . how could she blame him for it? She was hoping there were survivors from whatever Athanesin had done, but knowing how things had gone so far. . . .

"What is this second matter?" he said, distracting her.

"Oh, right." Reese cleared her throat. "Surela's alive. We rescued her from the Chatcaavan."

"Ah?"

To put the picture into proper perspective, Reese said, "She did it. Killed the Chatcaavan."

"With my pick!" Irine added. The tigraine shook her head and crossed the floor, bending down alongside Araelis. "My own pick. Can't you keep a single weapon a person gives you, Reese?"

"I have a knife now," Reese protested, but not with much enthusiasm.

"Perhaps she was meant to heal with her hands, and not kill." Hirianthial smiled a little for her, probably noticing her wide eyes. "Yes?"

"Honestly I feel like I haven't done anything useful yet," she said, crestfallen. "Except get thrown in a cell."

"It happens," he said, and was that a touch of humor? She hoped so, anyway. If anyone could say something like that about ending up in a prison, it was him. "So, you saved Surela. I presume you had good cause."

"It's complicated." Reese dug the medallion out of her inside vest pocket and offered it to him. "She said to use this to get her guards to give up."

"Did she," Hirianthial murmured, lifting it from her palm. He turned it, frowned at the back. "I would not have expected surrender of her."

"She's changed," Reese said. At the looks everyone gave her, she said, "Fine, she's chang*ing*. It's a process. But at very least, she should have some dignity before the Queen executes her."

"We will leave that matter to her, then," Hirianthial said. "We have enough work of our own to do, beginning here." He touched Val's chin, turning the younger man's face and examining it. "Many of us are not well enough to help in that endeavor. Irine? Sascha? Has one of you a telegem?"

"I do," Sascha said.

"Let us gather our allies and finish the work here. After that. . . ." He looked drawn. "We will have grimmer duties."

CHAPTER 22

Mopping things up in Ontine proved easier than Reese had feared they might. Surela's pendant earned them the surrender of her remaining partisans and guards, and after that it was a matter of ferrying the wounded up via Pad to the waiting battlecruiser—battlecruiser!—and getting the refugees away from Rose Point and back to the palace where they could provide an occupying force and help with the clean-up. Reese finally got a formal introduction to the Fleet Intelligence personnel, and the story they had to tell her about what had happened in orbit. . . .

Now and then, when their many errands brought them near enough, she considered her Eldritch healer and boggled at the things he'd managed to accomplish. And regretted, a little, ever condescending to him about needing rescue.

Reese hadn't needed the halo-arch herself, but enough people had that there was a brief period of quiet, one where she could use a modern ship's facilities to take an actual shower and request some fresh clothes from the genie. Half a day later in response to an invitation, she let herself onto the bridge of a warship, something she'd never thought to see in her lifetime, and found the Fleet people with Hirianthial. Stepping up beside him, she dared to glance up at him. She was not encouraged by the look on his face.

"Thank you for coming," the Seersa said, her own expression grave. Solysyrril Anderby, Reese thought, but everybody called her Soly. "We have some relevant news."

. . . hopefully good, Reese thought.

"Your Queen should be here in three days."

That surprised Hirianthial out of the stillness he'd been holding at her side. "Three days? I thought she was not due for two weeks?"

"That was before we captured a battlecruiser," Soly said, ears sagging. "There are a lot of vessels in Fleet, Lord Hirianthial, but most of them are smaller ship classes. We desperately need all the heavy hitters we can muster at the front. They're scrambling a crew to man this one and get it moving; the Queen's riding along with them, and the scout she was originally issued is coming along." She glanced at Reese. "She's in the company of two of your people, I'm told? A Glaseah and a Flitzbe?"

"Yes," Reese said, grateful that at least two of their number had been spared the fight in the palace . . . but glad they would be here soon, too.

The Seersa nodded. "The scout will stay and free up the *Moonsinger* to head coreward. That's the good news."

"And the bad news?" Reese prompted.

"Is that we have better sensor data on your province, alet," Soly said to Hirianthial. "And there's not much moving down there. We're ready to undertake search and rescue, though, and can bring a shuttle down so we have access to the portable medtech and a power plant to run it."

A heartbeat pause. "And the army?"

"Hasn't deviated," Tomas said. "It's still almost two weeks out, making its way north. They're not going anywhere quickly as long as they don't run into some tech down there that we don't know about."

Hirianthial was silent a moment longer, and she couldn't tell from his face what he was thinking. "Ready the shuttle, then, if you would. Let us see if there is anyone left to rescue."

"We should be ready to go in an hour, then."

He nodded. "Summon us then, then. Captain?"

When had she become "captain" again? She followed him off the bridge, uncertain, and jerked to a halt when he stopped outside the door, turning his face from her. She wanted to say something, but knew better by now—finally—and waited instead for him to reassemble his composure. When he had, he reached and took her hand, folding her fingers in his and then resting the other hand over it. "Forgive me, Theresa, if I am numb."

Since he very likely had lost his entire family and all the people he'd felt responsible for when he'd been in charge of Jisiensire, she couldn't see how he could be otherwise. So she said, "Let's get the rest of this done and then we can worry about . . . anything else."

"Yes."

She thought that would be all, but he brought her hand up, pressed her knuckles to his brow, and she almost had to go on tiptoes to let him though he ducked his head for it. Through that contact she could feel the fine tremor he refused to let develop into anything more visible.

"But I vow it you," he said. "We will speak of what we are, and what we should become."

Reese managed a shaky smile. "A real, bona fide relationship talk, huh."

His mouth curved a little. "The very thing."

A time and place for everything, she figured. And he already knew what was in her heart. "I look forward to it."

That moment . . . Reese held it close in the days that followed. She'd never done search and rescue before, and while she'd run the usual shipboard drills after leaving Mars, the process in space was sterile: lonely and cold, something to make you aware of the vast distances the universe considered trivial when compared to the tiny spark of human life.

Search and rescue in wet wreckage, where the chill humidity had turned the ash into icy black slush that stained everything it touched, where you had to physically shove bits of charred wood aside only to be confronted with a streak of paint, a knob of gilding, something that made you feel, like a punch to the chest, that this had been someone's home. . . .

It was horrendous.

Everyone came to the task who could be spared, who had the strength for it. Reese, the twins and Bryer followed Hirianthial down, and so did all the Fleet people, even the doctor who said the patients on board the ship were stable enough to do without him. Olthemiel's Swords came too— they didn't volunteer, they just showed up, as if there was no question they would be a part of the operation. So did all the refugees from the palace who felt they could help, even children who put themselves to work running messages to people without telegems. Reese watched them darting through the ruins and wondered what it must be like to grow up in a world where a child could be inured to violence this obvious. But then, if Hirianthial and Liolesa were right, this was a world accustomed to untimely death. She shuddered.

The first day was bad. Somehow the second was worse, because they knew how little there would be to find. It was sometime into that afternoon that Reese straightened, trying to work the kinks out of her back, and heard a familiar voice say, "I pray you're not afraid of the consequences."

She turned to the figure wrapped once again in a gray coat, if cleaner than it had been when she'd seen it last. "I thought you'd be up on the ship still."

Val smiled, but there was no humor in it at all. "The four-legged doctor yonder judged I am well enough and sent me away. Particularly once I started hovering over Belinor."

"And Belinor. . . ."

"Will be fine," Val said, softly. "But he has paid bitter coin for his defiance."

Reese glanced at him. "Like some other priest I know."

"Like some other, yes."

Reese nodded, surveying the mess. "So. Consequences of what?"

"Of this."

"I'd be more afraid if there weren't consequences for this," Reese said, but Val shook his head.

"You have seen your man kill yet?"

Thinking of the fight in Surapinet's compound, Reese said, "Yes."

"In cold blood?"

That gave her pause. "No."

Val nodded. "He won't be the same man afterwards, in every way but one."

"Which one is that?"

"The one that counts."

Reese scowled at him. "I thought you were more of a straight-talker than most Eldritch."

Val chuckled softly, walking past her. "I am more of a

straight-talker than most Eldritch. Most priests, now. . . ."

She sighed and trudged after him.

By the end of that day all that could be excavated of the remains of Jisiensire's country seat had been. They had found no survivors, and almost no corpses either: the fire at the estate had been fueled with too much eagerness to leave much of anything behind. What few bodies they did find were in pieces. Reese guessed the new esophagus Hirianthial had sewn into her had given her some unexpected resilience because she didn't vomit the way a lot of the unfortunates working alongside her did. She was guessing they were able to think of the pieces as parts of actual people. Reese was having trouble with that: it was so horrible that some part of her was convinced what she was seeing were props, bits of molded plastic made to look like someone's arm or hip.

Even knowing they were real, she didn't do a whole lot to convince herself otherwise. Better to keep moving than to cripple herself when there was so much still to be done.

Afterwards, the team split into smaller groups and went by Pad to the two separate sites Soly had pinpointed in her orbital scans. These were the villages Athanesin had razed, and here they found bodies, and the looks on the faces of the dead. . . .

That night, Reese took a break in a field far enough from the edge of the village to smell something besides the memory of ash in the air. She didn't say anything when the twins joined her, or when she ended up with one head on each of her shoulders. It kept her warm, having them close. They didn't talk, which for them was strange, and their bodies were slack with more than exhaustion. Depression, she thought, and couldn't blame them.

Bryer joined them not long after, bringing a sticklight

that left a trail of golden luminance in the purple twilight. That the Phoenix didn't say anything as he crouched across from them didn't surprise her either, except he broke his silence without being prodded.

"There will be a killing for this."

"Angels, I hope so," Sascha muttered.

"I know," Reese said to the Phoenix. "And yes, I know he's going to be the one to do it. I won't take that away from him. That was his family, his life, the people he took care of, the way you people have insisted I take care of you."

A quiet. Irine spoke into it. "But?"

"But it's a bleeding army of four hundred people, and they've all got modern weapons," Reese said. "I don't want him to die."

"I'm guessing they have some sort of dueling tradition here, from what I've heard," Sascha said. "That would probably be the way he does it. One on one."

"As if this guy hasn't cheated already, by their standards?" Reese waved a hand back toward the village, almost knocking into Irine's nose. "They're not supposed to kill what they think of as peasants, either."

"Bigger weapons," Bryer said. When they all looked at him, the Phoenix flared his crest and articulated. "We have them."

"I guess," Reese said. "But at some point there won't be any people left to use the weapons, if we keep just upping the power level." She sighed and rubbed her face slowly, dragging her fingers up and down her cheeks. "I just want this to be over, so we can figure out how to live through the days that are coming after."

"That part should be easy," Sascha murmured. "One day at a time, and all that."

That made her smile, and then her telegem chimed. She touched it. "Reese."

Solysyrril: "Captain? Your Queen's made it in-system. She should be in orbit within the hour."

"Thanks, Soly, we're on our way." She tapped the telegem off and didn't move, for long enough that Irine nudged her.

"Um, Reese?"

Reese shook her head. "Nothing. Let's get back." She pushed herself upright and ambled after the twins, listening to their subdued attempts at banter and thinking about Soly's casual comment. 'Your Queen.'

She had a Queen. And a castle. And a people deeply in mourning after the violence of this short-lived revolution, a planet now forced into permanent vigil against the incursion of pirates and slavers . . . and a man who'd beheaded his own brother and then lost almost all his family. Almost all of them: there was Liolesa. Thank freedom for small blessings. Reese caught up with the others and led the way back to the camp.

CHAPTER 23

The first thing Liolesa did on stepping through the Pad tunnel was scan for him, meet his eyes, and step toward him, extending her hands . . . and he took them, and with them her fury and horror and seething satisfaction at all they'd accomplished in her absence. He searched her gaze and let her study his, and then he let himself accept that she was home and that the greater part of the responsibility had at last passed from his shoulders. He sighed, judged that they were close enough to alone, with the people around them standing so apart, to use the more intimate name. "Lia."

"Hiran. Walk with me and tell me how it stands. I want to hear it from your mouth."

He inclined his head and let her pick the route. Inevitably, she moved toward the remains of the village. Two of the Swords detached from their posts near the Alliance shuttle and trailed them, and that was their duty and their diligence pleased him, in some distant place where he could be pleased past the numbness of the past three days. So they walked, and he told her of the pirate's stolen warship and the battle to retake it; of the war in the palace, and the deaths of the Chatcaavan and his brother; of the attempt to salvage anything from the atrocity Athanesin had perpetrated on Jisiensire's holdings and their estimation of how few of Jisiensire's populace had survived. He spoke exclusively in black mode, and shadowed, until the dark of it clogged his throat and painted everything in hopelessness and exhaustion.

When he had finished she said nothing, staring into the distance. He let her have the quiet, standing behind and to one side of her, his hands folded behind his back. The wind was stiff and wet, sticking his hair to his cheek and numbing his nose. Three days of laboring in it, and he found he forgot that he was cold, though it made him clumsy. Too much to distract him. Too much shock.

At last, she said, "Lesandurel's on his way with his fixed fortifications and enough engineers to go to work on them. That's settled. And the scout will be staying after the battlecruiser you liberated departs. They had not planned to leave it, but they need the cruiser more. We will have some protection thus, until we can push through any longer-term plans."

"Of which you have many," he guessed.

"Oh, one might say so." She did not sound satisfied, however. "They are bearing fruit somewhat too late to have saved us this grief."

He stepped up alongside her, feeling her awareness of him, her wariness, and her need not to accept any palliative words. So he did not give her them, and felt the prickliness of her irritation growing alongside the reluctant fascination that streaked her aura with tarnished silver. "Well?"

All he said was, "The chances of us living our lives without grief are nil. Our lives in particular."

"Because they are so long? Or because of who we are?" She turned her face away, clicked her tongue against the roof of her mouth. "Never mind. It hardly matters, does it. This is the situation we have, and it must be faced." She glanced at him, then. "You will kill Athanesin."

A command, a question, a statement of fact? All of these things, perhaps. "Is that to be his sentence?"

She turned her face back to the ruins, and her voice was low and hard. "Need you ask?"

What other reply? "No." Something else seemed important, and he remembered after a moment. "He has an army."

"An army that Corel's heir could not contain?"

Could he? Probably. While fighting a duel at the same time? Best not to push his limits, not when heartsore. "I have a better idea."

"Good." She considered the bleak vista for long enough that he became far too aware of the cold and the ache in his joints, in the fine bones of his fingers. "Tomorrow, you will finish this. And then we can begin the long process of remaking the world in its new image."

"How does it find you?" he asked, quiet, allowing his words to glide into neutral grays. "To at last be free to do so, without political impediment?" When she glanced at him, he finished, "You have been waiting so long."

Liolesa looked up at the firmament, her profile limned by starlight, revealing its uncompromising lines, glowing in her eyes. Then she looked at him and said, "I knew that I would come to this moment after bloodshed and horror, if I came to it at all. That my plans were never meant to grow slowly, but to be torn from the body, bleeding and screaming. But for all that, Hiran. . . ." She returned her gaze to the sky. "I am satisfied. The moment has come. I am here to seize it. And our people will survive this."

"My Lady," he said.

"You'll be my Sword?" she said. "Not the White Sword, who guarded my safety. But the Lord of War, who wards my people."

That made him smile, a little. "This from the woman who took the sword as her personal emblem in defiance of the customs that mandated that a woman should bear the seal and shield alone?"

She pursed her lips. "Sooth." She considered him, then nodded. "And a nuance deftly exposed. You are right . . . you are no sword, not anymore." A grin, fierce and focused. Words gone white for hallowed ground and holy vows. "The Shield, then. Of a world. That is a better metaphor for the Lord of War, who must direct the defense of a nation."

His heart paused. The world did not; the wind still dragged at the back of his exposed neck, teasing a chime from the prayer bell at the end of the hair chain. It seemed an unreasonably cold night, a quiet one, to hold such an offer in it. The healer who was also a warrior. A task suited to his talents. A responsibility, he thought suddenly, that would give him purpose after the woman he took to wife died. He closed his eyes.

"How well you know me," he said at last.

She set a gentle hand on his forearm.

Reese returned to the camp and among the silhouettes had no trouble identifying the one she most wanted to see. "Kis'eh't!"

"Reese?" The Glaseah brightened, then jogged to her and enveloped her in a warm, solid hug, smelling of cinnamon like the pies she liked to bake. "Reese! And . . . oh, Irine, Sascha . . . Bryer . . . I'm so glad to see you all well! Here's someone who's missed you, too, Reese—oh, where's Hirianthial?"

"Over with the Queen," Reese said and then stopped as the Glaseah deposited a soft, familiar weight in her arms. Her mind exploded with a trumpet fanfare and shimmering confetti, overwrote itself with a confusion of voices and the comforting warmth of blankets after having slept in them long enough for the fabric to go knobby. She laughed and cried, "Allacazam!" and pressed her cheek to the Flitzbe's body. "Oh, am I glad to see you too. Go easy on the talking, though, you're going to give me a headache!"

Chagrin fell like nightfall, soothing the excitation of her nerves. Reese sighed and looked up at Kis'eh't, hugged her again. "It's so good to see you."

"We missed you!" Irine added.

Surprised at the extra hug but keeping her arm around Reese's shoulders, Kis'eh't said, "I missed you too. Tell me everything?"

"Everything's going to take a while," Sascha said. "As usual."

"Come on," Irine said, tugging at Kis'eh't's free arm. "Over this way. There's not much left by way of buildings around here anymore, but Soly's given us some heaters."

"All the comforts of civilization," Kis'eh't said, amused, and allowed herself to be led away. Once they'd settled around one of the thin cylinders, stuck into the soil like a torch but radiating a far more consistent and powerful warmth than any fire, she said, "All right, I'm listening."

The story took a while to come out. Reese let the twins carry it, adding her bit when it seemed appropriate, and spent the time relaxing into the realization that they were all in one place; that somehow, they'd gotten through this and were together again. She loved her crew. How had it taken her so long to realize?

Allacazam's jab felt like a stubbed toe. "Hey," she said to him. "I'm getting there! Go easy on me." A laugh then, like the tinkle of windchimes. She grinned and petted him, and caught up with the story . . . almost over now.

When Irine finished—with less of a flourish than usual, given the desolation that they were camped beside—the Glaseah blew out a breath. "Well. That's an adventure, then."

"What about you?" Reese asked. "Did you get to spend any time with Liolesa on the way back?"

"A fair amount, yes," Kis'eh't said. "I like her. She's a thinker." That earned the Glaseah some guffaws, which she accepted with a good-natured grin. "I know. A very Glaseahn compliment. But you wouldn't believe the amount of work she's been doing out in the Alliance while everyone on her world was complaining about the evil influence of the alien. Lots of risks and research and investments, almost all of them against her world here falling apart. All the way here she was making calls. If it wasn't for Fleet having the lock-down on most of the military stuff, she'd have found a way to buy a navy and gone pirate-killing herself."

"Risks and research and investments," Reese said, quiet. "Sort of like. . . ."

"Us?" Irine's ears perked.

"I guess if you're betting your world's going to need supplies, you could do worse than rescuing a few freighter captains from debt," Sascha said.

"Yes." Kis'eh't nodded. "A lot of long-term thinking. I greatly enjoyed my conversations with her. In fact, she . . . ah . . . might have asked me how I felt about becoming. . . ."

"Becoming. . . ." Reese prompted.

The Glaseah rubbed the back of her neck, sheepish. "A royal advisor."

The twins laughed; even Bryer snorted.

"You!" Sascha exclaimed. "Really? When you were lambasting this place for its backwards, feudalistic culture only a few weeks ago?"

"That's just it. She wants me *because* I find the culture backwards. Because she wants to remake it into something that isn't, while keeping it true to the principles that drove the Eldritch here in the first place." Kis'eh't managed a weak smile. "How could I say no to a challenge like that?"

"You couldn't, obviously, because you didn't." Sascha laughed. "So that leaves the rest of us to figure out what to do around here."

Reese looked down at her hand on Allacazam's fur, reminded herself to keep petting him. "I hope you know you have a place with me. I have that entire run-down castle to fix."

"You should see it!" Irine twined her tail around her brother's. "It's covered in roses."

"I'd like to," Sascha agreed. "But . . . I also think . . . I might see what Hirianthial decides to do. I'm used to following him around, keeping him from getting killed. It would feel strange to give that up." He glanced at Reese. "Of course, that might not be a problem, if the two of you. . . ."

"I don't know," Reese said quickly. She took a steadying breath, the air cold enough to lift goosebumps under her coat. Calmer, she said, "But . . . I think things are going to work out there. After all this gets resolved."

"All this," Kis'eh't agreed with a touch of a growl, looking toward the remains of the village. "Barbarism at its worst." She shook herself until her fur smoothed down and said, "Not for much longer, though, if Liolesa has her way. Speaking of which . . . I think she's heading for us."

They all stood to await the woman's approach. When she drew nigh, the Queen paused and inclined her head to them before saying to Reese, "Theresa . . . if you could spare a moment to attend me."

"Sure. Of course." Reese started to put the Flitzbe

down and stopped when Kis'eh't waved her on. "If I can bring . . . ?"

Liolesa smiled. "Certes. I am acquainted with Allacazam from the voyage."

Reese nodded. "Be good, you people."

"We'll keep the heater warm for you, Boss."

There were more fields than forests in this part of Jisiensire and Liolesa led her some distance across them, far from the rest of the camps. Keeping pace with the taller Eldritch meant having to work a little harder than she was used to, but the exertion kept her warm, and Allacazam's soothing presence, like the trickle of a distant stream, was familiar and made everything feel far less alien.

"So, my liegewoman," Liolesa began without preamble. "You have acquitted yourself well on my behalf."

"If you count leading one only partially successful raid and then getting thrown in a dungeon successful," Reese answered, rueful. "I guess Hirianthial told you what's happened here since?"

"He has, yes." The woman slowed to a stroll even Reese found comfortable. "You think your efforts useless, but anything that agitates and distracts the enemy has value. You were also responsible for the eventual death of the Chatcaavan, without which my cousin would have fallen to his brother."

"I didn't have anything to do with the shapechanger dying. That was all Surela."

Liolesa stopped and faced her. ". . . and who gave Surela her only weapon?"

Stumbling to a halt, Reese swallowed and said, "It wasn't so much a weapon as a lock pick with delusions of grandeur."

"You succored my enemy."

"I. . . ." Reese stopped. She'd known this moment would

come and yet she hadn't prepared any speeches to answer for her own actions. "Yes. She was their pawn. They needed someone who hated you to help make this trouble, and she was convenient, and yes, she did the job. But when she realized she was wrong, she tried to fix things. She tried to stop Hirianthial's brother. And for that, she got thrown in a cell with me and beaten and raped, multiple times." Allacazam's muted support helped keep her spine straight. "She was willing to kill the Chatcaavan, my Lady . . . even knowing that the only way she could do it was to wait until he was lying on top of her and stab him. And you know what? She did it. She's probably never so much as killed a chicken to feed herself, but she put a nine-inch needle through a person's eye. A person who was still raping her. And when that didn't kill him dead enough, she ripped it through his throat. For an encore, she gave me her medallion so we could get her supporters to surrender, while she was still naked and crying."

"So you think she warrants leniency."

"I think she deserves a second chance, yes," Reese said. Her heart was hammering, but she kept going. "I've been a pretty awful person myself, but people gave me another chance to grow up and learn how to be a decent human being."

Liolesa's eyes narrowed. "You did not betray your entire nation."

"No," Reese said. "But I murdered a third of the entire population of a species of sapient crystals. The only reason I'm standing in front of you now and not in some jail waiting for extradition is that they didn't want to punish me; for whatever alien reason, they spared me. *I* haven't spared me, though. I still think about it . . . that I cut down a few hundred innocent beings just because I was too proud to admit that my life wasn't working for me.

Surela's life wasn't working for her . . . but some part of that is your fault, Lady, because you keep things so bleeding close to your chest that no one realized the world is going downhill."

"I beg your pardon?" Liolesa asked, brows lifting.

"Do you think Surela could have coasted to power had everyone realized that you literally need the Alliance to survive?" Reese asked. "Your ruling class was existing in some fantasy world where food came out of nowhere if the peasants failed to grow enough and the only penalty they earned for their mistakes was you being angry at them. Those people came to your palace on their fancy horses, in their fancy outfits, and they haven't known a moment of want in their lives because you keep compensating for their mistakes."

"Allowing their mistakes to go uncompensated for would have resulted in people *dying*."

"Maybe," Reese said. "But I'm betting it wouldn't have taken many people dying for them to realize it was your way or no way at all."

"I think you overestimate their sense of duty."

"And if I am, then what the hell are they doing still ruling any of this world for you?" Reese said, her exasperation edging painfully close to anger. She forced her fingers not to tighten in Allacazam's fur. "If they could just watch their tenants die and go back to playing darts or whatever the hell it is Eldritch nobles do with all their time, then you should have killed them and gotten it over with, rather than let it come to this . . . !"

Liolesa paused, then sighed. "All it would have taken, Theresa, was me killing one of their number, and then the rest would have allied and come for my throat." She smiled faintly. "And then truly the species would be extinct, since I really am the only one with the outworld contacts to keep the food in the larders. It is not as simple as you make it out to be."

Something in the other woman's voice . . . Reese said, hesitant, ". . . but?"

"But you are correct, in that I perhaps erred on the side of covertcy. I did so because I believed that half the world would rebel if they discovered where the aid was coming from . . . but perhaps I was wrong."

Reese grimaced. "Or maybe I'm being too hard on you. But Surela . . . Surela had a few days of being queen, and I think if you talk to her you'll find she doesn't want your crown anymore."

"And what precisely am I to do with her now?" Liolesa sounded tired. "You rescued her . . . very well. You must have some notion of why she might deserve it. I cannot give her back to Asaniefa because I cannot allow Asaniefa to remain whole."

"What . . . what does that mean?"

"That the province will be given to a new family to manage, or folded under another," Liolesa said. "The blood direct will be scattered and forced to take shelter with whatever House will accept them, but they will no longer be nobles themselves. I suppose if they prefer death, they will be permitted to choose that path."

"You'd let them commit suicide?" Reese asked, aghast.

"Rather than have them live to become my enemies?" Liolesa shook her head minutely. "Theresa. This is not the Alliance. We live under different codes. We may evolve from them to something saner—and I hope we do—but until then, we cannot force people to live by a standard of conduct they do not respect. Speaking of which . . . Hirianthial will be executing Athanesin, tomorrow."

"I figured," Reese said, subdued.

Liolesa nodded. "I intend to ask him to become my . . .

defense secretary."

"I bet that has a more flowery name here."

A smile. "Lord of War, if you will."

Reese sighed and smiled. "He'll do that well. He likes protecting people."

Liolesa nodded. "So he does. Prithee, marry him directly, and do not wait."

Had the woman slapped her, Reese wouldn't have been more startled at the sudden shift in the conversation. "W-what?"

"He will linger on the matter with Athanesin if given the opportunity. And this matter with Jisiensire. . . ." Liolesa's sigh was quieter, more personal somehow. "It is a bad, bad business, Theresa. Do not give him time to become mired in sorrow. He is already given to melancholy."

"Just like that, you want me to propose to him," Reese stammered.

Liolesa arched a brow, and Reese swore there was a hint of mischief in her eyes. "You do love him? Yes?"

"Of course—"

"Do you know that it can be a fruitful union?" This, more hesitantly, which Reese thought altogether fitting given the topic.

"Yessss," she said, slowly. "Surela told me. And that my children would be like you."

"Does this concern you?"

"A little?" Reese said. She flushed. "But . . . not enough to stop me."

"Then is there some other reason you would prefer not to wed him? I assure you, I can vouch for his character." Now she was teasing, Reese was sure of it. "I have known him a good six centuries. . . ."

"I . . . I just . . . I've never asked anyone to marry me!"

"Of course you haven't," Liolesa said. "If you had, you'd

already be wed and we wouldn't be having this conversation." She smiled. "Theresa . . . on this world, women ask men to be their husbands. You are the seal-bearer of a new House, and one with powerful royal favor. If you have chosen your man, let him know. He might assume a lack of interest otherwise." Liolesa paused, and added, exasperated, "Knowing Hiran, he will. The man is positively expert at self-effacement."

"I noticed," Reese muttered. "All right. I won't wait."

"Good. We no less than you can afford wasted time." Liolesa turned and began walking back.

Reese watched her, then blurted, "What if I took Surela into Laisrathera?"

Liolesa stopped and glanced over her shoulder with narrowed eyes. "You believe, truly believe, that she has changed so much as to be safe. You trust her enough to expose her to a House that will be composed almost entirely of the aliens she despises."

Did she? Reese thought back to their conversations in the cell, remembered her surprise that someone might want to give her advice on pursuing the man she'd once wanted for herself, remembered the courage it had taken to strike back against her abusers when all her upbringing had howled for her to give in and accept her ruination and death. Tried to image the kind of bravery it had taken to face that she'd been wrong about things, and to do something about them. "If she'll accept the offer, then I'll believe in her."

"And if she does not?"

"Then . . . I guess she's yours," Reese said. "But I hope she'll be mine. I hope she'll choose life, Liolesa."

The Queen considered her, then smiled. "Strangely, you make me so hope as well. This however does not absolve me of the responsibilities I have to my own people."

"Which means. . . ."

"If she accepts your offer, I will commute her sentence from death to exile."

"Exile!" Reese exclaimed.

"Better than dying, yes? And is exile to your own Alliance, where you have lived and loved, so horrible a sentence?"

"It might be to her!"

"And if it is, then she is not the changed woman you think her to be." Liolesa shook her head. "This is as far as I can go for you, Theresa."

What could she say? A second chance was still a second chance. Maybe Surela would see it that way. Reese drew in a breath. "I guess that's fair."

Liolesa snorted and headed on. "Consider it your wedding gift."

"Great," Reese muttered. "What I really need is about four or five hundred people to help rebuild a castle in time to get through a planetary winter, and she gives me one."

Liolesa's laugh trailed back to her. That was something, Reese thought. If anyone could laugh after all this . . . that was something.

CHAPTER 24

The day dawned cold and cloudless, a welcome respite from the unrelenting gray skies that had seen him bent in the wreckage of his childhood home, his pulse quick under his tongue with outrage and horror. He'd worked through a mounting headache brought on by that wrath, until at some point the emotion had grown too dense, too large for his body to hold . . . and then it had exploded, leaving behind a numb clarity.

Would Athanesin have been able to perpetrate this atrocity had Hirianthial remained home at the helm of Jisiensire after his wife's death? Or would he have fallen too, fighting modern weapons with the relics bequeathed to him by bygone generations? He would have worried at such imponderables in the past, he knew, but he had changed. The outworld had changed him; learning to heal had changed him, the *Earthrise* had changed him, and becoming heir to Corel's legacy had changed him . . . he was no longer the man he'd been. Baniel would have loved to see him fall prey to the guilt of might-have-beens.

Urise was right. It was a form of staggering hubris to believe that he alone could save the world from grief and pain. It was not for him to take on all the evil of the world.

But this one evil . . . yes. This one evil was his.

He had not expected Araelis, having left her in the *Moonsinger*'s Medplex with Jasper. But she had come down over the Pad, dressed in a simple but clean dress and wearing her towering anger like a banner, with two febrile spots on her pale cheeks and the blaze in her eyes.

"Cousin."

"Araelis."

She faltered, then said, "We searched for the swords. They must be in Ontine somewhere, but we have yet to find them."

And it would have been good to kill Athanesin with them, fitting. But he was no longer the head of Jisiensire, and it was not as its sword-bearer that he went to this duty . . . it was as the hand of Liolesa's justice. "I have a sword that will serve."

She nodded. Then said, quieter, "What will you do? When it is done?"

He hesitated. "I cannot come back."

"I know." She looked down at her arms, folded beneath her breasts and over the heir to Jisiensire, whose father's body had not been found in the ash. "What will we do, when it is done?"

"Live," Hirianthial said. "Live to spite those who wanted us dead. And thrive."

Her head jerked up.

"For your own sake," he finished, more gently, the words softly silvered. "Thrive."

She looked away, and he saw the bead growing at the edge of her lashes. As her cousin, then, and as a man who'd found a home in the Alliance when his own home and its memories had proved too painful to embrace, he drew her into his arms. She sniffled once, but didn't weep. That was Araelis: stern to the point of stubbornness. Perhaps he'd always had a fondness for strong, sharp-tongued women.

Stepping back, Araelis drew in a breath. "Go and make an ending for me, cousin."

He inclined his head and let her go, and was still standing thus when Sascha found him.

"Soly's got it all arranged. If you're ready to go?"

"Yes," Hirianthial said. One last chore. "Let us."

A Fleet assault shuttle could carry a good hundred people, and did, depositing their party on the hill Hirianthial selected and then lifting off again to provide the air support he'd requested. Heralds unfurled the banners: Liolesa's unicorn standard, blue and white and silver, and Jisiensire's wine and bronze hippogriff. The latter was torn and streaked with soot and blood that sang when Hirianthial touched it, desperate laments that recalled the hands that had tried to hold it upright even as they'd died. He'd resisted the urge to snatch his hand back and rested his palm on the fabric until he'd answered that desperation with promises. It did not silence the pleas, but it made them bearable.

Sascha and Val were eyeing one another on the crest of the hill when he ascended it. It astonished him that he could find some amusement, no matter how muted, in this situation . . . but the sight of the two men who'd both assigned themselves the duties of his squire trying to decide which of them had more right to attend him. . . .

"Both of you," he said. "Stay with me."

No argument or pithy comment from either of them for once; perhaps they felt the gravity of the situation. Standing at the top of the hill, he could see the approaching group, winnowed by their journey but not enough for their safety did Athanesin decide to use his stolen weapons against them.

But he would not. Hirianthial had seen to that.

Liolesa joined him on the hill, furred cloak hanging heavily over her shoulders, its hood thrown back to expose the clean, uncompromising lines of the face she shared with him, through blood and family. Across her brow was a narrow coronet of diamonds and sapphires, with a rim of pearls, set in the cold gleam of platinum; she so rarely bothered with the trappings of her title, save when she rode to battle. He responded to it instinctively, and if the White Sword training found him older, it also found him cannier.

"You must expect treachery, of course."

"Yes."

"And you have some plan for it?" She glanced at him, just a sideways flick of her eyes made tawny by the early morning light.

Hirianthial said, "I do."

She waited, and when he was not forthcoming, blew out a breath in an exasperation he could feel crawling over her aura like static electricity. "If you die, my liegewoman Theresa will spit me with that dagger you gave her, and this planet's future be damned."

That made a corner of his mouth turn up, just a little. "I won't die, Lia."

"See that you don't." Lower, harder, "You have a duty."

To execute her justice . . . yes. He answered, quiet, "I am your instrument."

"Are you?" she asked, eyes distant. "Is that pride, do you think, cousin? To think that I might order the fate of a world?"

"Haven't you?"

Liolesa was silent, her breath easing from her in

pale plumes. "Theresa would have me believe that some measure of this debacle is my doing, for sheltering our people from the truth of how precarious our hold on survival is."

"Do you agree?"

"I was going to ask the very question of you." The smile that curved her lips . . . wry and fond and tired, all at once. "I cannot answer it myself."

He glanced at her then. "Even with your talent?"

"My talent comes and goes at its own pleasure, not mine," Liolesa said. "And I still have the responsibility of action when it leaves me bereft of counsel. One cannot be paralyzed by the future's uncertainty, cousin . . . because the future is forever uncertain. That is our salvation, for otherwise we would surely be hunted by insanity. We live too long, to also live without surprise." She sighed out, but her shoulders were straight and her chin high, resignation in a proud woman. "I did what I felt needed to be done. And now . . . now I will take this data into account, and modify my plans accordingly, and see if a spirit of openness will prove more salubrious. I will need to anyhow, to do what comes next."

"Am I allowed to ask?"

Liolesa smiled a little. "If I told you I owned an extra planet?"

He looked at her sharply, his heart giving a great double-pulse.

"The Alliance has a colony bureau, of course," Liolesa continued. "I had the discussion with them not long after I was invested as Queen. Had we had ships of our own to discover new solar systems, it would have been easier . . . since we did not, I had to apply to have one awarded to us, as sovereign allies without a navy. It took some time, but I assured them I had the time."

"You will send some part of us off," Hirianthial said, stunned by the magnitude of her plans.

"Jisiensire's remains, if they're willing. I still keep some contact, now and then, with Sellelvi's descendants. I have cause to believe that they would welcome a closer association with Fasianyl's family. If they are amenable, they could depart for a new world and begin fresh, absent the associations of this . . . atrocity. And they would have Alliance support." Liolesa smiled. "Lesandurel has the Tams, of course, and the Tams will come home here. I think a world tended by Eldritch and Harat-Shar has a chance of developing a unique culture of its own."

"I daresay!" Hirianthial exclaimed. And then, low, "You will build an empire."

"I will. To remain trammeled on one world . . . perhaps we will be safe this month, or this year. But the year after? All the years to come? What if the pirates arrive in force? What if they steal more of the Alliance's warships? What if the Alliance loses to the Empire?" She lifted a gloved finger to forestall his commentary. "Yes, I know, it does not bear thinking on. But it must be considered. And even if the Alliance does win, they may be winnowed to the point of vulnerability to some other enemy. No, Hiran. We can take no more chances. The Alliance will remain a firm friend, but we must foster, as much as possible, a more equitable partnership."

For a long moment he couldn't speak for the audacity of it. At last, he said, "God and Lady, cousin."

She smiled grimly. "Yes . . . well, no one has ever accused me of a lack of ambition."

"I did not realize when you asked me to be the Shield to your Sword that you meant for several worlds."

"And does that change your answer?"

He thought of a vibrant Eldritch empire, spread across

several solar systems, integrating slowly with the Pelted, humans, and aliens who had learned to call them kin, creating something entirely new from the amalgamation of outworld cultures and the perspective that Eldritch longevity could afford, were it responsibly cultivated. He imagined their people thriving, not just surviving, and felt his heart crack. The grief over Jisiensire's loss scalded like a new burn, but only as part of a longing for that future so intense he was swept away by it.

Liolesa nodded. "As I thought." A smile. "You and I, cousin . . . we are more alike than you would admit."

From behind them, Sascha called, "Hirianthial? Soly says it's time."

The Queen said, "Go on, then, dear one. Let us put an end to this era in our history and move on to brighter days and better deeds."

He bowed to her and went to her work.

Athanesin brought his army arrogantly close, reining in his horse and staring up the hill with cold amusement. "What remains of Jisiensire has arrived, I see. Are you so eager to meet the fate of your sons and daughters?"

Sascha growled behind him; he felt Val's quelling hand as a shift in the colors of their auras, cool blue pacifying the spike of magma-orange.

Hirianthial said, "Your Queen requires your surrender, Athanesin."

"I recognize no Queen. I am my own master . . . and this world's. Or has Liolesa come running home with the aliens at her back?"

"Fine words from someone who has used alien weapons to break with all the laws and customs of our people. You have killed the innocent, Athanesin, and fired the homes of tenants beholden to a Lady in an act forbidden by precedents set in place since Settlement. What makes you believe you can escape justice?"

"The fact that I've gotten away with it?" Athanesin said with a sneer. He glanced past Hirianthial at the crest of the hill, where Liolesa awaited alongside her standard, hanging limp in a day gone windless and chill. "I see she's allowed you to speak for her while she remains at a safe distance. I suppose you haven't yet tired of being the convenient tool of a woman. But I have. And I am not the only one. It is long past time for us to cease to owe allegiance to the skirts of the realm."

Hirianthial considered his opponent for long enough that Athanesin's horse sidled, betraying the man's unease. Then he said, "As the bearer of Jisiensire's swords and the holder of the world's shield, I issue formal challenge to you for the wrongs you have perpetrated against my kin and those who dwelt beneath the banner of my protection."

Athanesin laughed. "You really think I would come down off this horse and indulge myself in single combat with you? With the men I have at my back?"

"Yes."

"How brazen you are! And so misguided! You think I would put honor over my own survival?"

"No," Hirianthial said. "But this is your only chance to survive."

"And you figure this because. . . ."

Hirianthial lifted his voice. "Sascha. Please tell Commander Anderby we are ready for her demonstration."

"Yes, sir."

Athanesin snorted. "If you think to sway me with some display when I hold all the cards, Hirianthial. . . ."

"In five, Boss."

Hirianthial stood absolutely rigid, steeling himself. One breath in, one breath out.

The earth behind Athanesin's army exploded.

As carefully as the Fleet personnel had calculated the shot, close enough to frighten but far enough to avoid casualties, it was still shattering: the noise, the clods of earth shooting through the air, some of the pieces as large as a man's torso . . . the sheer kinetic energy of it threw many of the men to the ground. Athanesin's horse reared, and only his frantic efforts to bend its head kept it from bolting with him.

Hirianthial gave the opposing force time to compose themselves, and for the echoes of the shot to fade, before addressing his opponent.

"The first man who fires on us will be responsible for the death of your entire force. You inclusive."

"Are you mad?" Athanesin hissed.

"You brought modern weapons into our world. Do you not blame me if I brought bigger ones."

"So if you could slay me so easily," the man hissed, "why are you insisting on single combat?"

"Because," Hirianthial said, cold, "I want to kill you myself."

"And if I win?"

"You won't. But if you do, you can take your chances with Liolesa's justice, rather than Jisiensire's revenge."

"Not much incentive," Athanesin said.

"Come down off your horse, Athanesin, before I kill it to force you."

"You wouldn't—"

Hirianthial said, soft, "Try me."

The other man stared down at him, eyes narrowed. Hirianthial saw the twitch in his knees before the movement was fully realized and said, "If you charge me, you will die in ignominy. They will say of you that you broke your neck, tumbled by your own steed."

"You really think that pride will be sufficient goad to put me on the field with you, Hirianthial?"

"I think you have no choice, if you wish to keep the esteem of the men you purport to lead. If men we can call them after their recent actions."

Athanesin's hesitation read in his aura, a slick muddy color over the flame of his arrogance and hatred.

"Make no mistake," Hirianthial said. "You cannot escape. You can fight me and perhaps earn yourself a clean execution and a pardon for your men . . . or you can attempt to flee and die to the very weapons you invited onto our soil. Do not think you can take us with you when you die. The fingers on the triggers right now are much faster, and their weapons instantaneous. You may manage to kill me, but I am the only one in range . . . and that would be the limit of your vengeance." Hirianthial settled into an open stance. "Make your choice."

The other man glanced behind himself at his people, now holding painfully still. Then forward at the people blocking the road. With a snarl, he dismounted and drew his sword. "Fine. We shall have your pretty duel. But mark you now—I am two centuries your junior, and I am better at this than you."

"Then you have nothing to fear."

Hirianthial backed away until they'd cleared the horse's restive hooves and then woke his Alliance sword, glowing a purple so bright it left streaking lilac after-images.

"And how is that fair?" Athanesin growled.

"It isn't," Hirianthial said, and leapt for him.

One parry, Hirianthial gave him, a disengage he allowed to slice the outside of his arm on its way past.

One parry.

Then he lunged into the other man, and his fingers stroked the hilt of his foreign sword, begged it to be true, to have the reach, to make the ending. It grew narrow as a needle and long as a lance, and took Athanesin through the chest. The man paused, shocked, grabbing for the wound and losing his fingers to the blade as Hirianthial pulled it out, rocked forward, and took his head.

The sword steamed its blood mist, dripping plangent drops in the utter silence that followed. Hirianthial darkened the sword, the obedient sword, until it clicked off. Then he put it back at his belt and looked across the field at Athanesin's men. He saw one or two begin to lift their hands . . . and stopped them.

No.

They thought about resistance, but he discouraged them. There was no gentleness in it. He did not need to kill to be implacable.

No.

They let their hands drop, and he released them.

The standards came down the hill, and in their wake, the Queen. She halted beside him, bringing the aura of her satisfaction, hot as banked embers. "Recommendations, Lord of War?"

He studied the lot of them. How many had been swept away by passion and the power of the mob into acts they'd regretted? How many of them had enjoyed the violence and cruelty? How to tell? "Put them to work burying the Jisiensire dead and towing away the wreckage," he said, quiet. "And when that is done, call for them to swear their fealty to you."

"With you at my side?" she asked without looking at him, and by that he knew what she was asking.

Could he do it? Police a man's thoughts? He could, but was he wise enough to forgive error?

Some privileges, he thought, must be arrogated only to God and the Lady.

"I can watch for signs of violence against your person," he said. "But what is in the heart of a man must remain between him and the Mysteries."

A faint smile curved her mouth. "I thought you would say as much. Well. Let us put these creatures to work, shall we? Then you must rest."

"Yes," he said, feeling the strain in his shoulders and wrists and back. How tired he was, and had not realized it.

CHAPTER 25

"Looks like they've got that crowd to work with," Sascha said, climbing the hill to join her. "And Soly and most of her people are going to come down to ride herd on them too. You want to join them, Boss?"

Reese tugged the collar of her coat a little closer against the rising wind. In her free hand, Allacazam seemed to be napping . . . was that the cold or the wan winter light? She would have to ask when he woke up. "I've got an errand to do upstairs, if things here aren't teetering on the brink of world-changing disaster or anything."

"Nah, I doubt that." Sascha drew abreast of her and gazed out at the tableau: the uncertain group facing the Queen and Hirianthial, the dead body of Athanesin, the twin standards beginning to shiver in the breeze now that there was finally one blowing: not strong enough to lift the heavy tapestries, but more than strong enough to make Reese wish she was somewhere more climate-controlled. "They're not gonna try anything with all the fire-power hovering overhead, plus Hirianthial's down there mind-maging at them."

"He's going to be tired," Reese murmured.

"Fortunately there's an enormous ship in orbit with real showers and soft beds." Sascha managed a grin as he ran a hand over his hair, tousling his own forelock. "I could use one of those myself."

"Which, the bed or the shower?" Reese asked, smiling.

"The rate I'm going, I'll fall asleep in the latter and save myself the trouble of choosing." He rubbed his arms. "I didn't sleep all too well last night on the ground. Thermal blankets and sister or not."

"We could have used the Pad to go somewhere more comfortable. . . ."

"Except then we would have been abandoning Hirian-thial, and we can't do that." Sascha smiled, one ear sagging. "We did what he had to, Boss. Go on and do your errand. I'll stay down here, tell him where you've gone if he gets done before you."

"Thanks."

Reese trudged through the cold toward the Pad being guarded by the Swords, keeping her chin down where the coat could protect it and her lips from the cold. She wondered how she should feel about seeing her Eldritch healer execute someone with such skill. No, she thought—be honest—how she felt about her future husband executing someone with such skill. Because she should feel some-thing, right? Other than a small, quiet satisfaction that he could defend himself. But that was all she had, and maybe that was all right. She'd spent so much time haranguing him for his helplessness and vulnerability, and then being afraid of his competence, that it was a relief to let go of all those things and admit that all of it was just fear: fear that she'd lose him, fear that he'd hurt her, fear that she was getting too involved, fear that she was living in a world that needed that kind of violence.

She was still scared—that she was going to mess it up, this time—but strangely that was a fear she could get her arms around. She'd been afraid of messing things up for so long that she couldn't really take it seriously anymore. Allacazam even woke enough to murmur a sleepy agreement, something that felt like an extra scarf around her throat. She sent him an appreciative response.

Crossing the Pad took her from the moist cold of the early Eldritch winter to the shocking warmth of a battlecruiser's Pad facility. There were two more Swords there, standing guard in lieu of the Fleet personnel that couldn't be spared, but they recognized Reese and saluted her, which was . . . startling. She didn't know how to respond to the courtesy and settled for nodding her head the way she'd read fairy princesses would, and that seemed to satisfy them. She was halfway out the room when she realized she didn't know where to look for her quarry.

"Um, Asaniefa?" she asked. "Surela. Is she in a cell or. . . ."

"In the Medplex."

The Medplex . . . still? Had her injuries been that severe? Reese said, "Thank you," and hurried on, shedding her coat as she went. Allacazam's neural fibers started wiggling in response to the heat, and she felt his vague curiosity. "Just worried," she murmured. "You'll see."

The last time Reese had seen the inside of a Medplex she'd been recovering from her emergency surgery on that first starbase. A Fleet cruiser's Medplex was smaller, of course, but not as much smaller as she'd been expecting . . . and it had an actual wall composed entirely of an aquarium with floating fish in it. She was shocked they'd survived the pirate takeover and was still staring at them when a sardonic voice said, "The tank was nearly dead when I got here. I restarted the water cycle and released a few of the cryo-stored fish to get it going again."

Her speaker was the Ciracaana from Soly's team, looming over her as he joined her to consider the wall.

"You restocked the aquarium?" Reese asked.

"Instead of doing something more productive?" Jasper chuckled, his ears sagging. "Trust me, Captain Eddings, it was productive. For me. I needed to calm down a little. And it helps the patients, which is why the ships have them, or something like them. Now, can I help you with something? Got a contusion or two that needs attention now that all the major problems have come through?"

"I'm here to see someone, actually," Reese said. "Surela Asaniefa, one of the Queen's prisoners."

"Oh." He eyed her. "I hope you're not here to agitate her. She's not up to agitation."

"No," Reese answered. "I . . . might be the closest thing to an ally she has."

He sighed. "Fine. Follow me."

At the threshold to the room, he added, "Don't tax her."

"No," Reese promised. After he left her with one more reluctant look, she cleared her throat and said, "It's Reese. Can I come in?"

A long pause. Then: "Yes."

There was no halo-arch pinning Surela to the bed, so that was a good thing. But the Eldritch was sitting with her knees drawn up to her chest, the same pose she'd defaulted to when trapped in the cell with Reese, and that seemed like a very bad sign. The woman looked physically well, but wan and disinterested in everything around her: for someone whose presence had snapped with the vigor of a flag in a strong wind when wresting the throne from Liolesa, that struck Reese as a signal that the game was over, at least as far as Surela was concerned. And how could Reese convince her to live if she'd already given up?

"Mind if I. . . ." She pointed to a stool.

"Go ahead."

Reese dragged it to the bed and sat, setting Allacazam on her lap and resting her hands in his fur to keep herself calm. "I guess asking you how you are is kind of gauche."

Surela looked away. "Just tell me why you have come."

The abrasive demeanor, the brusque comment . . . it reminded Reese strongly of who she'd been a year ago. It firmed her determination to give Surela the same chances she'd been given. "I talked to the Queen. Your crime still merits execution, but she's agreed to commute your sentence to exile if you're willing to go."

That got the woman's attention, along with as stunned a look as Reese imagined any Eldritch ever allowed herself to show. "I beg your pardon?"

"She also says," Reese continued, "that you'll have to give up your name. That's . . . not a punishment specific to you. All of Asaniefa's being disbanded, and the tenants are going to end up working for someone else, and the nobles will have to petition to be admitted to some other House. Or, I guess, end up working on a farm somewhere themselves."

"That . . . is . . . more mercy than I expected," Surela said, but she grimaced.

"I guess Eldritch don't work on farms."

"No." Surela touched her fingertips to her browbone, eyes closing. "That is how we ended up in this contretemps."

"Nothing wrong with a good farm," Reese said.

"If it bears fruit, certainly. But our soil does not yield what we need, and so we will remain forever indebted to you." Surela sighed then, pulling the blanket up closer. "What is it you want, Captain Eddings?"

"I just wanted to bring you the choice—"

"The choice," was the bitter reply. "And what choice

would that be? To die . . . or to go alone into a world I know nothing of, where I now intimately know to be particularly dangerous to people of my race? Liolesa had given me the choice between an immediate demise and a protracted one, probably preceded by enslavement of the kind I have only just survived." Surela smoothed the blanket down, wrist shaking. "I cannot do that again. I would rather die quickly than suffer that again."

"It doesn't have to be that way!" The vehemence in her voice lifted the other woman's head, and Reese went on, "Look, you can go out there and live and thrive. Other Eldritch have done it. Hirianthial did—"

"I am no Sword to be my own defense," Surela said.

Reese stared at her. "You stabbed a man in the *eye*, Surela." She paused, then reiterated, "*In the eye.*"

"I was under duress," Surela murmured.

"And then in the throat!"

"I wanted to make sure he was dead."

"You did!" Reese forced herself not to grab her braids. How could the woman be so blind? Allacazam whispered the music of windchimes into her mind, distracting her from her distress. "All that can be taught. Defending yourself can be taught."

"That would require money," Surela said. "Of which an exile has none. Nor does an exile have references, or friends. And who would sponsor me into the alien world-scape, anyroad? 'Former traitor to her country' makes a fine recommendation. I am certain to be trusted wherever I go."

"That part I can't help you with," Reese said. "That's the bed you made and have to lie in. But the rest of it. . . ." She sucked in a breath and said, "Look, I have a ship and I can't run her anymore. I have too much to do here. But I also can't let her sit idle when there are so many things I need brought back. The *Earthrise* is used to having an Eldritch on board by now. You could go with her."

Surela stared at her, eyes wide.

"You're not going to be expected to know anything about cargo-running," Reese continued. "You'll have to learn. And you wouldn't be in charge for the obvious reason that you don't know anything about ships, cargo or the Alliance." She thought back to Kerayle and said, "I have an idea where to find the seed for a new crew. And while they're going to be good at the cargo-running part, they could use a little instruction on how to do the social engineering thing. You probably had a lot of practice with that, running Asaniefa. It won't be very glamorous but . . . it worked for me for a long time, until I figured out what I wanted with my life." She petted Allacazam, feeling the tickle of the neural fibers beneath her palm, remembering those first lonely days when it had been just her, the echoing corridors, and for a while, the Flitzbe. "I'll give you my name. I'm sure that comes with . . . I don't know. Some expectation from me that I'll keep you clothed and fed. I don't know about my responsibilities yet, but Liolesa said you can't keep your name, and it would be cruel for you not to have one."

Surela whispered, "You . . . you would trust me?"

"Most of my life I've been the opposite of trusting," Reese said. "And that held me back. A lot." She looked up and met the other woman's eyes. "I don't know, Surela. You tell me you've changed. Were you right? Am I right to trust you?"

"If I said 'yes' I could be lying," Surela said, wide-eyed.

"You could be, sure."

"I could be conspiring to sabotage Liolesa's reign again, in revenge." The other woman was shaking now.

"You could, yes."

"I could be venal, a liar, a schemer, and. . . ." Surela turned away, pressed her face into her knees, and started sniffling.

"Hey," Reese said, surprised. She reached over and set a hand on Surela's knee. "Hey, no, don't cry."

"Oh, I am a woman ruined, and no mistake. I don't deserve a savior."

Reese shook that knee a little. "Stop that. You're stronger than this."

"Am I?" Surela said. A gleam ran across the wet trails on her cheeks as she looked up. "Yon four-footed creature thinks I may be with child. What then?"

"Oh, blood," Reese whispered. "Not them?"

"Who else? I had lain with no man before the violence." Surela wiped beneath her eye with the heel of a hand. "He is not sure of it, but the signs are leading, he says. So, you want to take a traitor into your House, Eddings, and with her a child born of violence?"

"You could. . . ." Reese trailed off, unable to say the words.

Surela snorted, and the indelicacy of the sound made her seem more approachable. "You would have me commit a crime you yourself cannot even speak? You think it a crime, don't you?"

"It's not so much that it's a crime as . . . my family never had children by accident," Reese said. "You got an implant when you started bleeding, and you left it in until you mail-ordered your sperm sample and took it to a clinic to get inseminated. Where I come from, children are all wanted." She thought of her mother. "Even if they don't grow up the way you want them to. You still want them, in the beginning." Allacazam tugged her memories away from the corpse of the eucalyptus tree. "It's not like that in every culture in the Alliance, though. If you wanted to take care of it, it could be taken care of."

"I could not," Surela said, quiet. "It is not done." She

sighed. "If it turns out that I am with child, Liolesa will
have to hold off on my execution until the baby is born
anyway. Though I am sure it would please her to exile me
with a child in tow, knowing how difficult it would be for
me to raise her alone with my memories of violence to
serve as her father."

"Liolesa doesn't strike me as actively cruel."

"You don't know Liolesa," Surela said and sighed. "But
then, I am beginning to think I don't either."

"Look, if you end up having a baby, you can leave it
with us here on the world," Reese said. "She'll grow up surrounded in Eldritch and I guarantee you, no one's going
to care who her father is. They're all going to be delighted
that you managed to bring a baby to term and that Laisrathera gets to keep her."

Surela said nothing, eyes lowered and chin resting on
her knees. "I still don't know why I deserve any of your
regard," she said, quiet. "I can feel it in your palm, though
I am no mind-mage to sense the specifics of it, or your
thoughts, anything beyond the confidence of your suit. I
was vain and stupid, and because of my machinations my
world is now exposed, Jisiensire set to the fires, my House
sundered, my liegewoman dead. . . ." She closed her eyes,
fine lines etched around them. "To be executed would be
a kindness."

"Because you wouldn't have to live with your mistakes?"

Surela jerked her head up.

"Look," Reese said. "I know a lot about mistakes. I've
made a lot of them. I broke my family's heart so badly
they disowned me. I murdered a bunch of aliens because I
needed money. I treated Hirianthial like the worst kind of
dirt, and my crew not much better, most days. It would be
a hell of a lot easier if I didn't have to deal with the consequences of my mistakes. I'm trying to be brave enough to

do that." She lifted her chin. "You showed a lot of courage once you ended up a prisoner with me. Was I wrong? Because I don't think the woman who could strike back against her own torturers is going to back down from this challenge."

"You are asking me to live my life as the Traitor," Surela said slowly. "The One-Week Usurper. To be known forever for my treason the way Athanesin will surely be forever known as the Butcher of Jisiensire."

"I am asking you to be a part of my family," Reese said. "And to give yourself a chance to be known for the restitution you made for your mistakes. And to prove that I'm serious about this, I am leaving Allacazam with you." She set the Flitzbe on the bed, encouraging him to roll over to the Eldritch's side. Surela flinched, but hesitated when Allacazam leaned on her.

"What . . . what is this—"

"Put your hand on him."

Bewildered, Surela touched the fur. "It's soft." She started. "It moves! The fur moves?"

"Listen," Reese said.

Surela frowned at her, then froze. "It talks . . . !"

"This is one of my best friends in all the worlds," Reese said. "His name is Allacazam. He's a Flitzbe, and I think you might find it useful to talk with him for a while. He's . . . well, when I've been at my lowest points, he's always come through for me. If you give him a chance, I think you might find him helpful."

Surela petted him, uncertain. "It . . . he . . . really is very soft."

Reese smiled and stood. "I'll be back. Or you can have them call me, if you have news about . . . you know."

"You would truly do this," Surela said softly. "Leave your . . . friend . . . with me. Issue me the protection of your House, knowing that my actions will reflect back on you, and you the Queen's favorite."

"Yes," Reese said. And smiled, wryly. "Though I don't know how favorite I am, having argued with her about you. She thinks I'm crazy." She lifted her brows. "Am I?"

"Yes," Surela said firmly. "Yes, you are." Rueful. "I think you are well made that way."

Reese grinned. "The rest of my crew agrees with you, so that's a good sign."

The other woman was still petting Allacazam with tentative fingers. She swallowed, then said, quieter, "I don't know what my answer will be. To you. About this. I don't know if I can live so long with my own ignominy. I don't know if it's better that I should live, when justice demands my death. Perhaps there can be no healing the world while I live."

"Surela . . . no one's that important." Reese shook her head. "And justice is important, but so is mercy. You swear by a god and goddess, don't you? What do you think they'd like better? To see you dead or see you doing something positive with your life?"

"I could spend my entire life doing something positive, Captain, and still not have made up for my errors."

Reese nodded. "So why are you so eager to die before you even get started?"

Surela froze again. Then winced. "Yes. It does sound selfish that way, doesn't it."

Reese glanced at Allacazam, who was turning a soft blue as if to reassure her. She raised her eyes and said, "I won't pressure you. I know all about trying to do things before you're ready, or having people push you into making decisions when you hate all the choices you've got. Think about it, all right? And call me."

"Very well, Captain."

Outside the Medplex, Reese paused to compose herself. Was she doing the right thing? She had no idea. Maybe she really was crazy. And yet . . . she remembered Surela's remorse in the cell they'd shared, the willingness with which the woman had admitted to her mistakes. It had taken Reese most of a lifetime to be able to own up to her own mistakes with that much forthrightness, enough to really grow. She had to believe that Surela had a future based on her ability to look her own failings in the eye that way . . . or what hope was there for herself?

Back in the quarters she'd been assigned, Reese called Sascha.

"Hey, Boss. What's cooking up there?"

"I was about to ask you that myself. How are things downstairs?"

"This . . . looks like it's going to take a while, to be honest. They're spreading out these people and putting them to work digging graves."

"Digging—" Reese stopped. "Ouch."

"Their fault."

"I know." She grimaced. "So, they're going to be busy a while . . . I'll stay up here. Are you staying?"

"Until things are done, sure. How else are you going to hear the news?"

"Send up the girls any time, then, and Bryer. I'll have work for them in a bit."

Sascha's tone turned curious. "Oh?"

"I seem to have inherited a castle," Reese said. "It needs a lot of work, though."

"Ohhh. Yes, you'll definitely want at least Bryer for that. I'll find them and tell them you're looking for them."

"Thanks, arii. And for looking out for him."

"Part of the job, hey?"

"No, which is why I'm thanking you."

Sascha chuckled. "Listen to you. You're even prickly about being not-as-prickly."

Reese huffed, but she was grinning. "You all went through all the trouble of redeeming me. I'd like some respect here!"

"Respect. Got it. I'll put that on the list."

"Oh, shoo. Some of us have work to do."

"Yes, ma'am!"

Reese shook her head and petted the console with her fingers, just once. How had she deserved such people? She was so lucky. At least she'd figured it out before they'd gotten tired of trying to tell her.

Still smiling, she spread a new blank message and tried to find the right words to entice Ra'aila, Clan Flait, to come be the captain of a new trading enterprise on behalf of House Laisrathera.

CHAPTER 26

Watching his enemies bury the evidence of his previous life and responsibilities was a nearly overwhelming experience; the symbol felt too obvious, particularly when the high, bright vault of the winter sky began to clog with gray tatters. He would have found the whole thing painfully melancholic had Val not insisted on dogging his heels.

"You are attempting to keep me from brooding."

"The significant word in that statement being 'attempting,' since so far you're managing it fine despite my efforts." Val drew up alongside him. "You should let me trim your hair."

"I beg your pardon?"

"I'm a fine hand at it, as you can see. And you might as well even it. You don't want to look untidy for your wedding."

Hirianthial eyed him, then allowed a low laugh. "Fine. You have coaxed a moment of brightness from me. Are you pleased?"

"Not yet," Val said. "Maybe when you finally admit what you're really feeling. To yourself, if not to me."

"And what might that be?"

"Relief," Val said. "And guilt, because you see all these bodies and all this wreckage and it hasn't destroyed you the way you feel it should."

Aghast, Hirianthial glanced at him, and felt a psychic tug, gentle but clear enough that he almost felt like leaning toward it.

"This still exists," Val said, exerting a soft pressure on the bond. "From our fight against Baniel. Anyone tell you about what it means to draw on someone else's energy that much?"

Urise's memories tinkled together, like chimes in a wind. He sorted out the notes. "That you make a link, of course. Apparently, that it is hard to sunder."

"It can be done. We haven't yet, though. And we'll have to sit down somewhere quiet and concentrate to do it."

Hirianthial considered him. "And you are telling me this . . . because of some other reason. Because, perhaps, in the past, such links were not things to be sundered, but to be nurtured. Am I right?"

Val inclined his head.

"I see." He returned to surveying the bent shapes of the men toiling with shovels beneath a sky increasingly grim and low with clouds. In the gloom, Olthemiel's men shone in their white uniforms. "That would be an entirely new way of doing things."

"I have a number of entirely new ways of doing things planned," Val admitted. "If, say, the Queen is willing."

"Such as?"

"The Lord's priesthood has always been devoted to the mysteries . . . at least, on paper. In reality, it was devoted to the talents, and their reaping. They lived at the Cathedral, where their victims were brought to them for questioning and then killing." Val folded his hands behind his back.

"They had a lot of power and money. I'm guessing you can figure why?"

"I imagine the property of the dead came to them in some fashion."

Val nodded. "I was thinking maybe the priesthood of the Lord should cleave to more humble roots. We can be itinerants. Wander in search of the talents, not to kill them, but to bring them to places to be trained."

"New ideas!" Hirianthial murmured. "How heretical."

Val eyed him.

"Put it to the Queen," he said, more seriously. "I think you will find her a sympathetic auditor. And Theresa as well . . . in case your new order requires a place to site its first school."

"In the frozen north," Val muttered.

"Where Corel died, yes? It seems appropriate." Hirianthial stopped and said, "You took that burden on yourself, Valthial. If you truly wish to hold on to it, then I would think the symbol pleasing."

"And we're all about symbols, aren't we."

Hirianthial smiled a little. "I think we always will be. Embracing the outworld will make us more Eldritch, not less. We will have something to pit ourselves against in contrast."

"May we survive the experience."

"We will."

They watched the grim work in silence, one Hirianthial found comfortable. He was well aware of the bond that remained fallow between them, narrow but promising, and through it, a sense of Val's heart. How much more sane would the Corels of their world have been, had they been embraced thus, rather than thrust away? And yet how hard it was to push through those fears and prejudices. His life for the past year had been an exercise in observing that oscillation: not just in himself, but in others.

"I hope," Val said, quiet, "that you're not planning on standing by yourself through some two hundred odd men swearing fealty to the Queen."

"I would not think of forcing you to stay behind."

"Knowing how much I'd enjoy it." Val sighed. "What can I say. I'm Eldritch. We love punishment."

Hirianthial's mouth quirked.

The door chime that Reese answered with an idle "Come in," did not herald the arrival of her crew, whom she'd been expecting. Instead, Solysyrril padded through the hatch and came to a halt just inside the room, her hands folded behind her back and her pale ears perked. Surprised, Reese rose and said, "Commander? Is there something wrong?"

"No," Soly said. "At least, not that I know of. Which is why I'm here, actually. Can I . . . ?"

Reese motioned her to a chair and rested against the table she'd been working at, hands propped on its edges.

"Things have been hectic, so I haven't had the chance to get you alone for this talk . . . but it looks like we have some quiet time, so . . . here I am."

"This sounds a little bit ominous," Reese admitted. "Am I in trouble?"

"No. The opposite, in fact. My superiors have made it known to me that you earned the Copper Sickle not long ago."

Fleet's sole civilian citation had been awarded to her in a situation so harrowing and bizarre that Reese often couldn't quite believe it had happened. But she had received a medal, not long after also hearing that she wasn't going to be extradited for accidentally killing off several boxes full of a previously unknown alien species. That might have been part of what made the whole experience feel surreal. "Ah . . . yeah."

"And we've done the base minimum to show our appreciation by waiving the mooring fees you'd ordinarily be paying at a starbase for the *Earthrise*," Soly continued. "But I've also been authorized to fulfill any reasonable request from you."

"You've been what?" Reese asked, astonished.

"As someone not only decorated by Fleet but also now the confidant of an allied sovereign of state, we are very interested in making an ally out of you." Soly paused, then said. "No, I'll be honest. An ongoing resource. Queen Liolesa has made noises about allowing us to put a permanent base in this system, which would dovetail nicely with our needs now that the Colony Bureau is planning to push out here, far, far away from the Chatcaava. Having a presence in what's currently the furthest corner of the Alliance would be awfully good for us. And we figure if we make you happy, we'll make her happy."

"Okay, I see that," Reese said, feeling her way into a chair. "Though I'll be honest, I don't know how much influence I have with her."

Soly snorted. "You're marrying her cousin, aren't you?"

"How. . . ." She stopped and folded her arms. "Does everyone know about this but me? I haven't even asked him yet!"

The Seersa grinned. "You know how scuttlebutt is. Everyone loves gossip, especially if it's about something happy. But to turn the topic back to how this can be of help to you, Captain Eddings—"

"—you might as well call me 'Reese' if we're going to be talking gifts."

"Reese, then. I've got a battlecruiser's power-plant, genies, and storerooms here. We're not talking unlimited potential, but we can set you up with a lot of very nice things before the replacement crew arrives to drive this thing out of orbit."

"That's . . . quite an offer," Reese said. "But blood in the soil, I'll take you up on it. We can start with a few spare Pads if you have them and as much gem grid flooring as you've got, and I'll get you a bigger list once I've had a chance to go downstairs and have a better look at what I'm renovating."

"Good enough," Soly said, standing. She held out her hand, palm up. "Chances are if we do get basing rights, me and my hold will end up stationed here for a while. It's looking like pirates are going to find this corner of the universe very tempting."

Reese stood, covered the Seersa's palm with her own. "And we'd be glad to have you keeping an eye out for them, definitely."

Soly nodded and let herself out, leaving Reese standing in the middle of the room. So much to do, so much she didn't know. How much capital did she have in addition to her own? Would Liolesa give her some? Would Liolesa care how many Pelted she imported to work on Rose Point? How many of them could she give land grants to, to convince them to stay?

The Pads she had to have, at bare minimum, because she foresaw a lot of meetings at Ontine, figuring all this out. Maybe she should have asked for a few space heaters too. With a rueful smile, Reese returned to her notes.

"So this is home," Kis'eh't said, for once taken aback.

"It will be, once we make it comfortable," Reese replied.

Bryer was already moving past them toward the profusion of roses, his wings flaring a watery gold beneath the pale winter sunlight. She remembered, sudden as a blow, the wish he'd divulged when they'd been trapped by slavers in the *Earthrise*'s closet: *a garden.*

"That's one happy Phoenix," Irine said. "And I never thought I'd say that about any Phoenix."

Reese smiled and started walking toward the keep. "All right. We have a job to do . . . in this case, going through this place and making lists of things we need to make it habitable."

"Technically it looks like some of it is already habit-able." Kis'eh't squinted at the stones as they passed beneath them. "This structure is sound, isn't it?"

"It is, but it's cold enough to crack your pawpads," Irine said. "Habitable isn't necessarily comfortable . . . !"

"All right. A list of things we need to make it comfort-able," Reese said. She stopped just inside the great hall, letting Kis'eh't look around. "Soly's offered to give us some things from the battlecruiser's stores, so we should take her up on that before the ship leaves for the front."

"Right," Kis'eh't said. She drew in a long breath and said, "Oh, it smells like flowers. Inside. Even in winter! It seems . . . well, a little magical."

"To me, too," Reese said with a smile, and started to speak when the sound of footfalls in one of the nearby cor-ridors feeding into the hall froze them all in place.

"Did you leave someone here we didn't know about?" Irine whispered.

"No?" Reese said, tense. "Maybe we should—"

"Sssh," Kis'eh't said. "They're coming."

. . . and from that hall stepped an Eldritch woman wearing a sheepish expression. Felith stopped at the arch and rested her hand on it, head lowered. "Ah . . . I hope you are not too wroth, Lady Theresa . . . but I came with the fugitives fleeing Ontine in Lady Fassiana's entourage, and when they all began to return I thought perhaps I might stay and begin cleaning the castle in preparation for your arrival." The woman blushed. "It did not occur to me until just this moment that this was presumption. I swear it you, I did not intend it thus—"

Reese interrupted her by crossing the distance and hugging her, Eldritch or not. Felith squeaked, and then hesitantly rested an arm across her back.

"I didn't realize . . . I didn't even think where you might have gone," Reese said, stunned. "Not since they told me that Surela wouldn't touch the servants. And all this time. . . ."

"I hope you did not think I was lost!"

"No. I mean . . . I don't know what I thought." Reese flushed and rubbed her cheek, wondering if she could polish the blush off. "That you'd run off, or escaped, or. . . ."

"Gotten eaten by bears," Kis'eh't offered.

"Basilisks," Irine corrected.

The Glaseah eyed her, curious. "Literal ones?"

"Apparently."

Felith covered her mouth to hide the twitching smile, then said, "I admit, when the betrayal occurred and the chaos erupted, I ran for the safest place I could find and hid there . . . behind Lady Fassiana's skirts. I should have been braver."

"You should have nothing!" Reese exclaimed. "You did exactly what you had to do. Blood, you did what I wish I could have done . . . !"

Felith shook her head. "You acted just as I thought you would, Lady. As a proper liegewoman to the Queen. Which . . . brings me to another question, as I believe you do not understand the implications of my decision to be here."

"She wants to work for you," Kis'eh't said.

"Okay? Really?" Reese turned from the Glaseah and said, "Sure. Absolutely."

Wide-eyed, Felith said, "That is all? Just so? 'Yes, be one of Laisrathera's'?"

"Is there a reason it shouldn't be that easy?" Reese asked. "I mean, I assume there's going to be some tiresome divisions between staff and labor and commoners and nobles and families and who knows what other Eldritch things, but I'm not Eldritch, Felith. I'm human. If you want to work for me, if you want to help me make Laisrathera a going concern . . . then absolutely. I could use all the help I can get. And Eldritch help? Someone who can walk me through all the traditions I'm going to accidentally trample? Yes, please!"

Felith was trying not to giggle, but she managed a sober expression. "You must not trample all our traditions, Lady."

"Only the stupid ones," Irine said, indulgent.

"Which is probably most of them," Kis'eh't muttered.

"Hush, you two." To Felith, she said, "So it's my turn to ask. Knowing that this is going to be an upside-down house . . . do you want to work here?"

"Oh!" Felith smiled to dimpling. "Yes. Absolutely. I think I could grow to like a . . . more unconventional lifestyle."

"Ha!" Kis'eh't shook her head. "Unconventional! Goddess save the poor creatures here. 'Unconventional,' my—"

Reese cleared her throat.

"—Tail." The Glaseah fluffed hers. "Speaking of which, we have a castle to inventory and map, don't we?"

"So we do," Reese said, grinning. "Let's go to work."

It felt good to be wandering through the castle with a checklist, with no agenda other than to consider how she planned to furnish the place, or whether she wanted to partition off the rooms to make them easier to heat and cool, or how she could integrate modern technology without losing the architectural feel. Here and there she saw signs of the refugees' passage, in a few blankets folded in a corner, or a floor that had been swept clean of dust . . . but other than that, the castle remained vacant, waiting for its own renewal. What would the gardens be like in spring, she wondered? Maybe she should plan the wedding for then. Come to think of it, if she wanted any of her crew's family or friends to have the chance to get here from off-world, she'd have to put it off at least a month or two . . . and that was without the threat of the pirates maybe or maybe not returning.

Reese sat abruptly on one of the benches scattered on what was left of the wall walk, on the battlement still intact enough to support them. So much to do. So much to fear, still. It was funny: she'd thought that not letting herself care about things would make the fear manageable, maybe even go away. But the fear never went away, whether she was enjoying her life or not. Closing her heart only meant she had no reward for living with it.

With a sigh, Reese rose and looked over the wall into the courtyard. She could just see the glint of Bryer's feathers amid the roses. How far back would he prune them, she wondered, and smiled. He could keep the whole garden if he wanted: an Eye-trained killer, now a noble groundskeeper. Would he bring a mate here from Phoenix-Nest and hatch a nest full of proper, tiny children? She imagined Irine's kits pulling their tail-feathers and running away giggling and smiled.

This was what she'd worked toward; to think she'd almost lost it because she'd been too afraid to admit to wanting it. . . .

"Hey, Reese!"

She looked up, found Irine jogging toward her with Allacazam in her arms.

"Here," Irine said, handing the Flitzbe over. "One of the Swords on the ship brought him over. Said that he—that's he the Sword, not he Allacazam—had a message, that she said, 'yes', and that you'd understand?"

"Yeah," Reese said, petting Allacazam's fur. She sent a wordless query and received back a satisfied sound, like the hum of an *a cappella* quartet warming up. "I do. Thanks, Irine."

The tigraine eyed her. "Should I ask?"

Reese grinned and put an arm around the other woman's waist. "Let's just say that after years of other people gambling on me, I've decided it's time for me to start gambling on other people."

Irine rolled her eyes. "This is about Surela, isn't it."

"And if it is?"

The other woman shook her head. "You're the boss."

Reese snorted. "Right. So that's why whenever I told you people to do something you didn't want to do, you found a way to talk me out of it, right?"

"Well. . . ."

"Or gave me ideas that you made me think were mine but were actually yours, and then let me go on believing they were mine?"

Irine looked up at the sky. "Well. . . ."

"Or outright badgered me when I was doing something stupid until I stopped doing it?"

"It was for your own good," Irine said, sagely.

Reese started to retort and then paused. Chuckled and said, "You know, you're right." And grinned at the tigraine's gape. "Come on. Let's go talk about a wedding."

Finding her voice, Irine said, "So there's going to be a wedding?"

"I hope so."

"Have you proposed yet?"

"We've been a little busy," Reese said dryly.

"Mmm. Might want to get around to that before you start sending invitations...."

Reese sighed and smiled. "I'm in trouble when the Harat-Shar start making sense."

"We always make sense, by our standards. But yes, absolutely, let's go talk weddings!"

"Before we do, though...." Reese stopped, frowned. "Is the Sword still here?"

"I don't know," Irine answered, one ear propped, the other sagging. "Probably? Why?"

Reese pulled the dagger out of her boot and turned it in her hands. This one was plainer than the blade Hirianthial had given her in Ontine, but felt older than the one from the Alliance she'd lost on Kerayle: someone had used this one, and taken care of it. She traced the white leather girdling the hilt with a fingertip and nodded. A woman alone in a new world should have a weapon. Hirianthial would understand.

She gave the dagger to Irine. "Give this to the Sword and tell him to bring it to Surela Laisrathera. A liege-gift, from her new lady."

"You're going to lose another dagger?" Irine said, rueful, but she took it.

"Not losing this time," Reese said. "Giving." She grinned a lopsided grin. "It's not like I have any luck keeping them anyway, right?"

Irine sighed and hugged her, but Reese could tell she was smiling.

CHAPTER 27

Liolesa hosted the fealty sessions in the mud of Jisien-sire's ashen fields, so lately turned for the graves. Beneath the pewter-gray sky with its oppressive clouds, she sat enthroned on a small bench padded with a blue velvet cushion, with her hands folded on her lap and her skirts arrayed around her; the grime streaked up their hems looked like a brackish embroidery, and made her seem as if her purity was rising out of the muck. The display grated on the raw nerves of the men who came to kneel before her, already abraded nearly past bearing by the hours of digging holes and setting not only bodies, but parts of bodies into them. Hirianthial had required them to try to match the pieces when they could. They often couldn't, and would break into frustrated tears at their failures.

There were some who cherished their resentments, and he marked those as men to watch in the future. But for the most part, the service had had the desired effect. The cold, the pathetic remains of children and women, the hard labor, all of it had bewildered them, worn them down. Liolesa's stately regard, stern and distant as any matriarch's, undid the majority of them completely. Their guilt made them hers.

The effort of concentrating on each petitioner as he recited the loyalty oath—concentrating and not affecting—was exacerbated by Hirianthial's own exhaustion. The damp cold was particularly enervating, and his knees and shoulders and wrists ached with it. Olthemiel was a welcome addition, standing watch over the Queen's physical safety at her opposite shoulder, though Hirianthial thought he could stay an attacker faster than Olthemiel could. Even so, his mental faculties were tired. *He* was tired.

/Not long now,/ Val offered from behind him, his voice colored with a gray softness.

/I know./

He felt rather than saw the younger man's nod and applied himself to the next stranger to drop to his knees before his cousin.

She was magnificent, Liolesa. A woman given to quick tempers, impatient with ignorance and stupidity and incompetence and often domineering, she was nevertheless invested with an air of command entirely owed to how far she looked into the future, and all she did to secure that future. Mistakes did not frighten her; inaction did. That assurance clung to her like a mantle, and Hirianthial watched her personally accept the allegiance of every single man Athanesin had put to the task of razing Jisiensire, knowing that they had but this one chance to prove themselves to her. Did they wreak such an atrocity again, their necks would meet a sword.

They knew it, too.

Afterwards, he took the group assigned to him and brought them to Lady Fassiana. The northern Galares had agreed to scatter the men amongst their numbers; it was not the best solution, but it was the only one they could all live with. Literally, in the case of the criminals. He was watching the last of them follow their new mistress toward the Alliance's Pads when Liolesa joined him.

"That's done," he said at last, wondering at the satisfaction in her aura. It seemed too soft a sunrise gold for the work they'd put in, no matter how glad he might be that it was behind them.

"So it is, and hopefully for good and true." She nodded. "Gather up your priest, then, cousin. There's a thing I'd like to reward you with." She held up a finger. "And do not tell me 'I have done nothing worthy of reward.' Or I will set your mortal family on you."

He narrowed his eyes at her. "You *are* cruel."

"Only to those what cling too hard to an improper humility," she replied airily. Was she? She was pleased, truly pleased. He wondered what had inspired her mood. "Meet me at the Pad."

Accordingly, he found Val and presented himself to her, and together they crossed onto the *Moonsinger.* There she led them to the lift.

/What's this about?/

/I have not the first notion. But one does not argue with a Queen./

/Even if she's your cousin?/

Hirianthial eyed him, amused despite his fatigue. /Especially so./

On the bridge, Liolesa joined Solysyrril in front of the enormous holoscreen: tall Eldritch, pale-hair wound on her head, pale nape of the neck exposed, alongside the much shorter white Seersa, her white hair brushing the shoulders of her dark uniform. "Is it about time?"

"It is, and I still don't know how you figured it out so quickly," Soly said, bemused.

"I'm good at guessing."

Hirianthial shook his head a little at the glint of merriment that danced over Lia's aura at the demurring. 'Good at guessing.' He supposed that was one way to characterize her talent for pattern-sensing.

"Can we see them yet?"

"We can if we magnify the image . . . they've been coasting in-system for long enough. Lune, will you put it up for us?"

"Yes, sir."

A series of pin-pricks in the tank swelled into focus, became an enormous vessel haloed in four smaller ships, barely large enough to be seen against its flanks.

"Lord and Lady," Val said. "What is that thing? A floating moon?"

"That," Liolesa said, "is Hirianthial's cousin, Lesandurel."

"Did he buy a colony ship, then?" Hirianthial asked, startled.

"That's a builder/wrecker, actually, Lord Hirianthial." Soly reached a hand into the display, grasping the ship and pulling a glowing blueline of it onto a different part of the tank. "Used for putting together other ships, or space stations. Mostly engineering and industrial capacity onboard, but a lot of storage, too. You could park it in orbit and have the beginnings of a very useful manufacturing platform . . . which I'm guessing is the intention."

"Did that use up the Meriaen fortune, then?" Hirianthial asked his cousin.

"Nine generations of investment off-world can accrue a great deal of money," Liolesa said. "I'd be surprised if your cousin is penniless even now."

"What about the other ships?" Val asked, stepping closer to examine them.

"Three of them are the couriers run by the Queen's

Tams," Liolesa said. "The last a personal transport. Probably Lesandurel's."

In their tongue, Hirianthial said, "You have brought a Jisiensire home, now that you are sending most of them away."

"Somewhat," Liolesa replied in kind, the words cautiously neutral in gray. "I doubt Lesandurel will want to stay."

"But?"

"But who can know every pattern?" she said. "Perhaps he will marry and start a homeworld branch of the Jisiensires to replace the ones who are leaving to colonize our new world."

Val glanced over his shoulder and said, "And Lord Hirianthial doesn't count as a branch of the Jisiensires, is that it?"

"That would depend entirely on him," Liolesa said, unfazed. In Universal, she said, "Commander Anderby? How long until they arrive, do you think?"

"Oh, two hours, maybe?" Soly glanced at Lune, who inclined her head. "Give them two hours. You can talk to them now, if you want. We've got the repeaters in-system."

Liolesa grinned. "Yes, let's."

"Hail them, Lune, and put them up when they answer."

The call went out, was received, was responded to. Part of the holo-screen blanked, reformed into an astonishing image of the wide bridge of a ship. Lesandurel was there, in a chair near the center seat but not in it, and he was surrounded—surrounded—by foxes. Golden Tam-illee and ruddy, milk-white and black, pelts gray and silver and sorrel; ears tipped in black or blond or unmarked; flat faces or more animal ones, green eyes and blue and golden and orange and brown. . . .

He was not the only Eldritch in this sea of foxishness:

Urise was comfortably resting in one of the high-backed chairs lining the edge of the bridge, beaming, looking—again—as if he had been merely transplanted from one seat to another.

"Meriaen," Liolesa said, amused. "You come in good time, and with gifts."

"As you see, my Lady. We are home."

"And you!" Hirianthial exclaimed to Urise.

The old priest grinned. "These are some fine young creatures your House cousin has yoked to his banner." The two Tam-illee beside him looked down at his head with expressions so merry Hirianthial could almost sense their auras dancing across the distance. "It has been a most rewarding excursion."

"We bring you the materials for our first orbital station," Lesandurel said, more formally, "as well as enough materiel to improve and enlarge the base on the moon. The three couriers came as escort, and my own personal ship I brought for when I make my inevitable escapes back to civilization." He pressed a hand to his breast and inclined his head. "No offense intended, my Queen. But our world is a touch backwards for someone accustomed to the Alliance."

"No offense taken, since you have come bearing the tools by which we might begin to address that," she said. "When you reach orbit, do come over that we might discuss the details?"

"It would be my pleasure, my Lady."

"And mine." She smiled. "Welcome home."

"Thank you. Meriaen out."

"And thank you, Commander, for this."

"My duty, Your Majesty."

Liolesa nodded and turned to the two Eldritch, returning to their tongue. "You need not stay, though at some point you should greet your kinsman, cousin. It need not be soon. There are things he and I need to discuss that will be of interest to you, but you have your own duties first."

"Do I?" he asked.

She smiled a little. "See to the succession, cousin."

That was as plain a dismissal as he was ever to receive from her, and as far as she would command him in matters of the heart. He smiled faintly and bowed to her, then left with Val at his heels.

"She always boss you around like that?" Val asked, switching to Universal—for its informality, Hirianthial guessed, and didn't blame him. The intimacy afforded by their own tongue seemed limited in its use, given the far greater intimacy of the occasional mindtouches they exchanged.

"She has a commanding personality."

Val snorted. "Now there's as neat-footed a dodge as I've heard in a while, and I've been living on this bloody planet all my life."

Hirianthial laughed. "It's fine. She would not be Liolesa, if she was not also Queen."

"Mmm. So now what?"

Two hours, she'd said, until Lesandurel arrived . . . and no need to rush his return. How strange it was to finally be free, to have a respite from responsibility and ugly duty. How to fill those hours?

How else?

"Now," Hirianthial said, "I think I will allow you to trim my hair, as you promised."

Reese was in the great hall when Hirianthial stepped over the Pad. And because he stopped to lift his head and feel the age and weight of the place, she looked at him, could look at him . . . and this time, didn't see the fancy clothes she could never have afforded, and the grace that used to make her feel awkward, and the gravitas that had humbled her, when being humbled had been a recipe for resentment.

Instead, she saw the lines around his wine-colored eyes, and let herself love him for the loss and hardship he'd lived through; her gaze glanced off the cropped hair and followed the length of the dangle the crew had made for him, and she was grateful that he'd allowed them into his heart. She let the tastes linger as if she could savor them with her tongue: what it felt to be willing to be vulnerable, and even better, to trust that her vulnerability would be cherished, protected. Her skin prickled, and the nerves in them seemed to pulse in time with her heart.

It made her realize that, as usual, the damned great hall was too cold. Heaters, first thing.

"Theresa," he said.

She smiled, shy. "Hirianthial. Welcome to Rose Point."

"It is well and truly a castle," he said, his eyes lifting to the rafters. "I have not seen one. There is stonework else-where, but only in the cathedrals and churches."

"Would you like a tour?" she asked. "We've done a pretty good job of mapping the place, though it's a bit of a walk. It's pretty big."

"I would be delighted."

Should she hold out her hand? She wanted to, and didn't; wanted the moment between their life before and the life to come to stretch out into this liminal space, where she could live with the anticipation of something good.

Would he understand? She glanced at him and found him smiling one of those little, quiet smiles, head lowered and eyes on the floor as he folded his arms behind his back.

Of course he did. Reese smiled too. "I'll get my coat."

They walked, then. On battlements combed by the brisk

wind rolling in off the bitter cold of the ocean. Through drafty halls, empty of anything but echoes and memories and the dust now disturbed by the passing of alien feet. Up stairwells and into towers with their stunning views of a countryside shrouded in pale grey slush. She didn't know the castle as well as she one day would, but already the stones spoke to her. Reese dragged a hand along the inner walls as she paced them, sympathizing with their strength and their sturdiness and their desire to keep everything out so everything in could be safe.

They came at last to the riotous spill of roses that crawled over the shattered tower, where the smell of the sea gamboled unfettered through the ingress, cutting the heavy perfume of the blooms with a sharp, briny scent. The sky fell toward the sea in a gradient of tarnished silver, softly lit steel, pewter gray, extending all the way to the faint, tired color of the sand. White petals framed the view, and the brambles, black and cruelly thorned, curved their talons close.

Everything about Rose Point made sense to Reese. It seemed ridiculous to say so about a place so wan when she'd grown up beneath a sky the color of butterscotch, on a world with soil ruddy as blood and rust, but that didn't stop it from being true.

"Come summer," Hirianthial said, "it will have color." His regard lingered on the vista, and then he surprised her by turning and holding out a hand. "Shall we go see the strand?"

"The wha—oh, you mean the beach? Sure?" She slipped her gloved fingers into his and let him help her over the tumbled stones, and then they were descending the short distance to the shore, leaving bootprints in the damp sand. His longer fingers were curved around hers, loose but present. It was the sole point of warmth in her whole body, and it made her feel the numbness of her face and the ache of the cold air when it flowed into her lungs.

Now and then, the little prayer bell Kis'eh't had sewn onto the bottom of his hair dangle tinkled, high-pitched against the low rush of the surf.

How to start this discussion? It had to be started. She had no idea how to start. "Can . . . I ask something?"

"Anything."

Did he mean that? Blood and freedom. Reese swallowed, then continued. "Your wife. What was she like?"

"Ah. . . ." He looked up at the sky, but he didn't loose her hand, nor did he stop walking. With her. "Laiselin was . . . a sweetness. A very gentle spirit. Kind and open-handed. She loved to sing, and embroider while listening to poetry."

Reese could see that as if he'd drawn her a picture: a young Hirianthial sitting in front of a fire, reciting verses of love to a blushing bride at work on her sewing.

"I loved her very much," Hirianthial said at last. "My Butterfly, my first wife."

His *first* wife. Reese tried not to shiver.

"You're cold," he said, gentle. "Let's walk back."

She followed because it was really was colder out on the shore, without the castle walls to bar the wind.

"Now I ask?"

"Sure." She smiled, nervous. "Anything."

"Why your change of heart recently? It seemed . . . abrupt."

That was a fair question. She walked alongside him, concentrating on matching his speed with her much shorter stride while the answer seeped up into her head. "It's . . . not going to be an easy thing to listen to."

Hirianthial glanced at her, somber. "We must become accustomed to the occasional ache of communication."

"Even when you can pull the answers out of my head?"

"Because I will not pull the answers out of your head," he answered. A little smile. "Because I respect your head, Theresa, and I would rather you advance your thoughts to me because I have justly earned them, not because you feel I will have them from you with your permission or not."

She shuddered and rubbed at her arm with her free hand. "You say things like that, and it makes me feel like. . . ."

When she didn't finish, he prompted, "Like . . . ?"

Reese laughed a little. "Like we're in one of my books." But better, she thought. "So, the ache of communication. Right." She steeled herself with a long breath. "There are several parts to it. The easiest part is that . . . it's hard to sustain that much pique. I lived on anger, but it's the kind of fuel that uses you up even when it's pushing you forward. Does that make sense?"

"Yes."

She nodded. "So, I was getting tired of being angry at you. Especially since you kept not giving me reasons. I mean, you gave me reasons, but they were accidental. Even I couldn't keep being angry about accidents, and the fact that those things made me angry because they revealed my fears and flaws. . . ." Reese focused on the spray of rocks they were approaching. "The only reason that mattered so much to me was because I didn't want you to think less of me. I might have the emotional intelligence of a small rock, but even I can see some things when they slam me in the face often enough."

He didn't answer for long enough that she glanced at him, fretful, only to find him hiding a smile against his fist. Noticing her look, he said, "A *small* rock."

"I know. Not even enough for a big one." She smiled too, then chuckled and shook her braids back. "Anyway. I ran out of energy to be angry, probably because I was using so much of it up resisting you . . . and don't give me the look you're about to give me. You had to know you were attractive to me."

His snort made him sound much younger than his years. She liked it, that he let himself sound normal, prone to frustration and amusement. "I knew nothing of the sort."

"Really?" Reese stopped, pulling him to a halt and lifting her brows. "I read stories about fairy princes and sleep in lacy nightgowns!"

"Storied princes are not much like flesh and blood Eldritch," he said. "As you yourself pointed out, now and then."

"No. You're far more attainable for one thing. And far more interesting, because you're real." Reese let herself reach up, pull the hair dangle over his shoulder and onto his chest. Her fingers trailed over the bits of metal and glass and wood the crew had braided into it. "You're more than a cipher in a fantasy. You can be loved."

"Am I?" he asked, softly.

She brought his hand to her cheek and rested her face on his palm until she felt his hand curve around her face. Something in his eyes relaxed: the lines around them, maybe. She kissed the inside of that hand, tasting the leather of the gloves and the sea-salt dampness that clung to them. Then she pulled him back into motion.

"Seeing you in that tent," Reese said finally, before she could lose her nerve. "That broke me. I had no right to be broken by it when you were the one that got hurt. I'd seen you in a prison cell, but unbowed by imprisonment. Resigned, maybe, but still sitting straight. I'd seen you half-dead from attack, from being fought by pirates and being howled at by dying aliens. And you still had a dignity. It made me feel like . . . all these setbacks you had, they were all some game that you could float above." Her heart was racing; admitting these things made her dislike herself. But she kept going before she could convince herself to stop. "All those things . . . they were like inconveniences, and I knew you weren't putting on some show specifically to make me feel like I was less than you, and there just to keep dragging you out of trouble, but I didn't understand then that . . . that stoicism under pressure is how you cope."

His hand remained in hers, but Reese could sense the tension in his fingers. "On Kerayle," she said, "I saw you lose it completely. And then it finally hit me that there wasn't any game here, that you weren't playing at something just to watch the mortals react. That it was as real to you as it was to me. That you could get hurt, just like me. That you could be shattered. And the terror of finding that out. . . ." She stopped walking entirely, because she was surprised to discover she was fighting not to cry. Pushing the words out past the trembling in her chest, she finished, "It made me realize how awful I'd been to you, and how stupid it was to treat you the way I'd been treating you."

When Reese was sure of her feet, she resumed walking, and he went with her, quiet until at last he said, "I would never have thought any good would come out of that encounter."

"You found out about your power there," she pointed out.

"Any unqualified good." A wry look, not quite a smile. "Becoming heir to Corel's legacy was not a choice I would have made, given the choice."

"You used it to help save the world."

He shook his head and didn't answer.

They reached the remains of the tower and climbed over the lowest pile of stones until Hirianthial found an unbroken length of them, enough to serve as impromptu bench. He sat and stretched out one leg, keeping the other

curled under. She joined him, sitting hip to hip, her eyes
moving toward the sea. He was warm, and near, and that
sufficed . . . except there were still things between them
that needed saying.

When she spoke, she surprised herself by choosing
none of them. "Why 'Butterfly'?"

"Ah?" A smile. "Ah. We have a tendency toward many
names. That was the song name I chose for Laiselin,
because she was the unexpected beauty that graced my
life. Song names are thus . . . things chosen from symbol
and myth."

"And everyone gets one?"

"Everyone who is loved by someone who wishes to
bestow one," Hirianthial said. "We also have sweet names,
or nursery names, or . . . milk names. I do not know how
I would translate it. Shorter than our full names, usually,
and employed only by intimates. Mine is Hiran. You could
call me that."

She blushed. "It seems so . . . informal."

This laugh was a good laugh. There was no memory of
sorrow in it. "It's supposed to be. We have titles and family
names and House names and all of it would be unbear-
ably long and exhausting if we only used them. To switch
between those names, and the formal names, and the song
names out of myth, and the milk names . . . that is part of
how we signal our relationships with others."

Reese started. "Wait, was that what all the 'my lady'
stuff was about? And then Captain, and then Theresa, and
I'd tell you to call me Reese, or at least Captain, but it felt
like you were always switching from one to the other. . . ."

"Yes," he said, nodding. "You understand."

"You almost never call me Reese," she added.

"Reese is your very informal name," Hirianthial
replied. He traced a gloved finger along her jaw. "But it has

a quickness to its intimacy. I will call you Reese when we are making love. Theresa most other times. If you permit."

Could he feel how hot her cheeks were? The idea of being in bed with him . . . ! She said, "And will I end up with a song name?"

"Certainly, as you are loved."

That gave her the shivers the mere thought of bedding him hadn't. "What do you think it'll be?"

He studied her face—no, she thought, he was seeing her in his own life, his wine-colored eyes unfocused, turned on some inward memory. "I think," he said at last, "I will call you my Courage."

She couldn't take much more of this. "I'm going to die long before you."

"Barring any accident," he agreed, quiet.

"I'm prickly and I act out when I'm afraid, which is often."

"Because you have not felt safe," he said. "Perhaps that will pass."

"It might not!"

"And if it does not, I will still love you."

She said, desperate, "I'll have your children, and you'll have to raise them without me . . . !"

"Then at least I will have them to remember you by," he whispered. "Theresa . . . Reese. My Courage, my Lady, captain of the ship where I had my resurrection. You know my feelings. You know your own. Will you accept them, though?"

"Marry me," she blurted.

He paused, startled. And then he laughed, and that was a good laugh, a great laugh, and she laughed with him as he framed her face in his long hands and kissed her. When he let her come up for air, he brushed his nose against hers and said, smiling, "How could I turn down such an elegant proposal."

She smacked his wrist, but she was blushing. "Is that a 'yes'? I want to hear it to be sure."

"Yes," Hirianthial said, smiling, resting his brow against hers. "Yes, I will marry you. Yes."

"Kiss me again?" she asked, wistful.

"You could kiss me yourself, if you wished . . . there is no reason you can't."

"Fine," Reese said, and tried it, and that was good too, really very good. Good enough that when they parted he rested a finger on her lips.

"Not here," he said. "And not like this."

"I guess a cold wet hunk of rock in the middle of winter is a bad place to lose your virginity," Reese said with a weak smile.

"We will do it properly," he said. "When we have a bed, and I can do it right." That expression . . . she'd never seen it on his face. Merriment, and a sort of smoky self-confidence that hinted at a lot more experience than she had in this arena, even with her very active imagination for company. Her entire body seemed to go liquid, wobble. "Let me do it properly for you."

"All right," she managed, her voice gone husky. "But only the first time. I hear 'proper' gets kind of boring in bed."

Hirianthial laughed and kissed her knuckles. "Oh! We will have fun, you and I."

"Strange thought!" She grinned. "But speaking of fun, or at least, not fun . . . let's get inside? It really is cold, and you're getting stiff."

"Am I?" he asked, startled.

"Well, you keep shifting a little, like you're trying to stretch your legs. . . ."

Hirianthial chuckled. "And here I'd thought Corel's

powers so much finer an instrument than the faculties of a normal being."

Reese tugged on him. "You should know better by now. Come on."

They experimented with walking arm in arm, and decided that would take practice, given their disparate heights. They settled for hand-holding, strolling toward the keep. Hirianthial stopped them halfway there to pick one of the roses and hand it to her, and she thanked him, blushing, thinking that she had never believed she'd be the recipient of roses of any kind . . . hadn't believed it even when Val had given her one as a challenge to be willing to reach for things, risking hurt and failure, because they were worth it. And here she was, with the flower in her hand, and now that she had one, the practicalities of it ran away with her. Should she put it in a vase? If she did, the thorns probably needed trimming . . . she'd never really thought through how strange a gift a flower was. Picking it meant it would die.

But then, everything died, didn't it? And there was no reason not to enjoy it, while you had it. Glancing toward the Eldritch, Reese caught him considering her and knew, somehow, that's how the gift had been meant. His own pledge to her, and a reminder to them both. To live in the love of the moment, and make it last while they had it.

She smiled at him, and accepted it.

Holding the door open for her, Hirianthial asked, "Will you give me a song name?"

"Yes," Reese said, after a moment. "But I'll need time to think up a good one."

He smiled and kissed the crown of her head, and they went into the castle together.

EPILOGUE:
ROSES

The weeks that followed took Hirianthial frequently from Rose Point, and this he endured because he knew the situations that warranted his absences were extraordinary. How often would his cousin be employed in setting up an empire, after all? He did not begrudge her the questions she put to him, for while she was savvy about the Alliance—was, in fact, more savvy about financial and industrial matters—she did not have his recent experience traveling it. He had spent almost sixty years abroad on various planets, had dipped in and out of several environments while doing so: the university, medicine, and then the itinerant lifestyle of a trader. His insights when blended with hers were more productive.

He accompanied her to the isle where the heir had remained sequestered, and freed the Chancellor and Bethsaida from their self-imposed exile there. Bethsaida remained unsuitable for her previous position; her nervousness riddled her aura with flaws, like brittle glass. Liolesa put her to work traveling to the churches and convents of the countryside, making a census of the clergy in preparation for the changes in policy the Queen planned in the wake of Baniel's power-play. It was Lesandurel's Tams she put to work in Ontine, cleaning out the debris of the battle and modernizing the building as much as possible. Hirianthial found himself walking the halls in winter and marveling that he did not need a coat, and that the water closets were no longer worthy of that name; even Kis'eh't proclaimed them proper bathrooms, and expressed gratitude that someone had finally seen sense about the renovation.

The flux of the political map remained troublesome. Scattering Asaniefa shocked the remaining Houses antagonistic to Liolesa's aims into wary retreat, but did not dissuade them from their views. Hirianthial thought that a few decades would accustom them sufficiently to the conveniences of the Alliance to prevent any uprising as obvious as the one Surela had spearheaded, but Liolesa remained unconvinced. He accused her of cynicism; she accused him of letting his forthcoming marriage fill his head with thoughts of unicorns and roses.

That he admitted to with good grace, because it was almost certainly true.

Reese he saw, though not as much as he preferred. She too was busy: renovating Rose Point, finding the best use of the gifts Fleet had bestowed, buying up supplies for the various industries she wanted her House to oversee in order to maintain its profitability. The Queen had awarded her seed money to furnish the House, and this amounted to more money than Reese had ever handled in her life. She confessed to him at some point, bewildered, that had that not been startling enough, she'd never had capital before, and she had no idea what to do with quite so much.

"Build me a hospital," he said.

She'd glanced at him, thoughtful, then grinned. "Get me an equipment list."

He found the time to make one, and sent it along with suggestions for Val's school of talents. He also sent Val, once Liolesa had finished with him, and Belinor, who was now apparently inseparable from the former renegade. On seeing the new high priest of the Lord, Hirianthial was amused at the younger man's hangdog expression.

"Ended up in charge, did you."

"All I wanted was to wander around and be of some modest use. . . ."

"Congratulations. Now you may wander and be of significant use."

Val had snorted and gone on, over the Pad and to Firilith where Reese awaited him with plans for a chapterhouse, and Belinor awaited him with the torment of his conservative wisdom. Hirianthial thought that would work out well. Val needed a Urise of his own, and if Belinor had granted himself that privilege, well . . . no one had gainsaid him.

The wedding itself he did not involve himself in, because he was barred from it with a strictness by Felith, Irine and Kis'eh't, all of whom insisted that men should have nothing to do with weddings. He'd considered protesting but decided he was not up to their combined intransigence. In lieu of that battle, he requested only that it involve at least some elements of the Eldritch ceremony. Since Urise had taken up residence at Rose Point, where he could watch the flow of colorful mortals pass, he thought they would have no trouble researching the particulars. The only thing they asked of him was a guest list, and that he provided before Liolesa tugged him away to discuss Fleet basing rights, and to help her bid a formal farewell to the *Moonsinger,* now properly crewed. The battlecruiser's departure left them with a scout and two Fleet courier vessels in orbit, and the Queen deemed that protection enough with Lesandurel's fixed fortifications building apace.

It was a gentle winter, and with each passing day he was aware of the promise of spring. Not just in the landscape as winter waxed and then began to release its grip on the fields and the skies . . . but in their society, as the Alliance began to trickle into their closed culture, like wildflowers drifting into a sheltered field . . . and in his own heart, as he prepared himself for the life to come.

To have a wife—to have this wife. To love again, fully. To have children . . . to grow old with family. To have a chance, perhaps, at the richness of aura that shone 'round Lesandurel like divine raiment.

In this, his work and his frequent absences functioned as a vigil. In his heart, he turned his face toward the coming light.

Irine had asked if she was ready to do this. Reese had told her the truth: that it had to be done, and putting it off wouldn't make it any easier.

That didn't make walking the corridors of the *Earthrise* feel any less bittersweet. Her chest ached as she wandered through it, observing the repairs Fleet had made while the ship had been nestled in one of its berths. Even the broken locks and blinky lights worked. It made her eyes prickle with tears she refused to shed.

This place had been home—no. A refuge. Home had involved the people she'd accreted while piloting this ship from port to port, never resting, always hoping that the next big thing would be the one to bail her out of yet another looming monetary crisis.

And it wasn't as if she was retiring the ship. Or even selling it. Ra'aila and her herd of crazy Aera, and the one or two other Pelted who'd chosen to answer her call for a crew . . . they'd take good care of it. The ship would be back in orbit at the end of every trip, delivering cargo to the new space station Hirianthial's House-cousin was working on. That part, Reese liked. That the ship that had striven so valiantly to be the home she'd needed would have a home of its own, a port to come back to.

So she walked the *Earthrise* from stem to stern. The echoing cargo holds with their spindles for the bins, waiting for something to haul. The narrow corridors with their metal mesh floors. The bridge, somnolent, all its boards glowing the subdued blue of a ship drowsing in parking orbit. She went through the crew quarters, finding them already empty: the rest of the ship's former crew had had time to come up, but she hadn't, not until now. She walked through the engineering deck, remembering the pirates crawling all over the machinery, looking for evidence of perfidy. She toured the galley and the mess, remembering apple pies and coffee and less satisfactory experiments that everyone had nevertheless eaten. She checked on Kis'eht's lab/clinic, brushing her fingers across the dents in the bulkhead where the equipment had been bolted.

She saved her own cabin for last.

Other than a set of crates by the door, there was no sign that anyone had come into the room. It was just as Reese had left it when she'd crossed over the Pad to Rose Point and given the ship into Sascha's hands. Her hammock hung in the corner, next to the unrumpled bunk; her data tablet was on the desk, long gone dim, and when she touched it awake she found the ship's accounts still bright on the surface. Her collection of jumpsuits and vests and a jacket or two hung in the closet, along with her boots, and in the bathroom, she found a bottle of chalk tablets and the box of wooden beads, fragrant still, redolent of Mars. She left the tablets and took the box with her, sat in her hammock, let it swing her gently to and fro.

In the beginning, it had only been her. No Flitzbe, no twins, no Phoenix or Glaseah . . . no Eldritch. Just this emptiness, the suffusive quiet. It had been crushingly lonely, but she had convinced herself that it was better than what she'd fled.

It hadn't been. But it had led her, somehow, to something that was.

Reese looked around at the room that had been the confines of her world for years, then pushed herself off the hammock. She began to pack.

An hour later, she toggled the antigrav on the crates and tethered them together, then pulled them into the corridor. The ship's new permanent Pad was in the cargo hold, so that's where she took them.

She brushed her fingers against the metal near the comm panel.

"Ra'aila will take good care of you," she whispered. "You take good care of her. And keep an eye out for Surela, too. Okay?"

The silence answered, and that felt like a good answer. Like waiting. Reese stroked the wall once, and then took the crate leash and walked over the Pad, and into her new life.

"That," Lesandurel said, "is a *horse*."

Hirianthial chuckled at the awe that set the other man's aura glittering. They stood together in the dusky warmth of Laisrathera's stables, which had gone from an empty shell of half-ruined stone to a fine complex for both riding animals and brooding in less time than he'd been able to credit even the Pelted with. It smelled sweetly of hay and leather, and reminded him of a youth spent breeding animals for Jisiensire. He ran a hand down the long neck of the mare studying them over the door of her stall, gathering the alert curiosity of her mind through the touch, like velvet over the nap of her skin. "Fine, is she not? And we have more on hold."

"How many did you buy?"

"These six here, and another ten in foal—or, perhaps I should say, in dish, since they have not yet been generated."

Lesandurel chuckled. "Alliance magic. I never tire of it. Show me the others, then. Is this one yours?"

Hirianthial grinned. "This one is my lady's, and the first I bought. A bet I lost, and a horse was the prize."

"And you spared no expense, I see. Well done. A woman should have a good horse. And a man, too, at that." Lesandurel considered the mare wistfully.

"Should Laisrathera be expecting a purchase from the Meriaen, then?"

"Ha! And where would I put a horse in my little empire?" Lesandurel pursed his lips, smiled. "Well. Maybe if I buy myself a little estate on-world."

"A man should have a good horse."

"Ha!" Lesandurel said again. He grinned. "Show me the others."

Hirianthial could not have wished for a more appreciative audience. The years away had not dimmed his House-cousin's knowledge or interest in horseflesh. While discussing the topic with the Pelted who'd sold him the horses had been enjoyable enough, in its own way, it was an entirely different matter to have the discussion with another Eldritch. Horses were a passion and a hobby for the Pelted. Here, they were livelihood, transport, life.

"Of course, all that will change," Lesandurel said when they'd repaired to two bales of hay at the back of the stables, there to share small cups of Tam-ileyan beer while watching the animals shift in their stalls and the golden light slowly creep across the floor, setting motes of dust a-sparkle. "The farms will have to be mechanized, if they are to yield a worthwhile calorie-to-effort ratio. And the Pads will make riding superfluous, except for short distances."

"The Pelted do walk," Hirianthial pointed out.

"The Pelted walk because it's healthsome, not because it's necessary. Necessity is the parent of many virtues." Lesandurel set his cup on the wooden board they'd pressed into service for a table. He leaned back, resting his shoulders and head against the back wall. "Things will change here, and I am not displeased with that, but . . . the life we knew, cousin . . . it will pass."

"Perhaps," Hirianthial said. "But we are not Pelted, Lesandurel. Those of us who lived with that life will not die tomorrow, to forget its lessons."

The other man chuckled. "No." He folded his arms behind his head. "I suppose we'll see how it comes to us."

Hirianthial half-closed his eyes, soaking in the contented auras of the horses, the comfort of his guest, the faint warmth imbued by the alcohol. "Will you stay, Lesandurel? Start a homeworld branch of the Jisiensires?"

"Andrel," the man said. At Hirianthial's look, he stretched his arms and said, "My nursery name. Hardly anyone uses it, but you may. And to answer your question . . . I don't know." He sighed. "I am no longer used to the country life, if you will permit the possible insult."

"I cannot take umbrage at an accurate characterization," Hirianthial said, still struggling with the unexpected offer of intimacy. "But you could do a great deal here."

"I could, I suppose. Jisiensire already has a head, though."

"So it does." He relaxed against the wall himself and offered, "An admirable woman, Araelis Mina."

Lesandurel eyed him. "The happy lover wishes to play matchmaker to all he espies, is that it?"

"You could do worse."

That earned him a snort. "I don't know her."

"She is here for the wedding—"

"Which is tomorrow."

"A man could do a great deal of listening and talking in two or three days."

Lesandurel laughed. "You won't leave off until I at least promise to introduce myself."

"I wouldn't think to ask it of you," Hirianthial said. "I'll make the introduction myself. It would only be proper."

A snort. But Lesandurel's aura developed a tinge of effervescent amusement. "I do admire the passel of pards she's surrounded herself with. Sellelvi's kin, I imagine."

"And much delighted to have rejoined their ancestress's Eldritch family, yes. I think they will find each other quite suitable."

"I have always preferred the foxes myself."

"Of course."

Lesandurel shook his head then, and his aura darkened, as if a cloud had passed over it. "I mean that just as it was said." He smiled a little. "I loved Sydnie Unfound." He nodded at Hirianthial's sudden glance and reached to refill his cup. "Yes, just as you think. I loved her, and she adored me, but not as a maid loves a swain. To her, I was ... something magical, and beautiful, something to be treasured and awed by. One does not marry an idol."

Was that why Reese had been able to love him, he wondered? Because he'd come into her life, not as something perfect and above need, but as an obligation and an inconvenience? His mouth quirked. What was it about their relationship, that always the negatives begot the positives? He said, careful, "And after Sydnie?"

"I don't know," Lesandurel admitted. "I became busy. The Tam-illee reproduce slowly compared to the Pelted, but compared to us? Soon enough I was drowning in the troubles of daughters and granddaughters, and that is what they were to me: people I'd known as infants, who grew into their adulthood in my presence. I could never think of them as possible lovers, when I had so lately been busy salving their adolescent traumas." He looked away, his eyes resting on Reese's golden mare. "Several of them loved me, I think. But all of them outgrew it. And that was for the best."

"You save yourself for an Eldritch love, then."

"I haven't been saving myself for anything, and well you should know it with your sorcerous insight." Lesandurel smiled, amusement beading his aura. "When I say I have been busy, that is precisely what I meant . . . ! But I admit, my mind turns more and more toward the thought of a companion. Perhaps I will meet one, as you have."

Hirianthial took a sip from his own cup. "One of the Pelted, do you suppose?"

"No . . . no. Most of them are very fond of children. We can be fruitful with humans, but not their progeny." Lesandurel shook his head. "No, I think I am curious if children of my own body will be any different than children of my spirit. Somehow I suspect not very, save that they will spend longer in the awkward ages, bedeviling me." He grinned, then allowed that grin to fade. "And you? What shall you do, when this has done?"

This being his marriage to Reese. Hirianthial held his shoulders taut to keep them from betraying him, knew that they did anyway. "Then, I suspect my cousin will keep me . . . busy."

"Ha," Lesandurel said softly. "A fair turnabout."

They drank together, unspeaking, enjoying the rustle

of the horses, the idle switch of their tails, their whuffles and soft shifting sounds.

"You could marry your cousin," Lesandurel said.

"Liolesa?" Hirianthial asked, brows lifting. "I hardly think she needs a man."

"No woman needs a man, arii." A grin at Hirianthial's start at the use of the Universal term, dropped into the middle of a conversation in their tongue. "Least of all her. But that doesn't mean she might not want one. Or find one useful at her side. Or to give her children, now that she is without heir again."

"Perhaps," Hirianthial said. "I wouldn't presume to that position. I have no desire to be King-Consort."

"No doubt. But would you accept her, if she offered?"

Hirianthial said nothing for a long time. He tried to feel the shape of his life after Reese and couldn't. Didn't want to, this close to its beginning. By this time tomorrow, he would be wed.

Finally, he said, "I love my cousin."

Lesandurel received that as the message Hirianthial had intended, and did not press.

After a time, Hirianthial added, "Hiran."

Lesandurel lifted his cup. "Hiran, then. I am sorry I missed your tenure as seal-bearer for our House."

Hirianthial tapped his lightly to the other man's cup. "Andrel. You need not. We will see more than enough of one another in the future we will make for our people."

"Eldritch and Pelted both."

"Eldritch and Pelted both."

"Angels, Angels, Reese . . . Allacazam is missing!"

Reese ignored Irine to peer at her own reflection in the mirror, resisting the urge to touch her eyes and smear all the hard work Felith had just done there. "Did you check my hammock?"

"Yes!"

"My bed, then?"

"Yes!" Irine grabbed her ears. "He keeps rolling away lately and hiding places, and it's driving me crazy."

"He'll turn up," Reese said. "He's not going to miss the wedding, he knows it's today."

"Does he?" Felith asked, entering from the room the Eldritch insisted was a closet. In Reese's opinion, it was about six times too big for the name. The room even had a padded bench in it, which struck her as particularly crazy. Who sat in their own closet? And why? To contemplate their mounds of clothing? Ridiculous. The dress they'd talked her into was fancy enough without adding enough clones to fill a cargo bin.

"Does he what?" she asked, distracted. She forced herself to admit she was nervous.

"Know that today is the wedding," Felith said, setting the gown on the chair next to Reese. "I did not perceive him to have much sense of normal time."

"He has ways," Reese said.

Felith was eyeing the gown with as close to a scowl as a well-bred Eldritch woman allowed herself. "I still think this would be far more proper with a corset."

"I am not wearing a corset under my wedding dress," Reese declared. "The first time Hirianthial kisses me, I'll faint."

Irine snickered.

"Kissing of that sort is reserved for the bedchamber," Felith said after bestowing a quelling glance at the Harat-Shar. "The kiss during the ceremony is a symbol of the union made manifest. It is supposed to be chaste."

Reese sighed, rueful. "Blood, Felith. It doesn't matter what kind of kiss he gives me. They all make me breathe too fast."

"Oh!" Felith colored. "Well. That's to be expected. He is the man you're wedding." Briskly, she continued, "Come, let us dress you. The bells will ring soon."

"Right," Reese said, and stood, allowing the ritual. Not just the gown, but over it, a new medallion of her own, Lais-rathera's, peach-colored stone clasped in white gold, with a bright star for an emblem: Earth as seen in the Martian sky. Felith threaded it on a long chain so that it fell past her breasts, hanging over her ribcage; it left her throat free for the choker of rubies and coral-colored moonstones the Queen had given her. All of it felt too expensive for Reese, but she supposed that was her fault for getting tangled up with royalty and Eldritch princes.

"You have a little time," Felith said once they'd finished the toilette. "If you'd like, we can stay . . . ?"

"No, that's all right. I wouldn't mind some time to myself."

Irine nodded. "And I'll look for Allacazam."

"He'll be fine."

"Then I'll look for Sascha. I need a cuddle."

Reese grinned. "Just so long as you remember to bring the ring."

Irine went into the pocket of her own dress and brought out the pouch, shaking it. "Still in there."

"Good. Then go have your cuddle. I'll be out soon."

Alone, she smoothed the silk folds down. It was traditional for seal-bearers to marry in their House colors, so she wore apricot, embroidered in white and honey-gold. Irine had assured her that it set off her brown skin beautifully, and she'd seen the admiration in Felith's eyes when the woman had drawn away to consider her handiwork. They'd seen to every detail, except her hair; Reese had handled that herself, using the beads from her box. The smell reminded her of home, knitted her past and her future together in a way that calmed her anxious stomach.

She was not the woman she'd been when she left Mars. Nor the one she'd been when she met Hirianthial. She'd seen it in her own face, sitting patiently while Felith had applied the cosmetics that had edged her eyelids in gold and gilt her lips. Strain had etched lines in her face, and worry. But she liked her eyes better. She didn't mind meeting her own gaze anymore.

The bells started singing, summoning the celebrants. She lifted her chin, brushed her skirts and answered the call.

The thing Reese remembered most about the ceremony was how little of it she did. In the days to come, it would fade into a pastiche of sensory impressions and a vague sense of overwhelming happiness . . . and that was fine with her. She had plenty of people to remind her of the details and she looked forward to their teasing and their company and the years of friendship those things implied.

Some parts, though, she did recall. Rose Point had once had a cathedral on the grounds encircled by the curtain walls, a building long since reduced to a rumpled stone foundation . . . but the keep's private chapel remained mostly intact, boasting three walls and enough of the roof to support its bell tower. The garden's vines had overgrown one wall, knotting through the mortar and spilling over the pinnacle into the nave. With the advent of spring, the roses had died off . . . but other flowers had bloomed, shining gold, tiny and fragrant. Reese had ordered the place swept, the stained glass windows replaced, and had the bell serviced, and liked the result: old and new, natural and man-made, sacred and somehow casual enough to be borne. That, then, was where they'd decided to host the ceremony.

She remembered the heady perfume of the flowers and
the sea, and the warmth of the sunlight on her shoulders
and Hirianthial's, the way it made the wine red velvet of
his coat seem to glow like garnets. She remembered—
vaguely—Liolesa, as the head of the Goddess's order, and
Urise, serving for the God's, saying something about love
and duty, posterity, joy.

She remembered the gifts, because those were important: she gave him one of the matched set of rings she'd
had made with the Laisrathera star-on-apricot field, and
a new dagger to replace the ones she kept misplacing: a
dagger, not a sword, as acknowledgement that while he
had accepted the role of Laisrathera's sword-bearer, he had
a greater responsibility now to the kingdom—empire—as
a whole. That dagger went on his belt alongside the sword
he'd used on his world's behalf, and she found herself okay
with the reminder of all that he could do, and had done. If
there was violence in their futures, she trusted that they
would handle it.

When it was his turn, he gave her his life, because that
was what men pledged to their brides, and she remembered him bowing his head to her when he vowed it.

She remembered sipping from a shallow bowl of honey,
symbol of the sweetness of the life they were to share. And
she remembered his lips tasting of it when he'd tipped her
chin up with gloved fingers: sweet gloss on warm, dry skin.

. . . Reese definitely remembered the kiss.

The priest had wrapped their joined hands with the
binding cloth, then, apricot and gold for Laisrathera,
bronze and burgundy for Jisiensire, and meeting in the
center the unicorn that spoke of Hirianthial's royal blood.
Hirianthial had removed his glove for that and she'd felt
his fingers warm in hers, close in the dim heat of the silk.

After that, there was the expected celebration . . . for

everyone else. The Eldritch, Felith had confided, expected the happy couple to leave the festivities for the guests and ascend to their rooms to consummate their bond. And then, if it pleased them, to return. The revelry would last for three days, and while they were expected to make an appearance it was not at all untoward for them to leave it until the last day. Indeed, it was something of a triumph if they did, hinting at many forthcoming years of marital bliss. Reese thought it all a little dramatic, and probably a way for people to enjoy the food and board of a rich family—Felith admitted to it without embarrassment. But when Hirianthial tucked her hand under his arm and suggested they depart, she thought there might be some merit in not having to suffer through a big dinner and hours of well-wishers before finally being alone with the man she'd married. The sounds of the party carried up through the halls as they left it behind, made it feel like they were escaping. Her heart raced, and she found she was grinning.

He surprised her by taking her by the waist and lifting her, twirling her. "That is how I like you," he said in that baritone that she now allowed herself to admit had always made the hair on the back of her neck rise. "Laughing."

"I'm not laughing," she protested, though by then she was.

"You're laughing on the inside," he said, and kissed her, and then she wasn't laughing—that was fine, though. Better than fine.

"Come," he murmured against her mouth. "Let us find our bed."

. . . and that was nothing like she'd imagined, because she wasn't capable of imagining just how good it could be. Except that it was tender and wonderful, and that maybe that cultured exterior was capable of hiding something untamed. And that was good, she thought with her hands wound through his short hair, tangled in the hair-chain that sang as she pulled him down. A man should always have something a little untamed in him.

"A woman too," he said against her sweat-glossed cheek, in a tone almost like a purr.

"A woman too," she agreed, gone all to goosebumps and not at all minding.

The light through the window had faded to silver in a dark sky. It was later—how much later, Reese didn't know or much care. The party was no doubt still going, but her crew could handle it, and what they couldn't, Liolesa surely would. There was no reason in the world to descend, and every reason to linger here with her cheek on this chest, with this muscled arm curled around her shoulders, keeping her close. How had the muscle never occurred to her? A light-gravity worlder who had learned the discipline of the sword, consigned to decades in heavier gravities? She should have known, but it was instead a delightful surprise. A delicious surprise. She traced a scar on his side, thinking that she would ask him about it one day, but not today, and that maybe she'd taste the skin there, but not just now.

"If you will permit," he murmured, brushing his lips against her forehead. "There is a custom. . . ."

This roused her from her pleasant drifting and she laughed, husky. "Another one! Sometimes I think you people are nothing *but* customs."

"Remove one and we may all collapse?" He smiled against her skin; she could feel it. "Sometimes I wonder myself. But this one is pleasing. I think you may find it so also." Rolling onto his back he stretched an arm toward the table alongside the bed and brought back a little box. "For you."

"A present?" Reese sat up, pulling the blankets up onto her lap.

"During the wedding is traditional for the bride to bestow gifts because she is invariably the one with the wealth," Hirianthial said, lying on his side beside her with his head resting on a palm. "But if a man is pleased with the match he will bring his own offering to the marriage bed. A troth gift, it's called politely."

She glanced at him. "And impolitely?"

He laughed. "A stud gift."

She couldn't help it . . . she laughed too. "You people and your horses. So do I open it now?"

"I would be pleased if you did."

The box was small enough to fit in her palm, but so intricately carved she couldn't fit her nail into some of the cuts. The pattern reminded her of something but she couldn't place it: leaves maybe? How long had it taken someone to make this box? Because, being Eldritch, someone had to have made it by hand. Knowing that made it incredible, like something out of a storybook.

Strange how wary she used to be of gifts, when looking at this one all she could think about was how it felt anticipating something new and wonderful. She carefully opened the lid.

There was a kernel inside. A kernel she would have recognized in her dreams, and yet seeing it here, in this context . . . when she touched it her fingers were trembling. "Is this really . . . ?"

His voice was low. "I took the liberty of having it engineered using the material in the bead you wove into the dangle. It is viable—you have only to choose where to plant it."

"It may be too cold here for a eucalyptus," Reese said, her eyes watering. Her voice was going hoarse on her.

"I'm given to understand that some cultivars thrive in the cold, so long as they have the right exposure. Or we could build it a greenhouse." He smiled. "The Queen has enough of them for her horticultural experiments. Why should not Laisrathera have one as well?"

She was going to cry. Was already crying, and didn't care that he could see it, because he'd resurrected *her eucalyptus,* the one that had given her comfort in her troubled childhood. Had come up with the idea, had somehow divined how important it had been to her, and he'd done that for *her,* and sacrificed the bead she'd given him to do it. That's what the familiar pattern was on the box—she looked a second time—those were eucalyptus leaves, as seen through the eyes of some Eldritch artist.

As she wiped her eyes, Hirianthial reached for her, gathered her into his arms. He didn't try to reassure her, didn't mistake her tears for an expression of some feeling that needed comfort. It didn't, because she was crying for release, for relief, for knowing that for every loss, there was a possibility of a returning. A potential for redemption, for a second try. She'd gotten hers . . . he'd gotten his. Everything was right with the world.

Everything was clear.

"Heart," she said suddenly against his chest.

He canted his head, just a little, to look down at her, and she met his eyes.

"That's your song name," Reese said, quiet. She curled her fingers around the kernel, bruising her fingertips on it to make the scent cling to the skin. "My Heart. That's what you are. And what you gave to me."

He touched his fingers to her lips and whispered, "Oh, love."

"Exactly," she answered, soft. And kissed his fingers. Then she thought, if she could kiss him first, maybe there were other things she could try doing first. So she set the box aside, and the kernel, and did, and smiled at his ardent welcome . . . and maybe they lost a few more hours.

In the morning, while he ran a bath in the mercifully renovated chambers because God and freedom help her if she was going to use another water closet no matter how much she liked this world, Reese donned a robe and dared to peek out into the corridor. She almost tripped over Irine, who was sitting crosslegged beside the door, reading a data tablet. At the sight of Reese, the woman set it aside and perked her ears. "You're out sooner than I thought!"

"I'm not out for long," Reese said, belting the robe closed. "I just wanted to find out how things are going."

"Oh, it's great." Irine laughed. "The crowd's over half-Pelted, you know, and those Harat-Shar who came to be Araelis's family are awfully charming. Felith's got everything running on a schedule for people who want events: picnics and little outdoor games and contests and feasts . . . something for everyone. But honestly, most of us are enjoying it for the chance to get to know one another. All the movers and shakers on this world are here, right now. We're seeing the future happen, you know?"

"I do, a little," Reese said, smiling. She sat next to the tigraine, leaned into her and sighed. This fur smelled like home, too.

"Happy?" Irine asked, gentler, nuzzling.

"Yes."

"Just like that." Said fondly, but with a little bemusement, too.

"Just like that, sure," Reese replied, finding it funny. "If 'just like that' means having to get through my whole life to make it to this point."

"Yeah," Irine murmured, sliding an arm around Reese's

shoulder. "I can see that."

"Worth it though."

Irine grinned and nudged her. "So I smell."

Reese colored and poked a furry side. "If you were anyone but Harat-Shar, I'd be embarrassed."

"But I'm not," Irine said. "So it's all good. Oh, and you know . . . I found Allacazam."

Allacazam! She had forgotten he was missing. "Where was he?"

"In a closet. Budding!"

Reese sat up, stunned. "Budding??"

"Budding," Irine said, satisfied with her shock. "There are now two more little Allacazams rolling around. Must be something in the air." She grinned. "Maybe we can send one of them off with Ra'aila and the *Earthrise*. It would be weird for the ship to be running without a Flitzbe."

"It would," Reese agreed. And added, "When they're older. Freedom." She laughed and rubbed her face. "God."

"And Goddess and Angels and all the good things in life," Irine agreed, and wrapped her tail around Reese's waist to go with the arm.

They sat like that a while, content, and then Irine bumped her hip. "Go take that bath with your man. And tell him that the Queen said something about him owing her a harp song or something."

"A . . . a harp song," Reese said, bewildered. Then the image of Hirianthial sitting at a harp with his fingers—his long and very knowing fingers—on golden strings came to her, and she wasn't sure whether her shiver was anticipation or something a little more blushworthy. "All right. Thanks, arii."

"It's my pleasure." She grinned and pushed Reese to her feet. "Go on, now. Work him hard! It's been too long for him. And since it's been never for you, work yourself hard too!"

Reese covered her face and fled.

When she let herself into the bathroom, Hirianthial was just setting out the towels, and the sight of him doing something so domestic, so normal . . .

. . . while naked . . ..

He took one look at her expression and started laughing, a real, deep laugh, unfettered.

"I like you laughing too," she said, grinning, her heart squeezing in her chest at the sight. "And if all it takes is me leering at you, I'll take lessons from the twins."

"You can try," he said, kissing her fingers. "But you can't leer, my Courage. It's not in you." Merriment pricked color from his wine-dark eyes. "But you are welcome to stop short in shock anytime you wish."

"You are terrible," she said, and pulled him close to kiss him, and let him draw her down into the bath. "So I hear there are events going on downstairs. Picnics and games and feasts and such."

"Mmm-hmm."

"A picnic actually sounds kind of nice." He was rubbing soap onto her shoulders and back, and all the tension was oozing from them. She continued gamely. "We could pack a nice lunch, go out in the sunlight."

"Mmm-hmmm."

"Take those horses you bought . . . they're kind of nice horses."

"Mmm." His lips were on her neck now.

"Hirianthial Sarel Eddings Laisrathera, I can't concentrate while you're doing that!"

"That was rather the idea."

She tried her last volley. "We could make love in the flowers?"

"Maybe later," he said, mischievous.

She sighed warmly and twitched her hair out of his way. "Okay. Maybe later. . . ." And after a moment, amended, "All right. A lot later."

He laughed that low, gentle laugh, and Reese smiled, turned in his arms, and reached up for him. The flowers would be there tomorrow, and if they weren't . . . well. She'd still have roses in winter.

THE SEVEN MODES OF ELDRITCH GRAMMAR

One of the unique features of the Eldritch language is the ability to modify the meaning of a word with emotional "colors." In the spoken language, these are indicated by the use of prefixes, which can be used as aggressively or as infrequently as the speaker desires; a single prefix can color an entire paragraph, or the speaker can use them to inflect every word. Uninflected language is considered emotionally neutral. This modifiers are not often used in the written language, but when they are, they take the form of colored inks.

There are three pairs of moods, with the gray mode not necessitating an opposite. Each mood in a pair is said to be the 'foil' of the other.

Gray (normal)   No modifiers are required to denote the neutral mood, however there is a prefix associated with it, and using it can be interpreted as a way of calling attention to one's lack of mood.

Silver (hopeful)   Silver Mode is the foil of the Shadow mood, giving a positive flavor to words. This is the color of hope.

Shadowed (cynical)   When Shadowed, most words bear a negative connotation, usually cynical, sarcastic, or ironic. It can also be used for dread/foreboding or fear.

Gold (joyful)   The best is always assumed of every-thing in the Gold mood, and all words take on that flavor.

Black (dark)   Black, the foil of Gold, tends to violent, angry, or morose connotations of words. Whole groups of words radically change definition when referred to in the Black.

White (ephemeral/holy)   Whitened words refer to the spirit, to the holy and pure. You often find this mood used for weddings and in the priesthood, and in the schools that teach the handling of esper abilities.

Crimson (sensual)   The carnal mood gives words a sensual implication, and inflect speech to refer to things of passions and things of the body.

THE SPECIES OF THE ALLIANCE UNIVERSE

The Alliance is mostly composed of the Pelted, a group of races that segregated and colonized worlds based (more or less) on their visual characteristics. Having been engineered from a mélange of uplifted animals, it's not technically correct to refer to any of them as "cats" or "wolves," since any one individual might have as many as six or seven genetic contributors: thus the monikers like "foxine" and "tigraine" rather than "vulpine" or "tiger." However, even the Pelted think of themselves in groupings of general animal characteristics, so for the ease of imagining them, I've separated them that way.

⇒ The Pelted ⇐

The Quasi-Felids
The Karaka'An, Asanii, and Harat-Shar comprise the most cat-like of the Pelted, with the Karaka'An being the shortest and digitigrade, the Asanii being taller and plantigrade, and the Harat-Shar including either sort but being based on the great cats rather than the domesticated variants.

The Quasi-Canids
The Seersa, Tam-illee, and Hinichi are the most doggish of the Pelted, with the Seersa being short and digitigrade and foxish, the Tam-illee taller, plantigrade and also foxish, and the Hinichi being wolflike.

Others
Less easily categorized are the Aera, with long, hare-like ears, winged feet and foxish faces, the felid Malarai with their feathered wings, and the Phoenix, tall bipedal avians.

The Centauroids
Of the Pelted, two species are centauroid in configuration, the short Glaseah, furred and with lower bodies like lions but coloration like skunks and leathery wings on their lower backs, and the tall Ciracaana, who have foxish faces but long-legged cat-like bodies.

Aquatics
One Pelted race was engineered for aquatic environments: the Naysha, who look like mermaids would if mermaids had sleek, hairless, slightly rodent-like faces and the lower bodies of dolphins.

⇒ *Other Species* ⇐

Humanoids
Humanity fills this niche, along with their estranged cousins, the esper-race Eldritch.

True Aliens
Of the true aliens, four are known: the shapeshifting Chatcaava, whose natural form is draconic (though they are mammals); the gentle heavyworlder Faulfenza, who are furred and generally regarded to be attractive; the aquatic Platies, who look like colorful flatworms and can communicate reliably only with the Naysha, and the enigmatic Flitzbe, who are quasi-vegetative and resemble softly furred volleyballs that change color depending on their mood.

SOME THINGS TRANSCEND

THE LONG AWAITED SEQUEL
TO *EVEN THE WINGLESS*

Coming in Winter 2014

Given a choice, Lisinthir Nase Galare would have stayed in the Chatcaavan Empire to help its reformed Emperor and Queen remake the worlds in their image. But when his presence proved a threat to the Emperor's attempts, he bowed to necessity and accepted an exile from love and purpose that he thought would kill him . . . for what was left without duty and the company of the beloved?

Adding insult to injury, his escort out of neutral space arrived with two psychiatrists to see to his mental health, as if he was something broken and in need of therapy . . . and one of them is another Eldritch. Do they expect him to spill his soul to anyone without the courage to make his sacrifices, and to a member of a species he now considers completely craven? And will he even have the chance, when the Emperor's enemies have a vested interest in never letting him see the other side of the border?

Xenotherapists Jahir and Vasiht'h of the novels *Mindtouch* and *Mindline* make an appearance in this second book of the Princes' Game, and the game is as large as the fate of three nations and millions of worlds. Perhaps there's a role for an additional prince on the playing field. . . .

ABOUT THE AUTHOR

Daughter of two Cuban political exiles, M.C.A. Hogarth was born a foreigner in the American melting pot and has had a fascination for the gaps in cultures and the bridges that span them ever since. She has been many things— web database architect, product manager, technical writer and massage therapist—but is currently a full-time parent, artist, writer and anthropologist to aliens, both human and otherwise. She is the author of over fifty titles in the genres of science fiction, fantasy, humor and romance.

The Her Instruments Trilogy is only one of the many stories set in the Paradox Pelted universe. For more information, visit the "Where Do I Start?" page on the author's website.

mcahogarth.org
www.twitter.com/mcahogarth

CPSIA information can be obtained
at www.ICGtesting.com
Printed in the USA
LVHW082131090123
736814LV00028B/855